THE LAST STREAMERS OF CONFETTI ON NEW YEAR'S EVE

Kenneth Nichols Fecteau
Judy Nichols Fecteau

Kinihood Publishing LLC

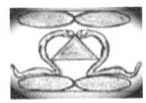

Kinihood Publishing LLC
Sequim, Washington
kinihood@centurylink.net

ISBN- 9798985059632

Cover art by: Kenneth Koskela
Copyright©A.K. Koskela, All Rights Reserved
www.kennethkoskela.com

Library of Congress Control Number: 2024918587

Printed in the United States of America

"The pain of parting is nothing to the joy of meeting again."

CHARLES DICKENS

PROLOGUE

My sister, Lizzy, and I have always been told that our high school years should be some of the most exciting times in our lives. Okay, I get it. Playing with our rock band, The Mols, along with our best friends, Hugo and Yerma, is unbelievably exciting. Our bookings during the holiday season this year have been at some of the best venues in the city. Sure, at school the classes are more challenging and our responsibilities at work are greater. Then, of course, there's dating, driving a car and all of the other perks that go along with getting older. Sure we have grown and learned, but the challenges and changes that we have faced over this holiday season are just not the same as the average teenager.

It began with a vision quest over the Thanksgiving holiday, when we were adopted by the Mistook Tribe. Our instructions by Rosethorn, Shaman of the Tribe, were to find "two bugs in a rock." Well, that turned out to be an ancient tribal artifact called the Crystal Heart. To find it, we had to time travel to another time and place during our vision quest. After posing as dancing girls in a saloon in Port Orion in 1888, we were abducted by Queen Ant LaRouge, a demented, self-proclaimed "Pirate Queen," who also sought the Crystal Heart. We were held at her mansion on Ant Hill Island until we agreed to help her find the treasure. With a whole lot of help from our friends, we escaped with our lives and the Crystal Heart. We thought our vision quest was over when we brought the artifact home to our tribe—Now we aren't so sure.

THE LAST STREAMERS OF CONFETTI ON NEW YEAR'S EVE

CHAPTER ONE

The sky was a vibrant blue. Wispy clouds looked like bleached driftwood floating overhead. A sandstone cliff, carved by violent winds and waves, towered over the sandy beach. The cliff's bare face of earth and rock was topped with tall spring grass and cowering scrub pines. Not far offshore, Mandy trained her binoculars on the cliff. Below, sat the deserted remains of a town. Only a few rotting dock posts and foundations were visible.

"You did exist," Mandy whispered to the wind. She wore a sad smile. "This town was really here, and I was once here too."

Mandy lurched, as her friend, Spring Rain, hit the throttle, and the boat zipped over the rough seas. "I think I know the island you are searching for," Spring said. "Once we get there, maybe it will relieve your troubled mind."

Storm clouds began to blot out the sun. Then suddenly, there it was. There was the inlet and a huge mountain in the sky. Its top disappeared in the gathering clouds. This was what was left of Ant Hill Island. The long gone ornate gargoyles and carved balconies left bare spots on the craggy walls, obliterated by wind, rain, saltwater … and a savage killer earthquake. All was silent, as the boat churned through the inlet on a leisurely turn around the bay.

"Look," Mandy yelled over the pounding surf. There was another boat not far away. A lone figure stood in the stern. He waved his hat. In the distance, Mandy thought she saw him smile.

"Please, Spring, please get us to him."

"I'm trying. But no matter how fast we go, we aren't gaining on him."

"Oh, my Lord, I think it's him!" A misty fog enveloped the inlet. Visibility became zero. When the fog lifted, the ship was gone.

Mandy's recurring dream had dogged her since returning from Port Orion. It was always about Ramone. Mandy had fallen in love with a pirate, more than a century ago. She could still hear his voice, still see his anguished face. She could never forget the heartbreak of her lover's farewell:

"Every goodbye is just the beginning of a new hello," he had said, as they embraced. "There's no such thing as never in forever. I will find you again, Mandy Elegant." Ramone's voice was ragged with torturous grief. "I promise, I will find you."

Every time that horrible scene ran through her head, Mandy would push it aside. But tonight that was impossible. It was a snowy Christmas Eve. By chance, Mandy and her sister, Lizzy, stumbled into the only place that was still open. Maybe it was the church bells, or the Christmas lights, or the desire for a piping hot cup of coffee before going home that drew them to their favorite coffee house. Or, maybe it was a blessed coincidence. Scant seconds ago, on a small stage, a total stranger sang his last song of the night:

"My love will keep its promise to the letter.
There's no such thing as never in forever."

His last chord hung in the air. His voice was a stranger's, but his words were Ramone's. Both sisters looked at each other with unbridled excitement. Could this really be Mandy's lost lover, returned to a different place with a different face?

"Is there anything else you need to know?" Lizzy asked with a huge smile.

"No, Lizzy," Mandy said dreamily. She closed her eyes, leaned back in her chair and sighed. "Now I know everything I need to know."

"Not quite," Lizzy giggled. "Guess who's coming over here?"

Mandy's mind struggled with metaphysical madness. As the stranger walked towards them, Lizzy wore an ecstatic grin. Mandy's smile masked pure panic.

"Hi," he smiled, "I know this probably sounds like a bad pick-up line, but do I know you two ladies?"

Mandy was speechless, so Lizzy quickly replied. "Maybe you've seen us perform before. We have a rock band called the Mols—an acronym for Mothers of Literature. We've played at a lot of the clubs and dances around town. Our next gig is at The Solstice Ballroom on New Year's Eve."

"Wow, that's terrific! I'm playing solo tonight, but I normally play with a rock band called The Phoenix. We're on winter break from college, and our agent lined up gigs for us throughout the holidays. I took this solo job because I've always wanted to see Tabula Rasa. My mom and dad told me that from the time I was little, I always talked about going to Tabula Rasa. They had no idea where I heard the name, but said I talked about it a lot. So finally I'm here in beautiful Tabula Rasa! By the way, my name is Zak Davis."

"I'm Lizzy Elegant ..."

"... and I'm Mandy Elegant. Please have a seat. I was absolutely mesmerized by your last song. Did you write it?"

Zak pulled up a chair next to Mandy. Their eyes locked, as he replied, "I did. In fact, it was the first real song I ever wrote. It was so weird, because it was like it wrote itself —I just started to write, and the whole thing came out of nowhere—maybe my subconscious. I really could never explain it, but it's my favorite of all of my songs. My band, The Phoenix, even does a rock version of it."

"Oh wow! Do you have a recording or video of that?" Mandy

asked.

"Sure, right here on my phone." Zak reached for his vest pocket.

Excitedly, Lizzy took out her phone for the transfer and asked Zak, "Do you mind if our band learns to play it? It would be great to do it on New Year's Eve, along with our fans' favorite song that we wrote, 'When Ya Gonna Wake Up?'"

As Zak transferred his video to Lizzy, he asked, "Do you have that one on video? I'd love to see it."

"Here you go," Lizzy smiled, as she transferred their video to Zak.

"You know," Zak said as he looked at Mandy, "On New Year's Eve, my band is playing the early show at a casino about fifty miles from here. Would you mind if I come to see you play and spend some time with you afterward?"

"N—No, that would be great!" Mandy flipped her hair and smiled shyly."

"And we'd love to have you come up and play your song with ours," Lizzy added.

"Okay, it's a date," he grinned. "I think we are about to be run out of here, so please let me get your phone numbers, and I'll stay in touch as I travel. I can't tell you how happy I am to have had the pleasure to meet you both."

"You too," both girls said as they got up, exchanged phone numbers with Zak and put on their coats.

Zak took each of their hands in his. "Merry Christmas, Mandy and Lizzy. This is a night I will never forget. I knew I wanted to come to Tabula Rasa, and now I think I know the reason why." He gave each of them a quick kiss on the cheek, before he turned to leave.

"Merry Christmas," they each replied.

The girls walked to their car in stunned silence, but while waiting for it to warm up, first Lizzy started to giggle, which caused Mandy to start to laugh. They laughed until tears were running down their cheeks.

"If Zak is who we think he is, this only confirms what we

suspected about ourselves!"

"I was Flora and you were Dora in a past life!"

"And," Lizzy said, romantic stars glistening in her eyes, "Ramone has returned to you … as Zak."

"And our vision quest rises from the ashes."

"Yep. Just like Zak's band name, 'The Phoenix,' the legendary bird consumed by fire, that rises from the ashes, reborn again."

Lizzy started the car and fishtailed out of the parking lot, not knowing they were headed, out into the great unknown.

CHAPTER TWO

Lizzy stirred and looked out the window. Gentle flurries danced by. She rubbed her eyes, stretched and yawned. "Oh," she groaned. She tousled her hair and sat up. "That was one heckuva dream … again!"

She remembered the day her frightening dream first began, because before that day, she had never been asked to visit her school advisor's office. Ms. Vale was her guidance counselor. She was a young, pretty woman with a mega brain and a marvelous sense of humor. She knew she needed it when dealing with a character like Lizzy. Lizzy knocked on the wooden office door with the covered window in it. Lizzy always wondered what Ms. Vale was trying to hide … what any of the teachers were trying to hide. They always covered up that little sliver of window in the door with stickers, or a sad looking curtain; or for those with no imagination, construction paper.

"Come in, Lizzy."

Ms. Vale motioned to the chair in front of her desk. Lizzy sat down, trying to look comfortable.

"Well, Lizzy, you look … um … fashionable as always."

Lizzy prided herself on dressing against the grain. But she knew that Ms. Vale was trying to soften her up. "Thank you, Ms. Vale," she said, with an angelic smile.

"I know you are wondering why I called you here."

"The thought had crossed my mind, Ms. Vale. Did I do something wrong?"

"No, no, not at …"

"Skirt too short? Clothes too bizarre? Makeup too freaky? Hair too distracting?"

Ms. Vale laughed. "I can see you're certainly not tired from your day in school."

"No, Ms. Vale, my adrenaline kicks in when the afternoon bell rings."

"Well, you aren't in any trouble. I brought you here because a few teachers have been concerned about your performance."

Lizzy broke into a devilish smile. "Ms. Vale! Aren't you getting a little too personal?"

That sent Ms. Vale into hysterics. She stared hopelessly at Lizzy. "Lizzy, what am I going to do with you?"

"I don't know, Ms. Vale, but I hope it's not discussing my performance anymore!"

"Lizzy. You're not in any trouble. Your grades are great, your attendance is great, your deportment …"

"Oh, no, Ms. Vale. I'm being deported!"

"Lizzy, will you be serious for a minute?"

"You have 55 seconds left."

"Everything is great … except for your lapses in punctuality."

"The late, great, Lizzy Elegant."

"Some of your teachers are concerned about your demeanor. They say your work is still excellent, but they say you seem depressed, distracted … staring out the window … and you, of all people, aren't speaking in class. Lizzy, knowing you as I do, not talking is a real red flag."

Lizzy had ceased to listen. A daydream that had become her recurring nightmare obliterated whatever Ms. Vale was saying. A sliver of moon tried to elbow its way through the cloudy sky. A million multicolored lights lined the shops and restaurants that ringed the windy, deserted plaza. A Spanish cathedral loomed in the distance. Its bell tower tolled the hour. Lizzy and her friend stood their ground in the damp cold. Their fingers tightened around the triggers of their guns. The sound of many footsteps approached from the black and blue shadows. Lizzy turned and was blinded by a lamplight. But in a split second of clarity, she saw a long arm raising a gun. Lizzy lunged and knocked her friend to the ground. She dropped her revolver, as a burning sensation shot up her hip. Lizzy looked up to see her companion was safe, firing his pistol and driving off their assailants. They watched the gunmen disappear into the gloom.

Lizzy squinted and rubbed her eyes, terrified at what she was seeing. Her friend had no face. Neither had their assailants.

"Lizzy? Lizzy!"

"I'm sorry, Ms. Vale, but I didn't hear what you just said."

"What do you remember last?"

"Something about me being deported."

Lizzy's thoughts were interrupted by a tapping on her bedroom door. She looked up to see Mandy's eyes peeping in, as she slowly opened the door. "Are you awake?" she whispered.

"Barely."

"Merry Christmas!" Mandy beamed.

"Merry Christmas to you, my dear sister!"

"I can hear Mom in the kitchen already. Are you ready to get up?"

Lizzy threw back the covers. "After the dream I had, I'd rather not go back to sleep. Just give me a minute to wash my face and get dressed."

"Was it a nightmare?"

"Yes, and one I keep having—but I'd rather not talk about it now. It's Christmas morning and time to celebrate."

As Eleanor closed the oven door, she was surprised to see Mandy and Lizzy appear in the kitchen doorway. Eleanor opened her arms wide to her daughters. "Merry Christmas my sweet girls! You're up so early!"

"Indeed, it is a Christmas miracle!" Lizzy exclaimed, as she and Mandy stepped into their mother's embrace.

Eleanor grinned, "I have some surprises."

"Well we just might have a couple of surprises for you too, but first I need coffee." Lizzy headed for the coffee pot and peeked into the oven. "What smells so good?"

"Oh, I'm baking a breakfast casserole and cinnamon buns for

you girls. By the way, the freezer and refrigerator are already full of food for next week, if you need it."

"Now I know where Mandy gets her need for efficiency." Lizzy poked her sister in the head, as she walked past.

"So where do you get your need for chaos?" Mandy grabbed her sister's hand, as Lizzy struggled towards the coffee.

"Some of us are just blessed with a natural, non-linear, creative mind." Lizzy grimaced, as she pulled her sister across the room. Mandy suddenly let go, causing Lizzy to lurch forward, banging into the cabinets. "If that leaves a bruise, you'll pay!" Lizzy poked her sister in the head again. This time a little harder.

"Enough," Eleanor threatened, "come and sit at the table."

Lizzy poured coffee for them and held out a cup to Mandy. "Peace."

Mandy flashed a peace sign and a smile, as she accepted the steaming cup.

After they were all seated, Eleanor got up and opened a drawer. "I'm so excited, I just can't wait. Merry Christmas!" she said, placing a small, green foil wrapped box in front of Mandy, and an identical package, wrapped in red foil, in front of Lizzy.

Mandy held up a finger and nodded at Lizzy. "Wait just one minute, Mom." They both dashed out of the kitchen and up to their rooms to get their gifts for Eleanor. Returning out of breath and excited, they placed their beautifully wrapped presents in front of their mother.

"Oh, they're so beautiful—too pretty to open."

"That would be thanks to the wrapping supplies at Antiques and Oddities," Lizzy laughed.

"Well," Eleanor smiled, "my store does have the best gift wrapping in all of Tabula Rasa. Thank you so much, but please, open your gifts first."

Without any more coaxing, Mandy and Lizzy gently removed the beautiful paper and delicate bows to find Victorian designed ring boxes. When opened, they looked at each other with wide eyes, when they saw the beautiful rings inside: golden bands with an exquisite filagree of flowers in figure-eights that wound around them. The rings were identical, except for the color of the flowers. Mandy's was a light citrine with diamonds and Lizzy's, a light aquamarine with diamonds. Mandy's eyes filled with tears, and Lizzy's hands trembled.

"Oh Mom, we saw these at the store and wanted them so much, but they were so expensive!" Mandy got up and gave her mother a hug.

Lizzy followed and did the same, saying, "I can't believe this, they are so gorgeous."

Eleanor radiated a beaming smile. "You know, I saw them at an antique jewelry auction and bought them for you two. I don't know how the package got mixed into the boxes you were unpacking for the store before Christmas. They were handmade in the mid to late 1800's and were probably wedding bands at that time. I had them sized to fit your right ring fingers. Did I guess correctly which color each of you would like best?"

"You have no idea how perfectly you chose," Mandy said, with a tear running down her cheek. These were the very rings the sisters had worn more than one hundred years ago, as Flora and Dora.

"Let's put them on and see how they look," Lizzy said, leading Mandy back to their chairs. They put on the rings, smiling and showing them off to their mother.

"Now it's your turn." Lizzy pushed their boxes in front of Eleanor who opened them carefully, folding the paper and placing the bows on the table's centerpiece. The packages contained boots from Lizzy and a jacket from Mandy.

"Oh, how did you two know exactly what I wanted for Christmas?" Eleanor left her chair to give each of them a big hug.

Lizzy smiled. "We saw you try them on, again and again, at Expressions. We knew you wanted them, but you never buy anything for yourself."

Eleanor nodded and said, "That is true sometimes, but you must have spent all of your savings on me."

Lizzy put her hands on her hips and stated sarcastically, "Yeah, but we're rock stars—We have money!" Mandy did a drum roll on the table, and they all started laughing.

The timer on the oven sounded, and Eleanor took the pans from the oven and filled their plates. As they enjoyed their breakfast, Eleanor began, "Okay, we need to have a quick family meeting before I leave for Grandma and Papa's. First of all, if you have any questions or problems while I'm away, call me. I don't care if it's in the middle of the night. I want to know what's going on with you. Thankfully, Aunt Billie has assured me that she will check on you from time to time. She also said that she's going to The Solstice for New Year's Eve and will make a video of your set for me." Eleanor paused and sighed. "I know you have to go to Manchester Castle Hotel to work on your article for the *Tabula Rasa Times*. One night would have been bad enough, but two! That place scares the bejeebers out of me."

"Mother," Mandy said, "you know you don't have to worry about us ... don't you?"

"I guess I just have to realize that my girls are growing up," Eleanor sighed. "I am so proud of you both, but it's hard to let go. Know that I do trust you, but I'll always worry."

As Eleanor got up to clear the table, she glanced at the clock. "Oh no, I really have to get dressed and out the door. I had to pack last night, so I didn't have time to clean up the living room after our Christmas Eve party. Will you do it for me?"

"Of course," Mandy and Lizzy nodded. "Go get ready!"

After hugs and kisses, Eleanor left for the airport, dressed in her new boots and jacket. Mandy and Lizzy walked into the living room to begin their first task.

"This place looks like a war zone," Lizzy sighed. She looked around the room with wonder. Scrunched up wrapping paper in festive fandango colors was haphazardly thrown everywhere. The blinking Christmas lights added to the chaotic color spectrum. There were mountains of half-open boxes with gifts and clothing still in them. Lizzy had draped her new skirt over a Tiffany lamp shade. With the light on, it looked like a headless showgirl with one leg. The centerpiece on the coffee table: a half-filled bottle of wine looked down on a tapestry of cookie crumbs, cold pizza, homemade fruitcake, assorted nuts, chocolate Santas, Christmas bows, eating utensils, a corkscrew and mangled cork. Lizzy picked up the half-filled bottle of chardonnay and took a big gulp.

Mandy reached out for the bottle and brushed aside some stray ribbons and bows. Lizzy joined her on the sofa as they passed the wine back and forth.

"I'm having that same recurring dream that's been driving me crazy," Mandy began. "I'm in a motorboat with Spring Rain, and we visit the remains of Port Orion and Ant Hill Island. Then we see a boat in the distance with a man whom I'm sure is Ramone, but I can't get any closer. What do you think it means?"

"Maybe, no matter how close you get to him, time and time again, you can never get any closer. He's dogging you like a shadow. He's also right in front of you, but you can't get any closer. Then again …"

"… There's Zak."

Lizzy nodded. "Maybe you're finally getting closer."

"We'll see."

Lizzy shook her head, groaned and sank back into the sofa.

"What?"

"Well, I didn't think it meant anything."

"What didn't?"

"My own recurring dream."

"How long has it been going on?"

"It started about the same time as yours."

"Why didn't you tell me?"

"I wasn't quite sure what the dream meant."

Mandy gave her sister an excited smile. "Ooh," she said, "tell me all about it—and don't leave out a single detail."

"Gossip monger …"

"Come on!"

"Okay, here goes." Lizzy closed her eyes and began. As her tale unfolded, she seemed oblivious to Mandy, and where she was. "It began as a daydream that I had when I was in Ms. Vale's office at school. But now, I have it almost every night. A friend and I are in a deserted plaza; nowhere that I recognize. It's damp and cold, and we are holding guns. Suddenly, armed figures emerge from the shadows, and one of them raises his weapon and fires. I lunge and knock my friend out of the way, but I think I was shot. I am in pain but am aware that my friend is on his feet and firing back. The weird thing is that when I look at my friend, he has no face. Neither do the attackers …"

"Lizzy …"

The sound of her sister's voice brought Lizzy back to the present. "What do you think?"

"Oh come on, Lizzy, it's so obvious. And it's nothing new. You know the friend who would take a bullet for you, and you for him."

"You mean Hugo?"

"Of course," Mandy replied. "I know that since our vision quest, and his obvious crush on you, you have been uncomfortable around him."

"That's because I know where this is all headed. Hugo's going to ask me out. So, what should I do? If I don't date him, I risk losing his friendship. If I do date him, and it doesn't work out, I risk losing his friendship. Not to mention what it might do to the Mols."

"Give it time and stop worrying. You two have a bond that is unbreakable," Mandy said. "And speaking of the Mols, we've got practice tomorrow. Let's get this joint cleaned up," she said as she finished off the last of the wine and tossed the bottle into the trash can.

CHAPTER THREE

The next day, the Mols reconvened for their final run-through for Friday's Solstice Ballroom, New Years Eve Gig. The Community Rehearsal Hall was downtown in the concrete and steel section of town—the shipyards. Frozen gray slush capped the parking lot and clung to the rusty barb wire fences. Lizzy and Mandy skidded to a stop. Lizzy left the car running and the heat on. A sense of weariness hung over them.

"What a week," Lizzy sighed.

"What a month," Mandy replied.

"Everything has changed."

"Well ..." Mandy said, " not everything."

The windows were fogging up. The heater hummed, as if it was listening.

"You've got to be kidding! How about finding out we lived past lives—a vision quest that almost got us killed." Lizzy paused and shook her head sadly. "Not to mention we can't even relate to our friends anymore."

Mandy was silent for a moment. "I suppose, you're right. Before we left on our vision quest, I was having so much fun with Matt. After we returned, I felt like we had nothing in common. That's why we broke up. It was a mutual decision by two people who had become strangers to each other."

"Yes ... and then there was the reaction to it. To a lot of girls, Matt Mitchell is a status date, class president, football star, expensive car ... and really good looking."

"None of that mattered. He's still a good friend and a really sweet guy."

"I know what you mean. I've been going out with Lou, for almost a year. Everything was going great. But when we got back … well … it just didn't click. It felt wrong…. It was wrong." Lizzy brightened up and gave Mandy a wink. "We remain friends … thank God for that! I love his Daffy Duck laugh … and his record collection! Speaking of record collections, Lou is coming over to pick me up after practice. We're going to go over to his house to listen to some of his new vinyl."

Mandy laughed. "He's such a wonderful guy. I'm so glad you remain friends."

Lizzy nodded. "Yeah, we spend so much time together, people don't even know that we've broken up."

"Well, I did tell Yerma."

"That's cool … she won't tell anyone."

Mandy hesitated. "That's true, but Yerma did tell me something that you might not like."

Lizzy gave Mandy a wry smile. "What could Yerma have said that I won't like?"

Mandy took Lizzy's hand. "Well, it's not really that bad."

"Well, don't keep me in suspense!"

"She said that she had talked to Hugo, the day after we got out of school for our holiday. She said that Hugo suspected that you and Lou were having trouble." Mandy hesitated to go on.

"What? Spit it out!"

"She said that Hugo told her that if you guys split up, he is finally going to have the courage to do something he has wanted to do since junior high—Ask you out."

"Oh no—Oh no—Oh no! This is awful! I knew this day was coming!" Lizzy wailed.

"Calm down!" Mandy said reassuringly. "It's going to be fine."

"No, it's not going to be fine, dunderhead. Remember my recurring dream? I took a bullet for a friend, Mandy—Not a boyfriend! Get it?"

Mandy nodded, reached over and shut off the car. "Let's not worry about that now. We've got a rehearsal to get through."

Both sisters got out of the car and tiptoed up the icy sidewalk. Hugo and Yerma were already on stage, tuning up. After exchanging a few hugs, "hellos" and "how was your Christmases," the Mols got down to business.

"How about we start with 'Too Much Stuff?'" Yerma asked.

Mandy laughed. "Good choice!" She knew the whacked-out song always put the band in a rocking mood. Mandy counted it off, and soon the band was lost in the volume and drive that bounced off the ceiling of the ancient hall:

"I've got stuff crammed in cabinets, and under the sink.
Some stuff smells funny, and some of it stinks.
There's stuff that is broken, and stuff we don't want.
Like that crappy gift, from your crusty old aunt."
Too much stuff, too much stuff.
Great God almighty, I got too much stuff!"

The hilarity of this rocker was like rocket fuel. The Mols ripped through the rest of their set list with passion, pizzaz and punch. The last song they worked on was Zak's," There's No Such Thing As Never In Forever."

Yerma shook with excitement. "That video you sent us … well … I was blown away by his group, the song, his guitar playing … and he is one gorgeous guy."

"Well," Mandy added nervously, "he might not be able to get here on New Year's."

"Let's hope he does," Yerma winked, "for our sake and yours."

The band tore into Zak's rocker. After a few takes, it was hard to tell any difference between their version and Zak's. The Mols were ecstatic—All except Hugo.

With the rehearsal ending, Lizzy noticed Hugo looking over at her. "Oh, no," she thought. She looked nervously at her watch."Where the heck is Lou?" Hugo had put down his bass and was walking over.

"Lizzy," he said shyly," I need to talk with you."

Lizzy looked away. "I am so screwed," she thought.

The stage door opened.

"Lou!" Lizzy cried. "I'm so glad you're finally here."

Hugo stopped and stared hopelessly at Lizzy.

"Hi, Lizzy!" Lou said. "Sorry I'm late. Are you ready to go?"

"Right now!" Lizzy replied, as she threw on her coat. "Bye guys, see ya later!" She grabbed Lou by the arm and hustled him out the stage door.

CHAPTER FOUR

After a long day, working on inventory at their mother's boutique, the sisters finally returned home. As the gray daylight gave way to a gloomy, cold night, the sisters packed their luggage.

"Mother will be gone until New Year's Day," Mandy smiled. "Meanwhile, the Elegant sisters will work on their teen scene, *Tabula Rasa Times* column."

"Yes, I'm really jazzed about that," Lizzy grinned. "It really fell into our laps—two nights in the Manchester Castle. And they're all paid for by the *Tabula Rasa Times*!"

"And now, we get to do our article on its hundredth anniversary! You know Mother was really frightened to death of us staying in that hotel ...."

"... until you began to work your magic, Mandy charm and reason on her."

"What choice did I have? When you were telling her about our article, you didn't exactly fill her with a sense of safety."

"What are you talking about?" Lizzy asked innocently.

"You know exactly what I'm talking about. All of your deliberately obvious innuendos like, 'Oh Mother, I promise we won't stay in room 420, where a guy was found hanging around.'"

"Well, I didn't tell her someone hanged himself in there."

"Then there was the, 'Oh, Mother, they say the view from the roof is to die for!'"

"Well, I didn't tell her someone did jump off the roof and die."

"Then there was the joke about room 566. Remember? 'You hear a lot of deadpan humor in there.'"

"Well, I didn't tell her that those people just disappeared."

"Mother knows about those stories. Every Halloween, they feature them in the *Tabula Rasa Times.*"

"Well ... I couldn't help busting her balloons a little bit."

Mandy frowned and searched Lizzy's face. "Speaking of busting balloons, are you still worrying about the New Year's Eve gig ... and Hugo?"

"Oh, please," Lizzy replied, shaking her head wearily. "Please, Mandy, I would rather not even think about that. Let's get going."

It was a short drive out of town along the coast road, with a magnificent view of the frozen bay. However, the ambience that surrounded them grew dimmer, the closer they came to their destination. A cold fog began to drift in. Wisps of clouds floated across the hillside, looking like evaporating ghosts.

"Look Lizzy!" Mandy pointed to the expansive lawn in front of the Manchester Castle's front wall. "We have never seen the painted metal sculptures of Atlantean soldiers and war elephants that they installed a few weeks ago."

Lizzy slowed and squinted through the fog. "Oh, wow! There must be fifty soldiers and what, three war elephants? Well, welcome to what is definitely going to be an unusual two night stay."

Mandy laughed as Lizzy turned the car into a long driveway and skidded through the filigreed wrought iron gates. The Castle was a fading pink, with a distinctly British architectural style. Three gables poked out of the darkness. They were hardly uniform in height, creating an illusion of turret-like mountains. An elaborate garden decorated with elegant ornaments and sparkling, golden Christmas lights surrounded the hotel. Lizzy idled the car. The sisters sat in silence, steam fogging up the car windows.

"There's that gnarly dead tree," Lizzy said

"It's been dead for years; I can't believe they never took it down."

"The Manchester family is superstitious regarding that tree. Mr. Manchester insisted that, dead or alive, that tree was not to be cut down ..."

"... and there are the sightings of Mr. Manchester's white, ghost cat guarding the gate."

The sisters parked their car, grabbed their bags and headed up the garden walkway, toward the front staircase. They stopped and looked up at the edifice. A chill rippled up their spines. Lizzy led the way up the stairs, as Mandy, uncharacteristically, lagged behind. When Lizzy reached the top of the stairs, she turned to see that Mandy was struggling. She ran back down the stairs and took her sister's arm. "Are you okay? You look so pale!"

"Let's sit for a minute. I just suddenly felt really dizzy after I saw those people."

"Umm, Mandy, we are the only people out here."

Mandy looked at her sister in disbelief. "You mean that you didn't see the couple coming down the stairs? They were dressed in old clothes, like from the early nineteen-hundreds, and complaining about Mr. Manchester not paying them enough for their work. Then they disappeared, and I got really dizzy—It felt like I was seeing into another dimension or something."

Lizzy felt her sister's forehead. "Well, you don't feel like you are running a temperature, but you are still trembling a little. I don't doubt that you saw or felt something. There are just too many stories of unusual events happening to people on this property. I'm just surprised that it wasn't me. Remember, you're the steady, rational one."

At that, Mandy began to laugh with relief. "Maybe instead of a performing arts career, I'm destined to become a parapsychologist.... Help me up and let's get inside to see what awaits."

"What probably awaits is a whole lot of weirdness! Only time, or out of time, will tell." Lizzy pulled her sister up and took her bag.

Upon opening the door, they were startled by a large, white

cat that hissed as it ran out the door. When they entered the lobby, they peeked into a sitting room to their left. There was a massive fireplace with Mr. Manchester's portrait above it, floor-to-ceiling walnut book cases, a large desk and comfortable chairs.

"Look at that library! I can't wait to take a look at that," Mandy whispered.

Lizzy gasped. "Yes, and look at that creepy portrait of Mr. Manchester gazing down on his guests. I sure hope they let you take books to your room. Come on, let's check in."

Lizzy led the way to a long walnut desk. A heavy-set man with slicked back hair and black-rimmed glasses watched their approach. With a forced smile, he greeted them. "Welcome to the Manchester Castle. I believe you must be the young ladies who are doing the reporting for the *Tabula Rasa Times*."

"We are indeed," Lizzy replied, with the same forced smile. "I'm Lizzy Elegant, and this is my sister, Mandy."

"I'm Richard Knox, and it's a pleasure to meet you both. We have your reservation and room 566 has been prepared for your arrival."

"Umm, Room 566," Lizzy said haltingly. "I think I heard that ... that room might have had some unusual events."

"Oh, of course. I supposed the two of you had read some of the past articles about the Manchester Castle in your research. I specifically chose room 566 for you, so that you could dispel the rumors. I'm sure you will appreciate the charm of our beautiful room. After your breakfast tomorrow, I will be available to take you on a tour of the entire property, and you can ask me any questions you have."

"Thank you so much. We look forward to interviewing you for our article. Have you worked here for a long time?" Mandy asked.

"Only 32 years," he proudly replied. "Mrs. Manchester Williams hired me when I was just out of school. I began as a bellhop and worked my way up to assistant manager."

"That's a wonderful story already. We can't wait to hear more about the hotel."

"Of course. I have also arranged time for you to interview Mrs. Manchester Williams and many members of the staff. We can talk about that in the morning, but for now, I'll escort you up to your room." He nodded to his associate to cover the desk and then brought the luggage carrier over and loaded their bags. Mr. Knox led the way down a short hallway and slid open a brass gate to an elevator.

Lizzy grimaced as he closed the gate and turned a crank to number 5. The old elevator stalled once before lurching back to life. Lizzy closed her eyes and held the safety rail with a white-knuckled grip as it bumped its way to the top, where it ground to a groaning halt.

"Here we are," Mr. Knox announced, "level five, west tower. The view of the bay from here is magnificent."

As Mr. Knox led them down the hallway, Mandy and Lizzy slowly followed, examining the paintings and photographs that lined the walls. Many of them were of the Castle during it's early days, and the omnipresent portraits of Mr. Manchester and other members of the Manchester family. As they approached room 566, Lizzy whispered to Mandy, "Are you feeling okay?"

In response, Mandy just held out her trembling hands and smiled weakly.

The key creaked in the lock, and the doorknob groaned with the twist. Mr. Knox had to put his shoulder to the door to open it. The door scraped across the carpet, as if it was afraid of going inside. Mandy and Lizzy glanced hopelessly at each other, but followed Mr. Knox into the room. As Mr. Knox opened the long, floral-patterned curtains to display the foggy view of the bay, Lizzy turned on a Tiffany lamp that sat on a rich mahogany table. A fire was burning in a gray, stone fireplace. Flickering shadows rippled across the dark antique furniture, floral bedspreads and sofa. Two high-backed chairs sat catty-corner to the hearth. Lizzy turned on two other Tiffany floor lamps and joined her sister at the fireplace. It was then that they noticed a huge oval portrait above the hearth.

"Charles Frederick Manchester … again," Lizzy said.

"Oh yes," Mr. Knox chirped cheerfully. "Isn't it a wonderful portrait? We have one in every room of the hotel to honor him and his great vision."

Lizzy shuddered. "Vision! It does look like his eyes are watching the room."

"You're funny," Mr. Knox laughed. "All right ladies, I'll leave you to unpack. Your complimentary meals will be served in the dining room on the first floor. It is open from 7 to 10 daily, and room service is available. You can ring the front desk if there is anything that you need, and I will see you at 9 tomorrow morning."

"Thank you so much," Mandy said, as she extended her hand.

Lizzy also shook Mr. Knox's hand, saying, "You have been so welcoming and helpful. Thank you."

As the door closed behind Mr. Knox, Lizzy turned to Mandy. "Do you think we should leave?"

"Why don't we just unpack our suitcases? Maybe we'll feel better after we're settled in."

"Maybe we won't. Then what?"

Mandy smiled and patted her sister on the back. "Then we run for our lives."

They went about the business of unpacking their things. Lizzy hesitated at the closet door, slowly opening it just enough so the lamp light would pierce the darkness. She heaved a sigh of relief. Only hangers and a laundry bag greeted her wide open eyes.

Mandy put their makeup case on the dressing table.

"Well," Lizzy said, sinking into an elegant love seat, "so far so good...." She looked around the room, as if she remained unconvinced.

Mandy flopped down next to her sister. "Yep, so far so good," she said uncertainly.

They kicked off their shoes and put four tired feet on some comfortable ottomans. It had been a long day. Each closed her eyes and smiled. When they opened their eyes, something had changed.

Lizzy nudged Mandy." Heh," she said uncertainly.

"Yes?" Mandy yawned.

"Doesn't Mr. Manchester's portrait seem a little different to you?"

Mandy squinted. "Oh, good grief, it is."

Lizzy leapt to her feet. "Mandy, let's get out of here."

"No wait, there must be some logical explanation for this."

"Logical explanation? You've got to be kidding!"

"Look. The portrait is really a big, oval, wide-screen TV!"

Lizzy sat back down and made herself comfortable. "Doesn't it look like some weird giant eye?"

Mandy nodded and grabbed the remote. "Let's see what's on."

"Hmmm," Lizzy said. "How come there's no menu on the screen?"

"Oh, this is quant," Mandy said sarcastically. "This remote has button controls."

"Oh well, let's just start with channel one."

On the screen, a bomb exploded, followed by gunfire and frantic screaming.

"Well. That's not very cheery."

"Yeah, let's try channel two."

A swarthy looking man in a straw hat was tearing up a newspaper and punching a table..

"He's scary looking!"

"Stop moaning Lizzy; let's try three."

Channel three was showing a muddy man in a sinking rowboat.

Channel four had an elderly woman in a towel turban turning over Tarot cards.

None of the programs looked mildly interesting. But surfing the channels kept coming up with the same unsettling shows. After going through all of them again, there was something wrong with what they were seeing. No matter what channel Mandy pressed, the same show was now on all of them.

"What is going on?" Lizzy asked nervously.

Mandy struggled, punching the buttons rapid fire. "I don't know what happened—It's all of the scenes from each of the other programs rolled into one."

Every channel had the same program. Suddenly Mandy hit a channel with a totally different show, in black and white. Two women, on all fours, were crawling in the darkness.

"This is so freakin' weird!"

"It's getting weirder," Mandy whispered.

The screen seemed to reach out, as if pulling Mandy and Lizzy into the movie.

"Mandy ... Do you have the sensation of crawling?"

" Yes! Just like the people in front of us!"

"Yes, that's what I was going to say."

"Oh, this is mind blowing!" Mandy gasped.

"Yes, and what's really scary is we seem to be gaining on them...."

"We are!"

In a flash, they caught up with the two shadows and then seemed to sink into their bodies, like they were cosmically fused.

There was silence in the hotel room. The TV screen just showed a still photograph of two shadows crawling under a black sky:

It was Mandy and Lizzy Elegant.

It was Zoey and Desiree Daniels.

CHAPTER FIVE

Like Mandy and Lizzy, on Christmas Eve Hugo and Yerma had visited Rosethorn, Shaman of the Mistook Tribe. When they asked the Shaman if their interpretations of their vision quest were correct, Rosethorn replied with one of his typically cryptic answers, "You decide." Hugo and Yerma walked away baffled.

That night, Yerma began to have a series of unsettling dreams. Day after day she tried, but failed, to put the images out of her mind. There were things about their vision quest that festered like sores in her subconscious.

Hugo's own nocturnal journeys had turned into nightmares. After a few harrowing, sleepless nights, he called Yerma.

"Hey, Hugo! I was just going to call you. What's up?"

"Well ..." he said and paused.

Yerma prayed that he would not ask her about his unrequited crush. Luckily, he did not.

"I've been having these weird dreams about Flora and Dora, and Mandy and Lizzy."

"So have I! How about Rosethorn and Moon-Sun?"

"Yes, them too!"

"At first I thought our vision quest was just about going back in time and retrieving the Crystal Heart. But now? I'm not so certain."

"Nor am I." Hugo scratched his head and frowned. "So what do all these dreams mean, and how are they connected to our vision quest?"

A bewildered Yerma shook her head. "I do not know, I do

not know. In my dream, I saw Ice-Fire and Moon-Sun walking toward each other out of this blurry mist." Yerma paused. "I don't know if this is going to make any sense, but … well … they kind of became the same person."

"Yes!" Hugo exclaimed. "Then Ice-Fire and Moon-Sun morphed into Rosethorn!"

Yerma nodded excitedly. "Then I saw the same thing happen to Mandy and Flora …"

"… and Lizzy and Dora! The more I think about it," Hugo groaned, "the more complex it gets."

"Not to mention, we're having the same dreams!"

"We've got to call Rosethorn."

The two friends contacted him immediately. They gave the Shaman a brief outline of their dreams, followed by a few questions. Rosethorn gave them no answers but agreed to see them the following morning.

"I'm a bit scared Hugo. What if the answers to our questions are worse than not knowing … or propels us into another part of our vision quest … another trip down the rabbit hole?"

Hugo nodded somberly. "It's kinda like what the native warrior, Bloody Knife, said. 'Tomorrow we go home on a road we do not know.'"

"Good night, Hugo."

"Good night, Yerma … pleasant dreams."

"Yeah, right."

****

There were flyers and circulars stapled and taped around a telephone pole. One advertisement announced the premier of a brand new Clara Bow movie. At a newspaper stand, headlines screamed of the gangland murder of three people. Model T cars went bouncing down the city streets. Men passed by in stylish hats, doubled-breasted suits with cuffs and wide ties. Flapper Girls strutted their stuff: bucket hats, high heels, lots of makeup and shockingly short skirts; smoking, laughing and spewing out profanity. Across town, Mandy and Lizzy were oblivious to their surroundings. They found themselves on top of a building.

"Why are we crawling across a roof, looking down on a fire?" Lizzy whispered.

"Why are you wearing a mask?"

"I might ask you the same thing."

Both girls stifled a laugh.

"Why are you wearing a gypsy durag on your head?"

"Don't you remember?" Lizzy giggled. "We got them at the two for one sale at the gypsy store!"

"The word 'remember'... when you said that word ... I've started remembering ... remembering so much that it's making me dizzy. I need air."

Lizzy was having the same problems. Both girls stripped off their masks. The reality of the moment came down on them like an anvil dropped off Mount Everest. In the moonlight, the faces they saw before them were not the ones they knew.

"Is that you, Mandy?" a terrified Lizzy asked.

"Oh, thank God, Lizzy. It's you!"

"Yes," she replied with a baffled look. "I'm still Lizzy Elegant ... but somehow ... I am Desiree Daniels at the same time ... and the year is 1928!"

"I'm feeling the same way. I am still Mandy Elegant ... but at the same time I am Zoey Daniels ... and yes, the year is 1928 ... and we are in the French Quarter of New Orleans."

The sisters shared a moment of relief. That moment disappeared. The memories of Mandy and Lizzy were eclipsed by those of Zoey and Desiree. A long past filled their minds like blood filling a plasma bag. They were Mandy and Lizzy living other people's lives. Most terrifying of all, they knew the danger they were in. Zoey and Desiree's problems had become Mandy and Lizzy's.

They leaned over the facade of the roof. Smoke billowed out of Josiah's Restaurant. Screams of terror echoed out of the burning ruins.

"People are trapped in the restaurant!" Zoey cried. "The whole ground floor is on fire, and they can't get out through the front entrance!"

"The side door must be jammed too!"

The sisters put their masks back on. They hung over the top of the roof and swung onto the upstairs balcony. They held onto the cast iron rails that rimmed the balcony and dropped to the ground. The sisters made their way to the side door. Sure enough, it was wedged shut. Zoey spied a tire iron in the back of a truck and retrieved it. Within seconds, Zoey and Desiree pried open the door. People staggered out, blinded by the smoke, coughing and stumbling. Fire trucks and police car sirens came closer and closer.

"Time to get out of here." Desiree whispered.

Suddenly, fire engines and police cars screeched to a halt and surrounded Josiah's Restaurant. The Midnight Shadows were already gone.

****

The following morning, two glamorous young ladies stepped out into the chilly November sunshine. Their neighbors called them "It" girls. These were girls who had that extra special something called "It" that earned them the envy of jealous women and the longing of lovesick men. Their meticulously applied makeup framed their lovely faces. Thick, dark eyeliner added an air of menace and mystery. In the French Quarter, the Daniels sisters were hard partying Flapper Girls. Last night they were the Midnight Shadows, dressed in black clothing and masks. Today, Desiree Daniels wore a dark purple coat and scandalously short dress. Her matching bucket hat and brown bangs made Desiree hopelessly cute. Her dark eyes were hypnotic and alluring. Zoey's black bucket hat accentuated her radiant blonde hair. She wore a matching coat and dress, fashionably short. Her beautiful smile was all light and love. That made Zoey irresistible.

The Daniels sisters made their way down to Josiah's

Restaurant. They didn't want to believe the morning newspapers. They wanted to believe that last night was nothing more than a bad dream. Tragically, in the daylight, the devastation was no longer cloaked in surreal darkness. Smoldering gray ashes smudged the bright blue sky. Glass was scattered across the intersection. The wooden doors had exploded into a million burned out match sticks. Both girls fought back tears for their dear friend, Josiah, proprietor of the restaurant that was blown to smithereens. Their sadness turned to contempt when they saw a familiar figure approaching.

Louis D'Quad was well known throughout the French Quarter as a man about town, wealthy and powerful. He claimed to be a pillar of the community. Zoey and Desiree knew D'Quad as a blustering loudmouth and liar. He was a lawbreaker and bully who used intimidation and worse to get his way. Prohibition meant alcohol was illegal—So was gambling and smuggling. D'Quad claimed he made his money in imports and exports, railroads, utilities and stocks. Savvy residents knew otherwise. D'Quad frequented Victoria's Place on North Rampart Street. It was a notorious speakeasy. Gambling, drinking, dancing and danger reined. Police and elected officials on the take, gangsters and women of ill repute were always in attendance. Fortunes were lost in rigged games of chance. Those same games made Louis D'Quad a millionaire. His palatial mansion, fancy cars and his huge luxury yacht, *The Eclipse*, attested to that.

Louis D'Quad wore his trademark white straw hat, omni present toothpick between his teeth and a condescending sneer. "Well, well, what do we have here? The Belles of New Orleans, my dear Zoey and Desiree Daniels. To what do I owe this pleasure?"

"Pleasure?" Desiree snapped. "Only an idiot would see this disaster as a pleasure."

D'Quad's smirk disappeared. "I was referring to you and your sister, missy."

Desiree didn't break stride. "Hey, big boss man, why are you here? Did you come to see a little of your so-called 'business associates' handiwork?"

Louis D'Quad spit out his toothpick and glared at the sisters. "Are you accusing me of something, Desiree?"

"Word on the street is you didn't have much use for Josiah," Zoey said.

D'Quad laughed derisively. "Ah, little ladies, all you gals are so obsessed with idle banter … especially you two with your little gossip column in the *New Orleans Nitpicker*."

"We don't have to look far for the gossip, D'Quad. Your friends are blabbermouths," Zoey replied.

Desiree nodded and smiled wickedly. "You're the hub of the bicycle wheel, and all of your blabbermouth friends are the spokes connected to you."

D'Quad tried to hold his temper. "First, you both know about the two vigilantes who stalk our streets, wreaking havoc on people and businesses, don't you? It might be them! They've brought terror to this city, and everyone is at risk. If it wasn't those crazy Midnight Shadows, it was Kongo Kaminga's gang, the Street Sweepers, that was behind the hit, no doubt. You both know old man Josiah was selling rotgut hooch. Kongo's gang smuggles in expensive imported stuff, and Josiah refuses to buy it. Kongo don't like that."

"Or," Desiree said, smiling coyly, "maybe it might be that Josiah was not buying expensive smuggled spirits from you."

D'Quad removed his straw hat, scratched his head and replaced it at a jaunty angle. He glared at the Daniels sisters with angry eyes. "Don't go printing that kind of accusation in your rag of a newspaper. That's slander and can only cause you a whole lot of trouble, little ladies."

"First of all, don't call us little ladies …" Desiree replied with angry indignation.

"… and why would we print anything about you in our flighty gossip column?" Zoey gave D'Quad a knowing smile. "Though you do have quite a reputation for, well …"

"… so many things," Desiree added.

It was clear the sisters had touched a nerve. D'Quad's face

was framed in fury. "I got no more time to listen to you," D'Quad said angrily. "But you play nice—or I'll play nasty." He turned and walked away. Suddenly, he stopped and looked at the smoldering ruins of Josiah's Restaurant, then looked back at the sisters. "You know—you are right about one thing. I do have a reputation for my fiery temper—and I know where you live." He turned, began to whistle and took a leisurely stroll down the street, past the site of the deadly disaster.

"We've got to keep an eye on him." Zoey said somberly.

"Yes," Desiree replied. "Sooner or later, we'll get the goods on him at those speakeasies. You know what that means."

"Yep. Dress sexy, bat eyeballs, dump drinks in potted plants, do the Charleston with criminals ..."

"... and just listen to the gossip."

"But what about our house? What about our safety?"

The pitter-patter of afternoon rain stopped their reverie. It soon turned into a downpour. Zoey and Desiree mince-stepped, uncertainly, over the slick pavement. Their home loomed in the distance. Window boxes hung from the second story balcony. Sad flowers sagged over the sides, pleading for help against the relentless rain. The sisters opened the cast iron gate and hurried through the courtyard to their front door. Zoey fumbled with the lock, then stumbled inside. Desiree followed. She locked the security latch on the door and struggled to remove her soaked coat. Zoey and Desiree went from room to room, checking the locks on windows and doors.

Satisfied that their home was as secured as it could be, Zoey said, "Come on. We're dripping water all over the place. Even my shoes are wet. Let's get out of these clothes and go out to eat. I'm hungry!"

"Me too!"

"How about driving over to Vida Pasada's for dinner?"

"I'm in!"

The girls changed into dry clothes, put on fresh makeup, bucket hats and overcoats and stepped outside. As they did, they noticed something hanging on the door. It was a red and black woven cord tied around a bloody rabbit's foot and a dove's wing —a juju charm—never a good sign.

"I think we better forget dinner and go straight to Madame Ravonjay," Desiree said solemnly.

Zoey revved up the car, Desiree jumped in, and they rolled slowly across town.

****

New Orleans is never what it seems, day or night. Spirits, good and bad, wander the ancient streets. Dark voodoo lurks in the shadows. There is the omnipresent danger of mob violence. The vigilante Midnight Shadows were wreaking havoc all over the city. But there was a place of sanctuary. Everyone knew of Madame Ravonjay's beautiful two story home on St. Ann Street. To the long-time residents of the French Quarter, she was a respected and saintly friend to everyone. For those who did not know her, she was a fake and a fraud. They would say Ravonjay could afford to be generous to everyone because she conned people out of lots of money with her phony cures and charms for any evil that befell them. That did not matter to the many she had helped and befriended. Her customers were the poor and the powerless who counted on her gris-gris bags and paranormal powers to protect them from danger or distress. Ravonjay never let them down.

Zoey and Desiree Daniels met Madame Ravonjay, when they first arrived in New Orleans. After a chance encounter in Jackson Square, she had became a close friend and trusted confidante. Tonight, Zoey and Desiree were beside themselves, as they entered Madame Ravonjay's parlor. The room was so warm, so inviting, so safe. The floors were unadorned oak, covered with an array of colorful carpets. Shelves rose from floor to ceiling with books, teak boxes with little brass locks, jars and hand-woven baskets. Statues of Jesus and angels mingled with those of voodoo icons, Marie Laveau and Bayou John. The entire living room was illuminated by scores of candles.

Madame Ravonjay was seated in a high-backed, cobra cane chair, behind an octagonal table. In the flickering candlelight, her radiant smile seemed to dispel some of the dancing shadows.

"Come in, come in," she said with a laugh." Get over here, my girls. Tell me what is on your minds."

Zoey and Desiree sat down. "Not anything good, I'm afraid," Zoey said.

"Someone put a juju charm on our front door," Desiree added.

"Do you have it with you?"

Desiree opened her purse, took it out and handed it to Ravonjay.

"Ah," she said with a frown, as she gently ran her fingers along the ribbon, blood stained rabbit's foot and dove's wing. She got up from her cobra chair and paced.

Both sisters watched her intently. Ravonjay wore a floor length, woven, striped dress and an African Tignon on her head. The turban was a swirling rainbow of colors. Heavy makeup could not cover deep scars on her forehead, face and throat. Ravonjay's voice was a gritty rasp. She walked with a slight limp and was barefoot.

Ravonjay returned to the table. "Each of you take hold of one of my hands." Her gaze swept Zoey's eyes, then Desiree's. She repeated the process twice.

Ravonjay leaned back in her chair. "This rabbit was trapped, and his foot was cut off — as was this dove wing. This charm is symbolic of a trap. The way this cord is tied in two loops means that both of you are in great peril."

"Oh, wonderful," Desiree said hopelessly. "What can we do?"

"Do not worry. Do not worry," Ravonjay said reassuringly. She went over to a bookcase. She scanned the shelves, found one, and pushed aside some debris. She unscrewed the lid of a stained glass jar, filled two small gris-gris bags and returned to the table.

"Put these on your doorstep. No evil shall enter your home." She looked pensive for a moment and said, "But remember there is a dangerous trap that you must look out for." Ravonjay handed the juju charm back to Desiree. She rose, walked over to the girls, kissed each on the cheek and ushered them out the door. "Go on home, my sweet girls, and have a wonderful evening."

"Thank you so much, Madame Ravonjay."

They hopped into their car and headed home. "I'm a little relieved. Are you?" Zoey asked as she drove.

"A little bit," Desiree replied, "but I think it was D'Quad who left the charm, and you know he means business. I can't get the image of the burnt-out remains of Josiah's Restaurant out of my head."

After a short drive home, Zoey and Desiree parked their car. As the sisters made their way through the courtyard and to the front door, they looked around nervously. Suddenly, they both stopped and stared.

"Oh, no …" Desiree shivered. "I can't believe this is happening again."

There, on their front door, was another juju charm with a blood red ribbon.

CHAPTER SIX

Near sunrise, Hugo and Yerma skidded their way into the Mistook Tribal Council House parking lot. They found a smiling Rosethorn waiting for them at the door. They exchanged hugs and greetings. "You look well," he said with a smile.

"As do you," they both replied.

Rosethorn's clothing was always strikingly unique. Unlike his ornate shirts, helix jeans and top hat, he was dressed in a beautiful, floor-length, buckskin robe with stunning bead work. He wore a single Steller's Jay feather in his braided hair. His eyes and face were heavily made up. "Come in, come in, that snow is really coming down," he laughed. "We will sit in the triangle. It will be useful."

The friends were so happy to be inside where an enveloping warmth took the chill out of their bones. They always marveled at the beauty of the Council House. It's massive cedar buttresses and hand-carved totems arched their way up the cathedral ceiling. Through the open skylight, the stars sparkled and lit up their eyes. Hugo and Yerma seated themselves on the cushioned floor, by the soothing fire pit. Rosethorn gave them a welcoming smile. "Last night you told me that you have had the same troubling dreams. That is a good sign!"

"Exactly how could it be a good sign," a tired Hugo asked, "if we can't get any sleep?"

Rosethorn gave Hugo a mischievous grin. "As a Mistook, you must know that these dreams are a continuation of your vision quest."

"The dreams are so hard to interpret," Hugo said.

"... and how are they connected to our warrior's path?" Yerma asked.

"Last night, you asked me questions about Lizzy and Dora, and Mandy and Flora ... and of course," he smiled, "Rosethorn, Moon-Sun and Ice-Fire." Rosethorn paused and looked intently at his Mistook brother and sister. "Much of what I say to you is what you already know."

Both friends nodded.

"Long ago, there was the great Shaman, Ice-Fire. He was a Two Spirit. A female spirit and a male spirit are present in one person. Ice-Fire, like Moon-Sun and myself, are Two Spirits."

"And Shamans and teachers," Yerma added.

Rosethorn nodded. The fire danced in the Shaman's heavily made up eyes. "Long ago, Ice-Fire had a vision. He found himself high up on a sacred mountain. He had left the earth and entered the spirit world. The air was so clean, the sky was the bluest blue, and the earth was the greenest green he had ever seen. Ice-Fire breathed deeply and smiled his most brilliant smile. From the spirit world, he could see the earth. He could also see his reflection running in crazy circles. He realized that the real world was the spirit world, and our world is its shadow. Sitting on his snow-white horse on a slowly drifting cloud, he was filled with a wisdom and joy that he had never known on Mother Earth. He realized that human beings go to the spirit world, and their spirits come back to Mother Earth, from time to time."

Yerma frowned. "So Ice-Fire's vision told the Mistooks that ... um ... spirits return to earth and take human form ..."

"... and then they return to the spirit world ... and repeat this process again and again?" Hugo asked.

A smile creased Rosethorn's lips. "Yes ... and no."

"Oh, please Rosethorn! Please, please, please explain," Yerma begged.

"The Great Spirits no longer need to return and rarely do. But for humans ... well, the elders say that is the way of the world and of the human beings."

A flash of understanding lit up Hugo's eyes. "So, what you are suggesting is that you are a spirit who has returned as Ice-Fire, Moon-Sun and Rosethorn?"

"Yes. In a manner of speaking."

"So ... are you also suggesting ..." Yerma struggled to make sense of what she was about to ask, "that Mandy and Lizzy lived a life as Flora and Dora?"

"If they did," Hugo added, "then it confirms what both of us have suspected. Mandy was Flora and Lizzy was Dora, in a past life."

"If that is how you define it, yes."

"Then why did Mandy and Lizzy have to go back in time to get the Crystal Heart, if Flora and Dora were supposed to?"

"My friends," Rosethorn said patiently, "despite prophecy, sometimes circumstances turn people toward the right place but at the wrong time."

Hugo looked puzzled. "Then Mandy and Lizzy went back to Port Orion to accomplish what they themselves had failed to do?"

Rosethorn nodded.

"But then, didn't we change history?" Yerma asked.

"You did not. You only changed the circumstance in which the task was accomplished."

Yerma leaned back on her hands on the cushioned floor, lost in thought. So did Hugo. Totem figures cast giant shadows on the three friends.

"Mandy and Lizzy were the instruments," the Shaman said. "This thing you call 'time travel,' only maintained what was." Rosethorn paused, pulled out his pipe and lit it. His smoke rings floated upward, past the massive cedar buttresses, drifting though the open skylight, destination unknown.

"If I understand you correctly, there is another matter," Hugo said. "Why did we go along?"

"Yes," Yerma said, "I have the same question. Unlike Mandy and Lizzy, neither of us can see anyone who might have been us in that past life. So, I ask you again. Why did we go along with them?"

"I will answer you with a question."

They both rolled their eyes.

"Considering the odds against you, and how you risked your lives for each other, do you really think Mandy and Lizzy could have retrieved the Crystal Heart alone ... without you ... without I'll-Go-Mine?"

"But if we didn't know Mandy and Lizzy then, why do we get the sense we have known each other before?"

"Come now," Rosethorn said. "You must know there are many possibilities."

The two friends grimaced with frustration.

Rosethorn smiled sympathetically. "You have reached another crossroads in your vision quest. This one will require the highest concentration of our energies. That is why we sit in a triangle. It is the strongest of geometric shapes. It has a peak, like a mountain. It has a rise and fall and a solid foundation. Manitou Mountain will help you find the answers you seek."

The Shaman picked up his drum. With a steady beat, the friends felt their hearts throb in time to the rhythm. They closed their eyes and breathed deeply. Rosethorn chanted the same invocation, over and over. "Across time, we remember the threads in our tapestry."

Hugo and Yerma sank into a deep trance. Slowly, all awareness disappeared. Their breathing and heart rate slowed. Their minds were blank. Down, down, down, they slid, from beta consciousness to alpha, to theta and then to delta, the deepest hypnotic state of long ago memories.

Soon, Hugo and Yerma were outside again, in the woods, following the trail up Manitou Mountain. There had been a few clear days that had melted some of the snow. As the temperature plummeted, it was now turning to ice. The wind was fierce and left their faces windburned and cold. The towering Hemlocks released a shower of snow flakes that stung their cheeks and noses. The ferns and rhododendrons bowed under a heavy white blanket. Soon, they came to a fork in the trail. Hugo and Yerma stood stock still, staring at each other. Each shared a somewhat bewildered smile.

"So now what?" Hugo asked.

Yerma shook her head. "Well," she giggled, "all we need to do is follow the trail up the mountain."

"Fine!" Hugo cried. "Which one?"

Yerma looked up. The snow spiraled down in a frosty cornucopia. There was no sound of any birds, no tracks in the snow. The only sound was the wind whistling through hollowed out trees, and the electric crackle of trillions of snow flakes hitting the ground. The forest looked like a black and white movie. Gray branches wore coats of ice, and tree trunks were bare and black. The silence exploded with the sound of the crack of a limb, breaking loose from a tree. The dark sky did allow for an ominous shadow of an incline.

"My gut tells me to take the fork to the left," Hugo said tentatively. "Right?"

"Rosethorn already gave me some wonderful directions," Yerma replied sarcastically. "We know our destination is on top of Manitou Mountain. Rosethorn has talked about this holy mountain many times before. Once, when I asked him how to get there, he replied, 'No one is really certain how to get there … until they do.'"

Hugo laughed, "Perfect! We'll know the right direction when we get there!"

"Good old Rosethorn."

The incline meandered up an icy trail. Aside from some slick passages that made them lose their footing, they had no trouble. They came to a footbridge that passed over a frozen creek far below. The cables that supported the bridge were ice-covered. The wooden slats they held up were old, icy and severely warped. Both friends looked down into the deep ravine. Then they watched the rickety bridge undulate, as the wind whipped its creaking frame.

"Well," Yerma said. "I am a liberated woman." Then she giggled. "That means you are not allowed to say,' Ladies first.'"

"Lucky me." Hugo took a deep breath and stepped out onto the bridge.

"So far, so good," Yerma laughed.

Hugo continued, the wooden slats groaning with his every step. Yerma waited, then followed from a distance. She didn't want to put too much weight on any part of this potential trapeze. Toward the middle, the bridge began to sag. Hugo concentrated on what was ahead and underfoot. Inch by creaking inch, he crossed the midpoint. Yerma followed. Suddenly, a rogue gust of wind rocked the bridge violently. Both friends quaked in fear. As soon as the bridge steadied itself, Hugo and Yerma were of one mind. They took off, taking tiptoeing steps at terrific speed, screaming at every creak and moan of every slat, grimacing when the bridge seemed to give under their weight. Hugo literally dove the last five feet, praying he would reach the other side. Yerma was right behind him. She too crashed to the snowy ground. Both friends gasped with relief, then burst into nervous laughter. The sound of their voices echoed off the bare-faced cliff, as they continued up the trail. The snow was coming down harder, covering their footprints as they walked. Their nostrils exhaled exploding vapor clouds, turned away by the wind. Visibility had gotten worse. Their path seemed to disappear under a steep incline.

"That trail section has collapsed!"

Yerma nodded. She put her hands over her eyes to shield them from the snow. "You're right, and now they have a log ladder to get up to where the trail continues."

When they reached the ladder, it was steeper than they had thought, and the logs were much wider and thicker. Hugo and Yerma stared up the icy ladder.

"Well. There's one good thing. We can go up side by side," Hugo said.

"Wonderful," Yerma replied dryly. "We can hold hands when we fall off the ladder and die."

Hugo patted her on the back. "Come on, Yerma. We both know you're a fitness freak!"

"Yes, but my workout regimen doesn't include climbing cliffs or high-heeling it across a rickety bridge!"

Hugo laughed. "Come on," he said, "let's rock."

The two friends hoisted themselves onto the first icy step and lost their footing. But they persisted, finally scrambling on hands and knees, pulling themselves up one step at a time. The climb was going perfectly.

"Almost there!" Yerma grunted. Her words were lost in the wind.

"What?"

"I said we're almost there —Oh no!" Yerma's foot slipped off the log, and she grabbed for Hugo's outstretched hand.

"Yerma, hang onto the laaaaaaaaaadder!"

Screaming and flailing wildly, they fell from the ladder, back first. As Yerma had predicted, they thumped into a deep snowdrift, hand in hand. Hugo stared up into a whirl of white. Yerma giggled and said, "Do you want to make snow angels?"

Hugo broke into relieved hysterics. They took the time to make two quite impressive snow angels.

Eventually, they made it to the top where the trail continued. Both paused to catch their breath. "The weather report said this snow is going to continue throughout the day," Yerma said.

"If we can't get back before dark ... the weather could kill us."

"I hope we are going in the right direction," Yerma said grimly.

"I hope we are too," Hugo whispered.

The winded friends searched for a sheltered place to take a much needed rest. Hugo squinted up through the driving snow. Even with the limited visibility, he saw a series of small caves, like pockmarks marring the black mountain. One wore an orange glow, with smoke rings billowing out into the angry wind.

When they reached the cave, they were greeted by a smiling face. As they drew closer, they could see a Mistook Elder they did not know. He had long silver hair and wore a fringed coat and knee-high moccasins. The smile lines on his face were deep as scars. He seemed oblivious to the cold. He had the same orange aura as the fire. He continued smiling. "Hello, I am Watching Owl. Come closer, my brother and sister! Come warm yourselves by the fire."

His smiling eyes studied them intently. The fire flickered and cast long shadows on the rock walls. "You are going up to the top of Manitou Mountain."

"How did you know that?"

Watching Owl laughed with delight. "Why do you think I am here?"

Both friends were clearly confused. This sent Watching Owl into a fit of laughter. "You want directions, and the Shaman has already given them to you! You do not understand them because you are thinking with your head and not with your heart. Listen to the spirit of the wind!"

At that very moment, the two friends were startled by a violent gust outside. They turned and looked toward the cave entrance. When they looked back, the fire was out and the ancient one was gone.

"Are we hallucinating?" a startled Hugo asked.

"Maybe we are," Yerma said laughing. "So, let's get going. Who knows where our hallucinations will take us?"

Both stepped out into the swirling madness. The snow was intensifying. The pair turned and continued up the incline. There were traces of two trails. One went up a steep rock face. The other wound it's way around the mountain.

"Why is it that Rosethorn has to keep putting us in this kind of situation? I'm sick of this," an angry Hugo cried.

"Ooh ... he really, really pisses me off sometimes."

"Wait," Hugo whispered, "Do you hear that?"

Yerma listened intently. "Yes," she said softly. "Yes, I do. It sounds like a Mistook flute and ... a drum."

Hugo and Yerma hurried up the trail, following the music. The flute and drum beckoned from the distance. As they struggled up toward the peak of the mountain, they ascended into the cloud cover. Visibility was worse. One wrong step could be catastrophic. Both paused at what they hoped was a wide ledge. Massive steel telephone cables were spiked into the rock wall. They would have to cling to them, as they inched their way around the precipice. Yerma looked over the ledge. It was, at least, a five hundred foot drop. She shuddered, looked away and closed her eyes. "Oh, boy," she said. "I hope the Great Spirits are smiling down on us."

"Amen," Hugo replied.

Hugo took hold of the cable with both hands, taking sideways steps along the icy ledge. Suddenly Hugo slipped. His feet landed on an outcropping shelf of snow and ice. Hugo scrambled to get some footing. Suddenly, the shelf gave way. A loud crack was followed by Hugo hanging onto the cable with one hand. Yerma tried in vain to reach him as a tsunami of snow tumbled down off the cliff behind her. For a moment, Hugo disappeared in a shower of white. When he came into view again, he had managed to pull himself back onto the ledge. White-knuckled fingers held the cable, as Hugo breathed a sigh of relief.

"Oh, my lord, Hugo! Are you all right?" Yerma cried.

Hugo leaned his forehead against the rock wall and tried to steady his nerves.

Yerma waited, inched over and patted her friend on the back. Once Hugo had calmed down, the two friends left the ledge behind and picked up the trail. They were immediately presented another problem. "Uh oh," Hugo groaned. "I can't hear the flute and drum anymore!"

"Neither can I!"

"What now?"

Shadows danced in the cloud cover. They had no substance, but there was something human in their movements. Shadow arms waved. A shadow head nodded.

"Do you see what I see?"

"Ghosts?"

Their speculations were suddenly interrupted. A flash of color appeared. It broadened the scope of what could be seen in the frosty mist. Soon they could see the outline of a single figure within a circle of stones. She wore a beautifully embroidered white robe around her shoulders. She sat by a fire, its flames waving in the hissing mist. A pastel rainbow outlined her figure.

"My name is Silent River," she said softly. "You have done well, my brother and sister. But this is as far as you can go on your own."

Yerma was frustrated and furious. "You mean that's it? We're done? We'll never get the answers to our questions?"

Hugo intervened. "Calm down, Yerma, she's going to guide us the rest of the way."

Silent River shook her head. "No human being can take you any farther to the sacred mountaintop. You have defied nature by coming this far. You have followed its treacherous path up the mountain. Only a creature of the forest can guide you to the top."

Yerma nodded. "I understand. We must follow our spirit animal. But I heard nothing of mine, nor did I see him."

"Nor did I," Hugo added.

Silent River smiled. "Your spirit animal exists in your soul. Its sound is first felt. Only then can it be heard and seen." With that, she rose, walked away and seemed to evaporate into the forest.

Yerma closed her eyes and took a deep breath. A feeling of warmth filled her body. The snow brushed across her face. It felt invigorating. She opened her eyes. "I hear it," she whispered. "I can hear the call of my spirit animal, the sparrow!"

"It's coming from up there!" Hugo cried.

The frigid mist engulfed them, as they stumbled through the snowdrifts and up the trail. Pulling themselves over an icy ledge, they broke into open air. They had reached the mountain top. The sparrow soared and sang from overhead. Bounding toward them, with joy, was Hugo Yerway's spirit animal, his beloved dog, I'll-Go-Mine.

CHAPTER SEVEN

Meanwhile, in room 566 of the Manchester Castle, the fire in the fireplace had burned down to smoldering embers. Mandy and Lizzy lay motionless on the love seat, with their feet still propped up on the ottomans. The screen on the unusual television showed Zoey and Desiree Daniels at the front door of their house in New Orleans. On the door, was a juju charm with a blood red ribbon. The screen went blank, and Mr. Manchester's picture reappeared, gazing down on the room. Mandy and Lizzy awoke with a start.

"Oh, my gosh!" Lizzy exclaimed. "I just had a dream we were in New Orleans in 1928, and my name was Desiree Daniels."

Mandy grabbed the arm of the love seat, as if awakened on a rocking ship at sea. "I had the exact same dream, and though I was still Mandy Elegant, I was also Zoey Daniels!"

They both kicked their feet off the ottomans, sat up stiffly and looked at each other in astonishment.

Lizzy was wide awake. "What just happened? Did we have the same dream? It seemed so real!"

A still groggy Mandy rubbed her eyes and nodded at her sister. "I'm afraid we did, and I'm afraid I'm going to be sick."

Lizzy sprang into action and helped Mandy into the bathroom. Mandy splashed water on her face. "I think I'm okay," she said as she dried her face.

"Well, I'm freezing!" Lizzy shivered. "I'll put some wood on the fire and make some coffee for us. We need to write down every detail of our dreams, so we don't forget what happened—

This is important!"

After an animated Lizzy had made the room more comfortable and started the coffee, they both changed into their warm robes. They sat down at a large round table with cups of coffee and laptops.

"Let's each write down exactly what we remember," Mandy suggested.

Lizzy agreed, and they both went to work. The room was silent as they both wrote page after page on their laptops and sipped their coffee. After some time, they stopped writing and their wide eyes met.

"You read yours first," Lizzy said.

After each of the sisters had read their memories from their dreams, they realized that they were essentially the same. Mandy's writings were strictly the facts, while Lizzy's were the facts, laced with her unsettling feelings about the juju charm with the severed wing of a dove and rabbit's foot: Mandy and Lizzy's Mistook spirit animals.

"So, was it a shared dream? Was it real? What happened to us?" Lizzy asked.

"Well," Mandy stammered, "it was definitely a shared experience, but I'm not so sure it was a dream. When we went on our vision quest, we traveled back in time, but we were still us."

"This time, we were two other people, or at least riding around in two other people's bodies." Lizzy sighed and rubbed her eyes. "It was like we were them."

"Maybe it was a past life regression," Mandy suggested. "I have read that people say they've experienced previous lives during regression hypnosis."

"But why here? Why now?" Lizzy asked. "When we went through the vortex to another time, we knew why we were there. This just seems random—Do you think it's just this place? You know the rumors."

"Maybe," Mandy nodded her head in agreement. "I have felt so dizzy and weak since we arrived, I'm not sure of anything. I do think we should get ready, so we can eat something before our interviews. We need to find out more about what other people have experienced at this hotel."

Lizzy glanced at her watch. "You're right. We only have an hour to get ready to meet Mr. Knox and become Mandy and Lizzy, super teen reporters." At that, they both laughed and headed to the closet.

After showering and dressing in tights, skirts, sweaters and low-heeled boots, they grabbed their laptops and wrestled with the creaky door to get out of room 566.

"See ya later, Charlie. Keep an eye on the joint," Lizzy shouted to the glaring portrait of Mr. Manchester, before pushing the door shut. As Lizzy locked it, she said, "There's no way I'm going down in that creaky elevator. Let's take the stairs."

The girls walked down an enclosed, spiraling staircase with ornate brass railings. The tall windows let in rays of golden sunlight that broke through the dark winter sky. "Wow," this is pretty amazing," Mandy said as she paused and admired the views of the gardens and the frozen bay.

"Yes, it's almost like being in a lighthouse. Look, it goes up past the 5th floor, maybe to the top of the turret. We'll have to check that out." Lizzy leaned over the railing and looked down at the spiraling stairs below. "Yikes, it's a long way to the bottom. This would be one great ride if we slid down the banister."

"Now that would make a great impression," Mandy giggled. "Walk Lizzy, we'll slide later."

When they reached the front desk, Mr. Knox wished them a good morning and told them that Mrs. Manchester Williams had come down for breakfast and was waiting for them in the dining room.

They walked down a long, wide hallway, attractively decorated with paintings and art deco era sculptures, displayed on long antique tables. Upon entering the dining room, they were greeted by a dark-haired hostess.

"You must be Mandy and Lizzy Elegant," she smiled. "Mrs. Manchester Williams has just been seated at her table. Please follow me."

On their way to the table, Mandy and Lizzy noticed the dark, antique tables and upholstered chairs that were arranged around the large dining room. Two of the walls were rock faced, but ample light streamed in from a floor to ceiling, thick, plate glass window. Mrs. Manchester Williams, wearing a long, loosely-fitting green dress with a colorful scarf tied around her neck, was sitting at a table in front of the window, sipping her tea and gazing out at the view of the bay front.

When they reached the table, the hostess made the introductions. "Mrs. Manchester Williams, these are the reporters who are writing the article for the *Tabula Rasa Times*, Mandy and Lizzy Elegant."

Mrs. Manchester Williams turned and looked them over. "Oh, aren't you two just so pretty …. and writers, too! Please sit down with me, and please, call me Lilly. Mrs. Manchester Williams makes me sound like an old lady. I may be eighty-eight, but I'm not gone yet," she said with a girlish grin.

Mandy and Lizzy were immediately put at ease by Lilly's warm greeting and were seated, as the hostess poured each of them a cup of tea.

"Okay, let's get to know each other," Lilly said. "Which of you is Mandy, and which is Lizzy?"

"I'm Mandy," she waved from across the table, "and this is Lizzy," she pointed. "We're twins and were selected to write this article together."

"Since we were born, it seems that we have done almost everything together. I guess we make a good team," Lizzy laughed.

"Well, from now on, we're Mandy, Lizzy and Lilly, and we're going to give them an article that they'll never forget! But first, let's order some breakfast. I'm starving."

As they enjoyed their breakfast, they talked about their interests. Lilly was delighted to learn that Mandy and Lizzy were both dancers, since she had studied dance in college at Tulane University. Mandy and Lizzy couldn't hide their excitement to learn that after college, Lilly had performed with the Rockettes in New York City, and danced on the Broadway stage in many plays directed by her husband.

"Oh, Alex and I had such a wonderful life together," Lilly said with sweet emotion. "We moved here after he retired, and I had to take over the responsibility of managing the hotel. It was sad to leave our home in New York, but what fun we had exploring this area together and meeting the new challenges of running the hotel. He passed away two years ago...."

"I'm so sorry to hear that," Lizzy said with such sincerity that Lilly reached out and took her hand.

Lilly then reached out to Mandy as well. "I have learned to live my life with losses but with no regrets. Let's go up to my study and talk about one hundred years of the Manchester Castle. I have stories, and you have an article to write."

The Manchester family had occupied the entire east tower since the Castle was originally built, and it was nothing short of magnificent. Lilly took them on a tour of some of her favorite rooms before they settled in her warm, comfortable study.

"So, what are your plans for your article?" Lilly asked.

Mandy glanced at her notes and began. "We are planning to use one of the *Times*' early photos of the Castle, and a current one that includes the most recent additions of the war elephants and Atlantean soldiers on the front lawn."

"Oh, my father would love that," Lilly beamed. "He found those sculptures in Egypt on one of our family trips, years ago, and wanted them for the Castle. I was able to acquire them recently and had them installed for the one hundredth anniversary."

"Great, I'm so glad you like that idea," Lizzy smiled. "We also want to begin the article by writing about the celebration planned on January first, describing the brunch, entertainment and tours that you have planned. Then we would like to include a brief history of the Manchester family and some interesting stories about the hotel. What do you think about that idea?"

Lilly thought for a few moments before answering. "Oddly enough, I don't know much about the early history of the

Manchesters, but I do know their history in New Orleans …"

Mandy and Lizzy exchanged baffled looks.

"… My grandparents owned and bred race horses. Racing was a huge business in the Storyville area of New Orleans, before World War I, and they became wealthy enough to buy other businesses, both in Storyville and the French Quarter. When my parents were engaged, his father built The Castle as a wedding gift and family retreat. Of course, the east tower has always been our family's residence, and the west tower was built for guests. Our family, friends and my father's business associates always spent time during the summer months here, to escape the heat in New Orleans."

Mandy finished jotting down notes and asked, "As you know, the hotel has the reputation of being haunted. Do you think there is any truth to that?"

Lilly nodded. "Yes, that reputation is both a blessing and a misfortune. It draws many people to the hotel but keeps others away. Of course, you have heard about the two suicides. Mr. Adams hung himself in room 420. After investigation, it was thought that it was most likely because he had lost all of his money during the stock market crash. Another man jumped off of the west tower turret after his girlfriend turned him down when he asked her to marry him. Both were such terrible events, and so widely publicized, that people came to the hotel looking for their ghosts. Of course, in a hotel one hundred years old, people have died of natural causes, including my parents and husband. Many have claimed to see ghostly figures, including my father, but I haven't. Sometimes in my rooms, I do see things out of the corner of my eye, or put something down and find it in another place later. Maybe that's just forgetfulness, but I do take comfort in thinking that my husband and family are watching over me."

Lizzy immediately remembered an article she had seen during her research. "I read that the hotel also has the reputation for occurrences of other paranormal events. Do you know why?"

"There are numerous reasons for that," Lilly began. "In the

nineteen-twenties, after the loss of life during the nineteen-eighteen flu and World War I, there was a resurgence of interest in the paranormal. Well-known clairvoyants, who made contact with the dead through seances, automatic writing or psychometry, came to the hotel so that guests could contact lost loved ones. That became news, so more psychics came to the hotel. Some predicted the future using tarot cards, pendulums, crystal balls or other means. As I said, once the reputation was established, it has continued throughout the years."

"We're staying in room 566. Have people staying in the room ever noticed any … unusual events?" Mandy asked.

"That room is just lovely, but it did gain it's own unique reputation. There was a widely reported, mysterious and awful occurrence about twenty-five years ago. A couple was staying in room 566, but when their check-out day arrived, their belongings were still in the room; but they were nowhere to be found. Their car was still in the parking lot, and they seemed to have just vanished. They were reported as missing persons, and the hotel and its grounds were searched. With the idea that they might have gone out on the bay, searches were continued for a week, but they were never found…. Out of curiosity, my husband and I stayed in the room one night, just to see if we noticed anything unusual."

"Did you?" Mandy asked.

"We thought we did," Lilly answered, "but it seemed to be more like we entered a time warp, experiencing another time. It felt like we were really there—Quite exciting for both of us. In fact, I would say that more guests have said that they have had 'time warp' experiences than have seen ghosts."

Mr. Knox tapped on the door, then stepped inside. "I hope I'm not disturbing you, but I have been able to arrange time for you to interview some of the staff and even some of our guests. I hate to interrupt …"

"Oh, you know me Richard," Lilly laughed. "When I'm enjoying my guests, I can go on talking forever." Turning to Mandy and Lizzy, she said, "I know you girls have work to do, but

I would love to meet with you again. I'd love to hear what you learn during your interviews today."

Lizzy looked at Mandy who nodded. "Well, it's a date," Lizzy confirmed.

"Wonderful! Let's meet in the dining room tomorrow around one o'clock for brunch, if it is convenient for you."

Mandy smiled and said, "That sounds great and thank you so much for spending this time with us. It has been so much fun to meet you."

"Oh, you two are just lovely girls. You have made my day." Lilly cheerfully rose from her chair to see them out.

By late afternoon, Mandy and Lizzy had completed their interviews, enjoyed a complete tour of the Castle and it's grounds, and taken the photographs they needed for their article. Exhausted, they returned to their room and wrestled their way through the stubborn door.

A warm fire had been built in the fireplace, and there was a beautiful basket of fruit, cheese and crackers on the table. The note on the basket read: "Thank you for a wonderful morning. Love, Lilly."

Lizzy turned to the portrait over the fireplace. "Charlie, you raised a great daughter, and thanks for watching over the room. Maybe you're a nice guy after all, but you should smile more."

Mandy laughed, as she ran to get the room service menu from the dresser drawer. "We missed lunch, and I'm hungry. What do you want?"

After their dinner was delivered, they looked over their notes and discussed their interviews as they ate. Returning the tray to the hallway after they were finished, Mandy turned to Lizzy.

"So, do you want to watch some more TV tonight?"

"Well, you said watching too much TV can be bad for us," Lizzy said sarcastically. "But you know there's no way I'm leaving here without getting the rest of the story."

"Me too," Mandy said, "I only have one request. Let's get changed first and get in our beds. Tonight, I'd rather not sleep in my clothes on the sofa again."

CHAPTER EIGHT

Hugo and Yerma watched I'll-Go-Mine step off the top of Manitou Mountain and onto the clouds. They hesitated to follow. A short distance away, I'll-Go-Mine stopped and stared back at his friends.

Hugo shrugged."We're scared, buddy."

I'll-Go-Mine barked, paused and proceeded on his way.

"Well," Yerma said. "A Bullador almost never barks, Hugo. That's got to be a sign. Let's go!"

Hugo nodded and smiled. "Rosethorn said the answers to our questions are up here."

"Yes," Yerma replied. "But he never said we'd have to walk out on clouds to get them."

Hugo rolled his eyes, and they both set off. Hugo's head seemed to be spinning. He marveled at all he saw. "This is the bluest sky I have ever seen. The sunlight makes me feel like I'm a battery being recharged."

"Yes, I know exactly what you mean," Yerma sighed, in a dreamy voice.

The clouds were so fluffy and firm below their feet, but looking closer, the pair could see they were translucent. Far below, the earth and its colorless inhabitants seemed to be running in mindless circles. Skyscrapers looked like toys, cars looked like pebbles and the inhabitants—little dots. The view did not unnerve Hugo and Yerma. In the transcendent bliss of the cloud trail, there were no circles to run through. Hugo's spirit animal led the way. Yerma's spirit animal, the sparrow, soared out in front of them. Her song beckoned the friends to follow. After some time, I'll-Go-Mine led them down through the clouds into an opaque mist. In minutes, the dog disappeared. The sparrow's song was no longer to be heard. Their sepia surroundings began to morph into color. The pair exchanged fearful glances. The face of the person standing next to them was not the face of the person they knew.

"Hugo …" Yerma whispered. "Is that you?"

Hugo nodded. Then, Yerma was gone, like she had evaporated into thin air.

Hugo walked alone down a dirty, deserted street. He stopped to study his face in a shop window. He could see his reflection in the glass. "I know … inside … I'm still Hugo Yerway," he thought. It was clear that the face he was seeing was not the face he knew. His thoughts were not his own. "It's 1928, and this guy is twenty-seven years old … and how the heck did I know that?" He studied his wide-lapelled jacket, matching pants, tie and collared shirt. His shaggy blond hair, that hung over his ears and collar, was parted in the middle. His awareness gave way to reflection.

"I'm Eric Strand," he said as he clutched the badge of a federal agent. He reached inside his coat and located his shoulder holster. Thoughts flooded his mind about who he was, where he was, where he had been, and where he was going. Hugo's consciousness was eclipsed. He was Eric—Eric was him.

The smoke was still billowing out of Josiah's Restaurant. Eric spotted something on the door frame. "How did this juju charm survive the blast and the fire?" he wondered. "Or maybe the question I should be asking is 'why.'" Eric took a camera out of his camera bag and snapped a few shots of the charred door frame and the charm. He took out a handkerchief, wrapped the charm in it and put it in his pocket. He heard footsteps on the shattered glass that littered the street. He turned to see a smiling face sauntering toward him.

"Hi, big guy," he said, as he extended his hand. "I'm Louis D'Quad."

"I know of you, Mr. D'Quad. Your reputation precedes you. I'm Eric Strand," he said as he shook Louis's hand.

"Please, call me Louis, and I'll call you Eric. How's dat sound?"

"Suits me fine," Eric replied with a warm smile.

"You're new in town."

"Yes, I moved here a few weeks ago," Eric replied.

"Since you're a rookie in town, I'm gonna do you a favor and clue you in. This is a dangerous place to be walking, any time of day. Especially for an amateur photographer ... you are a photographer, aren't you?"

"Freelance," Eric replied. "I'm doing a photo shoot of New Orleans during the Holiday Season."

"For the *New Orleans Nitpicker*?"

"They did approach me about my work. But I deal with clients all over the country and usually don't take on full time jobs." Eric maintained eye contact. "However ..." He could see D'Quad was getting nervous. Eric gave him a sly grin. "I did take a job with them as a feature photographer. They made me an offer I couldn't refuse—good money—off the books—no taxes. I start this week."

D'Quad's right eye twitched, as he cleared his throat. "Well, Eric, my friend, I have to warn you about the *Nitpicker's* trouble-making columnists, Zoey and Desiree Daniels. They're known gossips—and notorious flappers." D'Quad sneered. "Watch your back when those two are around."

"Thanks so much. I'll watch out for them." D'Quad smiled broadly. "Hey, friend. Why don't you join me this Saturday. There's a local soda shop ..."

"Thanks, Louis," Eric said, as he pulled out a flask and took a swig. "But I'm looking for something a bit stronger than soda pop."

D'Quad laughed as he picked up a piece of paper that Eric had purposely allowed to fall out of his pocket. D'Quad looked at it and smiled. It was a gambling sheet.

"Oops," Eric said nervously.

"No worries, my friend!" D'Quad said as he slapped Eric on

the back. "In fact I think I can help you quench your thirst and put a little money in your pocket." D'Quad took out his wallet. "Here," he said, handing Eric a business card. "There's an address on the back of a place called Victoria's. Stop by Saturday night, around eight. I'll make sure you have a good old time."

"Well, much obliged!" Eric nodded. "Eight o'clock would be perfect … give me some time to develop the day's photos." Eric smiled conspiratorially." Then we can put the cherry on top of the cake at Victoria's."

"You bet your ass," D'Quad said as he gave him another slap on the back. "See you Saturday."

As soon as D'Quad was out of sight, Eric said to himself, "D'Quad seems overly concerned about these Daniels sisters. I've got to find out about them." For a split second, Hugo's consciousness bubbled to the surface. "The more pressing problem," he thought, "is how the hell am I going to find Yerma?"

****

Amidst the bright lights of North Rampart Street stood an old two story plantation house that had seen better days. The giant Corinthian columns were pitted and gouged. The white paint was faded and cracked. The once great lawn was now flattened weeds, tire tracks and mud. Magnolia trees crowded the house. Spanish moss, swaying in the wind, dusted the shingles on the roof. Heavy curtains covered the windows. Above the double doors, a sign read, "Victoria's Place."

Victoria Guerrera was extremely dizzy. She was certain she was about to pass out. She gunned the engine of her Model T Ford and sideswiped a car before lurching to a stop. Victoria sat stock still in the driver's seat and stared, just stared. She was so confused and disoriented. A mental check list ripped through her head.

"It is 1928. I am twenty-five years old. I own this mansion—I live here—I run a speakeasy—The cops and feds leave me alone ——I consort with gangsters."

Her dizziness abated. She looked into the rearview mirror and studied her face. Her makeup was flawless, as was her bronze skin. Her long, jet black hair allowed for two little spit curls that framed her cheeks. Victoria Guerrera slid out of the car and hoisted herself up on the hood. She stared up at the ivory moon. The night air was cold and damp.

"I know I'm Yerma Wafermaker," she mumbled." But—I am Victoria Guerrera ... and my thoughts are hers." Suddenly, a wave of excitement fluttered in her stomach. "I am aware of Yerma ... she's still here ... but I am now Victoria Guerrera!"

She leaned back on the hood and howled at the dark sky. Yerma's consciousness bubbled to the surface.

"Oh wow! I must be living a past life!" she cried. "This is the lifetime when I will meet Mandy, Lizzy and Hugo for the first time!" Her joy quickly gave way to panic. She had a more pressing problem. "Oh no, New Orleans is such a big city with so many people!" she groaned. "How will I ever find Hugo?" A light went on in her head. She smiled. "This is not a problem, after all. If this is the life when we all first met, our paths will cross, sooner or later. " That said, Yerma's consciousness sank out of sight.

Victoria rolled a small cigar and lit it. She watched smoke rings rise and disappear in the moonlit sky.

****

During his first few days in New Orleans, Eric settled into his new home. He was careful about appearances. He wanted his neighbors to think he was just an ordinary guy who took photos for the *New Orleans Nitpicker*. He hired a gardener to fill the window boxes with fresh flowers and put potted plants on the porch and upstairs veranda. Meanwhile, he outfitted a makeshift darkroom in the attic and developed his photos for the newspaper and of the juju charm. He had dusted it for finger prints but found none. Eric hid the charm and photos under a loose panel of insulation, for safe keeping. The telephone rang, and Eric rushed downstairs.

"Hi, Eric —Agent Jim Hope here."

"Hi Chief. How's life been treating you?"

"Oh, you know. I'm a pencil pusher now. How's life treating you in your French Quarter home that the agency has paid for?"

"Grand! But you know, once I'm through here, it's going to be government property, and I'll be out on the street!"

Jim laughed. "Anything new with the case?"

"Not much. I did meet Louis D'Quad."

"Tell me more."

"I met him while I was shooting photos of a gang hit on a local restaurant. He was there too. His file does him justice. He's a not too smart con man. He swaggers like a gang boss. He invited me to this speakeasy called Victoria's' Place. He promised me some booze and money at the gaming tables."

Jim laughed. "So, the police don't care about prohibition either."

Eric laughed too. "It's like everywhere else. New Orleans police ignore it. Many of them frequent the speakeasies."

"Have you got any leads on who killed Agents Buck and James?

"Not yet. But I'll keep you posted."

"One more thing Eric. Could you send me a bottle of good Scotch?"

Eric chuckled. "Take care Chief."

CHAPTER NINE

Victoria Geurerro put the finishing touches on her hair and makeup. She leaned back in her vanity chair and studied her face. Sometimes, when alone, the consciousness of Yerma seeped into the overwhelming mind set of Victoria. These brief moments filled her with relief. She knew who she was, why she was here, and that she had to find Hugo. These moments of clarity were over in seconds. As always, Yerma disappeared under the weight of Victoria. Victoria went over to a full-length mirror. She primped and posed. The soft lamplight revealed the outline of her shapely figure under her floor length silk robe. She frowned.

"Well," she sighed, "this will have to do. You can't make a silk purse out of a sow's ear."

As she changed clothes, she could hear the sound of music, laughter and clinking of glasses downstairs. A wave of excitement rolled through her.

Resplendent in a red satin dress with a low-cut bodice, flounced sleeves and rows of shimmering ruffles on the full skirt, Victoria left her upstairs chambers and descended into Dante's Inferno. Her gaze swept the room. There was D'Quad holding court with his gangster buddies. Out on the dance floor, tipsy girls and guys were doing the Charleston, as if their lives depended on it. Each gyration was a flirtation. Waiters, armed with trays, flitted from table to table—stuffing big wads of tip money into their pockets. The gaming tables were swamped with rich, powerful men. Gold-digging debutantes hung onto them, fawning all over their would be sugar daddies. The tables were filled with half-eaten food and empty drinks. Ash trays were like funeral pyres, overflowing with smoldering cigarettes that filled the room with a gray haze. The whole place was a swirl of near chaos. A man sat alone at the bar.

Victoria took over for the bartender and went over to the stranger. "What can I get you?" she asked with a smile.

The stranger had been fumbling with his wallet and did not look up. When he did, there was a disquieting, strange and mutual recognition.

"Vodka," he said, staring intently. "Straight up."

"I wouldn't advise that," Victoria said nervously.

"And why would that be?"

"It's not imported quality stuff. It's … locally grown. Double distilled, one hundred proof, and it's got a kick like a shot gun blast."

"Seems to me you've got a whole army of quality bottles of spirits on the shelves behind you. Why the local vodka?"

Victoria leaned forward on the bar. She studied the stranger's face. "I like to buy from the locals.… It's hard times for a lot of them. I like to do what I can."

"So, you are the proprietor of the place."

"Yes," she said brightly. "My name's Victoria Geurerro."

"Pleasure to meet you, Miss Geurerro. My name is Eric Strand."

"Glad to make your acquaintance, Mr. Strand!"

"Call me Eric."

With no words and a trancelike meeting of the eyes, that rare and special instant arrived. Hugo's consciousness emerged from the shadows. So did Yerma's. They instantly recognized each other. But they were powerless to say anything about it. That awareness disappeared.

"Okay, Eric! What's it gonna be? Want some of the good stuff, or are you a man who wants to help the downtrodden?"

"Let me sample the local libation."

Eric drank the vodka, and almost spit it out as Louis D'Quad slapped him on the back. "Eric," he cried," so good to see ya!"

Victoria busied herself drying glasses. D'Quad made a sweeping gesture all around the club. "Look around you, big guy. Look around you! How's this for quenching thirst and putting money in your pocket? Ain't I right, Miss Geurerro?"

Victoria did not look up from the glasses. "Of course you're right, Mr. D'Quad."

"Well, Eric," D'Quad bellowed and slapped him on the back again. "Pick your poison, or all the poisons … and when ya get tired, you can sit down in front of those slot machines!"

Victoria watched D'Quad disappear into the crowd. "So, you're a friend of D'Quad are you?"

"Not really. I just met him the other day. He invited me over here. Is he a friend of yours?"

"No," she replied. "He's someone who helps me pay for the upkeep of this old place and employ some dear friends who have been going through hard times. A few years ago, D'Quad came by. He wanted a place to have a speakeasy for his cronies. His offer was too much money to refuse."

"Weren't you concerned about the police or civil authorities?"

"No one cares about speakeasies around here … not the cops, not the feds, not anybody. Louis D'Quad promised me he'd take care of any other problems that might arise. All I have to do is make sure that his guests are well taken care of. In return, my friends go home with a pay check."

"Your friends are lucky to have you."

"I'm lucky to have them, as well. Some of them, I've known since I was a kid; every one of them quirky in their own way." Victoria smiled and pointed. "You see that lady playing the trombone?"

"Yes."

"That's Old Mary. She likes using the rubber part of a toilet bowl plunger as a mute." Victoria laughed. "She says she does it cause it sounds so good. Her brother said their grandaddy gave her that old trombone. Old Mary couldn't afford to buy a mute and has never bothered to since. And," she pointed, "you see that old white-haired guy, sitting in front of the bandstand? That's Yappin 'Lips. He doesn't say much, unless he's singing. He's a legend around here, playing the blues in the streets for nickels and dimes. He lives in an abandoned shed." Victoria paused, a far away look in her eyes. "Just about every person I know has that same kind of story to tell … and they ain't good."

Eric nodded and frowned. "Give me another double of that flame throwing vodka."

"You're a glutton for punishment," Victoria said as she poured the drink. "It's on the house, Eric Strand."

"Thanks!"

"Newcomer discount …"

"How did you know I was a newcomer?" Eric asked, concealing his suspicions.

"Well, you're a first-timer here. You don't seem to know anybody except D'Quad, and just about everybody that's anybody is in this room."

"You've got me! I am a newcomer to New Orleans. I just bought a house here, and I'm a photographer for the *New Orleans Nitpicker*."

"Ah," Victoria laughed. "Your boss, Chuck Hines, is quite the character."

Eric flashed a smile. "Yes he is. Drinks, smokes, swears, intimidates and then makes you feel at home … and he's one helluva editor and newsman."

"I've known Chuck for years. I love him. He wants you to think he's a grumpy old bear, when he's really a big softie. You'll love working for him."

"He told me I'd really enjoy working with two of his columnists, though they were not present at the time. Odd thing, D'Quad warned me to watch out for them…. Their names are …"

"Zoey and Desiree Daniels! We've been friends for years! Oh, they are such sweet girls with so many talents. They're a pleasure to know. Sometimes they can be mischievous, flirty little girls. Sometimes they're glamorous flappers. And sometimes," Victoria laughed with delight, "they are hilarious columnists who love to take the air out of the powerful and pompous!"

"How so?"

"I cut out their last column. It's a riot ... typical of them. I'll get it from my office."

THE TENTH STREET SOUREE WAS A BLAST

"*Slugs sparkled like fireflies, as overly excited patrons ran for the exits in an impromptu, choreographed sprint. Mrs. Curbella's shimmering bouffant wig could not keep up with her. The wig decided, with obvious delight, to ride the wind of her wake and wrap itself around the turned up nose of Betty Anne McGraves, who was in hot pursuit. Miss McGraves did a delightful swan dive in her one of a kind, original, purple-shimmer, LaTete gown. Miss McGrave's stumble changed the colors of her gown to mud brown and green grass stains, which gave it a festive piñata look. Mr. Blunder, a hefty but accommodating fellow, was a popular figure, as evidenced by the number of people who were chasing him. Many caught up, and he was gracious enough to fall down and let them pass by him, over him, or on him. As the bullets lit up the sky, like a joyous fourth of July, the hellish chorus of the party goers was more memorable than any of those of the National Cathedral Choir. By the by, Mr. Blunder was wearing the latest in a husky man's mud foot-printed, gray, double-vented, gaberdine suit, wide at the lapels, perfect for the wide Mr. Blunder. A few cars left the parking lot with the ambience of Swiss Cheese, but otherwise this was an unforgettable event. Even though we've tried to forget it.*"

Ah, virtue, thy name is truth.

Zoey and Desiree Daniels.

Eric laughed. "These two are loaded pistols!"

"Yes, they are!"

"Considering how D'Quad feels about them, I assume they are not here tonight."

"No, they aren't, but they do pop in from time to time."

"D'Quad must hate that."

"He does, and he doesn't. He knows the kind of sharp tongues these two flappers have. What they say pulls weight. They've got a lot of very loyal friends, so D'Quad welcomes them … reluctantly."

"If they do come in, will you point them out to me?"

"Oh, I won't have to. The rare times when they grace us with their presence, every head turns. Their friends cheer, jealous women put on fake smiles, and men fall all over each other trying to get into their good graces."

Eric shook his head in bemused wonder. "These ladies are definitely not wallflowers."

Victoria laughed. "Just when you think you've seen everything, these girls turn up the burners on the stove, full blast."

Prophetic words. All hell was about to break loose.

****

As it turned out, the juju charm was nothing more than an invitation, tied in a crimson ribbon.

"So," Desiree said tentatively," it wasn't a juju charm after all."

"No–it's an invitation from D'Quad. He says he wants to put our differences aside and let bygones be bygones."

"This is the trap Ravonjay warned us about!"

"I think so too," Zoey replied. "D'Quad knows that our newspaper column depends on going to speakeasies. We need the power of alcohol to loosen the tongues of those creeps that are more than willing to talk too much and too loudly."

"I agree. But if we go to D'Quad's to get that gossip, we're walking right into the trap."

"How about we throw D'Quad off our trail? Why don't we go to …"

"… Kongo's Place! That's a great idea! We'll get the same kind of scuttlebutt there. Besides," she giggled, "I love Kongo."

"So do I ... even though he's a criminal!" Both sisters cracked up laughing.

"Saturday's the night, my dear sister. Let's dress up to the nines and give those poor men with those glassy eyes all the more reason to pine and yearn and tell us all we want to know."

****

That Saturday, two bedazzling figures strode down Bourbon Street, heading for Kongo's Place. They were dressed to kill: velvet bucket hats, overcoats and shockingly short dresses. Velvet high heels and purses completed their flawless ensembles.

"I hate these clunky heels!" Desiree said. "Clip-clop, clip-clop ... we sound like fat horses.... I hate these clunky heels, I really do!"

"Yes, I know you do," Zoey said wearily. "I've heard this same complaint about these heels a million times."

"Paris fashion says ..."

"... that thin and sleek heels will be all the rage this year. I can't wait for you to get some, so you'll stop moaning."

When they reached Kongo's Place, they stopped under a streetlight to check their makeup. Zoey saw Desiree pull out a compact, open it and dab powder on her nose.

"Oh, I love that thing!" Zoey exclaimed. "It looks exactly like a derringer. But when you open the handle, it's a compact! "

"Yes," Desiree smirked. "I'm hoping that if someone is coming after us, he'll be dumb enough to believe this is a real gun."

Zoey laughed, "I hope it doesn't ever come down to that!"

"Amen!"

Zoey looked over her sister and smiled. "You look divine!"

"So, do you!"

"Dressed to kill!"

"Or be killed."

CHAPTER TEN

Eric checked his shoulder holster, slipped on his vest and jacket and stepped out into the the dark and dank New Orlean's night. His footsteps mingled with the sound of partiers and music seeping out of shuttered windows. Voices, lights and laughter echoed down Bourbon Street. Eric spotted two young ladies standing outside Kongo's Place. Both were checking their makeup. Eric's whole demeanor changed. A chill of excitement rolled up his spine. From their column's newspaper photographs, there was no doubt about it. At last, these were the notorious Daniels sisters. They had spotted him too.

"Better put away your derringer," Zoey laughed.

Desiree giggled nervously as she stuffed the compact into her purse. The sisters locked onto the stranger who stepped into the lamplight. The girls glowed. They knew most everyone in the French Quarter, but they did not know this handsome man.

"Good evening," Zoey said, with a welcoming smile.

"Enchanté," Desiree whispered and extended her gloved hand.

Eric kissed it, and then took Zoey's hand and did the same.

"To whom do we have the pleasure of addressing?"

"I'm Eric Strand, your co-worker."

"Oh yes, of course! Your photos in the *Nitpicker* are beautiful," Zoey said. "Please allow us to introduce ourselves, I'm ..."

"Oh, there's no need to introduce yourselves. You are Zoey and Desiree Daniels." Eric tested the girls seemingly unflappable demeanor. "I read your column all the time and saw your photos

... both are quite impressive."

"Oh, you are too kind," Zoey said, as she batted her eyes and smiled.

Desiree just stared. "Don't I know you from somewhere?"

"I was thinking the same thing about both of you. I have traveled a lot doing freelance work and could have seen you any number of places. Have you ever been to Boston? Chicago maybe? Miami?

"I wish we had!" Zoey replied. "That would be so exciting!"

Desiree smiled wickedly, straightened Eric's tie and winked at him. "Well, my worldly Eric, don't start thinking we're innocent angels. We may not have been to all the wonderful places you've been, but we've been around!"

There was a moment of awkward silence. The consciousness of Mandy, Lizzy and Hugo, bubbled into their frontal lobes. For a millisecond, there was an overwhelming moment of mutual recognition—Then it was gone.

"We haven't seen you at Kongo's before," Zoey said. "Are you a friend of Kongo Kaminga?"

"No," Eric smiled. "I'm new here. I haven't met many people."

"Poor baby," Zoey said playfully. "We can't let you go in alone."

"That's right," Desiree said, with a pouty face. "We wouldn't hear of you sitting all by your little old self. You'll come and sit at our table with us!"

"We'll introduce you to all our wonderful friends. We know most everyone quite well!"

"Yes," Eric thought, as they led him toward the club doors. "Judging from your column, I'm certain you know everyone ... quite well ... maybe too well. That's exactly what I'm counting on."

The double doors opened into a scene of unbridled euphoria. Eric checked out his chaotic surroundings. Kongo's Place was much more intimate than Victoria's. The dark mahogany furnishings, crown moulding and convex ceiling were from the Victorian Era's grander days. The subdued lighting and table candles cast auras of light around Flapper Girls in all their finery. Gentlemen with slicked-back hair and pencil-thin mustaches lit ladies' cigarettes, with hungry, expectant grins. The radio blared out all of the songs on the current hit parade. A small bar rimmed the club. There were so many tables wedged together that it was a nearly impossible task to sidle through a sliver of space. While they did, patrons shouted greetings.

"Hey, Zoey. Where ya been, I've missed you sweetheart!"

"Desiree, you naughty doll, come on over here and join us!'

"Oh, Zoey and Desiree. You look divine, as always!"

****

Across town, Victoria Guererro was busy behind the bar. The place was jumping with jazz, Flappers doing the Charleston and inebriated patrons sitting at the bar. The sound of roulette wheels, groaning gamblers, clinking glasses, exploding corks and beer bottle caps filled the air. Louis D'Quad sat at the end of the bar, talking intently with a few of his cronies. Victoria was within earshot. D'Quad was bursting with bravado.

"Oh, yeah," he said with false sadness. "Ya know I sent those darn Daniels girls a special invitation to come here, and they didn't show up," he sighed. "This really hurts, boys."

"So, what are we going to do about it, Mr. D'Quad?"

"Well, I have to put this Daniels' insult out of my mind." Then he smiled and said. "Someone once told me, if you want to get something off your mind, doing a good deed always works!"

His companions laughed wickedly. "So, would you like us to do a good deed for you?"

"That's a great idea! Digger, I want you to deliver these gifts." D'Quad handed him a red cloth bag. "Addresses are inside."

Digger picked up a violin case, unlocked it and put the bag inside, next to a sawed off shotgun. He closed the latches, smiled and said, "On my way, Mr. D'Quad."

"Hey, Gizmo. How about rounding up a few of your boys and go for one of those good old fashioned moonlight drives."

"That sounds wonderful," Gizmo replied hungrily.

As his lackeys left, D'Quad rose, put a toothpick in his mouth, walked past Victoria, smiled broadly and said," One good deed deserves another, eh Victoria?"

Victoria watched D'Quad backslap his way toward the blackjack table and melt into the mayhem. Victoria motioned to a waiter. "Take over for me. I've just got to go upstairs and get a different pair of shoes. My feet are killing me."

Victoria looked around nervously. Not one of D'Quad's cronies was in sight. She carefully made her way toward the stairs to her private residence. But along the way, she was distracted by a number of those present telling her, in slurred sentences, how much they were enjoying her place. To avoid suspicion, she could not be rude. It seemed like hours before she locked herself inside her upstairs residence. Her delay had cost her precious time. Now, every second counted. Victoria dialed the number and placed her call. No one answered the phone. The noise drowned out the persistent ringing. But she wasn't going to stop calling. It was a matter of life or death.

****

After zigzagging their way through the Daniels' friends, the threesome was escorted to the head table. Once they were seated, Eric surveyed his surroundings. Kongo's Place was filled with laughing, drinking and dancing people. They were as inebriated and raucous as those at Victoria's, but there was something familiar and friendly in how they related to one another. Victoria's Place was nothing like Kongo's. Victoria's was a den of distant strangers, dangerous hombres, grasping gold diggers, cheats and bad vibes. Here, there was joyous partying.

Zoey's smile radiated in the dancing candlelight. "So," she said excitedly, "tell us all about yourself!"

"Yes!" Desiree batted her eyelashes and cooed, "please tell us, and don't leave out a single detail."

"Well," Eric began. "As you know, I am now the *Nitpicker's* feature photographer. Something new for me, as I've always worked freelance."

"You must have traveled around a lot." Desiree said.

"It's the nature of my business. I go where the best opportunities present themselves—Anything that's interesting or exotic."

"That sounds so exciting!" Zoey said. "Tell us about some of the more interesting and exotic —"

"—and erotic," Desiree added, with a wicked smile.

Eric cleared his throat, then turned to Zoey. "Well," he said. "The most exciting was a shoot at Yankee Stadium. I met Babe Ruth and Lou Gehrig!"

"Wow! The Babe and the Iron Horse. What a thrill!" Zoey exclaimed.

"The most exotic was for a private photo shoot. The gentleman who hired me was a descendent of Morgan the Pirate. He wanted a photographic record of Morgan's base of operations, so we went down to Port Royal, Jamaica. It was an exotic experience for me." Before either of the sisters could respond, Eric turned to Desiree.

"As for my most erotic photo shoot," he said, staring into Desiree's devilish eyes, "I got to photograph the famous Ziegfeld Follies girls."

Desiree laughed with delight. "We were Ziegfeld girls for a while! Are we in the photographs?"

Eric smiled. "I don't know. Would you like me to look?"

Desiree leaned over and patted Eric's cheek. "Why? Is it because you want to see us in our sexy little costumes?"

Eric was tongue tied. He struggled to change the subject. "Um … I was told by some of the Ziegfeld girls they took different names to protect their true identities. Did you have stage names?"

Both girls blushed with pleasure. "Yes, we did!" Zoey replied. "We decided to change our last name to Rivers. Not having a brain between us, we kept our first names!"

Eric burst out laughing. "It seems to me you didn't quite finish the job! What were you thinking?"

"What were we thinking? We were sixteen years old in New York City, we had never been away from home, men wined and dined us because we were young, pretty, innocent, naive, famous and having the time of our lives. That's what we were thinking!"

Hours passed. The threesome did not notice. Even a couple's fiery Flamenco on the dance floor was only a dazzling pause in their playful banter. Suddenly, their conversation was interrupted by a booming voice.

"Zoey! Desiree! How are my girls? Let me hug my beautiful girls!"

Zoey and Desiree stood up, and a big burly man wrapped his arms around both of them and literally lifted them off their feet. Both girls squealed with delight.

"Oh Kongo, it's so wonderful to see you!"

"It has been too long, my chicas guapas!"

"Kongo Kaminga," Zoey said, "I'd like you to meet our new friend, Eric Strand."

Kongo's big bandito mustache curled into an equally big smile. Both men shook hands. "It is a pleasure to meet you, Mr. Strand," he said with a gleam in his eyes.

"It's a pleasure to meet you, Mr. Kaminga."

"Let's drop the formalities, my friend!" You must call me Kongo, and I must call you?"

"... Eric."

Kongo smiled warmly.

"We just met Eric this evening. He's new in town," Desiree said.

"Well, Eric," Kongo said, "welcome to New Orleans. Any friend of the Daniels twins is an amigo of mine."

"We think Eric's a really wonderful guy!" Desiree cooed and patted Eric's hand.

"Eric's the new photographer at the *Nitpicker*," Zoey added.

"Oh, I have seen your photos my friend," Kongo said. "I'm an admirer."

"Thank you!"

"So tell me about yourself, Eric ..." Kongo suddenly seemed distracted. A man came screaming through the front doors, pursued by the grating sound of screeching tires. "It's them, Kongo! It's them!"

"If you will excuse me," Kongo said and hurried away from the table.

Suddenly, a titanic explosion blew out the front doors and windows of Kongo's Place.

CHAPTER ELEVEN

The blast shook the foundation of Kongo's Place. Zoey, Desiree and Eric were flung to the floor. Machine gun bursts sent a stream of bullets through the opening where the windows once were. The bullets strafed the table tops, like stones thrown across the face of a pond. Whiskey bottles, crockery, candlesticks, crystal chandeliers and ashtrays exploded into shards of glass, raining down on the crawling, scrambling, screaming patrons. Slugs bore into the mahogany tables with a dull thud. Then the gunfire abruptly stopped and was replaced with angry shouts, revving engines and screeching tires.

Zoey and Desiree struggled to their feet, just as the gunfire stopped.

"We'd better get out of here," Zoey whispered. "Some of the police don't like Kongo, and we don't want to be here when they show up. All of us might be hauled in on trumped-up charges."

Desiree nodded. "A lot of those cops on the take hate us and our column."

"Don't worry, we'll just blend in when people start leaving."

"No!" Desiree said and took her sister by the hand. "I've got a foolproof escape plan."

Meanwhile, Eric had edged his way to the front of the club. Kongo stood in the doorway, looking at two groaning men, lying in the street. He turned around, saw Eric's thirty-eight caliber revolver in his hand and broke into a big mustachioed grin.

"Ah, my good friend! You are an ally in our fight!" Then the big man put his giant arms around Eric and hugged him.

Eric patted Kongo on the back, then pointed at the two wounded men. "Either of those guys friends of yours, Kongo?"

"No, he smiled. "These are the unfortunate gentlemen who didn't know we were waiting for their hit. Those guys in the cars would have been gunned down immediately, but the attack was too sudden to prevent someone from lobbing a stick of dynamite at the building."

By the time Eric and Kongo went back inside, the patrons of the club were tending to those wounded. Except for a few cuts and bruises, no one was hurt. With Eric in tow, Kongo made the rounds, comforting those with frazzled nerves and fearful faces. Eric was intrigued. Kongo seemed to know everyone personally. He addressed everyone as amigo or friend, except for those he called brother, sister or cousin.

"I'm quite surprised," Eric said. "Do you know all of these people?"

"Not everyone," Kongo smiled. "Many are relatives. Others are friends I've known all my life, growing up in the Quarter."

"Hard times for you back then?"

"Hard times for us right now."

The two men watched waiters righting tables and chairs. The bartender sighed wearily, as he looked at his bullet-riddled bar. Vintage wines and twelve year old Scotch bled into puddles of beer on the floor.

"Who would do this to you?" Eric asked.

Kongo wore an air of melancholy. "It is a complicated situation, amigo. Suffice to say, some residents of the French Quarter do not like me or the people I associate with. One in particular, Louis D'Quad. Have you met him yet?"

"Yes, we've met."

"Then for your sake, mi amigo," Kongo laughed, "you had better not be seen with me! The police always rake me and my friends over the coals. Every time our interests collide with D'Quad's ... well ... the police rarely come down on D'Quad, because they fear him. Many of his enemies have disappeared. Standing with me, you are going to make a dangerous enemy of your own, amigo."

"Don't worry about me, Kongo. I choose my amigos as I see fit. I'm a photographer, no family, no strings attached to anyone. I've had a good life. Heck, what have I got to lose?'

Both men broke out laughing. "My friend, my friend," Kongo cried.

"Oh, no," Eric thought. "I'm going to get my ribs crushed again."

Sure enough, Kongo's hug knocked the breath out of him. Eric couldn't think about that now. The police had arrived and cordoned off the area. Kongo went over to talk to the officers, gesturing and pointing at the skid marks, and the club's blown out windows. The policemen examined the slug holes in the walls of the building. The two wounded men were whisked off to the hospital. Then the police began grilling the traumatized patrons.

While the police were occupied, Eric walked outside and noticed something out of the corner of his eye. There was a juju charm of a woven star, tied with a red cord. Eric was puzzled. "I saw this door frame before I entered the club. There was no juju charm on it. Just like at Josiah's, it was definitely put up after the bombing."

Eric stepped back into the club. His eyes searched for the Daniels sisters. They were nowhere to be seen. "How in the heck did they get out of here without me seeing them? Where the heck did they disappear to?"

****

Desiree led Zoey through the back door. "And we're free!"

"And we're trapped!" Zoey said angrily. "You idiot, this is a stone courtyard! There is no exit! Look at how high these walls are!"

"Don't start moaning."

Zoey gave her sister a withering look. "I'm not moaning! I'm furious!"

Desiree giggled wickedly.

"What are you laughing at?" Zoey growled.

Desiree shivered with nervous delight. "I've never been trapped before. It's so, so exciting."

"I can't believe it! You're getting cheap thrills out of possibly being arrested by the cops." Zoey looked around the dark courtyard desperately.

"Look!" Desiree pointed. "There's a little fish pond and a bench next to it! I told you I'd get us out of here!"

Zoey and Desiree hurried over to the bench and tried to lift it —again and again. "This is solid cast iron," Zoey grunted. "We'll never be able to lift this or drag it over to the wall for that matter!"

Desiree giggled nervously. "Don't worry! I said I'll get us out of here, and I will."

Zoey put her hands on her hips and glared at Desiree. "What do you plan to do?"

Desiree pointed. "There's a parapet shelf, midway up the wall. We can easily climb up on it and get ourselves up and over the wall."

"I'll go first. If one of us is to be caught, it should be you, since you got us into this mess!"

Zoey grunted as she managed to boost herself onto the shelf. She looked up and estimated how high she would have to leap. Still on her knees, Zoey turned around and looked at her sister with disgust. "I'm so, so mad at you."

"What you need is a good laugh," Desiree said sweetly.

Zoey glared at her sister. "What does that mean?"

Desiree grabbed hold of the hem of Zoey's dress and pulled it up. "Everybody can see your ass!"

Zoey pulled free, lunged for the top of the wall, straddled it, lost her balance and fell over. Desiree heard Zoey cursing. She hoisted herself onto the parapet, grabbed hold of the top of the wall, boosted herself up and looked down. Zoey was on her back in a bush, struggling to get up. Desiree laughed hysterically, lost her balance and crash landed next to Zoey.

There was silence for a moment. Then Desiree whispered, "I told you I'd get us out of there!"

Zoey gritted her teeth.

****

Across town, the night had turned into a nightmare for Louis D'Quad. Victoria's Place was still jumping. At the far end of the bar, D'Quad huddled with his cronies. The din of screaming patrons, the jazz band and people demanding drinks made it impossible to hear what he was saying. Only Victoria, who was close by, was privy to D'Quad's angry tirade.

"What I want to know is who tipped off Kaminga!" he roared.

"We don't know, Mr. D'Quad."

"You don't know? You don't know? What am I paying you for? Is there anything at all that you can tell me? Do any of you know anything about our two wounded men?"

"I just got word that they're at the hospital getting patched up," Digger replied. "When they are released, the police intend to arrest them."

"I've got the Police Commissioner in the palm of my hand," D'Quad cried angrily. "In fact, I'll take care of this right now." D'Quad stalked off to Victoria's office to make a call. He returned with a pompous grin on his face and an envelope in his hand. "Just like I told ya! One call and the boys won't be charged with anything." Then D'Quad took out his wallet, pulled out a wad of cash and stuffed it into the envelope. "Gizmo, I want you to take this over to our dear Commissioner. This is a little treat to keep him well behaved."

After Gizmo left, D'Quad huddled with T.M., Digger and some of his other cronies. "First of all, Digger, did you leave the juju charm on the door frame after the attack?"

"Yes, Mr. D'Quad. None of the cops pay any attention to a short, fat passerby with a violin case."

"Good. It makes it seem that Kaminga ignored the charm. Spread the word that Kongo's Place never sought protection from the charm, just like you did with Josiah's, and all those other places we hit."

Digger nodded. "I hope the Daniels sisters will concentrate on this voodoo protection angle. If not, I can only imagine the trash they're going to write about us in the paper tomorrow."

"I'm going to make those Daniels sisters pay dearly!" D'Quad railed. "It's time to get tougher. We've got to find a way to hit Kongo even harder too!"

His rant was interrupted by Victoria. "Telephone call for you, Mr. D'Quad."

D'Quad made his way back to Victoria's office. After some time, he returned. "Change of plans boys," he said with a nervous grin. "We're going about this all wrong. Since tonight's hit turned into a disaster, Kongo expects us to hit him again. The Daniels sisters snubbed me. They expect me to seek revenge."

T.M. was D'Quad's right hand man, a ruthless assassin and trusted confidante. T.M. was confused. "Isn't that the plan, Louis? To hit Kongo harder than before and make the Daniels sisters pay?"

"It was." D'Quad replied. "But I've had a change of heart. We'll do what they don't expect."

"And how do we do that?"

"Let Kongo sweat, worrying about when we're going to hit back," D'Quad replied. "With him plastered like a fly to fly paper at Kongo's Place, we'll make our monthly calls on his deadbeat friends who won't buy our spirits or pay protection money."

T.M. glared at D'Quad with blood in his eyes. "I've had it with this small time crap, Louis," he raged. "I want to end this cat and mouse game once and for all! I want to kill all of them—Kongo—his gang—yes, and just for the shear pleasure of it—the Daniel's sisters."

"That time," D'Quad said solemnly, "is not far off." He gave T.M. a twisted smile. "Did you see all those twinkling Christmas lights going up all over town?"

T.M. gave D'Quad a confused look.

"Well, 'tis the season to be jolly, and we're going to be jollier and jollier over the next few weeks!" D'Quad cried. "I've got a fool proof plan that will give us the best Christmas present of all. Before old man winter rings in the new year, we're going to own the French Quarter, and all of them: Kongo, his gang and the Daniel's sisters will be gift wrapped, buried and pushing up daisies."

CHAPTER TWELVE

Flamenco Dancers With Flaming Castanets
By Zoey and Desiree Daniels
New Orleans Nitpicker Columnists
Kongo's Place was really jumping last night! The intimacy of family,
friends and one curious stranger, cut through the smoky air. The
radio was blaring jazz and razzmatazz. Joyous dancers raised hell, in
the name of heaven. That rascal, dashing Diego Kaminga, in a shiny
silk suit, allowed his torrid romance to go public. His paramour,
Esmerelda, was resplendent in a low-cut, black satin dress with a
row of ruffled flounces. An embroidered slit up the side showed a
lot of luscious leg - and honey, Esmerelda has two of em! When the
lovestruck couple rose to dance, it was like the parting of the Red Sea.
All the other dancers stepped back. A switch of the radio station set
the mood. A Spanish guitar's soft strumming, and the gentle tones
of a single trumpet framed the moment. The couple's steps started
slow, sensuous, seductive, staring into the other's eyes. Moving
closer, face to face, their Flamenco fire burned hotter and hotter,
with every step. Esmerelda's heels punished the oak floor. Each step
was a rhythmic statement of power and passion. Diego responded
with an irresistible force of flashing footwork. Esmerelda's castanets
clicked in a frenzied flourish. One could almost see sparks of fire.
And wouldn't you know it? At that very moment, we did see sparks of
fire! Suffice to say that a firecracker, the size of a stick of dynamite,
turned out to be a real stick of dynamite! This created a mini
earthquake followed by a tsunami of machine gun slugs by a group
of thugs that couldn't hit the broadside of a barn. We must thank

these well known business associates of King Louis the 19th, for their gracious ineptitude. Alas, two of the visitors were wounded. Inside Kongo's Place, there were only cuts, bruises, and rumors of two patrons who took a nasty fall off a garden wall! Despite some bullet holes, damaged clothes and the moans and groans of both of us, we would not have missed this soiree for the world. You've just got to love Flamenco dancers with flaming castanets!

Ah, virtue, thy name is truth

Zoey and Desiree Daniels

****

It was an unseasonably warm, eighty degree day. Eric sat out on his upstairs veranda reading the newspaper, basking in the warm sun and gentle wind. "Well, I'll be darned," Eric chuckled, as he finished reading the Daniels sisters' column. "This is one nasty, naughty, innuendo filled tour de force!" Eric shook his head in wonder. "So that's how they escaped the club without my notice! They slipped out the back and," Eric laughed, "fell over the courtyard wall!"

Across town, in the Toulouse Street Inn, the patrons having lunch made it a point not to look over at Louis D'Quad's table. His deadly reputation made them tread lightly when this snake bared his fangs. The Daniels' column in this morning's *New Orleans Nitpicker* was already the talk of the town. The consensus was that Zoey and Desiree had made a mockery of D'Quad and his gang.

D'Quad tore the newspaper to shreds and threw it on the floor. His fury was hot as a blow torch. Everything he screamed was like liquid fire. Some patrons pretended that they couldn't hear him. Others left their unfinished food, hurried to pay their checks and made a fevered exit.

"I knew the Daniels sisters were there with Kaminga, or how else could these tramps have written this trash?" D'Quad slammed his hand on the table. "They called us 'thugs that couldn't hit the broad side of a barn! 'Then they called me King

Louis the 19th and thanked me for my 'gracious ineptitude.'"
D'Quad fumed. "By the way, what does 'ineptitude' mean?"

"It means you don't have the brains to run a gang," T.M.
replied.

D'Quad slammed the table again. "Do you know anything
about this guy Louis the 19th?"

"Yes, I do. It's you. The last King Louis of France was the
18th." T.M wore a mocking smile. "It seems the Daniels 'sisters
created a whole new incompetent, criminal monarchy with your
name all over it."

"This would be libel if those little floozies had just come out
and called me by my name."

"That's not their style," Digger replied. "They're sneaky,
backstabbing cowards —little girls who need to be put in their
place!"

D'Quad nodded and thought for a moment. "T.M., I want you
to send Gizmo and Bilious out on a little errand for me. I want
them to tail the Daniels sisters. And anything short of killing,
tell them to feel free to rough up those two brats."

****

The day dawned with brilliant blue skies and a warm sun.
Zoey parted the lace curtains and looked out the window. "It's a
beautiful day for a ride in the country."

"How about a picnic?"

"Great! Let's pack some food in our picnic basket—"

"—and I'll go get the wine!"

A few minutes later, they were cruising down the highway,
enjoying the balmy weather. The wind whipped through their
hair. The warm sun gave their skin a ruddy glow. In the distance,
they saw a car coming toward them.

"Well, it's great to see at least one person out for a drive, on
this beautiful day."

"Sure is moving fast."

D'Quad's goon, Bilious, had spotted them too. He pointed and cried, "Look, Gizmo!" A gleaming maroon Duesenberg X sped toward them. "That's the Daniels sisters' car!"

"Well, well, well," Gizmo sneered." We've finally found our glamorous 'It 'girls."

"Let's get em!"

"We'll let em pass us, then we'll do a huey and take em from behind. Get down, so's they don't see ya."

Bilious crouched low, and Gizmo shielded his face, as the Duesenberg sped by. Desiree stared into the rear view mirror. She saw the car make a u-turn. At first she thought nothing of it. Then all sorts of red lights went off in her head. "Zoey?"

"Yes?"

"You know that car that just passed us?"

"Yes."

"Well, it's made a u-turn, and it's gaining on us!"

Zoey turned around and watched. "Yes, it is! And I've got a feeling it's D'Quad's boys."

Desiree hit the gas, and the car literally left the ground. "To the Steeplechase Amusement Park!"

Zoey gave Desiree an evil smile. "Let's put a little distance between us and them. Once we get to the Steeplechase, we'll park and see if those morons pass us by."

"If not," Desiree laughed, "how about we let them chase us through the amusement park? We know it like the back of our hands."

"That's a great idea! They'll be bruised and battered by the time we reach the end of the fun house."

"Not to mention the bumpy slide at the end!"

"Speed up, speed up," Bilious cried, as he saw the Daniels 'car disappearing in the distance.

"That's a Duesenberg X, you moron! It can go up to 100 miles an hour. I'm just about flooring it!"

"Then floor it! Speed up, or we're going to lose them."

By the time Zoey and Desiree reached the amusement park, their pursuers were nowhere in sight. They pulled their car into a conspicuous parking spot with an unobstructed view of the road.

"Time for our picnic!" Zoey said, as she pulled out their blanket and spread it over the hood of the car. Desiree brought the picnic basket and bottle of wine and handed them to Zoey. Both sisters hoisted themselves up on the hood and began enjoying their lunch. It was not long before their pursuers reached the park and drove by slowly, searching the parking lot.

Both sisters laughed and pointed. "Hey, that's Gizmo and Bilious!" Zoey cried.

The sisters leaned back, made themselves comfortable and waited. They passed the wine back and forth, chugging right out of the bottle. It was some time before they spotted the goons' car. As it was passing, Zoey toasted their pursuers and screamed. "Let's drink to those who are about to be our afternoon entertainment." Zoey took a big swig and handed the bottle back to Desiree.

After she gulped down the last of the wine, Desiree shouted, "Yoo-hoo!" The car had doubled back and screeched to a halt. Bilious squinted out the window, trying to find out where the shout had come from.

"Yoo-hoo, big boys," Desiree shouted and waved. "Over here, over here! We so want to take you on the rides!"

"It's them!" Bilious cried.

Gizmo sped into the parking lot.

"We better put our picnic stuff back in the car and ..."

"...Why must you always be so neat? There's no time," Desiree screamed, as she took Zoey's hand and rushed toward the park entrance.

Zoey pulled free, stopped, opened her purse and took something out of her wallet.

"You're slowing us down! Put that junk back into your purse, or they'll surely catch us."

"They surely won't," Zoey said, as she grabbed her sister by the hand and dragged her to the ticket booth.

Desiree looked around nervously, then said to the gatekeeper, "Two tickets for ..."

Zoey put her hand over her sister's mouth and handed the cashier two cards.

"Ah," the smiling woman said, "season passes." She handed the cards back to Zoey, waved them through the turnstile and said, "Welcome to Steeplechase Amusement Park and have a great time!"

"See?" Zoey said with a smug look, as she put the cards back in her purse. "I told you they wouldn't catch us."

"You were so right! Quick thinking! I forgot about those season passes you bought. Look," she pointed. "There's Bilious and Gizmo on line to buy tickets!"

Zoey laughed. "They can't risk bursting through the entrance and attracting the police, so they have to buy tickets."

"Let's get the taunting going. Yoo-hoo boys!"

Gizmo and Bilious glared at the girls.

"We're right over here, you sweeter than honeys!" Zoey said.

"Catch us if you can, you hunkier than hunkies!"

The girls waited, giving the two men exaggerated limp wrist waves and blowing kisses, as their pursuers struggled to get through the turnstiles.

"You little trollops!" Gizmo cried.

Being much smaller, younger and defter than their pursuers, Zoey and Desiree weaved their way through the crowd with ease. Gizmo and Bilious stumbled around and into startled parents and children. In a matter of moments, crying kids and battered adults littered the ground. Shouts of terror filled the air.

"My word, Constance," a well dressed English gentleman cried. "I believe I've broken my arm!"

"Stick it up your ascot, Reginald," Constance groaned, as she pried cotton candy out of her hair.

Others joined in on the chorus of misery:

"Oh no, I spilled my soda pop all over my new dress!"

"Somebody stepped on my hot dog!"

"I got a footprint on my face!"

"Someone call security!"

"Someone call the police!"

"Constance, you must call a hospital!"

"Oh stick it in your humidor, Reginald."

Zoey and Desiree stood under a gothic stone archway at the entrance to the Haunted Fun House. The four story structure was cloaked in flaking black paint and crumbling wall boards. Jack-o-lanterns lit up the windows with an eerie orange glow. Silken spider webs undulated. Arm-in-arm skeletons grinned and waved. Witches and ghosts rode the yellow-moon-sky above the roof. Once you entered the house, the only way out of it was down the giant Loch Ness Monster slide, thirty feet wide and sixty feet high. That would take you to the ground floor. The polished surface was slippery as ice.

Zoey and Desiree laughed as they watched people careen off the sides of the undulating serpent of a slide. The reverie was interrupted when they heard screaming and cursing behind them. Gizmo and Bilious were in hot pursuit, shoving people out of the way. Zoey and Desiree ran through the Haunted House entrance and into total darkness. A single flash of a lantern revealed a long twisting staircase that spiraled up into the pitch black gloom. The sisters bolted up the stairs. Along the way, Desiree reached out, grabbed the lantern and ripped its wires out of the wall.

"Great idea! Even though we could get arrested for vandalism."

"No chance! If the cops come and see the bodies D'Quad's morons left in their wake, they'll blame those dullards."

The sisters reached the top of the stairs and opened the door. To cross the room to get to the next door, you had to walk across a series of wobbling tables. Parallel bars bordered the walkway on both sides.

"We might bust an ankle stumbling across those tables in these clunky heels."

Instead of running across the wobbling tables, the sisters hoisted themselves onto the parallel bars and hand walked to the other side. Bilious and Gizmo had finally stumbled their way up the winding stairs.

"Yoo-hoo, fellas," Zoey cooed. "Over here!"

Bilious stepped onto the first table, with Gizmo close behind. Bilious turned his ankle, stumbled and fell. "Oh, crap," he cried!" He shook his fist at the sisters and shouted," I'm going to kill you!"

Gizmo lost his balance and went down too. Bouncing up and down on the gyrating tables, Gizmo's voice sounded like turkey clucks. "Just ... wa ... wa ... wait ... till, I catch up... wi ... with you!"

"'Tis so sad, my handsome man, we can tarry no longer. Ta Ta!" Zoey laughed.

The sisters stepped through the door and closed it behind them.

Gizmo and Bilious grabbed onto the rails and struggled to catch up. They rubber-legged their way to the door and flung it open. They entered a maze of mirrors. The sisters, having been to Steeplechase countless times, easily found their way through it to the next door. Unfortunately, D'Quad's goons did not. As they cursed their way into dead ends, the hysterical sisters could hear them.

"We're over here, boys," Zoey shouted sweetly.

"You wanted us to wait for you, so here we are."

They listened to the swearing and shouting men's footsteps get closer and closer. They heard the screams of people who were flung aside by their angry and frustrated pursuers.

"Time to say, adieu," Zoey laughed. They turned and headed up a long dark hallway. They walked right into a dead end.

"Going down?" Desiree laughed.

"Going down," Zoey shrieked, as the floor gave way under them.

Zoey and Desiree slid down the trap door and landed on an overstuffed wrestling mat. "Quick," Zoey said, "we don't have much time."

Both girls tugged at the heavy mat, pulling it away from under the trap door. Desiree grinned. "Boy, are they in for one unhappy landing."

The sisters opened a door in front of them and looked back. It wasn't long before they heard the trap door open and Bilious and Gizmo crashing to the hardwood floor. For a few moments, they laid in the darkness, groaning in pain. That ended when they heard two prissy voices singing, "Humpty Dummies fell through the floor, Humpty Dummies are battered and sore!"

D'Quad's goons struggled to their feet, as the sisters headed for a huge revolving barrel. They stepped into the whirling cylinder, walking against the spin. Bilious and Gizmo attempted to run right through it. Instead, the revolving barrel flung them to the floor. Each time they tried to get up, the result was the same. Cursing and sweating, they attempted to crawl through the barrel. They were thrown from side to side, like sailboats in a tidal wave. The sisters watched as the pair crawled out, groggy and battered. Zoey and Desiree ran to the last leg of what had become a torture chamber for their two hapless pursuers. They had reached the Loch Ness Monster Slide. Excited children and adults sat down on little mats, closed their eyes, took deep breaths and screaming with terror, zoomed down the slippery, slick slide. Most lost their balance and slid down sideways, others found themselves sliding backward.

Zoey and Desiree waved at their unsteady pursuers. "See you at the bottom, boys!"

With that, the sisters plunged down the slide, their arms spread out like wings.

"Woohoo!" Desiree cried, as they zipped by startled parents. In and out, their wingspans gave them perfect balance as they slid to the finish and landed feet first. The sisters looked back and saw Gizmo and Bilious sit, give themselves a push and hurtle down the slide. Startled by their blazing speed, they tried to slow themselves down the only way possible.

"Aagh!" Bilious cried. "I burned my hands!"

Gizmo too had suffered the same fate, then lost his balance and fell on his side. Bilious was doing no better. He was flying down the slide head first. The pair hurtled into and over the unfortunate people who got in their way. Terrified screams preceded a human log jam of waving arms and legs. Like a spear, Bilious flew right through them and to the finish. Gizmo spun like a top. Dizzy and bruised, he struggled to get up only to fall down again. Bilious, who landed head first on the concrete floor, nursed a bump on his forehead.

"Yoo-hoo," Desiree waved. "Follow us, lover boys!"

"Yes, we've got one last ride, and it is so, so romantic," Zoey cried, as the giggling sisters skipped out of the Funhouse, hand in hand.

As they weaved their way through the crowd, they took backward glances, making certain D'Quad's goons could see them. The sisters raced toward the last ride in the park. Gizmo and Bilious had spotted them and were in hot pursuit. The sisters squealed with glee, as they carefully lowered themselves into a little boat and drifted into the Tunnel Of Love."

"Do you think they will follow us?" Desiree giggled.

"Two he-men like them?" Zoey laughed.

Gizmo and Bilious stood on the platform and watched the sisters disappear.

"Well, those floozies don't care what anybody thinks about two girls riding into the Tunnel Of Love— but if two men do it. ..."

"We ain't going to have to do it," Gizmo replied. He grabbed the arm of a startled passer by and shoved her into a boat.

"You cad!" she screamed. "Let me go, let me go!"

"Look, ya old bag, you ain't my first choice for a date, either. Now shut up!"

"Help, help," she cried, "I've been abducted!"

Bilious grabbed her companion and pulled her into a boat.

"Oh, you're in one heap of trouble," she cried and smacked him in the face. Bilious tried to fend off her flurry of punches. "So," his furious date screamed, "you forced me to go on this romantic ride with you. So, here's one right in the kisser!"

Gizmo's reluctant date was still screaming, as their boat emerged from the tunnel. "Police!"

"Don't worry, Madam, we are right here," Officer Peters said.

"That's him officers! That's the scoundrel who assaulted me!" Constance cried.

"That's the ruffian who assaulted all of us!" Reginald added.

The gathering crowd broke into a chorus of angry shouts and finger pointing. Gizmo stepped from the boat, furious when he saw the Daniels sisters.

"Are these the men who chased you and threatened you with bodily harm?" Officer Peters asked.

"Yes … officer." Desiree said, and pretended to sob.

"There, there, my dear sister," Zoey said, as she put her arms around Desiree. "Don't you worry a bit, the police will take care of these bad, mean brutes."

"Don't fret little lady, we'll protect you from these criminals," Officer Peters said reassuringly.

"Come on tough guys, you are under arrest!" The police cuffed both of the furious men. Behind the officers' backs, Zoey and Desiree waved and blew kisses to Gizmo and Bilious.

Gizmo's date whacked him on the head with her purse.

Bilious 'date reared back and smacked him across the face.

"What a lovely day this has been," Zoey sighed.

The two delighted young ladies ran like children through the parking lot, laughing under a gorgeous setting sun.

****

Bright and early the next morning, Eric arrived at the *New Orlean's Nitpicker*. Chief Editor, Chuck Hines, opened his manila envelope and studied Eric's photos. He looked up and gave Eric a crooked smile. "When the Feds sent you here to work undercover, I said to myself, oh great, another lousy photographer. But these prints are first rate work." Chuck winked. "Could be a great profession for you."

"Thanks," Eric chuckled, "but I already have a profession."

Chuck opened his bottom desk drawer and produced a bottle of Scotch and two tumblers.

"Isn't it a bit early to be drinking?"

Chuck laughed. "In the newspaper business, it's never too early to start drinking." He filled both glasses and passed one over to Eric. "So, anything new with the investigation?"

"I've got a few interesting theories, with no tangible evidence. I'm more or less going on gut instincts." Eric grinned. "The only place I seem to find any worthwhile leads are from the Daniels 'column."

"Yes. They always use a lot of similes and metaphors, but when you read their column, it's not hard to know who they are talking about."

Eric nodded. "You're right, it's not hard to know who they're talking about, but for me, it's hard to know who the Daniels sisters are. First, I read their column, and I was so impressed and eager to meet them. Then I met them at Kongo's Place, and my first impression was that they were flighty, flirtatious Flapper Girls. Then I found out they had been dancers in the Ziegfeld Follies. Suddenly, my impression of them changed again. These were streetwise girls who had experienced fame, fortune and the wild side of life in New York City."

"They're always full of surprises. They're like chameleons!"

"Yes!" Eric laughed. "I wouldn't be at all surprised if they were involved in piracy!"

Chuck emptied the last of the scotch into their glasses and toasted Eric. "Drink up me hearties, yo ho!"

CHAPTER THIRTEEN

After the excitement of their day at Steeplechase Amusement Park, the sisters partied till dawn. Zoey was asleep on the couch. She certainly needed her rest. Desiree was exhausted herself. Uncharacteristically awake before her sister, she showered, dressed, put on her coat and hat and grabbed her purse. Shoes in hand, she tiptoed down the stairs and to the front door. Each creeping step brought a groan from the old oak floor. The door creaked as she inched it open. Once outside, she locked the door behind her, put on her shoes and headed for Jackson Square. As soon as she reached the Cafe du Monde, Desiree ordered coffee and what she called, "those little slices of heaven,"—beignets. She found a table in a secluded corner. Comfort food always settled Desiree's rattled nerves. She wolfed down the beignets as if she had been stranded on a desert island, and this was her first meal in months. Lost in thought, she didn't notice the approaching stranger.

"Good morning!"

Desiree looked up. She slid her heart-shaped sunglasses down her nose and stared. "Eric! What a wonderful surprise!"

"Yes, it is," he said. "May I join you?"

"Please do," she replied with a delighted smile.

Eric sat down, took a sip of his coffee and lit a cigarette. "Well," he said, "I haven't seen you since …"

"… Kongo's! Yes! Everyone always has such a good time there. Sometimes people get a bit too happy … they drink too much." Desiree paused and giggled. "Why, even Zoey and I went a bit over the wall that night."

"Yes." Eric chuckled. "I read between the lines in your column, including the reference to the 'curious stranger.'"

"Ah, Eric," Desiree replied, her dark eyes sparkling, "I knew you were a boy with a brain!"

"I almost forgot to ask you. The other night, you never told me if you finally added a first name to your stage names. You only told me your last name, 'Rivers.'"

"Oh, you're going to love this! People began to call Zoey the 'Angel Of Allure,' and they called me the 'River Of Desire!'"

They both laughed so loud that people began to stare at them. Struggling to calm down, Eric finally said, "Tell me how the notorious Daniels sisters came to be."

"Well," Desiree began. "We were born and raised in Monterey, California. Our father was killed in World War I. He left us a sizable fortune, and a company we still own today. Our mother raised us alone. She taught us all the academic disciplines, as well as dance, music, gymnastics, self defense—even weaponry. Mother didn't pull any punches either," she said, an amused look on her face. "Once, when we were boxing, she hit me with a wicked right cross that knocked me to the ground. She did the same thing to Zoey! Thanks to her," she said with a big smile, "we could whip any boy in the neighborhood." Desiree paused and zipped her lips. "No more about me. Now it's your turn. Tell the River of Desire about Eric Strand's secret self!"

Erik thought for a moment. "Well. I grew up in New York City. My dad was a policeman. My mom was a nurse. Of all the gifts I received as a youngster, my favorite was my first camera. So, here I am, photographer for the *New Orleans Nitpicker*."

"No big dark secret, Eric?" Desiree pried. "No scathingly, scandalous secret that you left out?"

Eric put his finger to his chin, with a sly grin on his face. "There is one thing I left out." Eric reached across the table and took Desiree's hand. "I am a federal agent working undercover as a photographer."

Desiree giggled. "Sure you are. And I'm the Queen of

Atlantis."

Eric opened his coat, pulled out his badge and I.D. and showed them to Desiree. She was speechless. When Eric put the badge back in his jacket pocket, Desiree saw his shoulder holster. Her fear turned into a weird sort of excitement.

"So," she said, exuding charm, "why are you telling me this?"

"Because, Chuck Hines trusts you, and your columns are the only leads I have. He says your sources have always been reliable. Your columns imply that you are determined to take down D'Quad … and whomever else may be involved in this gang warfare. That's what I'm here to do."

Desiree gave Eric a suspicious look. "Two federal agents were killed here in the French Quarter. That's why you were sent here, isn't it … to find whoever killed them? Not to deal with the gangs."

"Aren't they one and the same?"

Desiree thought for a moment."I suppose you're right."

"I want you and Zoey to be my eyes and ears, my informants."

Desiree smiled. "I think what you're saying is you want us to risk our lives."

"It does come with risks. But I can minimize those risks. There are certain rules I must insist upon." Eric looked around to see if anyone was within ear shot. "The first rule is, no telephone calls between us, from home or from the *Nitpicker* offices. Our phones might be tapped. The second rule is you must keep my identity a secret."

"Your secret is safe with me," Desiree said with bravado. "I'll take your secret to my grave."

"Good," Eric said grimly, "because my secret could very well get you killed."

"Well, that's just wonderful! Is there anything else you want to tell me?"

Eric winked and smiled. "Yes. You have powdered sugar on you nose."

****

In Villa's intimate courtyard cafe, Zoey shared a midday brunch with her dear friend, the dashing Diego Kaminga, Kongo's younger brother.

As always, Diego handed Zoey a single rose and kissed her hand. "How have you been, my one and only?"

Zoey laughed, pulled her hand away and scolded him playfully. "Diego," she said, "behave yourself. Your heart belongs to Esmerelda."

"Ah, Esmerelda, my paramour, my queen of hearts, my dancing demon, Esmerelda. My world would be empty without her, and life would not be worth living." Diego twisted the ends of his mustache and sighed dramatically. "Then again, cannot a man such as I, with so big a heart, love many women at the same time, my dearest one?"

"I am not your dearest one anymore, Diego," Zoey laughed, as she patted his hand. "But I am your dear friend … always."

Diego tried to look heartbroken. Then he said brightly, "On the other hand, there is always Esmerelda! My paramour!"

Zoey shook her head in mock despair. "You are hopeless, Diego!"

"Tell me, Zoey, have you heard any new gossip from your sources?"

"Yes. Our sources have told us that D'Quad is planning hits on the Kaminga family and their friends … but nothing like last year's shootout on the pier or the bombings."

"But it could be lethal, none the less?"

"It could be."

"Ah," Diego said, "why do we talk of this, mi amore? There is an easy solution to this gloom and doom. Dancing!"

"Dancing?" Zoey searched Diego's eyes to see if he was kidding. He was not. "Oh, good grief, you can't be serious."

"Of course I am. Why worry about what might happen to any of us? Let's go dancing!"

"Okay," Zoey said hesitantly. "I'll bite—Where and when?"

"Victoria's Place on Saturday night. Alas, Esmerelda will not go with me, because she thinks I am a criminal. But I take some consolation that Kongo is coming with me. How about it, my Angel of Allure? Will you come with us?"

Zoey thought for a moment then broke into a big grin. "That would really piss off D'Quad. It would make him squirm. And he couldn't kill us with all those witnesses. Why not?" she cried. "I'm in!"

Diego laughed with delight. "Can we count on Desiree to join us?"

"Are you kidding?" Zoey laughed. "She's up for anything! But," Zoey cautioned, "this is not a date."

"Maybe not now," Diego said with a devilish grin. "But when we are at Victoria's, and I sweep you off your feet and into my arms, and we Tango, we will fall in love all over again."

Zoey broke into hysterical laughter. Diego did too. "You cannot fall in love with me again," Zoey cried, "because you are already in love with Esmerelda!"

"Esmerelda who?"

****

Louis D'Quad was not thinking about dancing at Victoria's on Saturday night. His mind was like a pincushion with bloody little holes. The hit on Kongo's Place had failed. Two of his men had been gunned down. His invitation to the Daniels sisters had been thrown back in his face. Zoey and Desiree had made him the laughing stock of the French Quarter.

"You idiots!" he cried. "All I asked you to do was harass the Daniels sisters," D'Quad said with disdain. "Look at you. Bruised, bloody, disheveled ..." D'Quad's face turned beet red. "Two little girls ... two little girls! They led you on a wild goose chase through the amusement park, and without laying a glove on you, they beat you to a pulp!"

Bilious said nothing. He rubbed the lump on his forehead and stroked his broken nose, courtesy of his bellicose "date" in the Tunnel of Love. Gizmo's black eye had closed shut, but he was not too battered to lash out at D'Quad. "Why don't you just stop talking and start listening. Those childish flappers must have been to the Steeplechase a million times. Any one of us could have fallen into the trap of fighting them on their own turf."

"Any one of us, but me!"

"Louis, none of this is doing us any good," T.M. said angrily. "We'll keep shadowing those two bimbos. But, for now, a little revenge and a little money might make us all feel better."

D'Quad's rage dissipated. He scratched his head and put his finger to his chin. Then he glared at Gizmo and Bilious. "Get out of my sight. You're useless to me in the condition you're in." Then he turned to T.M. and said, "Get me my calendar. I think I know the pigeons who are due for a little shakedown. Round up a few of your boys to pay our deadbeat enemies a visit. Tell them that even if these pigeons pay their protection money, I want them to rough them up real bad."

"How bad?" T.M. asked, with an insane look in his eyes.

"Bad enough to wish we had killed them instead."

****

Desiree was slouched on the sofa, looking out the open window. The afternoon sun played with the white patterned curtains, courtesy of a gentle breeze. The sunlight danced in Desiree's eyes. She wore a dazed smile.

"Hey, Desiree, what a beautiful day!" Zoey said, as she closed the front door behind her.

"Yes, it is a beautiful day," Desiree replied. "How was your lunch date?"

"Oh, Diego was his usual flirtatious self. I gave him the word on D'Quad's plans. But wait till you hear this. He said the solution to all this violence is to forget about it and go dancing at Victoria's on Saturday night!"

Desiree leapt up from the couch. "That sounds like a riot! Please tell me you said yes!"

"Of course!"

They hugged each other, jumped up and down and twirled around the room. After they were both quite out of breath, they collapsed on the sofa.

"So, what did you do today?" Zoey asked.

"Well. I went down to Cafe du Monde and ran into Eric."

"Ooh," Zoey said, "you alone with the handsome Mr. Strand ... any sparks fly?"

"Just one," Desiree replied, bursting with excitement.

"What? What? Tell me. Tell me!"

"Eric is an undercover federal agent!"

"Oh, come on," Zoey smirked, "he's no more a federal agent than I am the Sweetheart of the Rodeo."

"Well, saddle up the palomino, Sweetheart! I saw his badge and his I.D. I also spied a shoulder holster inside his jacket —looked like a thirty-eight caliber; common law enforcement issue."

Zoey was confused and disturbed. "Why is he here? Why would he tell you that he is an undercover agent?"

"He's searching for the killers who gunned down those two federal agents a while ago. He's linked them to the gangs. As for why he wants us, he read all of our old columns. He knows we have reliable sources with inside information that he can't get."

"He wants us to be informants." Zoey said somberly.

"Isn't this exciting?"

Zoey rolled her eyes and smacked her forehead. "I can't believe it! Informants get killed, and you're getting excited! Do you realize what kind of danger Eric has put us in?"

"Tsk, tsk," Desiree giggled. "That's not danger. Real danger is tonight, when we're masked and crawling across rooftops."

" My knees hurt already."

CHAPTER FOURTEEN

"It seems that D'Quad's shakedowns have a pattern," Zoey said, as she pushed her long blonde hair into an oversized black wool beret. "They rotate from neighborhood to neighborhood, on a monthly basis."

"Yes," Desiree replied. She wriggled into her skin tight jeans, black turtleneck sweater and leather jacket. "So where do you think D'Quad will strike?"

"Well," Zoey replied, as she opened a map of the French Quarter. "Look here," she pointed. "Judging from the places D'Quad has hit, the next in line should be Baca's Social Club. Baca has always said he would not pay protection money."

Desiree laughed bitterly. "Protection money from whom? No one preys on people like Baca. The protection money D'Quad's gang steals from them is protection from D'Quad's gang and no one else!"

Zoey nodded. "But tonight, if we're right, the only ones who are going to need protection will be D'Quad's goons."

"Hey," Desiree asked, "isn't Baca's next to that little boutique where I bought that scarf with that shimmery stuff on it that goes so well with my silver skirt?"

"Are you kidding me?" Zoey cried.

"Well," Desiree snickered, "I've told you I don't pay attention to street signs, I go by landmarks."

"Like dress stores?"

"Dress stores ... speakeasies ... pretty houses ... the Cathedral ..."

"Well, Desiree, you might be in luck. If we have to crawl across roofs tonight, you'll be able to see all of your favorite landmarks—the dress stores, speakeasies, the pretty houses and the Cathedral."

"Ah, the scenic tour. Let's go!" Desiree cried, as they both put on their long black masks.

Leaving the house lights on, the Daniels sisters stepped out their back door. Desiree opened the garage, and they guided two sleek, black motorcycles down the dark alleyway behind their home. They hopped onto their bikes, and the pair sped off. Physically, mentally and spiritually, Zoey and Desiree ceased to exist. The blood of the Midnight Shadows pulsated in their veins.

Zoey and Desiree came within a block of Baca's Social Club, idled their bikes, and switched off their lights. A black limousine was parked across the street from the club. Zoey opened her saddlebag and pulled out a lasso. She unravelled it, and each of the sisters tied one end of the long thick rope to their handlebars. "Okay," Zoey whispered. "Ready?"

Desiree nodded. "Let's get these bikes to the middle of the street—and don't forget to keep them ten feet apart and the rope slack."

The girls could hear yelling and screaming sounds coming from inside the club.

"It'll only be minutes before D'Quad's boys make their escape," Zoey said. "Keep your lights off, till I yell, 'now.'"

"Show time!" Desiree cried, as two men emerged from the club. Startled by the rolling thunder heading toward them, D'Quad's men froze.

Desiree and Zoey bored down on them, the rope hanging slack between the two bikes.

"Now!" Zoey screamed.

The sisters turned on their headlights. D'Quad's men fired blindly into the glare. Seconds before they did, Zoey and Desiree veered off toward opposite sides of the street. The rope pulled taught. D'Quad's men, still blinded by the bikes' headlights, never knew what hit them. Both men were slammed to the ground and knocked unconscious. Zoey and Desiree hopped off their bikes. They searched the mens' jacket pockets and quickly found the cash they had extorted from Baca. Hearing the gunfire in the streets, Baca, followed by a few patrons of the club, crept timidly outside.

Zoey slipped a rubber band around the cash, tossed it to a startled Baca and roared off into the night.

****

The following day, headlines screamed of the previous night's violence at Baca's Social Club. D'Quad's bag men were bruised and battered. Despite their fear of D'Quad, with so many witnesses, the police had no choice but to arrest them. Baca had told the officers about the brutal shakedown, and the two masked motorcyclists who had gotten back his money. A few patrons, not fearful of D'Quad, told the same story. All asserted that these were the notorious Midnight Shadows who had taken down D'Quad's enforcers.

It was a sunny day, and Eric Strand sat on a bench on the levy. He grimaced as he put down his newspaper. "It seems that there are more than just two gangs involved in this war of retribution," Eric said to no one. "Now there are two vigilantes who have joined the fray."

Over the past few weeks, Eric had done his homework, gathering more information on the gangs, and recently, the Midnight Shadows. There were a few commonalities in all of the vigilantes' exploits. Not once had the Midnight Shadows killed anyone. Not once had they robbed anyone. Now, they had even retrieved stolen money and returned it to its rightful owner. So far, their fast as lightning hits on the gangs seemed indiscriminate. Now, it was apparent that their target was D'Quad. As to why, Eric could only speculate. Eric put the Midnight Shadows out of his mind. He took out his camera and binoculars. He focused on D'Quad's massive sixty foot long yacht, *The Eclipse*.

"Another overnight cruise," he mumbled, "and it always seems to come into port around the same time." Eric stared intently through his binoculars. D'Quad's men were loading crates into trucks and driving off to his Import Export Warehouse in Market Square. Agents Buck and James had already gone over that place with a fine-toothed comb. They found nothing but consumer goods.

Eric frowned. "All my instincts tell me that D'Quad's booze is being smuggled in on the *Eclipse* and offloaded somewhere along the Mississippi. But all my instincts aren't worth a damn, unless I find a good riverboat man."

Zoey and Desiree did not share Eric's frustration. They had decided to take down D'Quad by going shopping. Magnificent in their attire, both girls were the epitome of that special "It" girl charisma. They entered Louis D'Quad's Antique Jewelry Store. A clerk looked up from behind the counter. "Zoey and Desiree Daniels!" He exclaimed. "Welcome to D'Quad's!"

Desiree smiled shyly. "Thank you so much."

"Can I help you with anything?"

"Well now," Desiree said, putting her finger to her lip and gazing down into the locked display case. "Let me see, let me see," she said and abruptly looked up just in time to catch the clerk's leering eyes. It was clear that he had bought her flirtatious, "poor little old me" act. She smiled to herself, as she pretended to look over the jewelry. "I've got this little fish hooked," she thought.

While Desiree kept her lovestruck prey occupied, Zoey wandered around the display cases. She looked at every piece of jewelry like it was manna from heaven. After she was satisfied that she had wasted enough time, Zoey excused herself and went to use the powder room. Once inside, she locked the door behind her. She went over to the window, unlocked it, lifted it slightly, shoved a small sliver of wood under it; then closed it, unlocked. After waiting a sufficient amount of time, she reemerged. With promises of their return to the lovestruck clerk, they hurried home.

That night, the Midnight Shadows slithered down the alleyway outside D'Quad's Antique Jewelry store. Zoey reached up and opened the powder room window she had left unlocked during their bogus shopping spree. They climbed inside. The curtains were drawn on the shop windows. The sisters entered the back office and switched on small flashlights. They made their silent way to a desk. The file drawers were locked.

"Now, where would King Louis hide the spare key?" Desiree asked sarcastically.

Zoey reached under the desk and found the key taped to the underside of the top drawer. The sisters unlocked all the drawers and searched them thoroughly, careful not to disturb anything.

"Here are D'Quad's financial ledgers!" Desiree whispered.

The sisters looked through them, shivers of excitement ripping up their spines.

"Sure enough," Zoey whispered. "D'Quad's got one ledger with records of his acquisitions, and whom he purchased them from, for tax purposes."

"Yes," Desiree replied, "but this other one has total acquisitions, including ones that he, no doubt, does not want the law to find out about."

Zoey nodded. "I'll bet some of the names in the secret ledger are people who have 'disappeared.'"

"These ledgers could link D'Quad's gang to some of the murders that remain unsolved."

Zoey locked up the file cabinets and re-taped the key under the drawer. Confident they had left everything as it was when they entered, they returned to the powder room window and climbed outside. Zoey closed the window.

"We've got to get these to Eric!" Desiree whispered excitedly, as Zoey stuffed the ledgers into her saddle bags.

As they revved up their bikes, Desiree said bitterly, "We're coming for you, King Louis!"

"First, we've got a delivery to make," Zoey shouted over the roar of the engines. "Let's go."

Minutes later, an oversized envelope marked, 'C. Hines F.Y.I.,' plunged down the *Nitpicker* mail chute.

The next morning, a mail room clerk delivered the strange looking parcel to Chuck Hines' office. As he drank his first cup of coffee of the morning, Chuck opened the envelope and read through the ledgers. As the reality of what was contained in these pages sank in, Chuck reached for his phone and dialed frantically.

"Hello?"

"Eric, Chuck here. I have something that you need to see—Get over here right away!"

CHAPTER FIFTEEN

As soon as Eric walked into the *Nitpicker's* offices, he knew that something was up. Chuck's office door and blinds were usually open, but today they were closed. Eric tapped on the door and asked, "Hey Chuck, everything okay in there?"

"Yeah, come on in," he replied, as he stretched and leaned back in his chair.

"What's up?" Eric asked. "Problem with my photos?"

"No, it's this." Chuck picked up a package and dropped it on his desk with a thud. "It was on my desk this morning, dropped down the mail chute sometime after we closed last night."

"What is it?" Eric asked, as he walked over to take a look.

"It's two sets of accounting ledgers from D'Quad's Antique Jewelry Store. One seems to be for tax purposes, and the other for the real transactions—In other words, for his eyes only. It's pretty much common knowledge that the store is more like an underground pawn shop for fencing stolen jewelry than an antique jewelry store."

"I'm assuming that the police know what's going on there?"

"Oh yeah. D'Quad pays them off, and even helps them out —He lets them know when somebody fences goods from theft cases they care about. He also uses it to get his enemies arrested."

Eric shook his head in disgust. "D'Quad seems to have developed a network of crime and protection that is going to be hard to crack. Maybe these ledgers will give me a foot in the door."

"I'm glad to get them out of here. They're all yours," Chuck sighed.

"Any idea where they came from?" Eric asked.

Chuck shrugged. "I don't have a clue."

Eric lifted the package off of the desk. "Okay, I'll go over the ledgers with a fine-toothed comb. Do you have police reports I could take a look at? Maybe, I can match some of the crime reports, or their dates, with the real ledger entries."

"Sure, I'll be right back with them."

After Chuck returned with the reports, he put all of the materials into a bag.

"Thanks Chuck. I'll get out of here and get to work on this. Is there anything you want me to shoot today?"

"Well, there is one job that shouldn't take too much time. From noon until three, tomorrow, they are giving away food and other donated items at the Community Center. It's a big pre-Thanksgiving, annual event and always front page news. Zoey and Desiree are going to be there and will be writing the article."

"I'll get some good shots for you," Eric smiled.

"I know you will. Remind Zoey and Desiree that I need that article by seven—same with the photos."

"You got it, Chief." Eric tipped his hat and was out the door.

****

Bright and early the following morning, Zoey and Desiree arrived at the Community Center. Trucks were parked outside, and food and other donated items were being unloaded. Inside, a team of volunteers was arranging the food into boxes to be given away to the residents of the French Quarter who were in need. As always, Madame Ravonjay headed the project and was seated at a table near the door when they entered. Due to her long experience with the community food project, all questions came to her, and the project ran like clockwork.

"Here you are and right on time!" Madame Ravonjay opened her arms wide and hugged Zoey and Desiree.

"We have been so busy that we almost overslept," Desiree

said, "but there is no way we were going to let you down."

"I thought I was going to have to drag Desiree down here in her nightgown!" Zoey laughed.

"I think I might still have it on," Desiree said, as she peeked down her dress.

"Oh, I know," Ravonjay agreed. "I have been so busy too. Most importantly, I have had to make all of the arrangements for today. Of course, I have done it for so many years, I have a dedicated group of donors and volunteers to contact. But still, it takes a lot of time and planning. Along with that, I have had so many people coming to me, seeking protection after the rash of juju charms that have been left on doors all over town. I have hardly gotten any sleep for the last two weeks."

"Well, your gris-gris bag on our front step worked like magic for us."

"You make all of us feel safe when we are threatened and alone. Do you have any idea who is putting the charms on the doors?" Zoey asked.

"No, it is unusual. People usually come to me asking for charms regarding love, money or health. I'm sure whoever is leaving the charms on doors isn't someone who practices Voodoo. It is just a way to scare people, and it's working."

"Do you think it could be D'Quad's men?" Desiree asked.

Ravonjay shook her head. "No, he is a businessman with no interest in Voodoo. I have known him for many years, and he has always helped with this charity event and many others. I can't see him doing that."

Zoey nodded. "By the way, we need to get down to a little newspaper business, before we all get too busy. Do you mind if we ask you a few questions for our article?"

Ravonjay smiled. "Ask anything you want."

"Why don't you tell us some things about yourself that people in the community might not know," Desiree suggested.

"Many don't know that I was actually born here in 1863. So yes, now I am sixty-five years old. When I was a young woman, I traveled the world before setting up my own merchandising business. I loved that life but suffered a life-threatening accident in my twenties. I returned home to recuperate from my severe injuries. After I was fully recovered, I dedicated my life to helping others, using my psychic abilities and practicing my religion. This is my twentieth year of directing the community food alliance. So many kind and generous people have helped me over the years, it has been an honor to do this work. I sincerely hope that I can continue for many years to come."

Zoey tucked her pencil into her notebook. "What a beautiful statement— You certainly have made our job easy."

"I agree," Desiree nodded. "All we will need to include in our column is a description of today's event."

"Okay, then as director, I'm putting you to work! Since I'm no longer able to lift the heavy food boxes, I greet people as they enter and give them a gift bag for their children. They contain cracker jacks, animal crackers, an apple and a toy of their choice. This year their choices will be: small dolls, cars and trucks, or stuffed animals. I need for you two to start filling up the bags and organize the toy table. I thought it would be the perfect job for you two, because we can work together, and it will be so much fun!"

Just as Zoey and Desiree were beginning to set up the tables and bring the boxes of toys from the back, Victoria rushed through the front door and gave Ravonjay a big hug. "I can't stay too long but wanted to help."

"Oh, my dear child," Ravonjay said as she patted her on the cheek, "I know how hard you work every day and appreciate you thinking of me and coming to lend a hand."

"Yes, and as you can see," Zoey laughed, "Ravonjay has put us to work, and we can sure use your help."

With Ravonjay's direction and the three girls' energy, the tables were set up and organized long before the doors were to open. Just as they were finishing, they heard a familiar voice.

"Hello, Madame Ravonjay. I have heard so much about you. My name is Eric Strand, photographer for the *Nitpicker*. It is my pleasure to meet you."

Ravonjay extended her hand saying, "It is wonderful to meet you too. I have seen your fine work in the paper.

"Well, that's good news. I have had the pleasure of meeting your three helpers, and I can only hope that they have had good things to say about me," he said with a wink.

Desiree's eyes lit up, as she gave Eric an evil grin. "Oh yes, we have, but also remember that if you don't take pretty pictures of us, that could change."

"Well, let's get you three over here with Madame Ravonjay, and I'll do my best."

The girls circled around Ravonjay, and Eric looked through the viewfinder to focus the camera. As he did, he couldn't take his eyes off of Desiree. He waited for the sparkle to appear in her eyes, and when that beautiful smile appeared on her face, he clicked the shutter. "Oh no," he thought, "am I ever in trouble—I cannot let these feelings happen."

"Absolutely beautiful ladies! You can rest assured that this is a photograph you will love."

"I would like to ask you a favor," Madame Ravonjay said to Eric. "Would it be possible for me to buy a copy of the photograph from you?"

"Definitely not ... but it would be my pleasure to give you as many copies as you would like."

"Well, in that case, how about one for each of us?"

Eric nodded. "Of course, I'll make sure you all get a copy, and you can bet I'll be making one to keep for myself. I want to always remember this day. Ladies, I would love to stay, but now I need to get shots of the volunteers and then, of the people as they come in. I'll be around, so call me if you need help with anything. Desiree and Zoey, I'll see you at the office before seven today. If I'm in the darkroom, give me a knock on the door. I have a couple of things I wanted to ask you."

"You bet," Zoey nodded. "See you then."

Desiree, once again, flashed that beautiful smile. Eric felt his heart beat faster as he returned her smile.

****

Before it was time to unlock the doors for the event, Madame Ravonjay got up to walk the floor and check the status of the preparations. To her surprise, in the back prep room, the boxes had been filled and were being moved to the front.

"I have never seen such a wonderful and efficient group of volunteers," she announced to the group.

Maria, one of Ravonjay's friends, responded. "Well, there's a reason for that. Come on everybody, let's take that break we talked about."

At that, some of the volunteers unfurled a banner that they had hung from the ceiling. It read: "THANK YOU, MADAME RAVONJAY!"

A beautiful three-tiered, white cake, embellished with pink roses, was rolled out from the kitchen, as Maria took Madame Ravonjay by the hand and led her to the center of the room. Maria lifted an engraved brass and walnut plaque from the lower shelf of the cart and began to speak:

"We are your friends and neighbors. You have helped each of us in some way, by providing your candles, gris-gris bags, herbs and potions when we were troubled or scared by the violence in our community. You have provided food for us when we were hungry and needed to feed our families. You have never turned anyone away from your door when we needed your advice. You have always been our shelter from the storm. To thank you and commemorate this twentieth anniversary of your work as Director of The Community Food Alliance, we want to present you with this plaque that Henry made in his shop, and this cake that Ursula, Amy and I baked last night. We have high hopes that it is edible."

At that, everyone laughed and clapped. Madame Ravonjay wiped tears from her cheeks and spoke to her friends. "Thank you so much for this lovely banner, plaque and cake, which is too beautiful to eat. I love this community, and I can assure you that over the many years that I have lived here, you have done much more for me than I could ever repay. I am truly honored."

Eric shot a picture of the group, and then the volunteers crowded around Madame Ravonjay to congratulate her and give her their personal thanks. Tears continued to run down her cheeks as she thanked each one for this wonderful honor. After everyone enjoyed a piece of cake, which was highly praised as very edible, the remaining boxes were stacked on the tables. When she was certain that everything was prepared, Madame Ravonjay smiled at her volunteers, walked to the doors and unlocked them.

****

After their work was finished at the Community Center, Zoey and Desiree rushed to the *Nitpicker* to write their column. Hearing them arrive, Chuck called them into his office. "Hello ladies, how was your day?"

Desiree began to laugh "Oh, it was so much fun! Our job was to help give away gift bags and toys to the children, and it was absolute pandemonium."

"Yes," Zoey agreed. "We had everything perfectly organized, but as soon as the kids saw those toys, they were uncontrollable."

"So what did you do?"

"Oh, we just got right out there with them and helped them choose toys," Desiree said. "They were adorable and so happy. There is nothing more wonderful than hearing children laughing."

Eric had joined them in the office and said, "That's so true. Take a look at these photos that I took of the two of you out on the floor, playing with the kids. They are great."

Zoey and Desiree rushed over to see the pictures.

"Don't worry, I made a copy for you to keep, if you like them."

"Oh, you're a doll," Desiree said as she squeezed Eric's arm.

"Thank you so much!" Zoey added.

"You're welcome." Eric looked at Chuck. "Is it okay if we close the door for a couple of minutes, so I can ask you something?" Chuck nodded, and Eric closed the door. "It's really nothing mysterious," Eric began, "but have you ever been to D'Quad's Antique Jewelry Store?"

Zoey flinched slightly—A fact that Eric, as a trained agent, did not miss.

Desiree never lost eye contact with Eric or showed any reaction to his question. "Yes, we've been there," Desiree confirmed. "I think it was a week or so ago. Zoey found this beautiful silver hair clip with a filigree of flowers and leaves that she loved, and I was looking for a silver bangle bracelet. I found one with a great geometric design that I may go back to buy. You know, we always take some time to think about jewelry before we buy it ..."

"That is always a good idea," Eric smiled. "But I was wondering if D'Quad is there often. Who runs the store?"

During Desiree's long answer, Zoey had calmed her nerves and replied, "When we were shopping, there was no one in the store, except us and the gentleman who helped us. He was about fifty, with brown hair and wearing gold-rimmed glasses. He seemed very knowledgable about all of the jewelry. Why do you ask?"

Eric looked at Chuck, and Chuck began the story. "We don't know who, when or why, but during the night, someone dropped a package down our mail chute. When I opened it, I found two ledgers for D'Quad's Jewelry Store—One with the dates, amount paid and names of the people he bought from. The other was, let's say, adjusted for tax purposes. I called Eric, and he has taken a look at some specific dates—Tell them what you noticed Eric."

Eric began in a quiet voice. "Well, as you know, I came here to investigate the murder of two of our agents. They were my colleagues and also my friends, so this case means a lot to me. The first things I looked for in the 'real' ledger were the dates and entries made, just after their bodies were found. I found some items that were very suspicious." He lifted his sleeve to show them his Bulova wristwatch. "This isn't known publicly, but a lot of the agents are given these watches as gifts by their superiors. They come in different types of gold and with a selection of bands, but they are all the same model, and their serial numbers can be traced through the Agency. I noticed in the ledger, that two Bulova watches were entered during the week after the agents' murders, as well as a ruby ring with a gold setting. I remember that Agent Buck had a ruby ring—I'm thinking that I'm going to have to do a little shopping over the next few days. If my hunch is right, we're heading toward a messy war with D'Quad and his gang."

"Oh, boy," Desiree cried."Shopping! Can we come too?"

"No!"

CHAPTER SIXTEEN

At half past eight, a magnificent automobile slid into a parking spot in front of Victoria's Place.

"Wow! What a boat!" an attractive Flapper exclaimed.

Her date stared slack jawed and muttered, "That car does 100 miles an hour!"

The car was a dark maroon Duesenberg X, with whitewall tires and two silver rimmed spares mounted over the running boards. Its rumble seat was inlaid with sparkling chrome, as were its fenders, grill and bug-eyed headlights. It was the most expensive and coveted automobile in the world. As mesmerizing as it was, it paled in comparison to the notorious ladies getting out of the car. It was as if all those watching had fallen under a voodoo spell.

"Oh, my God," one lady groaned. "There's always trouble when they show up. They shouldn't have come here!"

"Well, I don't know about that," her delighted companion replied. "You've got to admit, these girls have got to be fearless to willingly walk into the lion's den!" She smiled and patted her friend on the back. "Don't you worry one little bit. They can handle D'Quad."

"Look at Zoey Daniels," another lady said. "Look at that beautiful long, blonde hair, her angel face and that gorgeous white overcoat—And she acts so smug about how she looks. I simply hate her—I do!"

Her husband nodded, but for a far different reason. "Yes, Zoey is truly a gorgeous sight to behold! And look at Desiree," he sighed. "That cute little face, that scandalously short dress … and those legs!"

His wife gave him a withering look.

Zoey and Desiree's fashionably late, grand entrance was working like a charm. It was deliberate. They wanted to be the center of attention. They were bound and determined to let everyone know that they were not afraid of D'Quad or his gang. D'Quad's brutal enforcers, Gizmo Vincente and Bilious Dubois, stood in front of the entrance.

"After what they did to us, I'd like to smash those angelic smiles off their back-stabbing faces," Bilious said.

"Sure," Gizmo replied. "We could do that. Or we could let them inside. That way, if they cause any trouble, we've got them trapped."

"Then we can we rough them up."

"We'll do a lot more than just rough them up."

As they approached the entrance, Desiree giggled and said, "I'm so scared, I think I'm going to pee myself!"

"Thank God!" Zoey laughed. "I thought I was the only one."

"I don't know how much longer I can keep up my brave face."

"I know exactly what you mean." Let's think of something funny."

"You mean like, tonight, we might die laughing?"

To their surprise, Gizmo opened the door and made a sweeping gesture to the two sisters. "Mademoiselle Zoey and Mademoiselle Desiree," he said. "Welcome to Victoria's."

"Thank you Mon-sewers," Desiree replied, as they stepped inside.

"I think we've just been insulted," Bilious said.

"Yes, we have," Gizmo replied with a nasty grin. "But I got a feeling that payback time ain't far away."

As Zoey and Desiree entered the speakeasy, patrons recognized them and exchanged worried looks. They whispered to each other, gesturing at the girls. The Daniels sisters ignored them and made their way to the bar.

"Hey!" Victoria cried. "I'm so glad to see you!"

"We're glad to see you too!" Zoey replied.

"Hey, ya know what? Eric got here about an hour ago."

"That's great!"

"He was acting a bit peculiar. He asked if he could use my phone, and of course, I said 'yes.' He came back from the office, grinning like the Cheshire Cat. He said, 'One down, one to go!'"

Zoey wrinkled her nose. "I wonder what he meant by that."

"Beats me. But I think he's over at the poker table. He said he has a date with lady luck."

"I hope so. He lost quite a bit of money the last time he was here."

" Where's D'Quad?" Desiree asked.

"Oh, Desiree," Victoria laughed. "Don't tell me you want to start trouble already. You've just gotten here!"

"Victoria's right," Zoey said with a mischievous smile. "Maybe we should have a drink first. Give D'Quad some time to spot us."

It was unlikely Louis D'Quad would spot them. He was occupied elsewhere.

"Eric! It's so good to see you back at the gambling tables," D'Quad exclaimed. "Maybe seven card stud is your game, and your luck will change tonight, eh?"

"Well," Eric replied with a glimmer in his eyes," I certainly hope so. And don't worry, I'm going to pay you back every penny I owe you."

"Don't you worry about the money, mon ami," D'Quad said with a crocodile smile. "There are many ways that you can pay me back. Now," he said as he patted Eric on the shoulder, " you need to concentrate on the game."

During the first hour, Eric made a sizable amount of money. D'Quad was joined by T.M.

"How's everything going?" T.M. asked.

"Everything is going as planned. The dealer let him win a few hands. Soon, he'll start losing. Then he'll get desperate and lose everything he's won and then some, hoping he can recover his dough. I've seen his kind of pigeon many times before."

"It's all in the cards, right?" T.M. sneered.

"Oh yeah. My dealer's special deck will ruin him."

"Wait a minute," Eric said to the croupier, as he stared intently at the back of one card. Then he examined all of the cards in his hand. "This is peculiar."

"What is?" the croupier asked.

Eric showed the card to the dealer. "Look here," Eric said. "In the upper left hand corner of each card, there are little markings that identify what card it is. Like this one. See the little 'A 'and the tiny black symbol next to it? That's an Ace of Spades." He showed the card to the other players. Then they examined their own cards and found the same kind of markings. All of the players rose in anger, threatening the dealer with bodily harm. D'Quad and T.M. rushed over to the table, but Eric had the situation under control.

"Gentlemen, gentlemen, please sit down," he said calmly. Eric looked over his shoulder, smiled at D'Quad and then back at the croupier. "I'm sure it was an honest mistake, right? Someone must have slipped you a marked deck."

The croupier looked at D'Quad with terrified eyes. D'Quad looked away. "Yes," the dealer finally said. "Yes! I never noticed they were not sealed. I apologize profusely."

"Well, Eric smiled, "you're in luck." He pulled out a deck of sealed cards from his jacket pocket and showed it to D'Quad. "Do you think it would be all right if the croupier used this deck?"

D'Quad was trapped. He knew the deck of cards was legitimate. There was no way out. "But of course," D'Quad replied with a sick smile.

Eric opened the pack and passed the deck around to the other players.

"These seem fine to me," one of the players said, and the others nodded.

"Well then, let's play some poker!"

Meanwhile, over at the bar, the Daniels sisters had become a vortex of attention. Their charm, bawdy wit and "It" girl outrageousness made friends out of strangers. They marveled at the sisters 'reckless bravery. They knew, all too well, that the Daniels sisters 'column had made them the mortal enemies of Louis D'Quad. The sisters seemed oblivious to the imminent danger.

"Let's get away from the bar," Zoey said. "Let's cut the rug and dance!"

The sisters rushed over to the crowded dance floor.

"Yay! The band's playing the Charleston!" they both screamed.

Zoey and Desiree's limbs came loose, as they danced themselves into a frenzy, shrieking with joy. The other dancers joined the sisters, laughing and screaming louder than the house band. People poured onto the dance floor, flapping their arms wildly.

At the poker table, Eric's deck was working magic. D'Quad and T.M. watched with rising concern.

"How is he doing this?" T.M. shouted over the dance floor's deafening pandemonium. "His chips are really stacking up."

"Relax," D'Quad replied, with an uncertain smile. "Eric's on quite a winning streak, but give him time. Sooner or later, he's going to get greedy and lose everything. Just you wait and see."

Digger joined his cohorts. "Hey Louis, guess who's here?"

"Who?"

"The Daniels sisters!"

"You don't say," D'Quad grinned. "Where are they?"

"When they first came in, they were at the bar. But I think I hear their big mouths singing over there on the dance floor."

"Well, whaddya know, my brazen little Daniels sisters. It's outrageous they would have the crust to come in here after they've insulted me and slandered my good name."

D'Quad handed Digger his drink and headed for the dance floor. He had not gone far, when a hush fell over the room. Victoria dropped a beer mug, and the echo of shattering glass cut through the silence. The dancers stopped dancing. The house band stopped playing. All eyes were on the two gentlemen who had entered the crowded club. Tension filled the air.

D'Quad wore an arrogant smile as he walked toward his unwelcome guests. "Kongo, Diego," he said as he shook their hands. "To what do we owe the pleasure of your company?"

Kongo smiled broadly. "Ah, amigo, Diego had an irresistible urge to dance."

D'Quad motioned to the band to start playing again and shouted, "Everything's all right folks! Let's have fun!"

"So," D'Quad continued, "you're here to dance, but I don't see no dance partners."

"Oh, I'm sure we will find some," Kongo replied. "We still have a few close friends here, if you know what I mean," he said with a deadly grin.

D'Quad stared back at him with menacing eyes.

"I believe you are right, Kongo!" Diego cried. "In fact, I see one lovely dancer now! Zoey, you sexy muchacha, I am coming, my love!"

Kongo followed Diego to the dance floor. He spotted Desiree and tapped her on the shoulder. "Desiree, my sweet, may I have this dance?"

"I would love to dance with you," Desiree said, with sparkling eyes and a shy smile. Kongo took her in his arms, and they whirled away.

"I think Desiree has a boyfriend," Digger said.

"So," D'Quad replied with rising fury. "This explains why the two little tramps are tearing me to pieces in the press and say nothing about the Street Sweepers. Desiree's making all lovey dovey with Kongo."

Diego Kaminga caught Zoey unawares. He came up from behind, put his hands around her waist and spun her around.

"Ah, my love," Diego whispered.

Zoey was too startled to resist Diego. He took her by the hands and pulled her toward him.

"It is time we dance, my one and only," he said with a debonaire grin.

"Diego," Zoey laughed, "you scared me to death."

"Ah," Diego replied," your brush with the eternal has fueled the flames of desire. Heaven has anointed our love with the sweet nectar of passion."

"You are a hopeless flirt, Diego! You've mistaken heaven and nectar for a pit of stinky horse manure. I doubt you're even aware of how much you lie!"

"Alas, I am aware, but that should demonstrate to you that I would tell any lie to prove my love for you."

Zoey rolled her eyes. "Just shut up and dance Diego!"

"My lips are sealed! And soon my lips will be sealed on your's … but for now, we dance the dance of passion! Maestro!" Diego yelled to the band. "Please play the tango!"

The Cathouse Caterwaulers' conductor smiled and raised his baton. Diego took Zoey's right hand and spun her around and into a dip, then placed his left arm around Zoey's back in a close embrace, their bodies touching. She pushed him back, and they began to step in unison.

"Why do you continue to resist me, my sweet lotus blossom," Diego asked, as he once again pulled her closer.

Zoey pushed him back again. "Because you're more like poison ivy, says your sweet lotus blossom."

"Ah, then what you are saying is that I infect your soul with love."

Zoey's performed her perfect footwork, creating a sensuous figure-eight pattern on the floor as she answered. "No, what I am saying is you infect my soul with an itchy rash!"

"But I did leave my mark on you."

"Yes! If you don't stop stepping in front of my leg, you are going to leave a bruise on both of my buttocks when I fall!"

"And what beautiful buttocks they are," he smiled, as he pulled her closer again. "Do you not smell the sweet scent of my lips of desire?"

Zoey turned her face away and performed a stunning set of footwork flourishes. "No, the sweet scent on your lips smells like Budweiser!"

Diego moved his face close to her again. "Kiss me, my Angel of Allure!"

Zoey lifted her knee and gave him a forceful blow to his leg. "If you try to kiss me, I'll bite your chin!"

"Ah," Diego cried with a delighted grin as her spun her around and into a dip, her head almost touching the floor, with her right leg suspended. "So you like it rough!"

"Yes! Let's get rough! You know the part when our tango ends, and I'm supposed to lift my leg and put my heel on your shoulder?"

"Yes, yes," Diego said, shivering with excitement.

" Instead, I think I might kick you in the head."

"We have enough people around here who want to do worse than kick me in the head," he laughed, as Zoey's shapely ankle made a sensuous landing on his shoulder.

The crowd clapped and cheered in appreciation of their amazing performance. The couple acknowledged their applause by joining hands with a curtsy and bow.

As soon as they found a place to sit down, Zoey said, "Diego, I'm worried about your safety—D'Quad's boys seem to be everywhere."

"Fear not, my fair damsel. Do you really think Kongo and I would walk in here without muscle?"

"What do you mean?" she asked uneasily.

"We've got good and loyal friends in here."

"I know. I've seen a few friendly faces, and that's what worries me. You don't seem to understand that D'Quad has you badly outnumbered."

Diego reached out, kissed Zoey's hand and said," You need a little entertainment, my Angel of Allure, to take your mind off of this imaginary danger. There is quite a commotion over there at the poker table. I think I see your friend, Eric."

A crowd had gathered around the poker table. Tension mingled with excitement. Two sweating players removed their jackets, loosened their ties and stared at their cards with desperate eyes. Eric sat behind a mountain of chips. Kongo and Desiree found two empty chairs behind the croupier. They had a clear view of Eric. They also saw D'Quad, T.M. and Digger standing behind him.

"I think that deck Eric brought along is also a marked deck," D'Quad growled. "Look at those chips. He's made back everything he owed me. He has to be cheating!"

"While you were away," Digger replied, "the dealer brought in another deck. All of the players checked it. It was legit. This guy just keeps on winning."

"Legitimate cards or not, he lost big before. At some point he's gonna push all his chips into the pot—One last desperate bet, and he'll lose everything."

"I'm going to help him along," T.M. replied, as he went over to the table. One player had cashed in his chips. T.M. filled his empty seat, right in front of Kongo and Desiree. "Deal me in," he said.

D'Quad watched as Eric lost a few pots in a row. T.M. had taken him for a lot of money. "T.M.'s about to wipe this guy out," D'Quad whispered to Digger.

T.M. stared across the table and smiled at Eric. With Eric's luck turning, T.M. was certain that last desperate bet D'Quad had talked about was about to go down.

Zoey and Diego had joined the mesmerized audience, sitting across from Kongo and Desiree.

"Ante up," the dealer said.

"Wait a minute," T.M. replied. "How about we change the bet limit?" He stared intently at Eric. "How about we say the sky's the limit?"

"I think I'll call it a night," one player said, as he took his chips and vacated his seat.

T.M. looked around at the remaining players. "Anyone else ain't got the stomach to mix it up with the big boy? Harry? Robert?" Then he stared at Eric. "How about you Mr. Strand?" he asked tauntingly.

"I'm comfortable right where I am," Eric replied.

The dealer dealt one card up and two cards down to each player.

Eric showed the Ten of Hearts, T.M—the King of Diamonds,

Harry—the Nine of Hearts and Robert—the Eight of Hearts.

T.M. looked at his hole cards and smiled. Eric was expressionless, studying the cards face up on the table. T.M. raised the bet. His fourth card was the Queen of Diamonds. Eric's was the Jack of Hearts. Harry drew the Nine of Spades, Robert—the Eight of Clubs. Each had a pair showing. Nevertheless, T.M. raised the bet again. He watched Eric intently. With every card dealt, T.M. looked for some facial expression, change in body language, anything that might indicate how Eric was feeling about his hole cards. But whether betting or calling, Eric was the picture of calm. The pot was becoming sizable. With each face-up card, it was becoming increasingly apparent that the payoff for this game was going to be huge. The play went on. The tension grew. Fifth card, sixth card; whenever he could, T.M. raised the bet. Eric studied the cards each player was showing. Finally, the last card, the seventh card, was dealt face down.

T.M. stared at his three hole cards and looked up at Eric with eyes of cold steel. "Well, Mr. Strand," T.M. sneered, "here's the bet." He pushed all of his chips into the center of the table. Immediately, Harry and Robert folded. It was down to Eric and T.M.

Desiree whispered to Kongo. "This is so tedious, it's like watching grass grow."

Kongo was amused. "Do you not enjoy this battle of wits, my dear one?"

"No. It's so hot in here, and I'm beginning to perspire. My makeup must be a mess." Desiree opened her purse and searched for her compact.

T.M.'s face up cards were the Queen of Diamonds, King of Diamonds, Jack of Diamonds and the Ten of Diamonds. Eric showed the Three of Spades, King of Hearts, the Jack of Hearts, and the Ten of Hearts.

"Here, we go," D'Quad said gleefully to Digger. "Here's comes Humpty Dumpty falling right down into my lap."

Desiree gazed into her mirror and powdered her nose.

"Well, Eric," T.M. laughed. "Let's see what the cards say—Let's see what the future holds for you."

Eric was expressionless. "I think all the answers about my future can be found right here in the present moment."

T.M. tested his resolve. "Take a good long look, Eric. You're looking at a potential Queen high straight flush. Who knows what cards are hidden from you? I saw the Nine of hearts and the Eight of Hearts on the table, when the other losers were playing. Odds are you don't have nothin' in the hole. All I need is either the Nine of Diamonds or the Ace. You need an Ace of Hearts and the Queen Of Hearts. Don't be a bigger fool than you are already, thinking you could mix it up with me."

Eric sighed. "Well then, I am resigned to my fate." He pushed all of his chips into the center of the table. "Let the better man win."

"Oh, I am the better man," T.M leered. "Read em and weep."

T.M.s 'hole cards were a a Deuce and Four of Spades and… the Nine of Diamonds! Those watching gasped. It was a Queen high straight flush. "Beat that, photo boy."

Eric stared at T.M. and did not look away. He seemed hesitant to turn over his cards. T.M. smiled at Eric's reluctance to show his hand, as a ploy to forestall his inevitable, humiliating defeat.

Eric turned over the Seven of Spades—and the Queen of Hearts—and the Ace of Hearts! The crowd went wild, screaming and clapping. It was an unbeatable royal straight flush.

T.M. jumped to his feet, pulled out his gun and pointed it at Eric. "You're a cheat, and you're gonna pay, pretty boy. Get up!" T.M. growled.

"I'm up," Desiree cried, as she grabbed T.M. by the collar. "And I think you feel the barrel of my gun in the back of your head."

"Oh, my God, oh my God, Diego," Zoey whispered. "She's gone insane. She'll never get away with this bluff. She's going to get herself killed."

"What do you mean, Zoey?"

"Diego … Desiree has a makeup compact that looks exactly like a derringer. That's what she's holding to the back of T.M.'s head!"

Diego chuckled and whispered, "Knowing Desiree, this should be interesting."

"You won't shoot me, Desiree," T.M. sneered. "Now put that gun down before you get hurt, little girl."

"This little girl is going to put a hole in your head, if you don't put your gun on the table."

T.M. reluctantly put down his weapon.

Desiree turned to Eric and said, "Get out of here now! Kongo —Diego—and your friends —get out of here too." Desiree turned to D'Quad and said," I'm doing you a favor, Louis. A lot of innocent people will get hurt if these boys stay, and you all start shooting at each other."

Kongo and Diego hesitated. "Move," Zoey growled, as she picked up T.M.'s gun. "All of you, get out. Now!"

Eric rose slowly and turned to D'Quad. "Thanks for the credit, Louis." Then he pointed to the pot. "It's all yours. We're square. In fact, there's a lot more there than what I owe you. Keep it," Eric said with a sly grin. "Think of it as a thank you for your hospitality."

The room had gone silent. The band watched. Eric, Diego, Kongo and his friends gave backward glances at the sisters as they left the club.

"T.M.," Desiree said loud enough for everyone to hear, "is coming with us. If any of you try to follow us, T.M. will be in a world of trouble. Otherwise, your boy will be returned safe and sound."

Kongo, Diego and a few friends were waiting outside when the sisters emerged with their prisoner. "We'll take it from here, Zoey," Kongo said. "Give me the gentleman's gun."

Zoey handed it over.

"Now, I want you and Desiree to leave right now."

"But ..."

"After what you did tonight, you are D'Quad's primary targets. Now go!"

Kongo and Diego insisted that Eric leave as well. "Please, my friend," Kongo said, "it would be better for all of us, if you get out of here too."

Eric nodded reluctantly, then turned and headed toward his car.

"He better leave," T.M. growled. "He's a cheat, and one day I'm going to make him pay." Then he turned to the Kamingas and said with disdain," And you boys are just two bit crooks!"

"Ah, mi amigo," Diego replied. "We are many things, but thieves we are not." Diego emptied T.M.'s pistol and handed it back to him. "Now, go back inside and take your mind off this unfortunate incident. Play a little poker," he smiled.

"This is far from over, Diego. We will meet again, and when we do, you will regret it," T.M. said. He turned and walked back to the club.

Once Zoey and Desiree were inside their car and had started up the engine, both girls shared a sigh of relief. They leaned back in their seats and stared up at the dark buildings that surrounded them. Their hearts were still racing.

"I can't believe you used your derringer compact to get us out of Victoria's alive!" Zoey patted her sister on the leg. "Good work," she said. "But what would you have done if T.M. found out that your gun was a compact?"

"I would have powder puffed him to death!" Desiree laughed as she gunned the engine, and they roared away into the night."

CHAPTER SEVENTEEN

Sunday dawned with a dismal downpour. Fog was like a leaden weight, dragging down the spirits of those who lived in the French Quarter. The residue of the showdown at Victoria's Place had spread like a plague. People were uneasy, walking to mass at St. Louis Cathedral. The joyous Voodoo rituals in Congo Square were replaced with ghosts, dodging the relentless raindrops. Shoppers crept from shop to shop, crouching, as if hiding from some invisible enemy. Restaurants were filled with nervous patrons. With so many witnesses to the chaos at Victoria's, everyone in the Quarter feared a war of attrition. Chief Editor Chuck Hines reread the Daniels sisters 'column for the *New Orleans Nitpicker*. Chuck shook his head and with an ironic smile, said to to no one in particular," This column is surely going to make the situation worse."

Gaudy Gowns And A Golden Gun
By Zoey and Desiree Daniels
New Orleans Nitpicker
Saturday night at Victoria's Place was a night of simple pleasures ... dancing, debauching, flirting, fighting, imbibing and making love to Lady Luck. Envy, anger, hatred, jealousy and inebriation shared a table. They gleefully poured gasoline on the human kindling around them. A gleaming automobile hypnotized the glitzy debutants in their overpriced gowns, gaudy jewelry and sledgehammer shoes. Pomposity made us wonder why these young ladies did not have each item's price tag pasted to their foreheads. A torrid tango

spared our eyes the horror of having to look at the nouveau riche for one more second. Flappers seemed to have lost their minds, as they danced the Charleston with flying feet and flapping arms. Seeming to have wingspans of giant birds, it was amazing that no one was flapped to death. And speaking of death ... The King with the toothpick and straw hat saw to that. His guest of honor was the 'Wayward Wanderer,' an associate and dear friend of the King. The Wayward Wanderer always goes about his business, doing King Louis's business, which is giving other people the business, which is what their businesses are all about, in the first place. Well, last night, 'business' was booming. Speaking of booming, a petite derringer in a pretty lady's hand, and a wandering gentleman with a tingling skull, gave birth to wisdom. You'd have to have a hole in your head, if you don't get going while the getting's good.

Ah, virtue, thy name is truth.

Zoey and Desiree Daniels

Zoey and Desiree were enjoying a somewhat quiet day at home. The only noise was Desiree, blowing out hit tunes on her kazoo. Zoey was oblivious to the melodic racket. She was immersed in a book about boomerangs. With the remnants of a pencil, Zoey plotted ellipses, calculated distances and aerodynamic forces. Then she studied the dimensions, weight and curvature of two boomerangs. "Toys from our youth," she finally said," still in perfect shape."

Desiree stopped playing and smiled at her sister. "Yes, they're about to come out of retirement!"

"So, what do you want to do today?"

"How about you come over here, and we practice our kazoos and tap dancing."

"Great idea! We never know when we'll need our toots and tappy toes!"

Desiree handed Zoey a kazoo.

"Suwannee River?"

"A ona, a twoa, a threea...."

Across town, Eric awoke with a blinding headache and mind

numbing hangover. A freezing cold shower and freshly brewed coffee helped him ease into the day. Somewhat revitalized, he checked his phone for bugs and found none. He picked up the telephone and called headquarters.

"Agent Jim Hope speaking."

"Hi Chief, how are you?"

"I'm still alive," he said wearily. "What's up?"

"Well, first of all, I bugged the phone at Victoria's Place. D'Quad uses that phone quite a lot."

"I'll set up a monitoring system right away."

"Second, I need some information. Do you have files on two guys named T.M. and Digger O'Doul?"

"Oh," Jim said with a frown, "both are well known around here. Miss Quarters," he called to his secretary. "Would you bring me the files on Tony Maroni and Francis O'Doul?"

After Miss Quarters returned with the files, Jim opened Digger's first. "'Digger' is a nickname. He has a reputation for making the bodies of D'Quad's enemies disappear. Some, have been found floating in the Mississippi, some in bayous, marshes and estuaries. We've found some in unmarked graves, thus his nickname, 'Digger' . T.M. is an nickname for Tony Moroni, an enforcer for the mob. However, T.M. does not refer to his given name. He's known as the 'traveling man, ' because he's a prime suspect in the murders of lawmen and business owners in New Orleans, Natchez and Vicksburg. The problem is we don't have enough evidence to link either to any crimes."

"Any priors?"

"Misdemeanors—assault, theft, that sort of thing." Jim frowned. "Why in God's name did you ask me about those two?"

Eric told Jim the story of last night's showdown at Victoria's Place.

"So," Jim said, letting out a hearty laugh, "now, you've made three deadly enemies: a mob boss, a hit man and a grave digger."

Eric smiled. "Lucky me."

"Tell me something. Did you use that counting card thing to beat T.M, and if so, how does that thing work again?"

"Seven card stud is a memory game. You've got to memorize all the face up cards of each player, their rank, and their suit. Depending on the value of the cards on the table and your own, in the hole, you can guess what cards the dealer has left. Then you estimate players' hole cards and bet accordingly. Add to that, which player is raising bets along the way and any tells. With this information, you can predict the hands of all the other players."

"So you will win all the time."

"People with photographic memories can. I don't have one, so unless I have focus, I'll lose."

"Seems you did pretty well last night."

"A little concentration, a little luck and Desiree Daniels with a derringer at the back of T.M.'s head."

Jim laughed and said, "That doesn't bode well for your reckless friend. You got anything else for me?"

"I've gotten ahold of D'Quad's ledgers from his jewelry store. There were two books for each year. There is quite a discrepancy between them. One is for tax purposes, the other contains all the actual purchases he made and from whom. That one might connect him to a few murders."

"That is fantastic news! How in the hell did you get ahold of those ledgers?"

"They were dropped into the overnight mail chute at *The Nitpicker*. No one has a clue who delivered them."

"That's bizarre, really bizarre. So, what's your next move?"

"I'm going shopping."

****

Before entering D'Quad's Antique Jewelry Store, Eric walked up and down the street, making sure he didn't see D'Quad's car parked anywhere nearby. Hoping he could go into the store when the clerk was busy, he waited at the corner until he saw that there were a number of shoppers going into the store. The bell on the door jingled as he entered. He was immediately impressed with the expensive furnishings and beautifully displayed cases of jewelry. He noticed that the busy clerk who looked up and nodded to him was the man that Zoey had described.

Eric first walked towards the back of the store—"Good," he thought. The office light was off. D'Quad was not there. He then walked from case to case, pausing before the ones with items he wanted to see more closely.

"Can I help you sir?" the clerk smiled, as he greeted Eric.

"Yes, I'm buying some gifts today, and I have a few items I would like to see."

"Of course, what would you like?"

"There are two in this case. First, the silver bangle bracelet with the geometric design … the third one from the left. And I'd also like to see the silver hair clip with the engraved flowers and leaves," Eric said, as he pointed through the glass.

"Very good choices, Sir," the clerk nodded as he placed them on a velvet cloth in front of Eric.

Eric lifted each piece, examining them closely. "Yes, I think I'll take them both. I'm sure my sisters will love them."

"Oh, certainly," the clerk agreed. "All of the young ladies love the silver accessories. They can't seem to have enough bracelets and clips for their hair. I have to admit, they look lovely on them."

"Indeed they do," Eric smiled.

"Is there anything else I can show you?"

"Yes, I need a watch, and I saw a few in the front case that I'd like to see."

The clerk motioned for Eric to follow him to the front case.

When Eric arrived, he pointed to a display of six watches. "I'd like to see those."

Eric lifted each watch and examined it closely. "I'll take this Bulova with the gold case and black band. It's for my father, and this is just like the one he broke about a month ago. I had given it to him for his birthday a few years back, and he loved that watch so much that he always took it off when he was working in his shop. Well, that worked out fine for him— until he dropped a hammer right on top of it and smashed it. You can't imagine how upset he was when he showed it to me—I can't wait to give him this new one."

"Those are fine watches. I wear one myself." The clerk raised his shirt cuff to display his watch. " Come over to the register, and I'll total this up for you. You may have noticed our sign in the window. Today, we are having a ten percent off sale."

"Fantastic, I appreciate your help."

After his purchases were completed, Eric left the store and immediately went to the *Nitpicker*. Chuck, as usual, was hard at work in his office.

"Are you busy?" Eric asked, as he tapped on the door.

"No, come on in." Chuck pushed his chair away from his desk, stretched and put his feet up. "Word on the street says you had one heck of a night at Victoria's."

Eric rubbed his face and nodded. "Well, the good news is I left enough money on the table to pay off my gambling debt and more. The bad news is that T.M. wasn't too fond of losing and seemed pretty determined to blow my head off."

Chuck rolled his eyes. "I heard about how that ended, but I have to hear it from you."

"Well, considering the situation I was in, what happened is unbelievable, even to me—Desiree saved me and ended the whole situation."

"I heard she pulled a gun on T.M. — I never imagined that she even owned a gun."

Eric smiled. "She didn't really pull a gun, or so I was told. She has a compact that is shaped like a derringer. That's what she pulled out of her purse and put to the back of T.M.'s head."

Chuck doubled over in laughter. "That girl is crazy! After all of that, she and Zoey turned in a column this morning, mocking D'Quad and his men."

"Matter of fact, that's the reason I'm here. I want you to call them to come in. I went shopping this morning and found those two watches and the ring I was looking for at the jewelry store. I bought one of the watches, but thought it might be suspicious if I bought all three items at once. I wanted to ask them to finish up my shopping for me."

"Son, you're really getting the evidence on D'Quad. He's so slick, no one else has ever been able to pin anything on him."

Eric was stoic in his response. "Well, I've still got a long way to go. I need a lot more evidence to prove that he was behind killing the two agents here and the others upriver. I want to shut down his whole smuggling operation and put him and his gang behind bars. It's going to take a lot of work and a lot of patience."

"You're a good agent, and I think you have the smarts to catch them," Chuck said. "Let me call the girls. I'm sure Zoey and Desiree will be delighted. There's nothing they like more than shopping."

****

Zoey and Desiree arrived at the office a short time later, dressed fashionably in their wool skirts, short jackets and cloche hats that accented the color of their outfits. They immediately hurried in to see Chuck.

"What's wrong?" Zoey asked. "Did you hate our column?"

"No, I did not, although I'm pretty sure that D'Quad is not going to like it at all. Zoey, how on earth did you let your sister pull a compact on T.M.?"

With that, all four of them started to laugh.

"So," Desiree said, as she walked up to Eric and poked him in the chest. "I risk my life to save you, and you ridicule me and my fake gun!"

Eric grabbed her finger and gently twisted her arm behind her back. "Oh, so you don't think I can handle a bully?"

Desiree quickly pivoted to the side and slammed her elbow into his stomach. "Well, I know that I can," she replied with a smirk. Eric let go of her arm and grabbed his stomach.

"Children," Chuck scolded, "a little self control please! I know you all had a tough night, and I'll tell you one thing for sure.

I couldn't be more proud of you and will definitely take you along the next time I have to go into the rough side of town. Sometimes I could use a little protection, fake gun or not."

"Don't worry Chuck, we got you … and Eric," Desiree laughed.

"Well in that case," Eric said, "I could use your help on a little shopping mission in the better part of town."

"Shopping," Zoey and Desiree exclaimed. "We're in!"

After Eric described the watch and ring, and their location in the jewelry cases, he gave the girls the money they would need. "I have to do a little work here, but when you're finished shopping, why don't you meet me at the diner across the street, and I'll buy you something to eat."

"It's a deal," Zoey and Desiree agreed. Excited to complete Eric's shopping and help with the case, they set out in high spirits.

The bell jingled as they entered the store, and the clerk smiled when he saw the pretty pair. "Hello ladies, welcome, back!" he said.

"Oh, thank you," Desiree replied.

"We saw your sale sign, and thought that we would love to find some gifts," Zoey added. "Do you mind if we look around for a few minutes?"

"Of course not! Call me if you find something you like."

Zoey and Desiree moved from case to case, asking for help to see different rings and watches before settling on the two they came to buy.

When the clerk led them to the cash register, Desiree improvised. "Oh, I think this watch is perfect for Uncle Laurel …

"… And Uncle Hardy only wears gold jewelry, so I'm sure he will just love the ring," Zoey added with a giggle.

Desiree pinched Zoey and stifled a laugh. "We do get a twenty percent discount, don't we?"

"Well," the clerk answered, "the discount is only ten percent … but for you two lovely ladies, I'll make it fifteen."

"Oh that is so nice of you!" Desiree batted her eyes and smoothed her hair. "We have a lot more shopping to do and will definitely come back to do it."

"Oh, I always look forward to seeing the Daniels sisters," the clerk said, as he put the purchases into attractive boxes. "I hope your Uncles Laurel and Hardy like the jewelry."

The girls bit their cheeks until they left the store, then burst into laughter. "Uncles Laurel and Hardy," Desiree hooted, "I could have keeled over when you said that."

"Well, you set me up with the Uncle Laurel stunt," Zoey laughed.

They continued to talk and laugh until they entered the diner where Eric waited, sipping a cup of coffee. He smiled and waved when he saw them arrive.

Desiree's eyes sparkled as she greeted him. "Hey, we got everything, and I even talked the clerk into a fifteen percent discount."

"Flirted her way into a fifteen percent discount." Zoey mocked her sister, batting her eyes and smoothing her hair.

"Oh, I'm aware of your sister's irresistible charms," Eric admitted. His cheeks reddened, when he saw the bright smile that lit up Desiree's face when she heard that. He quickly changed the subject by taking two small boxes out of his jacket pocket and handing one to Zoey and the other to Desiree. "A little thank you gift from me," he said.

The girls sat down and opened their gifts with delight.

"Oh Eric, my hair clip! You're such a doll," Zoey exclaimed, as she wrapped a coil of her golden hair around her finger and secured it with the clip. "How does it look?"

"Beautiful as always," Desiree grinned, "but how about this bracelet. It's the one I wanted so, so much. Thank you my dear and generous Eric!" Desiree slipped the bracelet on her wrist, and reached out and touched Eric's hand.

Again, Eric's cheeks reddened at her touch, and again, he quickly changed the subject. "Umm ... I'm ordering a burger. How does that sound?"

"We love burgers," Desiree said, "and we must have pecan pie for dessert!

Zoey nodded. "Got to keep our energy up. Shopping is hard work!"

CHAPTER EIGHTEEN

On the days leading up to Thanksgiving, the violence continued. There were hits, retaliations, random assaults, robberies and homicides. The people of the French Quarter hoped, at least on Thanksgiving Day, there would be a truce between the warring gangs. Eric was exhausted and far from any relatives or friends. The holidays made him feel lonely. Zoey and Desiree came to the rescue.

"We've been meaning to ask you: why don't you have Thanksgiving dinner with us?" Zoey asked.

"Yes, you must!" Desiree added.

"Thank you, ladies, but I believe that should be time alone, with your family."

"We have no family here, so you're not intruding. Every year we go down to the South City Mission and help Madame Ravonjay serve Thanksgiving Dinner to the many homeless and destitute people of the French Quarter. Over the years, we've come to know many of those people. They've become family to us. Won't you let us introduce you to our family?"

"Then you'll be family too!"

"Well then, when you put it like that," Eric said, "I would be honored to have Thanksgiving dinner with you."

"Wonderful! Dinner is at noon!" Desiree cried.

"When will you be getting there?"

"Six a.m.," Zoey replied. "We need time to get everything ready."

"I'd like to help out. I'll be there at six o'clock sharp."

"Great!"

"Why do we have to get there so early?" Desiree moaned.

Zoey sighed like a deflating tire. "As I have to remind you every year, princess, we've got to cook the dinner, before we can serve it."

"Well, with all that time, we'll be able to hunt down the turkeys, shoot the turkeys, clean the turkeys, stuff the turkeys, cook the turkeys and serve the turkeys ..."

"... and," Zoey groaned, "we'll have time for your yearly pout."

The following morning, when they arrived at the mission, Eric was already inside, carrying boxes of produce from the storage area and refrigerator to the kitchen. The volunteers were putting on their aprons and starting work on the dinner preparations. Madame Ravonjay had positioned herself at the sink, washing vegetables. She greeted Zoey and Desiree with a big smile.

"Good morning my dears! Can you believe it's already another Thanksgiving?"

"Oh, I know. I'm so happy to be helping you again this year," Desiree said, as she patted Ravonjay on the back.

"Happy Thanksgiving!" Zoey added. "What can we do to help?"

"Well, the turkeys need to go in the oven as soon as possible, so why don't you grab an apron and help with that. After we get everything started, we should have plenty of time to talk and catch up."

"Okay! Let's go," Desiree said, as she and Zoey headed for the prep area.

"Hey, Desiree and Zoey," Eric waved, "if you're on turkey duty, I could use some help bringing them out."

When Zoey and Desiree went into the refrigerated room, Eric closed the door behind them.

"Are you locking us in?" Desiree laughed.

"I hope not!" Eric tested the door, relieved that it would open from the inside. "Whew, it's okay. I just wanted to give you an update. I sent the jewelry by special courier to the Agency. The serial numbers on the watches check out, and Agent Buck's wife identified his ring."

"So, when are you going to make the arrests?" Zoey asked.

"Not yet. We want to solve the case the agents were working on. We need to find out how D'Quad's gang is smuggling in the alcohol and nail them. That's the only way we can end the violence in the Quarter."

Desiree said nothing. She was furious at Eric for insisting he had to wait before making any arrests.

"We're all in to help any way we can," Zoey replied, though she too was disappointed with Eric's insistence that they bide their time.

"I'll keep you up to date on the case, but I'm going to stand pat for now."

Eric opened the door and started handing the turkeys to the girls, who delivered them to the cooks. As the morning progressed, Eric and the girls kept moving food to the prep area. Exhausted and hot from the exercise, they finally decided to take a break on the back porch. Outside, they saw Madame Ravonjay walking towards a familiar black sedan, carrying a brightly colored red woven bag.

"That's Digger's car," Desiree whispered, as she pushed Eric and Zoey back and out of sight. They peeked around the wall and saw Madame Ravonjay hand the bag to Digger through his open car window. Then she gave him something else. It dangled from her fingertip. Digger took it, started his car and drove away. As Madame Ravonjay turned to walk back to the building, the three onlookers ducked back behind the wall, unseen.

"What was that?" an astonished Zoey asked. "It looked like a juju charm! Why would she give it to Digger?"

"I don't know," Eric said, "but don't say a word about this to anyone, or let it affect how you act with Ravonjay today. There's got to be some explanation, and maybe she will tell you about it. I'm sure it's something innocent ... but it's definitely strange."

"It may be strange, but there is no doubt in my mind that this is something innocent," Desiree replied. "We'd trust Ravonjay with our lives."

Zoey agreed, though she was baffled by the whole incident. Desiree was clearly upset. Eric could not help but notice. "Desiree, look at me. Everything is fine. Let's pull ourselves together and get inside to work. It's Thanksgiving, and we're going to have a great time."

Desiree squeezed Eric's hands and nodded. "Okay, I know you're right ... I'm fine. I think I'm just tired and need to eat. Let's get this dinner ready, I'm hungry."

Eric got up and headed inside. Zoey grabbed Desiree's arm and held her back.

"Don't you see what's happening?" she asked excitedly.

"What?"

"The way he took your hand to reassure you. Didn't you see the sparkle in his eyes? I often see him take a glancing look at you, then quickly look away."

Desiree blushed but said," You're out of your mind!"

"I've seen that same sparkle in your eyes whenever you're around him."

" Oh Zoey, I do like Eric ... but we're never going to be more than friends."

"I think you and Eric keep telling yourselves that, but the heart wants what it wants."

Desiree frowned. "My heart wants him to be a good friend and nothing else."

Zoey gave Desiree a knowing look. "We'll see."

Desiree laughed. "The only thing you're going to see today is me hauling turkeys, eating like a pig and flirting."

"Flirting?"

"Yes! I love flirting with Eric. I get him so flustered. It's so much fun."

"Fun?"

"Sure, you don't see him complaining do you?" Desiree asked, as she took Zoey by the hand. "Let's go inside and have some fun"

"Flirt," Zoey said and poked her sister.

"I suppose your flirting with Diego is different."

"No," Zoey laughed. "But he isn't here today!"

****

By noon, the tables were beautifully decorated with festive arrangements of carved, lighted pumpkins and colorful fall flowers. Just before the crowd entered, the turkeys, stuffing, cranberry sauce, gravy, rolls, desserts and side dishes were loaded onto the tables to be served family style. Eric moved from table to table taking photographs, as everyone found seats with their families and friends. When everyone was seated, Madame Ravonjay rose to greet the happy crowd.

"Welcome everyone and Happy Thanksgiving!" she said. The crowd clapped, and she continued. "We are so thrilled to have you all here today to celebrate and give thanks for this wonderful dinner. May it bring hope and optimism to our wonderful community."

"Amen," they all said in unison.

The food was passed around, and lively conversation and laughter filled the air. Zoey and Desiree introduced Eric to all of their friends at their table. Eric sat next to an elderly lady, who introduced herself as Marie, a longtime friend of Madame Ravonjay.

"I have known Ravonjay, since she first arrived here. It is an honor to know her," she said proudly. "She had a terrible accident, many years ago, and suffered some bad injuries. She came to the Quarter to recuperate. I helped her as best I could, til she was on her feet again."

"So, do you still help Madame Ravonjay?" Eric asked.

"Oh yes," she said. "I work for her now. I gather materials for her to use in her elixirs, potions, charms and gris-gris bags. Ravonjay is such a blessing. She helped me buy a house just down the street and pays me well for my work. With all of the gang violence and juju charms found on people's doors lately, we have surely been busy helping everyone—Makes me proud to be able to help make people safe."

"Well, you should be." Eric agreed. "I haven't been here long, but this seems like a community of fine people."

Overhearing their conversation, a lady sitting next to Marie joined in. "As soon as I got one of those juju charms on my door this week, I ran right to Madame Ravonjay. She gave me one of those gris-gris bags she makes to put on my doorstep, and this one to wear around my neck." She removed it and proudly handed it to Eric. He examined the bag and the uniquely woven red cord that was tied with a slip knot.

"I haven't had a bit of trouble or bad luck since. Madame Ravonjay always gives me a big discount. She calls it my 'friend's' discount," she said with a radiant smile.

"Well, this is quite attractive." Eric nodded. "I'm a photographer. Do you mind if I take a picture of it?"

"Of course not. I think it's very pretty."

Eric carefully laid the necklace on the tablecloth and took the photograph, then got up and gently slipped the necklace over her head and tightened the slip knot. "Let's get this back around your neck, so that you stay safe."

"Oh yes! I will wear it until all of this trouble in the streets passes," she said as she patted it.

"How about a picture of you and Marie?" Eric asked.

They moved their chairs close together, and their smiles showed their delight at having their photograph taken.

Eric returned to his chair, leaned back and studied Madame Ravonjay closely, as she talked to her many customers and "friends."

****

Hope springs eternal, even in the middle of a bloodbath. There were rumors Kongo Kaminga and Louis D'Quad had brokered a shaky truce for Thanksgiving Day. The French Quarter prayed the rumors were true. Their prayers were answered. The day passed without a whisper of violence anywhere. The residents were ecstatic and looked forward to a peaceful evening. The Daniels sisters did not.

"It's too quiet," Zoey said.

"I think all of this quiet is to lull all of us into a false sense of security."

Zoey nodded. "D'Quad's done this kind of thing before. With no one expecting anything, he has the element of surprise."

"Yep. And considering his lack of imagination, he'll do the same old thing. Hit some more business owners and shake them down."

"After your derringer bluff at Victoria's, the monthly rotation of D'Quad's hits have remained the same. The only difference is that random violence is more frequent. As for tonight, we have two possibilities ..."

"Dominique's Restaurant or Fishbowl Head's Nautical Shop," Desiree said.

"Yes," Zoey replied. "I think they'll hit Dominique's first. What do you think?"

"Well, I think it's cool that Fishbowl Head named himself that because he thought his big head looked like a goldfish bowl, and no hat could fit it. That's hilarious!"

"No, you dunderhead!" Zoey snapped. "I'm asking you which place do you think will be hit first. Stop kidding around!"

Desiree laughed and patted Zoey on the back. "Calm down! I think we should trust your instincts."

Zoey frowned. "Okay, it's Dominique's, and it's not going to be easy. There's a long, wide, roofless courtyard in front of Dominique's. If there are only two guys going in for the protection money, we can take them down anywhere we want. But if there's someone waiting in their getaway car, we have to get them in the courtyard and stop the car ..."

"... It's time to be gun-toting aborigines!"

The ride across town was eerie. With death stalking the night, the streets and sidewalks were empty. The Midnight Shadows, masked and dressed in black, melted into the darkness. Their ebony motorcycles left a split second of sonic sound behind. Speeding down the deserted streets, their rip roaring arrival quickly became a disappearing echo.

About a block away from Dominque's, the Midnight Shadows found a narrow alley and parked their bikes. Zoey pulled a lasso from her saddlebag and tossed it, hooking it around a crowned cornice on top of the building. They each grabbed their weapons, then shimmied up the rope to the roof. It was not long before two shadows looked down into Dominique's courtyard.

"I just hope I'm right about the hit being here and not at Fishbowl Head's shop."

"I'm sure you are," Desiree replied.

Zoey nodded uncertainly. "All we can do is wait."

An hour passed before Zoey said, "I think I was wrong. We might as well go."

Desiree shook her head. "No, not yet. There's a car coming down the street. It might be D'Quad's bag men."

Sure enough, the car came to a stop and parked. Two men stepped out.

"Oh, crap," Zoey said, "there's another guy in the getaway car."

" We'll just have to get the two in the courtyard first ..."

"... and hope we'll be in time to get the car."

They could hear shouts coming from Dominique's. A man came crashing through the plate glass window. Two other men rushed outside after him.

"That will teach you to make us wait for the protection money," one bag man said.

"Hey," his companion laughed, "he'll get a real kick out of this," then stomped the groaning man on the ground.

"One ..." Zoey whispered slowly, " Two ... Three!"

"What's that whirring sound?" Both men asked. They had no time to think about it.

Two loud cracks sounded like hatchets splitting coconuts. Both of D'Quad's goons sank to the concrete.

The startled patrons congregated at the window. Seeing the men out cold and motionless, they stepped outside. Dominique's sons, Juan and Alexandro, first helped their father to his feet, then examined D'Quad's men. One had a deep cut across his forehead. The other had a lacerated ear and bloody scalp. The brothers reached into the goons' jackets and retrieved the protection money. Then they tied them up. Suddenly, they were startled by a hail of gunfire coming from the roof. A car screeched down the street.

Juan and Alexandro rushed to the black barred gate.

"He's riding on rims!" Juan cried. "Someone blew out his back tires!"

Both brothers looked up to the roof, where the gunfire had come from. There was no sign of anyone.

As they walked back to the onlookers, Juan spotted two strange objects in the shadows. He stooped to pick them up and started to laugh. "You've got to see this," he said.

"Are you kidding me?" Alexandro cried. "Boomerangs? Somebody whacked these guys with boomerangs?"

"It had to be the Street Sweepers."

"With boomerangs?"

Juan and Alexandro stared at each other in disbelief and broadening smiles. "The Midnight Shadows!"

At that very moment, both sisters made their way back down the rope and into the alleyway.

"It's too bad that we lost our boomerangs," Desiree said sadly. "Mother gave them to us."

Zoey patted her sister on the back. "Well, in Mother's honor, we'll order new ones."

"Where? I don't think they sell boomerangs in the Sears' Catalog!"

CHAPTER NINETEEN

The next morning, Eric paced the floor of his attic room. He always did his best thinking when he was moving, and he had a lot of loose ends that needed to be tied together. First, was the information he had about D'Quad and his gang: He knew their money came from his gambling operations and the high interest he charged on the gambling debts. Next, there was the protection money that he demanded from the local businesses. Eric knew D'Quad's jewelry store records indicated that he paid little for the jewelry he sold, since most of it was stolen, and he sold it for a big profit. The one area that he knew less about was his shipping and import business. "Obviously, a front for his illegal alcohol operation," Eric muttered, "but how do I get the proof I need?"

The other thing that was really bugging Eric was those darned juju charms. He walked over to the loose panel of insulation where he had hidden the photos and charms he had removed from the bombed buildings. He inspected the two identical charms he had collected. They were woven stars attached to a red cord tied in a slip knot. He closely inspected the cords and slip knots. "Just like the one on the necklace," he said to no one. Eric frowned and scratched his head. "The only difference is the ornamentation." After returning the charms and photos to their hiding place, he grabbed his camera bag, put on his jacket, headed downstairs and out the front door.

****

Zoey and Desiree were also up early, still stoked with energy after their successful midnight run. They sat in their living room, watching the sun rise on a brilliant, clear morning.

"I'm sick of waiting," Desiree exclaimed. "Eric has said that he won't make any arrests, until he finds the source of D'Quad's alcohol smuggling. We found the jewelry store ledgers, so there must be other ledgers in his import-export business office."

"Yes, an office that is surely watched at night by his men. We were lucky at the jewelry store. Finding those records in a locked drawer was easy. I'm sure getting our hands on the Import-Export ledgers won't be."

"I know, and I share your concerns. I just don't know another way to get the records that Eric needs."

"Okay," Zoey nodded. "Let's write the column for the *Nitpicker* on yesterday's Community Thanksgiving Dinner, and the one Chuck suggested on holiday shopping trends. After we turn them in, we'll take a casual walk along Canal Street and check out D'Quad's office. By late afternoon, they returned home, confident they knew every detail about the Canal Street area. But they had missed one crucial detail.

****

Over the past few weeks, Eric's attention had been drawn to D'Quad's sixty-foot yacht. *The Eclipse* was a massive, nautical masterpiece. The main deck was resplendent with elaborate crystal chandeliers, a fully stocked wraparound bar, a starlit dance floor, and tables for gambling, drinking, eating and carousing. The second deck was filled with luxurious state rooms. On top was the wheelhouse. At night, The *Eclipse* displayed a carnival of lights that rimmed the ship and portholes. A glowing crown topped the wheelhouse. The hold was enormous.

Aside from D'Quad's occasional afternoon jaunts to Chalmette, *The Eclipse* took overnight cruises. Eric knew D'Quad used the ship for his import-export business. But he suspected that it was also used for his illegal imports of alcohol. That spawned a lot of questions: If D'Quad was smuggling contraband, where did he unload it? How was he getting it into town? Where was he storing it? Eric had noted *The Eclipse* followed a fairly regular schedule. Those overnight jaunts left at sunset and returned at sunrise.

"If my calculations are correct," he thought, *The Eclipse* should be docked this morning. Eric parked his car and walked over to his usual observation point. "There she is," he said to himself. He took a few photos, recorded the time and date in his notebook, then headed to the *Nitpicker* office to turn in his photographs of the Thanksgiving Dinner. When he arrived, he found Chuck in his office talking to one of his reporters. Eric dropped his photos into the inbox.

"Just the man I was getting ready to call," Chuck said. "Ed here just told me that he talked to Fishbowl Head this morning, because his nautical shop was hit last night. Ed is writing the article, but I could use some photographs of the damage."

"Good timing," Eric smiled. "I have my camera with me, so I'll go right over."

"Thanks Eric. It seems like every year, as soon as the holiday season begins, everything gets crazy around here. I appreciate your help."

Eric took a walk across town, and when he approached the door of the nautical shop, the first thing he noticed was a juju charm hanging from the door frame. He took out his camera and took a photo, noting that it was exactly the same as the two he had at home. Eric peered through the window and saw the floor was strewn with glass and debris. The store had been trashed. Behind a wooden counter, he saw the back of a bald, perfectly round head. "Mr. Fishbowl Head, I presume," he thought, stifling a laugh. "All he needs is a couple of tattooed goldfish on that noggin, and he'd be a walking advertisement for his shop."

Eric tapped on the door frame and said, "Hello, I'm Eric Strand, photographer for the *Nitpicker*. Ed interviewed you earlier, and they sent me to take some photos of your shop for his article. Do you mind if I come in?"

"I reckon you can come on in, but I didn't tell that boy nothin' except I didn't know why my store was torn up, or who did it. 'Course I do, but I'm sure not havin' it in the paper. Heck, everybody knows who done this. Come on in but be careful. There's glass everywhere."

Eric removed the charm, carefully stepped inside and asked, "Did you know this juju charm was on your door?"

"No, it wasn't there when I came in this mornin', but I'm not a bit surprised. I thought I saw Digger O'Doul walking down the street carrying that violin case, a little while ago. He's the one always hangin' those things on the doors. It's funny, they trash my store because I won't pay D'Quad for protection. Then put one of those charms on my door, thinkin' I'll run to Ravonjay to buy one of her bags for protection. What a scam!"

"Do you mind if I keep it?" Eric asked.

"Heck no, I don't want the danged thing!"

Eric tucked the charm in his pocket and asked, "So you know Digger, D'Quad and Ravonjay?"

"Sure do! I've lived here all my life, and I know most everybody."

"Well, now you know me," Eric said. "I've just moved here recently and started working for the paper. It's a pleasure to meet you, but wish it was under better circumstances."

"Nice to meet you, Eric. You can call me Fishbowl." He took off his heavy gloves and shook Eric's hand.

"Do you mind if I go ahead and take some shots of this mess? Then I'll help you clean up, if you have another pair of those gloves for me to use."

"Sure, shoot away. Just make sure I'm not in any of them. Don't need my big head in any picture in the paper," Fishbowl laughed.

Eric took his photographs and said to Fishbowl, "I'll make copies of all of these for you—Might help when you file for insurance."

"Thank you, that's mighty kind. I done had the agent come by this mornin'. I surely hope they'll pay for some of this."

Eric put on the work gloves and started picking up glass and items that weren't destroyed. "Hey, why don't you bring over that big trash can. I'll pick things up, and you can put the good stuff back on the shelves and racks."

Fishbowl smiled and shook his head. "Eric, you're one fine man. I had people comin' by all mornin', peeking in the window, but you're the only one that's offered me some help. I appreciate it."

"I'm happy to help," Eric smiled, "and maybe you can help me. You've lived here all your life, and I've just arrived. I'd like to hear some of your stories."

"Oh yeah, I know most of what goes on here in the Quarter and out on the water. Since I got old, I only sleep a few hours a night, so I walk around a lot. Sometimes, I even go out in one of my boats and do some fishin'. There's a lot that happens after dark in the Quarter."

"Yesterday, Desiree and Zoey Daniels invited me to the Community Thanksgiving Dinner …" Eric began.

"… Desiree and Zoey! I love those gals. They come in and buy all sorts of stuff from me. Such pretty girls and sweet as can be. They say they want to give a nautical design to one of their rooms. I also see them zoomin' around at night."

"They do have a fast car," Eric agreed.

Fishbowl nodded. "Yeah, they're some classy women."

"I met Madame Ravonjay and Marie at the dinner. So, do you know them?"

"Yep, I've known them most a my life. Marie's a good woman. But she's too trustin'. She does everything the Madame tells her to do, thinkin 'Ravonjay is some kinda bonafide, blessed, God fearin', Voodoo queen." Fishbowl scratched his head and said sarcastically, "I grew up with Voodoo. My grandpappy knew Marie LaVeau, the Queen of all Voodoo Queens! Marie LaVeau helped people, cured people, no charge. She would give you the shirt off her back … give you her last biscuit. Ravonjay does everything for money. I've known people here who practice the real Voodoo religion, but she ain't one of them."

"What about D'Quad?" Eric asked. "Do you know him?"

"Yeah, I know more about him than I want to know," Fishbowl laughed. "He wants all of us to pay him for protection, and as you can see by this mess, I won't do it. He runs that big yacht up and down the river, carryin' that hooch he picks up offshore. When I was out on the river one night, I seen that ship put in at a hidden dock south of Chalmette to unload. A bunch of men come out and carried them barrels and crates down a dock and to a warehouse there. The Sheriff in St. Bernard turns a blind eye, as long as they pay him off. One night I was out there on the river and seen it when they almost got caught. There were two men with guns who tried to arrest them, but D'Quad and his boys shot them and dragged them off. Guess they was the ones they found in the swamp a few days later."

"Did you tell the police?" Eric asked.

"No, there's only two of the cops that I know can be trusted, Baker and McGhee. Far as I know, the rest get paid off by D'Quad. I didn't want no part of that mess."

"What about Kongo and Diego Kaminga? What about the Street Sweepers?"

Fishbowl smiled slyly and winked. "Oh, I do a little importing for them, now and then, if you know what I mean.... Anyway, they're good people; always have been. They bring in a little of the imported stuff, but mostly buy from the local bootleggers. They protect people in the neighborhoods and never ask for nothin' in return."

The floor was cleared, and Eric moved the trash can out of the way. "Do you have a broom?"

Fishbowl smiled, "Sure do. You know, you do good work. If you're lookin' for some extra money, I could sure use some good help like you."

Eric laughed. "Well I don't need a job, but I could sure use a new friend."

"Well, buddy. You've got one. You come on by anytime, and

I'll buy you a drink and tell some more tales."

Eric nodded, as he finished sweeping and took off his gloves. "I sure will. Are you certain that you're going to be safe after this? Do you think you should talk to one of those officers you say you can trust?"

"No, the police came this morning, and I filed a report. One of them was Baker, so I know he and McGhee will keep an eye on the place without me askin'. I'm pretty sure D'Quad will leave me alone for a while—He's mostly just using me as a warning to other shop owners who don't want to pay him off." Fishbowl shrugged. "Everybody just kind of knows how things work down here without sayin 'much."

"It's an interesting place all right," Eric agreed. He put out his hand, and Fishbowl gave it a firm shake.

"Thank you, Eric."

"You bet, buddy." Eric picked up his camera bag and headed out the door. "Hey, how about the door?"

"I've already got somebody comin' in about an hour."

Eric shook his head as he walked down the street, wondering if he had hit the jackpot or just spent a couple of hours listening to the ramblings of a crazy old man.

****

Across town, Louis D'Quad's palatial mansion shimmered under the silver-dewed Magnolia trees. An eight foot stone fence surrounded the property. A black-barred, wrought iron gate stood like a sentinel. The house had a massive stone fireplace and grand Hollywood staircase. Mrs. D'Quad had decorated the home with oversized plush furniture and expensive antiques. Original paintings adorned the walls. The dining table could have fit King Arthur and all of the Knights of the Round Table. King Louis the 19th was meeting with his enforcers, in his elaborately decorated study.

D'Quad stared at his henchmen with angry eyes. "So, tell me, how's it going with our enemies?"

"Well, our boys destroyed Fishbowl's Nautical Shop. Windows shot out of Kongo's cousin's home. Two of the Street Sweepers were ..."

"Enough!" D'Quad screamed. "Stop right there! Our boys have accomplished nothing! Let's start with Dominique's. If not for my call to our corrupt police chief this morning, our two bagmen would be rotting in jail. The cops got them on attempted robbery, extortion and assault with a deadly weapon —All in front of a gaggle of witnesses, more than willing to talk. We didn't get our protection money from Dominique's—And don't brag about what your guys did at Fishbowl's. He wasn't even home! They got no money from him, either."

"In all fairness to our boys who were arrested, they were ambushed from the top of a building," Digger said.

"... and," T.M. added, "their getaway car's tires were shot out from behind."

"Whoever did this to our boys was also guilty of assault with deadly weapons ... plural," Digger added.

"What weapons were they carrying, pray tell?" D'Quad asked, still fuming.

"Well," Digger said tentatively, "they shot out the tires of the getaway car, and ... well, you're not going to believe this— They took down our men in the courtyard with ... boomerangs."

"Boomerangs!" D'Quad raged. "You mean they cracked my boys' skulls open with boomerangs? What am I missing? Has Kongo lost his mind? Boomerangs? What have Kongo and his boys turned into, lunatics from the land down under?"

"No," T.M. replied. "The witnesses say it was the Midnight Shadows."

D'Quad slammed his fist into his desk. "I'm getting sick of this! I hear more and more about those crazy vigilantes, and yet, no one is positive they've really seen them."

"Assuming it was the Midnight Shadows," T.M. said, "they also have to be in cahoots with Kongo and the Street Sweepers. The Midnight Shadows have only been going after us, not them."

"So," D'Quad said, "Kongo has some allies. That's a first."

"No, it isn't." Digger replied. "All along, the Daniels sisters have attacked us in the press but never said anything about the Street Sweepers. On top of that, the Daniels sisters are all lovey dovey with the Kaminga brothers. Look how Zoey and Desiree risked their lives to make sure the Kamingas and their friends escaped from Victoria's."

"The battle lines are drawn. Let the war begin!" D'Quad cried.

T.M. pulled a knife out of his jacket and ran his finger down the cold steel blade. "I smell blood on the wind."

CHAPTER TWENTY

All along the avenues, Christmas lights blinked like winking eyes, eliciting a sense of joy. Menorahs glistened. Red-berried, green holly hung over door jambs. The giant Christmas tree in Jackson Square was a tower of light, reaching up into the heavens. Storefronts were resplendent in silver tinsel and gold ornaments. In store windows, little mechanical elves clutched brightly colored Christmas presents. A giant statue of Santa Claus stood on the levy, waving to ships as they passed. The Midnight Shadows roared by, oblivious to the joy that surrounded them. Within a few blocks of D'Quad's Import and Export Office, the sisters coasted to a stop and parked their bikes behind a newsstand. Zoey took binoculars out of her small backpack and focused them down the street.

"It's just as I thought," Zoey said. "There are two security guards patrolling in front of D'Quad's."

"Any snipers?"

Zoey's binoculars swept the rooftops. "None that I can see."

Desiree searched her sister's face. "What do you think? The rooftop?"

Zoey looked around and spotted a retractable ladder hanging from a second story balcony. "Come on and give me a boost."

Zoey reached up and grabbed the bottom rung. She slowly lowered it to Desiree. Once they were both on the balcony, Desiree pulled up the ladder. Both looked around for a way to get up to the roof.

Desiree pointed. "That's a pretty hefty trellis. Let's go."

Zoey hoisted herself onto the railing, stepped out onto the ivy-covered trellis and climbed up to the roof. Desiree followed.

"So far, so good."

Two shadows crouched low, as they tiptoed from rooftop to rooftop, closer and closer to D'Quad's. Halfway there, they ran into a dead end.

"I never noticed there was an alleyway here," Desiree whispered nervously. "We're going to have to go down to the street."

Zoey estimated the distance between the two rooftops. "I'd say it's about nine … ten feet across. With a running start, we can jump over."

"We're going to have to make one heck of a running start. I don't think I can make it."

"Sure you can." Zoey said.

"I hate heights!"

"So do I. But what other choice do we have? They'll kill us if they see us coming down the side of the building. Besides," Zoey giggled, "you're always complaining about our unfashionable outfits. Once we get those ledgers and put an end to D'Quad's gang, we don't have to be the Midnight Shadows anymore."

"That would be great," Desiree sighed. "This mask has ruined my makeup, this crawling around has ruined my nails, and it's not doing wonders for my fabulous knees!"

Zoey just rolled her eyes and said, "Listen closely, Miss Sexy Knees. First, we've got to make as little noise as possible. Second, once we stand up, we've got to run and jump as fast as we can, or we may be spotted."

Zoey stood up and backed away from the ledge.

"I can't watch," Desiree groaned as she closed her eyes tightly. She listened to Zoey's footsteps, and then there were none.

Desiree slowly opened her eyes and looked. Zoey was kneeling on the opposite side of the alley, motioning for her to come.

Desiree crouched low as she stood up, made a running start and jumped. But when she landed, she lost her balance. She was about to go over the edge, but Zoey grabbed her and pulled her back, both crashing to the roof.

"Hey!" one of D'Quad's men shouted. "There's somebody over there … in the alley!"

The Midnight Shadows could hear the two men running toward them.

"I wanted to wait until we were on D'Quad's roof, so we could get a clear shot at those two. But now we've got no choice," Zoey whispered as she drew her weapon.

"It's so dark down there, we're going to be firing blindly."

"I don't think we will. What would you do if you were looking for someone in a dark alley?"

"Ah, a flashlight," Desiree said as she drew her weapon.

"Wait for it, let them get within range."

D'Quad's security guards entered the alleyway. One switched on a flashlight, searching the garbage strewn passage. Scanning each wall with the light, they came closer and closer. When they were just about underneath them, one laughed and said, "Come out, come out, wherever you are."

"It's gonna be worse for you, if we have to find you."

"Open fire," Zoey whispered.

"Oh!" One guard cried out, rubbing his neck and cursing. "I've been stung by a bee!"

"No!" his companion moaned. "It's not a bee.… It's some kind of dart. And I feel so … so … woozy."

Both men started to stagger out towards the street, weaving like they were drunk. They belly bumped each other, fell backward, lost their balance and crumbled to the ground.

Zoey and Desiree put their dart guns back into their backpacks. Zoey smiled. "Those darts are coated with Indian Pukufa. That stuff should keep them out for a while."

The sisters continued tiptoeing across the rooftops, inching closer and closer to D'Quad's. Once there, they crawled to the edge of the roof and looked down. The coast was clear. The sisters lowered themselves to the second story balcony, stepped over the wrought iron rail and dropped to the ground.

Zoey gave a nervous look around, as did Desiree. The street was deserted. Then headlights pierced the darkness. A car was rolling slowly toward them. There was nowhere to hide. They pulled back against a building and hugged the shadows. Cigarette smoke billowed out of the car's open window. Yells and curses punctuated an angry argument. As they passed by, the couple did not notice the sweating vigilantes, fly-papered to the wall. Once at D'Quad's, Desiree stood watch in front of the building. Zoey examined the periphery of the front door and windows. "I can't be sure, but I don't see anything that would indicate an alarm."

"That sounds kind of iffy."

"D'Quad's stupid, sloppy, overconfident and predictable." Zoey picked the lock, and within seconds, they were inside.

There were floor to ceiling curtains over the front windows. It was pitch dark. Desiree turned on a flashlight and searched the room. Behind a long counter, they spotted D'Quad's desk. Oddly, the file drawers were unlocked. Other than office supplies and a bottle of Scotch, there were no ledgers in any of them. Desiree tapped her sister on the shoulder and pointed. "I know where the ledgers are." There, against the back wall, was a Brinks safe.

"Now what? We don't know the combination!"

Desiree giggled and said, "Well, I never thought I'd be asking you this, but did you bring the dynamite?"

"Yes," Zoey laughed, "and my new lighter too! But I don't think it will come to that." Zoey searched the bottom of the desk. She found a sliver of paper taped underneath. Desiree shined her flashlight on it.

"Yes!" Zoey whispered. "This has to be the combination to the safe."

Zoey knelt down. Slowly, she turned the tumbler: seven-clockwise, nine-counterclockwise, three-clockwise. The safe did not open. After a few tries, she looked up hopelessly and asked, "Got any ideas … other than blowing the door off?"

Desiree examined the slip of paper again. "Look, Zoey," she smiled. "This number is smudged. It looks like a three, but it's really an eight."

Zoey entered the combination, and she heard the lock click open. "We're in!"

"Yes," Desiree said nervously. "Now, let's just get the ledgers and get the heck out of here!"

Zoey pulled open the door. The instant she did, an ear-shredding alarm tore through the stillness of the room. Both sisters screamed, as they lunged into the safe. They looked like two hounds digging out a box turtle. In a fitful frenzy, they flung stacks of cash, gold bars, rolls of silver dollars and files over their shoulders. The debris was scattered all over the floor. The alarm blared on.

"Oh, come on, come on, come on," Desiree groaned. She was on the verge of panic. "Where are those damn ledgers? We've got to find them and quick."

Zoey reached far back into the safe. "The ledgers!" she said with a sigh of relief. "Put these in your backpack, and let's make a run for it."

As they stepped outside, they could hear the distant sound of police sirens.

"Oh, no! We're going to be caught!" Desiree screamed.

"Well, we're going to be, if we don't get out of here. Stop screaming and start running!"

The sisters sprinted up the street. In their wake, they heard a car screeching to a halt. They looked back and heard men shouting.

"What happened here?" Gizmo cried. "Bilious! Someone's broken into the office!"

"And look over there, Gizmo. Our security guys are out cold!"

"What the heck?" Gizmo shouted. "Hey Bilious! There are two guys running up the street. They must have been the ones who broke into the office, and they're getting away!"

"Get in the car!" Bilious cried.

Zoey and Desiree reached the newsstand. They revved up their motorcycles and waited, hoping they had not been spotted. Gizmo and Bilious sped by. The sisters eased out from behind the newsstand and headed in the opposite direction. "We're going right back toward D'Quad's!" Desiree yelled, above their roaring engines. "That alarm is still blaring, and the cops are surely on the way!"

"What choice do we have?" Zoey shouted. "Bilious and Gizmo are sure to double back."

Desiree looked over her shoulder. Sure enough, in the distance, Bilious and Gizmo were turning around. The buildings on both sides of the street seemed to be closing in. The lights of the car behind them were getting brighter. Out in front of them, police car sirens were getting louder and closer.

Both sisters looked at each other. "We've only got one chance of getting out of this," Desiree cried.

"Lead the way! I'll be right behind you."

The police cars came screaming toward the intersection right in front of them. Bilious and Gizmo were closing in. Bullets sprayed the pavement around them, pinging off their bikes like stones on a gravel road.

"Let's go!" Desiree screamed.

Zoey and Desiree made a hard right. The alleyway was too narrow for cars to get through but perfect for their motorcycles. Their bikes bounced over the curb and streaked into the alleyway, flying over garbage and debris and heading toward the open end of the alley. When they emerged, they opened up their throttles. Their bikes leapt forward, streaking through the glittering city.

The sisters took a round about route to get to the *Nitpicker* to avoid any chance of capture. Once there, Desiree leapt off her motorcycle, shoved the ledgers into a large envelope marked, C. Hines. F.Y.I. and dropped it down the mail chute. She ran back to her bike and remounted.

"Hey," Zoey shouted. "I'm so glad you remembered that alleyway had a rear exit!"

"I didn't! But it sure was exciting!" Desiree laughed as she hit the gas and sped off.

****

Around one a.m., the telephone rang at Louis D'Quad's home. "This better be important, Bilious," he growled. "You woke up Mrs. D'Quad!"

"It is real important," Bilious replied. "Someone broke into the Import Export office."

"You stay where you are Bilious. I'll be right down."

D'Quad frantically pulled on his clothes and raced to his office. The police were there when D'Quad arrived.

"What's going on?" he asked the officers.

"Someone broke into your office. The alarm went off when they cracked the safe."

D'Quad broke into a cold sweat. He tried to remain calm. "Any suspects or eye witnesses?"

"There are no suspects, and the only witnesses were your two friends, Gizmo and Bilious. Each of them gave us a statement. I'd be happy to read them to you."

"Don't bother Officer. I see Gizmo and Bilious inside. I'll get it from the horse's mouth."

"What happened?" D'Quad growled as he walked into the office. "Where are my security guards?"

"Last night we just happened to be a block away, when we heard the alarm," Gizmo replied. "When we got here, the security guards were lying by the alleyway, out cold. They had been shot with darts. They must have been coated in some kind of knock out drug."

"Dart guns? Dart guns! Are you kidding me?" D'Quad screamed. "Who in the heck would come up with an idea like that? Did you see anyone?"

Bilious nodded."We were checking out the guards, when we saw two guys running up the street. We chased them, shot at them; even the police were involved. We had them boxed in, but …"

"But what?" D'Quad shouted. "Two guys on foot! And you're

trying to tell me that you and the cops couldn't catch them in cars?"

"Before you get all bent out of shape, those two fugitives didn't run very far. They hopped on motorcycles. Knowing our cars wouldn't be able to pursue them into the alleyway, they roared off and disappeared."

"Good God," D'Quad cried. "Why didn't you morons ride around the block and cut them off, when they exited the alleyway?"

"We did," Bilious replied angrily. "Those motorcycles they were riding were SS100's. They go a hundred miles an hour! By the time we went around the block, they were long gone."

D'Quad hung his head and nodded. "Boys, I need a few minutes alone."

"We'll be outside," Gizmo said.

Once he knew they were gone, D'Quad ran to the safe. Stacks of cash, gold bars, rolls of silver dollars and files littered the floor. "They weren't here to rob me, so what were they after?" He had a sick feeling in the pit of his stomach. His heart was pounding so loud he could hear it. D'Quad fell to his knees and reached into the safe. "Oh, no!" he cried. "The ledgers are gone— The ledgers are gone!"

D'Quad rushed over to his desk and picked up the telephone. His shaking hands could barely dial the number. The person on the other end, answered the call but said nothing. "Someone broke … uh … into the … uh … Import Export office," he stammered. "The ledgers are gone."

In the minutes that followed, a furious reply ripped through the telephone line. D'Quad quaked with fear.

****

Eric sat back in his chair, put his hands behind his head and stared at the ceiling. He sighed and said, "You know Chuck, you have a knack for making my blood pressure soar whenever I answer the phone."

"Sorry about that," Chuck laughed. "But you have to admit my call was worth a stroke!"

"You bet! I was just about to leave the house when you called. I'm glad you caught me in time. These ledgers are another nail in D'Quad's coffin."

"The only thing I can figure is whoever dropped them off, wants me to start printing this stuff."

"That time will come. For now, we've got the records for D'Quad's Jewelry Store and Import Export businesses. One ledger tracks his import of luxury goods. The other has the same thing, as well as smuggling transactions. But we have to know how D'Quad is getting the booze into the Quarter."

"I'll bet the people who dropped off these ledgers would know."

"The only thing I can say with certainty is, whoever they are, they seem hell bent on taking down D'Quad."

"Maybe, it's the Midnight Shadows."

Eric grinned and shook his head. "Who knows? But if it's them, they're some strange birds. They've risked their lives to get back the money for those who have been extorted by D'Quad. They aren't vigilantes at all. They're like two shadowy Robin Hoods, hitting and running back to their own secret Sherwood Forest."

"Speaking of Robin Hood," Chuck said, as he got up, "I've got to go to the Little John."

CHAPTER TWENTY-ONE

Jewels and Jesters, Constables and Kings
By Zoey and Desiree Daniels
New Orleans Nitpicker
Last night, King Louis the 19th's Castle had an open house for travelers who seemingly came down from heaven. Unfortunately, they landed in hell. Though we were not present, our sources say the King's soiree was the epitome of poor planning. The Castle lights were not on. The drawbridge was locked. No joint of mutton, no mug of mead was served. The King did not even bother to show up to greet his guests. Only his court jesters made merry, with those who attended. Their bizarre ballet was brief. The weaving buffoons's grand finale was to bounce their heads off the sidewalk. Neither court jester rose to take a bow before their audience. We believe the clowns were unconscious, and so we can forgive them for their rudeness. Despite all of this, the King's cohorts gave the buffoons a twenty-one gun salute. Gotta love those all purpose machine guns! The guests joined the celebration by breaking into the castle and joyfully flinging everything they could grab, all over the place. The police sirens blared with joy. And why not? King and cops, share a mutual love of all that glitters. Only the King knows the IMPORT of what his gleeful guests may have taken as souvenirs. Only the King knows what a JEWEL he truly is. But everyone knows that it's only a matter of time before the King, himself, becomes an EXPORT. His Majesty will be going on a long royal cruise upriver, with his loyal buffoons.

Ah, virtue. Thy name is truth.

Zoey and Desiree Daniels

Once the sisters were made aware of what Eric had told Chuck, Desiree's ire exploded into a furious tirade. "I've had it with Eric!" she railed. "Even though he's got the ledgers from both businesses, he has no plans of making any arrests. He just calls them 'another nail in D'Quad's coffin. ' How many nails does he need to make an arrest? This coffin must be the size of Noah's Ark!"

Desiree started up their gleaming Duesenberg X, and the sisters eased out of the driveway.

"I'm just as frustrated as you are," Zoey replied, "But unless we find where D'Quad's booze is brought ashore, how it is smuggled into the city … and where it's stored, Eric isn't going to arrest anybody. And we don't even know where the boat brings in the booze."

"We both know what Fishbowl told us. He believes the landing is somewhere south of Chalmette."

"I found this old map in my collection …."

"Another of your weird hobbies."

"… There was an old coast road that runs from the river into the outskirts of the French Quarter. Once the Port Of New Orleans was moved here, the road was abandoned. But there are sketchy coordinates on this map."

Desiree looked out the car window and broke into a grin. "Well, it's a beautiful day for a drive in the country. We're going on a scathingly marvelous, mysterious scavenger hunt!"

"Yes," Zoey said somberly.

"What do you think we'll find?" Desiree asked.

"Something … nothing … or a whole lot of trouble."

****

"Hello, Agent Jim Hope, speaking,"

"Hi Chief, how are you doing?"

"I'm alive and kicking."

"Did you hear anything on the bug at Victoria's?"

"Sorry Eric, but we had a technical glitch on our end. D'Quad's voice was muffled, and so was the voice of whomever he was talking to. How about you? Any new leads on the case?"

Eric proceeded to tell him about the ledgers from D'Quad's Import and Export Business.

Jim whistled. "How the hell did you manage to get ahold of those?"

"Same way as before. Down the mail chute at the *Nitpicker*."

"Any idea who dropped them off?"

"Well," Eric smiled, "there are two vigilantes called the Midnight Shadows who have been going after D'Quad's gang. They dress in black, ride black motorcycles, wear face covering masks and usually strike from rooftops. They've been pulling these stunts for over a year. On the night the ledgers were taken from D'Quad's Import Export office, eye witnesses saw the Midnight Shadows fleeing the scene. That was the same night the ledgers were dropped off at the *Nitpicker*. While there are no eye witnesses of the ledgers being taken from D'Quad's Jewelry store, the handwriting on both sacks the ledgers came in are identical—no finger prints. "

"That's very, very intriguing."

"It's baffling." Eric told Jim about the Midnight Shadows' recent escapades, including their wacky choice of weapons.

Jim's incredulity gave way to booming laughter. "A lasso, boomerangs and dart guns! These aren't your run of the mill, business as usual, vigilantes!"

"No, they're not. And Jim, honest to God, I'd love to have those two on my side when I take down D'Quad."

"You might be taking on more than you can handle. What about the Kamingas? We both know they're smuggling in hooch, too, and they've done their fair share of killing. It's gonna be hard to take D'Quad down and the Street Sweepers at the same time."

"I've checked the files at the *Nitpicker*. In the articles I have read, D'Quad's hits came first. Kongo's retaliations came second."

"Are you saying the Kamingas only act in self defense?"

"Yes. I've gotten to know Kongo and Diego, and I'm beginning to trust them. They helped me get out of that jam at Victoria's place. The Daniels sisters vouch for them. So does Chuck Hines at the *Nitpicker*, and I've been to Kongo's speakeasy. There was a different atmosphere. Victoria's Place was a pit of vipers. At Kongo's, it felt like some sort of illegal celebration. It was like a big extended family. They got drunk together, danced together and enjoyed each other's company. The Kamingas are no danger to me. In fact, the Street Sweepers would make good allies in a fight with D'Quad. Sometimes, you've got to deal with one devil to get rid of a worse devil."

"It's a risk, and with anyone else, I would say no, but I have faith in your judgement—But be careful. If you get in a crossfire between two enemy gangs, you are to get out of there immediately."

"Thanks Jim, I appreciate your concern."

"No need to thank me. You're of no use to me, if you're dead," he said with a laugh. "So, this Kongo and the Street Sweepers alliance, what's your next step?"

"Well. I plan to rent a boat and get drunk with Kongo and Diego!"

"Can I come along?"

"Goodbye, Chief."

****

It had been a miserable, sleepless night. As soon as the police were done questioning him, Louis D'Quad jumped into his car and sped over to his jewelry store. Cursing and swearing as he fumbled with his key, he finally bulled his way inside. The little bell above the door clanked like it was being strangled. D'Quad rushed over to his desk and reached under the top drawer.

"Oh, thank God! The key is still here! The ledgers are safe!"

D'Quad slumped into his desk chair. Sweating and shaking,

he remembered he had a bottle of Scotch in one of his desk drawers. "I really need something to steady my nerves. Besides," he thought, "I want to hug my good old ledgers!"

Louis D'Quad unlocked the drawers, retrieved the bottle and a tumbler, but nothing more. The ledgers were gone! D'Quad jumped, as the ring of the telephone tore through his body like a lightning bolt.

"Louis, this is T.M. I heard about the break-in last night. Anything taken?"

D'Quad felt he had better keep the stolen ledgers to himself. "Nothing of consequence," he said casually. "But I want to see you pronto. Meet me at the Toulouse Street Inn."

"On my way."

When T.M. arrived, D'Quad was already seated at his usual table, staring into space.

"Hey Louis, what's cookin'?"

"I just finished reading this," D'Quad said with disgust, as he flung the *New Orleans Nitpicker* across the table.

T.M. began reading. It was the Daniels sisters' column. When T.M. was finished, he looked up at D'Quad. "They say it was the King's Castle, but he was not there. They're talking about you, Louis."

"No shit Sherlock! They called my guards 'court jesters' and 'clowns' who were out cold and lying on the pavement."

"Yeah, and after Bilious opened fire with his machine gun, they accused 'King Louis' of ordering this 'twenty one gun salute' and imply the cops are in cahoots with him.'"

Digger arrived and took a seat next to T.M.— D'Quad's blood was boiling. He pointed to the last few lines of the article. "Three capitalized words: 'IMPORT,' 'EXPORT,' and 'JEWEL.' What do you make of them?"

"Seems they all boil down to the last line: 'His Majesty will be going on a long, royal cruise upriver, with his loyal buffoons.'" T.M.'s face flushed with anger. "They know more about our business dealings than I thought. They know something that could put us in federal prison."

D'Quad shot back a furious reply. "Yes! They seem to know every move we make. I smell a big fat rat. We've got to find out who it is!"

T.M. and Digger went through the most likely suspects in the gang: Pancake Face, Zoned Out Tony ... Platter Puss ... Momma Mayhem ...

"Na ..." Digger finally said.

"Cops?" D'Quad asked.

"If any of the cops had ratted us out, we'd already be in jail with them."

"Anybody else?"

"Well," T.M. replied, "there's only one suspect left, Victoria Guerrero. When she's bartending, she ain't far away from us when we're shootin 'the breeze."

"Oh, come on T.M., Victoria wouldn't rat us out. She needs our business to keep all her dead-beat friends afloat. What would be in it for her?"

"A lot. All her precious, deadbeat employees are her close friends. Every one of them has Street Sweeper friends, relatives or neighbors. Seems to me that Victoria," T.M. said sarcastically, "might very well have them too."

"Yes, that's true," D'Quad replied.

"And, she is very close friends with the Daniels sisters."

"Yes," D'Quad sneered. "It all adds up. I believe you're right. It's time to shut Victoria's mouth—permanently."

****

"Let me check this map again. It's so old, and some of the print has been worn off." Zoey took out a compass and traced the coordinates.

"Take your time," Desiree replied, the sunlight flashing off her sunglasses, the wind tugging at her shoulder length curls. "It's such a wonderful day to cruise to wherever fancy takes us."

Zoey looked up and squinted through the windshield, then back at her map. "We're getting close. I think the road has to be somewhere around here."

Desiree slowed down. Zoey studied the woods as they inched by. After some time, they found nothing.

"The road's got to be overgrown by now. Why don't we double back and check this stretch again?"

Desiree did a screeching u-turn on two wheels.

"You're tilting me!"

"Oh, stop complaining and look!"

Zoey stared intently into the dense underbrush. The woods on the side of the road were a mixture of marshland, groves of tangled brush, towering Live Oaks and Cypress trees. The darkness of the forest was pierced by spears of light that sliced through the dense canopy. Zoey noticed something she had not seen before. "Pull over."

Desiree eased onto the jagged shoulder. "What do you see?"

Zoey pointed. "Look at the ground over there. I think I see some tire tracks. I'll go check them out. Keep the car running."

Desiree watched as Zoey walked up to a pile of brush and tree limbs. She pushed some of them aside and stepped into the shadows.

When Zoey finally returned, she wore an excited smile. She hopped back into the car and said, "Those are tire tracks, and it is a man-made barrier. The limbs are sawed off at the bottom, and they are Bald Cypress and Slash Pines. There were no Bald Cypress or Slash Pines anywhere near the blockade."

"That's fantastic! Any sign of a road?"

Zoey nodded excitedly. "Yes! I walked down a ways, and I could see it was once two lanes, but much of it is overgrown with brush and dead trees— It's still wide enough for trucks to get through. The tire tracks continue down a slope toward the river! I saw what looks like a warehouse down there."

"Tonight?" Desiree asked with a smile.

"Tonight."

Desiree hit the gas and fishtailed back onto the road.

"You're tilting me again!"

CHAPTER TWENTY-TWO

It was almost time for Fishbowl Head's Nautical Shop to close when Eric arrived. When he opened the door, he saw Fishbowl singing an old sea chanty, as he swept the floor.

"Hey buddy," Eric said as he entered. "You're taking my job away." Eric reached for the broom, and Fishbowl grinned.

"Hey, Eric! So, have you decided to take me up on that job offer?"

"Can't do that, but I can help you clean up and take you up on that offer of a drink."

Fishbowl handed him the broom. "You got it. You okay if we go over to Kongo's Place?"

"That's perfect! I've got some business to talk about with Kongo and Diego. Now I can kill two birds with one stone."

Fishbowl phoned Kongo and got an enthusiastic invitation to come on over. Fishbowl grabbed his coat, locked up the store and the pair set off. As they walked down the street, Fishbowl set a lively pace. "Since I got the store restocked, business has been great. Everybody heard about the hit, and they've been comin' in to help me out. I seen my police buddies, Baker and McGhee, patrolling the street real often. It's nice to know I've got so many friends."

"Are you still taking those night fishing trips down river?" Eric asked.

"Oh yeah, I was thinkin 'about going out tonight."

"Well that's a coincidence, because I was going to ask you about taking me out on the river tonight."

"Sure Eric," Fishbowl said with a nod and a wink. "After we talked, I was thinkin' you might like to take a little trip down past Chalmette sometime."

Reaching their destination, Fishbowl knocked out an SOS on the door.

Kongo opened it, and when he saw Fishbowl and Eric, a huge smile appeared on his face. Eric braced himself for one of those huge bear hugs, and that was exactly what he got. So did Fishbowl.

"Eric, my friend!" Kongo exclaimed. "It has been too long. I have seen your fine work in the newspaper and hoped that you would visit us."

"Great to see you, Kongo! I've been so busy, I haven't had a lot of time for going out since that night at Victoria's."

Diego arrived on the scene and exchanged warm greetings with the pair. "Come in, mi amigos, let us sit down at the big table and enjoy each other's company." Diego retrieved a bottle of twelve-year-old Scotch and four tumblers.

Eric gave Diego a sly smile. "Is this imported stuff?"

Diego returned Eric's sly smile. "You already know the answer to that question, do you not, mi amigo?"

Eric shrugged his shoulders and winked. "Now, how would I know that?"

"What a magnificent beginning to our night. Our new friend, Eric, and our friend of so many years, Fishbowl," Kongo said as he filled the four tumblers.

"We appreciate your visit," Diego added, "but it is quite all right if we mix pleasure with," Diego paused and grinned at Eric, "a little business?"

Fishbowl began the conversation. "I've had enough of all this violence, and all I can say is it's 'bout time those of us who are in the know take care of D'Quad and his men—All we need is the evidence that will lock 'em up for good."

There was silence, and everyone stared at Eric. He thought for a moment and then said, "Okay, I'll tell you what I know, because I'm sure it will be as useful to you as it is to me." Then he added grimly. "But if anything I say goes out of this room, there will be consequences."

Eric put out his hand, and each man shook it in agreement. "I'll take that handshake as a word of honor, and I believe you all are honorable men.... I'll lay all my cards on the table—I'm a federal agent, sent here to find out who killed our two agents, Buck and James. I already have a lot of evidence against D'Quad, but I could use your help." He looked at Kongo to see his reaction and was surprised to see a smile on his face.

"Eric, I knew you were an agent from the minute I saw you pull out that thirty-eight revolver, after the bombing on the night I met you." Kongo paused to see Eric's reaction. When Eric started to grin, the tension was broken, and everyone at the table broke into congenial laughter.

Kongo continued, "I'm aware of the fact that you know that I am doing some modest smuggling and could put me in jail, but I have trusted you from the moment I met you. Diego and I will help you any way we can, and I pledge to you, our honor, our loyalty and our trust."

Fishbowl nodded. "Eric, I've been suspicious of you since I met you. I've been around feds all my life. I'm glad you come clean with me, because I've been honest with you 'bout everything I've told you. I trust you, and you can surely trust me."

Eric looked at his new allies. "Thank you," he said. "Losing the two agents was awful for me and the agency. They were my friends, and so far, I've been able to buy and identify some of their jewelry that D'Quad put in his store the day after their murders. His records also show some other pieces of jewelry that he got just after some of the Street Sweepers were murdered. Kongo, maybe you could help me with confirming that the jewelry belonged to your friends. Fishbowl, I need for you to take me downriver to try to find that warehouse you told me about—I don't know what help I might need in the future, but I appreciate your trust in me. I don't want any harm to come to any of us."

"A toast," Diego smiled, "to solidarity among friends."

****

It was dark by the time Eric and Fishbowl left the Kamingas and walked to the marina where Fishbowl kept his boats.

"So Eric, what are your plans if we find the dock downriver?"

"Well, it depends, but ideally, I want to sneak ashore and take a look at what's going on at the warehouse. The more I know about their operation, the better."

"Okay, let's take this; my big ship with the dingy. If you want to go ashore, we'll lower it down, and you can row to the river bank."

"That sounds like what I had in mind."

"Okay," Fishbowl smiled, "I'll get her started, and you can untie the lines."

As they rode downriver, Fishbowl told Eric what he knew about D'Quad's operations in the French Quarter. "From what I seen and heard, after the *Eclipse* picks up the booze offshore, it unloads at the warehouse we're lookin' for. After that, D'Quad trucks it in at night to a place in the Quarter. Next day, his men move it to his customers throughout the city. Wish I knew exactly where he stores it in the Quarter, but I reckon it's somewhere central, so they can move it quick."

When they approached the area where the dock was located, Fishbowl slowed down and gave Eric a pair of binoculars. "Take a look and see if anything is goin' on—Look right past the dock where there are some lights."

Eric focused the binoculars, squinted and said, "Jackpot! I see trucks, and men moving around. I'll bet they're loading up."

Fishbowl cut his lights. "Okay, I'll drop anchor here. This steamy fog that's comin' off the river should keep both of us from being spotted."

Eric nodded and took a deep breath. "See you in a little bit, Fishbowl."

They lowered the dinghy into the river. Eric scrambled aboard and started rowing ashore.

****

There was no traffic on the highway. There never was. After the Port of New Orleans was moved upriver, this once busy thoroughfare might as well have been as overgrown as the road that led to the Warehouse. The Midnight Shadows cut their lights as they approached the hidden road. Just short of the entrance, Zoey looked for a dry path through the marshes. The sisters kept their flashlights low, as they walked their bikes down the jagged shoulder. Zoey abruptly stopped and pointed.

"Down there." she said. "It looks like a deer path that should go right through the swamp. We can use it if we have to make a quick getaway."

"We better hope that we can find the other end."

"We will."

"You have no sense of direction."

"But luckily, you do."

"We'll be on foot."

"We're armed," Zoey said, as she slid her fingers down the weapon strapped to Desiree's back. "If we get in trouble, we've got our thirty-eights and lightning bolts!"

The sisters stored their bikes in the dark shadows of the trail, then went back to check the Warehouse Road. The blockade had been pushed aside. The muddy entrance was gutted with fresh tire tracks. Zoey and Desiree made their stealthy way down the road. Once Zoey had a clear vantage point, she trained her binoculars on the Warehouse. "Looks like there's a lot of activity down there."

"Let me have a look." Desiree squinted through the glasses. "There are trucks and men too."

"Luckily, there aren't any on this road."

Desiree nodded. "Let's head for that grove of trees behind the Warehouse."

The marsh around them was silent and foreboding. Only the splash of a gator cut through the ominous distance. They made their way toward the grove of trees, then paused to take a good look.

"We're in luck," Desiree whispered excitedly. "That roof has a decided pitch on this side. We can surely get up that."

Zoey nodded. "Once we make it to the top, we'll have a perfect view of everything D'Quad's boys are doing down there."

Zoey took one last look around to make certain there was no one behind the Warehouse. The sisters left the safety of the tree line and sprinted to the back of the building. Desiree gave Zoey a boost and then she hoisted herself onto the roof. Zoey reached down, grabbed both of Desiree's hands and pulled her up. They crouched low, as they made their way to the top of the roof. They peeked over the edge and looked down. Men were pulling crates out of the Warehouse and loading them into trucks. Out of the corner of Desiree's eye, she spied a dark figure inching his way along the riverbank. She nudged Zoey. "Someone's making tracks down there on the banks of the ole 'Mississip'."

Zoey was startled. "Do you think it's Kongo ... Diego ... a Street Sweeper?" she asked nervously.

"It doesn't matter who it is. If he's spotted, D'Quad's boys will kill him."

Desiree pulled the weapon from her back, loaded it and wrapped the tip of the projectile in gauze. She took out a little vial from her backpack and soaked it. She did the same with a second bolt. Zoey pulled out her thirty-eight and trained her binoculars on the man. "Oh good grief," she whispered. "It's Eric."

Suddenly, one of D'Quad's men shouted," Look, there's a guy down there heading for the dock."

D'Quad's men converged on the figure, opening fire as they ran.

"We've got to create a diversion!" Zoey cried.

Desiree lit the end of the crossbow bolt, stood up, took careful aim at the loading dock and fired. The flaming projectile streaked through the sky. D'Quad's startled men watched it slam into it's target in a blazing flash. A second flaming bolt turned the dock into a fiery inferno. Eric was startled by his good fortune. He looked up to see two masked figures giving him a quick salute.

"The docks on fire!" Bilious roared, as D'Quad's men scrambled to get buckets to put out the flaming timber.

"Where the hell did those arrows come from?" Gizmo cried.

"Up there! Get them!"

They had been spotted. Zoey and Desiree pulled out their thirty-eights and opened fire, driving off the men. It gave them enough time to scramble down the roof and jump to the ground. They sprinted toward the main road. They could hear one of the men shout, "Look, they're over there! Let's go get those guys, and make sure they get got!"

Machine gun bullets hammered the trees around the sisters. They kicked up clods of earth, exploding against their boots.

"We can't take this main road and hope to get to our bikes," Desiree shouted. "They're sure to catch us."

Zoey nodded.

The sisters sprinted into the brush and sprawled to the ground under the cover of giant ferns, Cypress trees and tall cane. Zoey and Desiree listened as the men came closer and closer, searching the perimeter of the road. Every once in a while, there would be a burst of machine gun fire and shouts of "Come out, or sooner or later some of these bullets are gonna find ya!"

Once they were certain D'Quad's goons had passed, Zoey and Desiree made their stealthy way back up the deer path to their motorcycles.

While the Midnight Shadows made their death defying escape, Eric was running for his life—D'Quad's men were right behind him. Eric scrambled through the brush and down to the dinghy. Machine gun fire strafed the bank, sand spitting up all around him. Eric splashed through the water and got into the dinghy. As he cast off, a spray of bullets hit the boat, boring tiny holes into it's side. Knowing the dinghy was taking on water, Eric rowed for his life. Mercifully, the boat did not sink until after he had grabbed hold of Fishbowl's tow line. Fishbowl hoisted Eric out of the water, slapped him on the back and smiled broadly. "It is so good to see you alive! Did you find what you were looking for?"

"More than I bargained for."

"Well good, cause it's gonna cost ya. You have to buy me a new dinghy," he laughed.

"No problem," Eric said in a somewhat distracted voice. "I'll buy you any boat you want, spare no expense."

"That's one heckuva offer! What did you find?"

"D'Quad's men were loading crates onto trucks when they spotted me. I thought I was dead in the water, until ..." then he smiled at Fishbowl, "until the Midnight Shadows took them on, while I escaped."

"Well, if that don't make the bird crow!"

"They saved my life!" Eric smiled, turned and looked back toward the shore. "Who are these darned Midnight Shadows," he wondered, "and where did they go?"

Seated on their motorcycles at the top of the deer path, the Midnight Shadows watched and waited.

"Those trucks are going to be up here shortly," Zoey said nervously.

"If I know D'Quad's arrogant sloppiness, they'll drive off like a little string of ducks."

"Remember. We'll keep a distance behind them and keep our headlights off."

Desiree nodded.

They heard the roar of engines coming up the hill. One by one, the trucks emerged and turned onto the road.

"Yep," Desiree laughed, as they revved up their bikes, "just like little ducks in a row."

"Just like shooting ducks in a barrel!"

CHAPTER TWENTY-THREE

The next morning, just as Eric was pouring his first cup of coffee, his telephone rang.

"Hello," he answered.

"Hello Eric, it's Jim. We picked up some useful chatter last night on that phone tap you did at Victoria's."

"Any thing of consequence?"

"Well, the conversation wasn't long enough for us to get a good trace on who D'Quad was talking to. But he was talking to someone local and someone of equal stature. The stranger's voice was purposely muffled. D'Quad said he was working on finding the ledgers, and who took them—He said that he would kill whoever it was. Then he said that the goods were being moved from the river Warehouse to what he called, the Carriage House. I assume that's the smuggled booze."

"Yes it is ... and I came darned close to getting my butt blown off. I got this guy, Fishbowl, to take me downriver, and I rowed ashore to get a look at the Warehouse. D'Quad's boys were loading trucks to move the booze to town. Unfortunately, they saw me—but fortunately, the Midnight Shadows appeared on the roof of the Warehouse and gave me cover, so I could escape."

Jim burst out laughing. "So, a pair of masked vigilantes saved your life? Are you sure you weren't drinking some of that contraband hooch?"

"I wish I had been, then all of this would make more sense."

"Well, this whole yarn of yours will keep agents laughing for a hundred years!"

Eric chuckled. "I'll try to get some information on this Carriage House and get back to you. I'll also sniff around and see if I can get any info on D'Quad's ally—That throws a whole new wrinkle into this case."

"It sure does, Eric. We'll keep listening in on D'Quad's phone calls, 24-7. As soon as I hear anything, I'll contact you immediately. Keep me posted on what's going on at your end."

"You've got it, Chief."

****

For the Daniels sisters, the incident at the Warehouse had been a death-defying roller coaster. Tailing D'Quad's trucks had taken the Midnight Shadows straight to where the contraband was being stored. From a distance, they had watched D'Quad's goons unload the trucks and haul crates into the Carriage House. Since it's heyday in the 1890's, it had fallen into disrepair. There was a "closed for renovation" sign that had turned to rust. Residents saw trucks pull in, from time to time, and assumed they were carrying materials for restoring this architectural treasure. The only overt evidence of any renovation, however, was the windows were painted over.

Tonight, Zoey and Desiree were getting dressed and ready for a night out on the town—A midnight run to the Carriage House area. The Kaboom Saloon was a known hangout for D'Quad's goons. Their propensity for drink and pretty young girls might provide the sisters with some insight in getting into the Carriage House. But, they could not go and mingle with the goons as the Midnight Shadows, so they would use what weapons they had. Their new purchases, four and a half inch Colt Pistols, were tucked under their dresses in little velvet holsters attached to a garter. The only other weapon they had was being irresistible flirts.

"Let me look you over before we set out," Desiree said. Zoey's beautiful blonde hair flowed out of a silver bucket hat and down the back of her sparkling silver dress. Her black boa and strands of pearls were the perfect compliment." Desiree smiled. "Zoey, you are truly transformed into the Angel of Allure."

Zoey flashed a brilliant smile. "Let me look you over," she said as she scrutinized her sister. "Makeup - check, your boa is a little crooked ... maybe too many strands of pearls, but a great choice of shoes."

"... With clunky heels, clip-clop, clip-clop ... perfect for going to a house for horses."

"... A beautiful winter white dress, still fashionable after Labor day, but it's way too short."

"It makes it easier to lift up if I have to pull out my gun," Desiree said with a mischievous smile. "So, Zoey, what's the verdict?"

Zoey gave Desiree a thumbs up. "Desiree is no more! You are, once again, the River of Desire."

There was manic excitement in Desiree's eyes. "Well then, let's go! Let's finally get slow-butted, drag-his-heels Eric all the information that he keeps whining about, so he'll finally arrest somebody—anybody!"

The sisters cruised across the Quarter and turned onto Saint Peter Street. They parked on a side street, just across from the Kaboom Saloon. They had a clear view of the Carriage House. Desiree checked her watch. "You were right about waiting to come here after midnight. There are very few partiers still out on the street, and most of them are staggering."

"And most of them are going into the Kaboom Saloon."

"Time to sashay!"

As they got out of the car, they were startled by a stranger who seemed to come out of nowhere.

"What in blue blazes are you two doing here?"

"Oh, good grief, it's you, Eric, and you scared the daylights out of me."

"Good, Zoey! You should be scared. You could get killed out here." Eric stopped for a breath and tried to calm down. "Why are you here, anyway?"

"We might ask you the same thing."

"No, you may not ask me the same thing. I am a federal agent. You are columnists."

"Yes," Desiree replied furiously, "we're just columnists … but," she said with a sneer, "these little old columnists got a message from one of our sources that brought us here. We have friends in high places …"

"… and we came to visit the Kaboom Saloon, and," Zoey pointed, "check out the Carriage House."

"That's where D'Quad's booze is being stored, hotshot!" Desiree added.

Eric was shaken by Desiree's angry response. "I didn't mean to upset anybody," Eric replied." I apologize, but right now, I want you to get out of here and go home."

"We're not going anywhere." Zoey replied.

"You can stuff that notion." Desiree growled.

Eric shook his head in defeat. "Well then, since you're too stubborn to leave, maybe you can help me out. About a half hour ago, I saw D'Quad's guards walk down from the Carriage House and into Kaboom's. I want you to try to keep them there. You're," Eric stammered and looked away, "you're very … um … you know … attractive ladies."

Both girls nodded and smiled, enjoying Eric's discomfort.

"It's an uneducated estimate, but I need about forty-five minutes to try to get into the Carriage House, open a crate or two, turn the lights on and photograph some of the booze. Do you think you can stall them for that long?"

"Of course we can, Eric," Desiree replied with a coy smile. "You just told us how attractive we are."

"Yes … well … er … let's synchronize our watches. We'll meet back here around two thirty."

"Yup."

"Are you armed?" Eric asked. "I mean other than Desiree's magic derringer."

"Colts … would you like to see where we keep them?"

Eric cleared his throat and ignored Desiree. "The two guys you've got to keep entertained are Billy The Goat and Big Boy.

You'll notice Billy right away. He's a really tall, skinny guy with a long face, a Vandyke beard and close set eyes—He looks like a goat. Big Boy is huge. He's an ex-professional boxer with a pushed in face. He always wears a white boutonniere. You can't miss them."

"By the way," Zoey asked, "how did you know about the Carriage House?"

Eric chuckled, as he walked away. "I bugged Victoria's phone. Our boys in the agency have really fine hearing and sleep in shifts."

As Eric disappeared from view, the sisters crossed the street and entered the Kaboom Saloon. The smoke-filled room was packed with inebriated patrons, laughing, shouting and screaming. A radio was turned up to the point of distortion. The sisters made their way to the bar. They immediately recognized Billy and Big Boy, sitting at an adjacent table. They pretended not to notice, but D'Quad's goons noticed them.

"Why don't you come over here, ladies, and we'll get acquainted," Billy the Goat shouted.

The girls turned around, and Zoey said in a sultry voice, "Oh, what a wonderful invitation."

"And from such handsome men!" Desiree added.

"Yes, we accept your invitation, and as a way of saying thanks," Zoey said, "we'll buy you some drinks. What's your poison?"

"Well, that's right neighborly of you gals. We'll have whatever you're having."

Zoey ordered the drinks. The bartender raised an eyebrow and stared at the girls condescendingly. "You should steer clear of absinthe. It might be a bit unsettling for your delicate constitutions."

"Well," Zoey replied, as she paid the man, "these delicate ladies will take their chances."

"I'll bring over the bottle and four shot glasses, right away."

"Perfect," Desiree whispered, as they went to join their dangerous admirers. "We've got potted plants bordering the two empty seats at their table."

"Those ferns are going to have a heckuva hangover."

The sisters gave each of the leering men shy smiles. The bartender arrived with the bottle. Zoey filled their glasses.

Both men knocked back the shot. "Well," Billy burped, "this tastes like black licorice."

"Yes," Big Boy roared, "a candy drink for our fragile flowers!"

"Well, you big strong men, would you like to have a drinking contest with little old us?" Desiree cooed.

"Not much of a contest yet, eh little ladies?" Billy laughed. "You still haven't drank yer first shot."

"Yeah," Big Boy added. "Scared of a little drinky poo?"

The sisters smiled defiantly and downed the shot.

The men poured another round. While they knocked it back, each of the sisters dumped their glasses into the potted palms.

Big Boy poured another round and proposed a toast. "Here's to our two sexy broads," he yelled, "all ready for a little hanky-panky. Cheers!"

Both men drained their glasses. Zoey and Desiree dumped their drinks into the potted plants. The minutes ticked by, as the men downed shot after shot.

"Bbbboy ..." Billy drawled, his head weaving from side to side. "Every b ... b ... broad in the place is glowing."

Zoey nudged Desiree. "The absinthe is working."

Desiree looked over the glassy-eyed men. "The hallucinations have started."

"Look ... look," Big Boy howled, "the bartender's head is on fire!"

"The whole place is g...lowing with fire. It's so beeee ... beautiful."

"It's more like ... so wonderful ... glowing fire.... It's getting hot ... in ... here ... and I need some air."

"I need some air too ... so les go outside!"

As both men wobbled up and staggered toward the door, Zoey said," We've got to stall them! We've got to give Eric some more time."

Desiree took Zoey's hand and pulled her up. "How about we go outside and do a romantic dance for them?"

"Do you have our instruments?"

"Yes," Desiree replied. She reached into her purse, pulled out two kazoos and gave one to Zoey.

"Come on!" Zoey cried, as both sisters rushed to the door.

Once outside, they found both men staring up at the sky.

"Howdy girls," Billy howled. "How many stars ... da ya think there are up dere?" Billy started finger counting, repeatedly losing track.

"Don't bother counting the stars ... I did all 'eddy," Big Boy slurred.

"How many?"

"Two...."

Both men burst out laughing. "Les ... go take a walk." Big Boy took Zoey's hand, and Billy grabbed Desiree's arm. "Come on, it 'ill b-b-be fun!"

Zoey pulled away. "Sure, boys, we'll come for a romantic stroll with you, but first we have to set a romantic mood. We want to do a dance for you!"

"Whoopy!"

" Whoopy, whoopy, whoopy, woo, dance!"

"Well," Zoey said, "not here, we need some stage lights."

The girls pulled their hallucinating friends toward a street lamp. They stood underneath the light, making certain the men had their backs to the Carriage House. They gave each a sexy smile.

"Way Down Upon The Suwannee River," Zoey said to Desiree.

Both men howled, as the sisters broke into a tap dance, while blowing out the tune on their kazoos. "Dee ... Deeta deeta... de... de de de... de dete de de...." Their instruments farted and honked like raspy geese, as they danced in unison: step-ball change, step-ball-change, shuffle, shuffle, step-ball-change They danced with perfect timing and enthusiasm. Even as the two men sang off key and off beat, their experience allowed them to perform the perfect dance routine: step, kick, ball-change-kick, step, kick, ball-change-kick.

All the time they danced, they kept an eye on the Carriage House. As they reached their choreographed, honk-farting climax, the lights in the Carriage House went off. Zoey and Desiree gave their drunken dates a leg baring curtsy. Billy and Big Boy hooted, hollered and howled, along with trying to clap their hands, but missing. Their glassy eyes were red as rubies, as they sank to the pavement and laid down, fast asleep.

The sisters looked at each other, in disbelief.

"It had to be absinthe," Zoey smiled.

"No," Desiree giggled, "it was our terrific performance!"

"Yes, our kazoo farting, tippy-tappy, dance of romance!"

They took dainty steps over their victims of lust and black licorice, and ran across the street. Eric was already there, sitting in his car.

"I have to admit," he said, "that while you insisted on staying here and putting your lives in jeopardy, you really came through for me. Thanks!"

"No problem!" Desiree replied with a sly smile. "It was all a matter of our irresistible allure and a little licorice."

"Candy?"

Zoey tilted her head and smiled innocently. "Of course, silly. Men just adore a little sugar."

As Eric waved and drove off, Desiree said, "We were so lucky tonight. Maybe it's a sign of good things to come."

Desiree couldn't have been more wrong.

****

As the sun rose on a new day, the sisters' luck ran out. It was barely dawn when the telephone rang. "Hello," Zoey yawned.

"Hi, it's Chuck. I want you to go over to Victoria's Place, right now. Eric's on his way down there too."

Zoey was jolted awake. "What's going on? What's the matter?"

"Victoria's was hit last night. Get over there and see what you can find out."

"How bad is it?"

Chuck hesitated for a moment, then said, "From the little I know, it's an ungodly mess."

Zoey filled in Desiree as the sisters got dressed. Ignoring every traffic light, speed limit and stop sign, the sisters raced over to Victoria's. They skidded to a stop in front of her unrecognizable home.

"Oh, my God!" Zoey exclaimed.

Desiree shook her head, as they stared at the smoldering ruins that were once Victoria's Place. The only things that remained standing were the scorched, bullet-riddled, Corinthian columns that fronted the entrance. The sisters spotted Eric, peering into the charred remains. They walked over and joined him.

"When did it happen?" Zoey whispered.

"The cops said it was ..." Eric looked away, then said somberly, "around the same time we were at the Carriage House."

Zoey was overcome with emotion. "We could have done something!"

"Yes." Desiree said, a single tear running down her cheek. "We should have known D'Quad would turn on Victoria ... and now this! Oh, my God, oh, my God, oh, my God!"

"I know how close you were to Victoria. If there's anything I can do ..."

"There is one thing you can do for us, Eric," Zoey said in a hoarse whisper.

"Name it."

"Take pictures that will show the horror that is being inflicted on innocent people by D'Quad's gang."

While Eric shot photos of the smoldering structure, the sisters seemed riveted to the ground. With glazed over eyes, they slowly inched closer to the house. Bullet casings littered the ground. The steel gray dawn illuminated the gruesome disaster. Wreckage from the roof and massive beams from the second floor had collapsed and buried the speakeasy.

"There's no chance that anyone is alive under that rubble."

Zoey shuddered and nodded without expression.

"In all the time we've been the Midnight Shadows ..." Desiree said nervously,

"... we have never seen death up close."

"D'Quad killed one of our dearest friends. This has become personal! D'Quad is going to pay for this. Victoria will be avenged!"

As Eric shot his photos, his lens picked up a disturbing image. He walked over to a bullet-riddled column. Attached to it, was an unscarred juju charm. Eric removed it and studied it intently. He wrapped the charm in his handkerchief and slipped it into his jacket pocket. As he turned around, he saw Fishbowl emerge from a group of local residents and begin walking towards him. As he approached, Eric could see Fishbowl's anguished expression. "I'm just too darned old to help anybody," Fishbowl said, as tears began to stream down his face. "I was out walkin' last night and saw Gizmo and Bilious runnin 'away from the house. I knowed somethin 'was up and tried to run to the house to warn Victoria, but I couldn't make it—It blowed up."

Eric put his hand on Fishbowl's shoulder. "It's not your fault, buddy. There's nothing you could have done, except get yourself killed."

Fishbowl wiped his face and nodded. "I suppose you're right. I'm just an old man—But I'll see to it that justice is done here."

"One thing's for certain. If they hit Victoria's this savagely, the Kamingas might be next. I've got to get over there and warn them."

"I'm going to come along."

Eric smiled. "I wouldn't have it any other way, my loyal friend. And ... although I'd rather they stay out of this fight, I know it's hopeless to stop them. Zoey and Desiree have got to know what's going on."

"Yeah, I see those sweet girls over there on the sidewalk. I'd like to talk to them too. They might need a shoulder to cry on."

There were more hugs and tears, as Fishbowl greeted Zoey and Desiree. "Some of these people are sayin' they think the Street Sweepers done this," Fishbowl said. "You make sure when you write your stuff in the *Nitpicker,* you say that I seen D'Quad's men running away last night, just before Victoria's Place blew up."

"Don't worry Fishbowl. We know the Street Sweepers wouldn't hurt Victoria," Zoey assured him.

Eric joined them. "I was just telling Fishbowl that with what happened here, there's a good possibility that Kongo's place will be hit next. We're going over there. Care to come along?" Eric asked.

"Of course, we will." Zoey replied. "We just finished the last of our interviews with Victoria's neighbors."

"These people are terrified," Desiree said.

"On top of this disaster," Zoey added, "some of them found juju charms on their doors this morning. They're afraid they'll be hit next."

"I guarantee these people are in no danger," Eric replied. "Trust me on that. If D'Quad is going to hit anyone, the Kamingas will be next."

"We have to bring Kongo this horrible news," Desiree said, with a dead eyed stare.

"We'll follow you over there, Eric," Zoey sighed.

On the way to Kongo's Place, the sisters were silent and lost in their own thoughts. As Eric and Fishbowl drove, both men wore an expression of grim resolve. Eric frowned as he parked the car in front of Kongo's place. The Daniels sisters pulled in behind them. Without a word, they walked slowly toward the door and knocked. Kongo opened it immediately and led them inside. Diego was with him and studied the ashen faces of his four friends.

"I think I know what you want to tell me. We already know about the hit on Victoria's," Kongo said softly. "What you do not know, mi amigos," he added with a delighted smile, "is Victoria and all of her employees are alive and safe."

"Oh, thank God!" Desiree whispered, as she put her hands over her face and started to cry.

With tears in her eyes, Zoey took Desiree's hands in hers and squeezed hard. "She's okay, they're all okay!" she exclaimed, laughing and crying at the same time.

"How did they get out of that terrible destruction alive?" Eric asked.

Kongo began with a smile. "Well, as you all know, our Victoria is a very smart and savvy lady. Yesterday evening, around eleven, D'Quad went into her office and removed a strongbox that contained all of his cash and records; something he had never done before. He gave Victoria a lame excuse about needing to check all of the earnings, but she was suspicious. As he and all of his goons were leaving, Andre, one of his men who is a dear friend of Victoria and a spy for the Street Sweepers, whispered in her ear, 'Get Out.' As soon as D'Quad's men left, Victoria called all of her staff together and told them she thought there was going to be a hit, and they should leave immediately. As soon as they were out, she locked the door and left as well. She arrived on our doorstep around midnight. Soon after she told us her story, we heard the explosion."

"Oh! Where is she? She must be devastated," Desiree exclaimed.

"We put her in a safe house, where she will be comfortable and protected as long as it is necessary," Diego assured them. "Of course, she is upset after losing her home and business, but she is family here. She knows we will always take good care of her and all of you."

Eric waited for everyone to process the good news, then broke the silence. "I guess while we're all together, it's a good time for me to get everybody caught up."

Everyone's head turned to Eric, anxious to hear his news.

"First of all, I know that someone, probably the Midnight Shadows, dropped off the ledgers from D'Quad's Jewelry Store and Import-Export Businesses at the *Nitpicker* offices. I turned those over to the Agency's accountants for review. Second of all,

Fishbowl helped me find D'Quad's Warehouse, and he and the Midnight Shadows saved my ass down on the river."

Fishbowl laughed, "Yep, you was like pullin 'a big catfish out of the water, when you made it back to my ship. By the way, I found a nice dinghy to replace the one you got shot up."

"Fishbowl, I'm so sorry about that. I'll write you a check before we leave."

"I appreciate that Eric. Now, what else have you found out?"

"Well," Eric began, "last night, Zoey and Desiree helped me get into the Carriage House where D'Quad stores his booze in town. You guys wouldn't have believed how these two distracted Billy The Goat and Big Bob, so I could get inside—It was like watching the Ziegfield Follies under a street light—Only they were tap dancing with kazoos in their mouths, squawking out the melody to 'Suwannee River.' If I hadn't been under so much stress trying to get out of there, I would have died laughing."

"Those are our brave chiquitas," Diego laughed, taking Zoeys hand. "Their courage and cunning is only exceeded by their great beauty."

"So true," Eric agreed, with a smile that made Desiree's heart race. "Anyway, there are a couple of other things I can tell you all. I had a bug on the phone at Victoria's Place, but with her house blown to bits, I'm going to have to rely on good old detective work to solve the most important piece of the puzzle…. During the tap, we found out that whomever D'Quad was talking to, he's a very powerful ally. The guy was royally pissed at him for losing those ledgers. Any idea who it could be?"

Kongo shook his head and replied. "None of us know, amigo. With his Import-Export business, he's constantly meeting with big shot businessmen. But I do know that we all have enough connections to find out who this dangerous collaborator is."

Eric nodded. "But everybody be very careful. Don't let anybody know what we have discussed. As we all know, from what happened at Victoria's, anybody who gets tangled up in this could get killed."

"Eric, let us not be so gloomy. Victory is near at hand! I think we could all use a drink," Diego laughed.

"Amen to that!" they all said in unison.

CHAPTER TWENTY-FOUR

After the destruction at Victoria's Place, the community was in an uproar. Citizens of the French Quarter, tired of the violence, called for the removal of the Police Commissioner and Police Chief. They were indicted and forced to resign. With pressure from the Mayor, the police were assigned to double-duties during the weeks leading up to Christmas. Finally, the streets were safe and quiet. Christmas lights twinkled from homes and shops across the city. The glistening Christmas tree in Jackson Square bathed the Saint Louis Cathedral in a cascading rainbow of light. Madame Ravonay's gris-gris bags were placed on doorsteps for protection against the ominous aura of violence that permeated the Quarter. With Victoria's gone, D'Quad's gang was holed up in their new speakeasy, The Kaboom Saloon. Eric's daily surveillance records showed that *The Eclipse* remained in port.

"All is calm, all is bright," Eric thought. "Time to call the agency and get this train a rollin'."

"Hello, Agent Jim Hope speaking."

"Hi Chief, this is Eric."

"Howdy Eric, how's life in the Big Easy?"

"Unusually calm and quiet," Eric replied. "It's all peace on earth and goodwill. The spirit of the season prevails."

"I just hope it holds until after Christmas. You know you can call me at home if something comes up, but it would be great to get to spend one uninterrupted Christmas with my family."

Eric chuckled. "I'll do my best to leave you alone. Our corrupt

Police Commissioner and Police Captain are under indictment and had to resign. Until a replacement is named, new Police Chief, H.T. Franks, will be wearing two hats. He's an upright fellow, and he's making certain that the police are out on the streets and doing their jobs."

"I know H.T. Franks. We go back a long ways. With him as police chief, he'll make a great ally when you go after D'Quad. Funny you mentioned him. I got in touch with him this morning to let him know this is now a federal investigation. He said he would give you anything you require."

"Great," Eric said, "do you have any idea when another contraband shipment is arriving at the Warehouse?"

"Yes, we were tipped off. The Coast Guard expects an offshore delivery on the twenty-ninth, by night. They will make sure *The Eclipse* makes it through. Once it gets to the Warehouse, two Coast Guard cutters will stop the *Eclipse* if it tries to escape. The rest is up to you. I know you will use your best judgement."

"I'll get with Police Chief Franks, so we can coordinate our plans."

"I hope you can wrap this up soon. We've been having trouble shutting down a smuggling operation in Baton Rouge. Assuming you wrap this up by New Year's Day, I want you to head up there immediately."

Eric was taken aback by his upcoming assignment. His mind swam with images of Desiree; the sound of her voice, the touch of her hand, her smile, her hypnotic eyes. He had said nothing to her about his feelings, and now his time was almost up. A sense of longing and despair left him speechless.

"Eric, are you there?"

"Yes," Eric stammered and cleared his throat. "I'm sorry, my mind was drifting. Any other info on your end?"

"Yes. With the new wiretaps we've gotten permission to install through the phone company, we're monitoring the calls to and from D'Quad's offices, home and the Kaboom Saloon. I'm hoping we can identify the powerful ally who D'Quad is talking to over the phone. We don't know how many men this ally has, or what his role might be in moving the booze into the Quarter. A criminal alliance could turn this whole affair into a blood bath. If I get any new information, I'll contact you immediately and vice versa."

"Will do. I've got my gang of locals putting out feelers, and we're all watching D'Quad's every move. Hopefully, I'll have something for you soon."

"For that information, feel free to call on Christmas—It would be a gift."

"It would be a gift for us all," Eric agreed. "Give my regards to your family, Jim"

"Sure will Eric. Relax and have some fun over the holidays. You deserve it."

****

With the swirl of chaos and catastrophe they had been swept into, Zoey and Desiree had been oblivious to the passage of time. It was already Christmas week, and the eerie inactivity of D'Quad's gang filled them with a sense of dread. The Midnight Shadows watched, waited, and worried. As predictable as D'Quad had been, he was not even making his monthly hits to extort protection money. His only activity was to move product from the Carriage House. Fishbowl made nightly runs to D'Quad's dock down the river. He found nothing but silence and darkness. It all seemed like some human chess match, each side poised for the checkmate, each one certain they'd win— especially D'Quad. For now, he would sit tight.

"What the hell do you mean that the Import-Export ledgers were taken by the Midnight Shadows?" T.M. screamed.

D'Quad looked at him with scorn. "What did you think they took from here? The files and the money were all over the floor. I assumed you could put one and one together."

"Yeah, that makes two," T.M. replied angrily. "I hope that 'two' doesn't mean that someone robbed the jewelry store and took those ledgers too."

"Well," D'Quad replied, "as a matter of fact, they were stolen too, and the only ones who could have stolen those ledgers were one of the clerks. Our boys took care of all of them—Dead men tell no tales."

"Did those guys confess to stealing the ledgers, or where they went?"

"They pleaded for their lives. They said they didn't steal anything or know who might have done it, but we didn't believe them."

"Well, that's just great." Digger sneered. "Those ledgers are still out there and could put all of us in jail."

"And, why didn't you tell us about the ledgers being taken?"

"Because you didn't need to know at the time." D'Quad's angry eyes scanned the faces of each of his most trusted confidantes. "Don't forget," he screamed, "you don't run the show. Before you met me, you were two-bit gangsters running from the law. Got it?"

Both men were seething but held their tongues.

"Besides," Louis said with a satisfied smile. "The papers haven't printed anything from the ledgers, so they didn't get the ledgers. Our disgustedly honest police chief, Captain Franks, hasn't busted us either, so they don't have the ledgers—So where did they go? To Victoria's. She was the one who ratted us out. Victoria was just itching to give those ledgers to the authorities and the *Nitpicker*. But she hesitated, for fear we might catch her. But we surprised her! We didn't catch her," he laughed. "We killed her."

"Fine," T.M. said angrily. "The ledgers burned up with her, we get all that crap. So, what's next? When are we going to get that big Christmas present you promised. When are we going to kill them all, once and for good."

D'Quad smiled at his second in command and said, "Unfortunately, your present has been delayed until after Christmas, December 29th to be exact. That is the the night my foolproof plan goes into action. You have my good word, and my promise as a gentleman."

"Well, Mr. Gentleman," T.M. said as he got up to leave," you'd better keep that promise. Because I'm promising that if you don't keep your word," T.M. said, poking D'Quad in the chest, "I'll take you down any way I can. Ya got that ... Boss?"

****

The following morning, Eric got dressed, hopped in his car and drove downtown. As soon as he entered the station, Police Chief, H.T. Franks, was there to greet him. "It is a pleasure to meet you, Eric. Let's step into my office and talk."

"Lead the way."

Chief Franks closed the door behind them and motioned for Eric to sit down. H.T. Franks gave Eric a broad smile."So, Mr. Strand. You are a top federal agent and a talented photographer. I would have never guessed."

"I'm glad to hear that. Photographer is a rewarding cover. Working for the *Nitpicker* has given me first hand access to news in the Quarter."

"Agent Jim Hope called me yesterday. Since this is now a federal case, I am here to facilitate whatever you require. What do you have in mind?

"A simultaneous operation on the 29th. According to our sources, the *Eclipse* is due to bring up the contraband to a Warehouse down past Chalmette."

"There have been rumors of a Warehouse down there. But after some investigating, we found nothing."

"A friend of mine who skippers a ship on the Mississippi, spotted it a while back."

"Could this be Fishbowl and his ship, the *Goldfish*?"

Eric nodded.

"He is one helluva river man. You couldn't have chosen anyone more reliable and more skilled."

"Fishbowl took me down to reconnoiter the Warehouse. There are good places to put ashore, so we will access the Warehouse by water. The night of the 29th, the Coast Guard will allow the *Eclipse* to enter the river. The Coast Guard cutters will shadow it. They will send you a message, ship to shore, when the *Eclipse* has reached the dock and is preparing to unload. When you get that message, you are to raid the Carriage House and take down D'Quad's men."

"I'll get all the necessary warrants. How about you? Need any warm bodies?"

"I need a contingent of police officers to blockade Warehouse Road and assist me in making arrests." Eric handed Chief Franks a map. "This is the location of Warehouse Road. We will hit the Warehouse the same time you leave for your raid on the Carriage House. But we will need a signal from you."

"We will flash a few considerably bright searchlights into the sky."

"What happens if it's too cloudy to see those searchlights?"

H.T. laughed. "This is New Orleans, Eric. We know how to throw a party. We'll set off fireworks, if we have to! Anything else?"

"That night, we will need a second signal to let us know when you have taken the Carriage House."

"Done."

"I've got two things you need to know," Eric said firmly. "First, Kongo and Diego Kaminga and the Street Sweepers are my allies in this raid on the Warehouse. If you've got a problem with that …"

H.T. smiled broadly. "Ah, Kongo and Diego. I have known them since I was a kid. Great guys. True gentlemen. In a situation like this, if you're asking me to look the other way, you don't have to. Truth of the matter is, there would be no Street Sweepers, if there was no D'Quad."

"There is another matter that complicates the whole operation. The agency has a wiretap to monitor D'Quad's calls. The agency thinks the guy on the other end of the line is a very powerful friend and ally of D'Quad's. Any idea who it might be?"

H.T. leaned back in his chair, looked up at the ceiling and whistled. "An alliance… that puts a whole other spin on this case. I cannot imagine who that could be."

"That's the wild card. We know when and where to hit the Warehouse and the Carriage House, but we don't know what D'Quad and his ally might have in the works ... or where they will be."

"Assuming the *Eclipse* is blocked in by the Coast Guard, and we are successful at the Carriage House, D'Quad's alliance will look for an escape scenario."

"You know his gang better than I do. Where are they most likely to go?"

"My best guess is they'll try to access the docks to escape."

"I agree, but it's not safe to speculate."

H.T. smiled. "So, Eric, I suppose you are going to tell me that if anything goes wrong, we'll just have to wing it."

"Just like all police work."

"Ain't it so."

Eric rose to leave. "This needs to be our last meeting. We don't want to arouse any suspicions."

H.T. nodded, stood up and shook Eric's hand firmly. "See you on the twenty-ninth ... after my fireworks show."

CHAPTER TWENTY-FIVE

It is a truly rare sight to see in New Orleans, but Christmas day dawned with a light but steady snow. The marshmallow sky was streaked with dark gray. The clouds hung heavy and low. The temperature had fallen below freezing. Early in the day, the gloom and doom of the past week was temporarily forgotten. The sisters lounged around their cozy home, reveling in the joy of Christmas. They exchanged presents with the many dear friends who stopped by. They danced to the music blasting out of the radio. They basked in the glow of a warm fire and shimmering lights on their Christmas tree. As the French Quarter's sky turned from gray to black, the sisters made careful preparations for Kongo's much needed party. They took extra time and care getting ready. Each checked the other's flawless makeup, hair, dress, shoes and accessories. Both put on long cashmere overcoats, Zoey in winter white and Desiree in black. Matching knitted cloche hats and scarves were held tightly, as the sisters parked their car, stepped out into the cold, and mince-stepped across the street and into Kongo's place. Diego greeted them with an overjoyed smile, and with a sweeping gesture, waved them inside.

"My most precious senoritas, Merry Christmas!" Diego cried, as he gave each of them a warm and lingering embrace. After the sisters removed their coats, Diego whispered, " You have the faces and bodies of angels, but they bring out the devil in me. Please, save my soul and give me a spin!"

The girls just shook their heads and laughed at Diego's

predictability. They both broke into a slow twirl, holding the edges of their dresses, all the while smiling with sultry eyes.

"Oh, I have just seen heaven!" Diego sighed.

"Have you seen a table?" Zoey asked sarcastically.

" Ah, always my spitfire of desire!"

"Desiree's the "desire one. ' What I desire is to sit down!"

"Your wish is my desire, and your desire is my wish," Diego said with a come hither smile. He led the ladies to the head table. Kongo was already there, surrounded by family and friends. They all cheered when they spotted the girls.

"Welcome, welcome. Merry Christmas!" Kongo cried. He rose, picked up both girls at once and gave each a kiss on the cheek.

Moments later, Eric arrived and exchanged warm greetings with Kongo and Diego. Eric embraced Zoey, then turned to Desiree. Sheer terror shot through Eric's stomach. He was praying his feelings for her would not show through. Eric reached out, took Desiree by the hands and pulled her toward him. She did not resist. Eric held her in a lingering embrace. When Eric finally let her go, there were a few awkward moments of silence. Eric was mortified that his feelings for Desiree had been exposed for all to see. Desiree was in a panic. For the first time, she realized that Zoey had been right. She could feel it when they embraced. Eric wanted far more than a friendship. Desiree rebounded quickly.

"Ah, Mr. Strand," she said with a playful smile and batting eyes. "You do expect a lot of embrace from a girl, though I must say you are a delightful embracer."

Eric had regained his composure, somewhat. "I hope you'll remember you called me a 'delightful embracer,'" he blurted out.

"Touché, Mr. Strand! Now, how could I ever forget that?" she replied with a nervous smile.

Each sat down, shaken by what had transpired. Zoey had watched the whole nerve-wracking scene. She was not going to allow a bad start to turn into a bad evening. "Hey, you two, isn't this place decorated beautifully?"

Zoey's momentary distraction worked like a charm. A sense of wonder and warmth came over them. Couples crowded the small dance floor, dressed in their holiday best. A huge Christmas tree bathed the room in flashes of green, red and gold. Tinsel sparkled like the finest silver. Fragrant evergreen garlands lined the perimeter of the walls. Mistletoe was strategically hung from the ceiling. Embarrassed patrons, who inadvertently wandered under it, laughed nervously and surrendered to the inevitable kiss. The radio filled the air with the sounds of Christmas. Servers hopped from table to table with trays of food and endless rounds of drinks. Family and friends, even strangers, were all treated the same; as if they were the most important person in Kongo's life. Diego flitted from table to table, entertaining his guests with his wit and charm, but always keeping one eye trained on Zoey. Occasionally, Zoey felt as if someone was watching her. She looked around, and sure enough, someone was. Diego smiled mischievously as he walked towards her.

"My sensuous goddess of beauty!" he cried. "Come, let us be close in body. Let us greet Christmas with a dance of love, my one and only."

Zoey looked up at Diego. She couldn't help but smile at this romantic rogue. "I will dance with you on one condition. That you stop calling me your 'one and only.'"

"Of course, my love! But you will think differently when our passion and pulses rise."

Desiree's pulse was already rising. "When Zoey gets up to dance," she thought, "I will be left alone with Eric." Desiree's mind worked feverishly. "Well," she said," I'm getting antsy in here. While you hopeless flirts do your dance of love, I think I'll get some air."

"But it's dark and freezing out there!" Zoey replied as Diego took her hand.

"You needn't worry. I won't go far."

"Well … okay," Zoey called over her shoulder, as Diego dragged her to the dance floor."

"It's not okay with me," Eric stated. "It's dangerous out there. We don't know where or when D'Quad's gang will come after us."

"I'm armed," Desiree replied, as she put on her coat and headed for the door.

Eric was frustrated with her, but knew that Desiree only took orders when it suited her. "Alright, you win! Nothing will stop you from taking your walk, but nothing will stop me from coming along!"

Desiree stepped out into the bracing cold. The snow had covered the sidewalk and street. "Great, this is just great," she muttered to herself. "I came out here to get away from Eric. If I was wearing my Midnight Shadow boots, I could outrun him. But in these shoes, even walking is dangerous."—Desiree was right. As she stomped down the steps, she slipped. Eric stepped behind her, and when he tried to catch her, he fell too. Desiree landed right in his lap.

"Aren't you going to say, 'I told you so?'" Desiree asked.

"No. Before you fell, I was going to say I'm sorry for being so overprotective of you. But now that you mention it ..." Eric paused and couldn't help himself—He started to laugh.

Then Desiree broke into hysterical laughter too. "I hate these shoes. They're going to get me killed. Please, help me up."

Eric pushed her up, and when he made it to his feet, Desiree wrapped her arm through his, and they carefully made their way down the sidewalk.

"Seriously Desiree," Eric said, "I do owe you an apology. I know that I upset you with my overbearing behavior at the Carriage House, and again tonight. I am sorry. You are the smartest, most competent, brave person that I know. Heck, you saved my life."

Desiree blushed. "Thank you, Eric. Our mother raised Zoey and me to be strong and independent. Our father was a wonderful man, but after he passed away, Mother took over his clothing business and made it more successful than ever." Desiree paused, as she wiped snowflakes from her eyelashes and tugged her hat over her hair. "As I told you when we first met, Mother insisted that we were well educated and well read. We had lessons in everything from dance and acting to self defense and firearms."

"You must miss her, especially at this time of year." Eric took off his scarf, turned Desiree to face him and wrapped it around her neck. "Oh no, I'm doing it again, being overprotective."

"Oh, I have no problem with you giving me more protection from the cold. I have never seen snow in New Orleans—This is unique and wonderful." Desiree wrapped the scarf more tightly. "To answer your question, we do miss our mother. We would have gone home for Christmas, but felt we should stay, considering everything that's going on here. We hope to get out of here for a while after everything in the Quarter calms down. Who knows? Maybe we'll see her next Christmas. How about you Eric? What's your family like?"

"Well, now it's just me, my mom and my sister. Dad was a great detective. Even when I was little, he brought home his evidence files, and I helped him solve cases." Eric smiled wistfully. "There was never any doubt that I would become a detective. When I was a teenager, my father got sick and passed away. He made me promise to be the man of the family and take care of my mother and sister. I guess that's where I get my overprotective nature towards you and Zoey."

"That's sweet Eric. Don't think that we don't appreciate that you care."

"In this business, I've tried not to get too close to anyone. It's dangerous, and I have to move from place to place so much, I don't have the pleasure of many long term relationships.... But Desiree, I guess now is the time to fess up. I have tried not to fall for you ... but I have. I have to leave for a new assignment in Baton Rouge on January first, and it breaks my heart to leave you. I want to have you in my life. Come with me."

They had been so involved in conversation that they had lost track of time. They had walked all the way to Jackson Square. Desiree took Eric by the arm and led him to a covered gazebo. She turned, took him by both hands and said, "Eric, I'm too young and have too many plans to be in a serious relationship. You're too busy with your career to be in a serious relationship, so we're really in the same place. I think you know that I have feelings for you ... and I do want you in my life, as much as possible. Baton Rouge isn't that far away, so I'm sure we can still see each other once in a while."

Eric pulled Desiree close, and as their eyes met, he lowered his head towards her for a kiss ...

"Eric, Desiree!" Zoey yelled, from across the Plaza.

Startled, Desiree and Eric quickly pulled away from each other. When they turned, they saw Zoey and Diego approaching.

"What timing! Let's get them!" Desiree laughed, as she started making snowballs and lining them up on the gazebo rail.

Eric joined in the fun. As Zoey and Diego got closer he whispered, "Wait, wait, wait"— "Fire!" he yelled, and their armed assault began.

Zoey and Diego were unarmed and pelted by the attack. In retaliation, they gathered armloads of snow, ran up and threw it all over Desiree and Eric.

After Zoey had rubbed a handful of snow in Desiree's face, Desiree surrendered, but did manage to smash one last snowball into Zoey's hair.

Diego laughed and said, "This is some thanks we get for coming out in the cold to find you."

"I didn't know we were lost," Desiree quipped back.

"For New Orleans, this is a blizzard," Diego exclaimed. "We thought you might have frozen to death."

"Seriously," Zoey said, "people are starting to leave, and Kongo was looking for you."

Desiree shivered and nodded her head repeatedly. "Okay, let's go. I'm wet and freezing."

When they returned to Kongo's, he was waiting for them. "There you are! I thought you had all run away."

"No!" Zoey removed her hat and shook out her wet hair. "Diego and I were just delayed by a nasty snowball attack."

Diego took a towel and helped her dry her hair, while Eric and Desiree huddled by the heater.

Kongo laughed. "I wish I had been there. This Christmas snow is a delightful surprise, but I have an even better surprise for you, Zoey and Desiree."

"Surprise," Zoey giggled. "We love surprises!"

"Wonderful," Kongo nodded. "Eric and Diego, I need for you to stay here and keep the music blaring and the lights on bright. Zoey and Desiree, follow me."

Kongo had parked his car just outside. "Okay, be silent, get in the back and lie down," he said.

"Why, are we being abducted?" Desiree whispered.

Kongo poked her in the forehead and put his finger to his lips to shush her. After a short and winding ride on the silent back streets, Kongo parked the car, opened the door and hustled the girls into a small, white house. When they entered, it was dark; then suddenly the lights came on. They were greeted with a familiar voice shouting, "Surprise!"

Zoey and Desiree blinked, and there on the sofa, looking more beautiful than ever, was Victoria. Zoey and Desiree shrieked with joy and ran to their dear friend, crushing her with hugs.

"Oh Kongo!" Desiree cried. "Thank you, thank you for abducting us!"

"Thank you for the best Christmas present ever," Zoey said, as she wiped a tear from her cheek.

Kongo beamed. "You are most welcome. I want you girls to have a wonderful time together, but I can't stay. I'm going back to my house to talk to Eric and Diego. I'll be back in an hour to pick you up, so have fun! Merry Christmas, my loves!"

CHAPTER TWENTY-SIX

In the days following Christmas, it was back to work for everyone in the Quarter. Zoey and Desiree had columns to write, while Eric worked to coordinate all aspects of the upcoming raids, continue surveillance of D'Quad's operations and develop photographs for the newspaper. A sense of calm and Christmas joy remained among the residents, as they strolled down the busy streets.

Eric's suspicions compelled him to make a last ditch effort to find out who D'Quad's ally was. Something in his gut told him that Madame Ravonjay might know something about his identity. As he paced his attic room on the morning of the raid, he realized he had the perfect excuse for making a visit to Madame Ravonjay; the photograph he had promised to give her.

Eric arrived on her doorstep with the photo in hand and a smile on his face, as he knocked on the door.

Madame Ravonjay opened the door and greeted him warmly. "Why, Mr. Strand, it's so nice to see you. Please come in. How was your Christmas?"

"Oh, it was beautiful. I couldn't believe the snow. I didn't know that it was even possible to have a white Christmas in New Orleans. Even though it was short-lived, it made the day special, and I was able to get some great photographs for the paper. Speaking of photographs, that's why I'm here. I had promised you this one," Eric said, as he presented the framed photograph to her.

"Thank you so much!" Please, let's sit down so I can look at it."

Madame Ravonjay took a seat in her high-backed, cobra cane chair, and Eric sat across the table from her. As she studied the photo, he looked around the room at the attractive decor, and the shelves of herbs stored in colored jars and wooden boxes. One thing he couldn't ignore was that all around the chair where he was seated, several toothpicks with chewed ends were scattered on the rug. Pretending to scratch his leg, he quickly picked one up and slipped it into his pocket. "There is no doubt in my mind," he thought, "that Ravonjay is in cahoots with D'Quad. Those juju charms his gang puts on the doors help put money in her pocket."

"My sweet girls," Ravonjay said, as she studied the photo. "Oh, and my dear Victoria. There has been no word from the police, and I am so worried about her. I have hardly slept since that horrible bombing."

"I took photos the next day, but the structure was so dangerous, I wasn't allowed to go into it."

"At least I have my prayers and this photograph," she said in a soft voice. "Thank you. This is a special gift that I will treasure."

As Eric rose from his chair, he noticed more chewed toothpicks in and around the trash can near the table. "Well, I have a photo assignment, so I have to run."

"You're so thoughtful to have remembered me." Madame Ravonjay rose from her chair and handed him a gris-gris bag on a leather cord. "A little something from me for your protection."

"Thank you," Eric smiled as he took the bag and headed for the door. "Hope you have a wonderful new year," he added, before stepping outside. Walking down the street to his car, he noticed a slight tingling in his fingers. He dropped the gris-gris bag in the first sewer vent he passed, and upon reaching his car, washed his hands with a bottle of lens cleaner from his camera case. "Better safe then sorry," he said to himself.

Eric's next stop was to talk to Fishbowl. When he entered the shop, Fishbowl greeted him with a huge smile. "Eric, so good to see you. Come on into my office and let's talk for a few minutes."

Fishbowl closed the door and began. "Since I seen you last, I been keepin' an eye on ole D'Quad. Somethin' is up, because late last night when I was out walkin', I seen him park on a side street; then start walkin' towards Ravonjay's place. I hid out of sight and waited. About forty-five minutes later, he came back to his car and zoomed away."

Eric laughed. "You're some detective, Fishbowl. I think I should hire you as my assistant." He removed the toothpick from his pocket and showed it to Fishbowl. "I just stopped by to give Madame Ravonjay a photograph that I had promised her, and I found chewed toothpicks scattered all over her rug."

Fishbowl clapped his hands in delight. "I swear that D'Quad's half beaver. Always a trail of those darned toothpicks wherever he goes. It looks like he got somethin' goin' with Ravonjay."

Eric nodded. "Have you got the ship outfitted and ready to take us downriver?"

"Sure have, and here's the key to the cabin and the hold. You can put any equipment you need to have aboard in there."

"Thank you so much!" Eric rose and gave Fishbowl a warm handshake.

"See you soon," Fishbowl grinned and saluted, as Eric walked out the door.

****

As the weeks in the safe house passed, Victoria began to go stir crazy. Each day, as light gave way to night, she became more and more frantic. Each time Kongo and Diego came to visit, she pleaded with them to let her go outside, to take a walk, to go anywhere. Each time the brothers gave her an uncompromising, "No." This afternoon was different. As soon as the Kamingas arrived, Kongo assured her, "The time to reenter the real world has come. Tonight, we take down D'Quad's gang, once and for all … and," Kongo smiled, "we knew we couldn't keep you out of the fight."

Kongo told Victoria that Eric was an undercover federal agent and explained his plan in detail. Victoria listened carefully, but her concerns were elsewhere. As soon as the Kamingas left, Victoria sprang into action. She had to call Andre. She dialed and dialed—No answer.

"Please, please, please pick up!"

She was finally rewarded with a harried hello.

"Come right away, there's big trouble brewing!" Victoria cried.

"I'm glad you caught me. I was just about to leave on a matter of great urgency. Are you still in the safe house?"

"Yes, and hurry," she pleaded.

When Andre arrived, the dear friends shared a long and lingering embrace.

Victoria told Andre about the Street Sweepers alliance with the police and Federal Agent, Eric Strand, and their plan to raid the Carriage House and Warehouse tonight. "If you stay with D'Quad, you could be killed by your own friends. And if D'Quad finds out you're a spy, he'll kill you!"

"You could be killed too."

"How so?"

Andre frowned. "About a half hour ago, I overheard D'Quad, T.M. and Digger in a heated conversation about instructions from the Big Boss. Turns out, D'Quad is not the head honcho. Hard as it is to believe, they all said the Big Boss is Madame Ravonjay."

Victoria backed away from Andre and put her hands to her cheeks. Her shock left her speechless.

"There is no time for you to be surprised. Madame Ravonjay knows of your close ties to Zoey and Desiree. She believes you are the person who tipped them off about her gang's operations —Thus, the hit on your place. Ravonjay believes you are dead. As long as she continues to believe that, you will be safe. But with you out of the way, the Daniels sisters are her next two targets."

"Oh, my Lord! Zoey and Desiree have been talking about going to see Madame Ravonjay. I've got to go and warn them!"

"I was on my way to warn Kongo, so I've got to go right now."

Victoria nodded, a manic look in her eyes.

"Be careful," Andre whispered, as they shared a hurried embrace.

As Andre sped off, Victoria ran out to the hidden garage behind the house, jumped into her car and hurried across town. Ominous wisps of fog danced in her headlights. Wet steam spiraled out of the pavement. She eased into a spot in front of the Daniels' home. Victoria's worst fears were realized. The Daniels sisters' car was gone. "But the lights are on inside. Maybe one of them is at home." She rushed into the courtyard. A small lamp illuminated the doorway. Victoria pounded on the door. There was no answer. She turned to leave and spotted something. It was a nail hole in the doorframe with a strand of woven yarn stuck in it.

"This is the same kind of yarn Madame uses on her charms."

Then Victoria looked down. There was the nail that had dropped out of the hole, along with a longer piece of woven yarn. Victoria bent down and picked it up. Next to it was a dove's feather and white fur."

"Oh, Santa Maria," she cried. "This is part of a juju charm. The sisters must have seen it and headed over to Ravonjay's for protection!"

As she gunned the car and lurched it into gear, she did not know that death was only a few hours away.

****

While Victoria's afternoon unfolded, Eric returned home to gather equipment for the night's raid. His plans were suddenly thrown into chaos by a call from Chief Jim Hope that hit like a sledgehammer. The bugged phones had struck pay dirt. Eric's suspicions were more than confirmed. Madame Ravonjay was, not only in cahoots with D'Quad, she was the Big Boss. He had to risk a meeting with the police chief … and with Kongo and Diego.

A surprised H.T. Franks ushered Eric into his office and closed the door behind them.

"I had no choice but to come see you in person," Eric began. "We are going to have to modify our plan for tonight. The agency called, and the bugs on the phones struck gold this morning. It turns out that D'Quad is not the gang boss. The Big Boss is Madame Ravonjay."

"The saint turns out to be the sinner," the veteran policeman chuckled.

Eric nodded. "We can't risk arresting Ravonjay before we move on the Carriage House. If we do, and D'Quad finds out, he'll ship to shore the *Eclipse* and call off the delivery to the Warehouse."

"My thoughts exactly. But don't worry. We'll cast a wide enough net to trap her and her lieutenants, after we raid the Carriage House."

Eric nodded. "Assuming Ravonjay has an elite guard, along with whatever men escape from the Carriage House or Warehouse, I want you to cut off the streets that border Jackson Square and lead down to the docks."

"No problem. With the roads blocked, they will have to try to escape on foot and down through the Square."

"Exactly. And me and the Street Sweepers will be waiting for them."

After Eric went over some street maps with the Chief, he rushed over to Kongo's Place.

"I have news." Eric said.

"Just minutes ago, mi amigo, I believe we received the same news." Kongo told Eric about Andre's message.

"Perfect," Eric replied. The two friends went over the modified plans for the night.

"Do the Daniels sisters know about Madame Ravonjay?" Eric asked.

"Andre told us Victoria was on her way to their house to warn them."

"That's good news," Eric said with a frown. "I hope they will remain there and safe."

Kongo gave Eric a sad smile. "That is my hope too."

The Midnight Shadows would demolish both their hopes in a pillar of fire.

****

Zoey and Desiree's day paralleled those of their friends. It had been a long and sleepless night, finishing their columns and dreading what danger might await them at the Warehouse. Dawn was humid, and the sky was torn by jagged clouds. A fine drizzle tickled the windows. After they exchanged two weary, "Good mornings," Zoey said, "We've got to deliver our columns to the *Nitpicker* no later than four this afternoon."

"Fine," Desiree yawned. "But I'm exhausted, and I'm not going anywhere until three."

Their breakfast was yesterday's coffee and some stale beignets. Then Zoey curled up in an overstuffed chair, and Desiree flopped on the couch. Desiree slept soundly. Zoey catnapped. Each time the clock chimed, it awakened her. She kept count of the passing hours. At three o'clock, she woke up Desiree.

"Time to get ready," she whispered.

Desiree sat up, stretched, yawned and nodded.

They sleepwalked their way into their rooms. Their fashionable outfits seemed to call to them from dresser drawers and closets. Brushes turned into wizard wands, as their makeup magically appeared. They cruised over to the *Nitpicker* offices, dropped off their columns, then made their way back home. They tiptoed down the driveway and peeked into the courtyard, not knowing what to expect. They saw nothing.

"Whew," Desiree said, "I thought one of D'Quad's assassins would be waiting for us."

"They're all too busy making preparations for the big haul at the Warehouse."

"Oh, no!" Desiree cried.

"Shhh," Zoey growled. "The whole neighborhood can hear you!"

Desiree pointed. Zoey approached the door frame and pulled a small object off a nail. "Oh, good grief," she whispered in shock. "It's a juju charm!"

" Oh, my God! It's gruesome!"

"The head of a dove," Zoey said with disgust, "and the head of a rabbit ..."

"... eyeless and mutilated."

"We have got to go to Madame Ravonjay, now!"

As the sisters drove, Zoey said, "We know D'Quad put that juju charm on our door. He must know that each time we get one, we go to Madame Ravonjay. We can't park the car in front of her house. This could be a trap."

A half a block away from Ravonjay's house, Zoey eased into a parking spot. As the sisters got out of the car, three black cars pulled into spots in front of them. They immediately recognized D'Quad's goons.

"Pretend you don't see them," Desiree whispered. "Let's just sashay over to Madame Ravonjay's, like we don't have a care in the world. We'll be safe once we get inside."

As they walked, Zoey and Desiree took a quick look over their shoulders. They saw D'Quad's boys gathered around their car.

"Well." Desiree said. "It looks like Louis the 19th wants to make certain we have no way of escaping."

The sisters walked up the steps to Madame Ravonjay's house. The stained glass windows flashed in the sinking sun. It matched the girls' sinking feeling. As always, the door was open. The girls stepped inside.

"Hello, my innocent flowers, come over here and sit down!" After the sisters joined her, she asked, " To what do I owe this pleasure? Another juju charm?"

"Yes," Zoey replied. "We assume they are coming from D'Quad. But it had your yarn design. I'm confused because ... um ..."

"... On Thanksgiving, we saw you out back by the loading platform giving a charm to one of D'Quad's men. Why?"

Ravonjay chuckled. "Just as you have come to me for

protection, many of D'Quad's business associates come to me, uncertain about their futures. Please, show your charm to me."

Zoey took the charm out of her purse and handed it to her. Ravonjay studied it for some time, stroking the mutilated heads.

"What can this possibly mean?"

Ravonjay smiled. "My Tarot cards will tell you all you need to know." She shuffled the deck and drew three marked cards. She gave one to each sister and one for herself. "You first, Zoey, turn over your card."

Zoey turned it over. "What does the Moon signify?"

Ravonjay's expressionless gaze held Zoey's eyes. "Something in your life is not what it seems. Your intuition can't see though the subterfuge. Your past is turned away by present perceptions."

"I don't get it. What does that mean?"

Madame did not answer. "'Desiree, turn over your card."

"The Tower?"

"Something terrible is going to happen to you, and those you love. It could be disastrous, unless ..." Ravonjay sneered, "unless you have the bravery to face it and end it once and for all."

"I'd be willing to die for those I love."

Ravonjay gave Desiree a savage smile. "Prophetic words, my child." Madame leaned forward in her chair. She pushed her card over to the sisters. "Turn it over, Zoey."

"The Devil," Zoey whispered. "What the heck?"

"The Devil is a master of entrapment. He fills his prey with fear, doubt and temptation. He is the spinner of spiderwebs and lies. Inevitably, his prey is trapped. The devil is an evil clairvoyant, who knows the victim's inevitable end."

"And who is this devil?"

"The devil is the Big Boss," she laughed. "And I am ... surprise, surprise, The Big Boss of D'Quad's gang!"

Both sisters were flabbergasted. "Is this some kind of joke?" Zoey asked.

"Only on you."

"Then it was you that ..."

"Are you so ignorant that you thought D'Quad was smart enough to run a gang? Your columns alone have chronicled his inept attempts at carrying out my plans. I was the one who had Digger put those juju charms on the establishments after the hits. I knew people would believe those unfortunate fools were harmed because they did not seek my protection."

Zoey and Desiree stared at her in disbelief. "How could you do all this, after you have done so much for the poor … all the people in need?"

"Doing those things made me look like a saint, so I could gradually take over the Quarter. All my wonderful charms and gris-gris bags were money makers for me. I provided the fear, and then they paid me for protection. But not you two," she leered. "I have always given you my services for free. And sure enough, my little door prize has brought you here again."

There was no fear when Zoey asked, "So, now that we know you're the Big Boss … what now?"

"The Big Boss is the least of your problems!" she cried. Ravonjay shook her head in disgust. "You would not know the real danger, if it was staring you right in the face."

A chilling apprehension flowed over the sisters.

"Speaking of staring you right in the face," Ravonjay cried madly. "It is!"

"What … what do you mean?" Desiree stammered.

Ravonjay leaned back in her chair. A sigh of satisfaction oozed out of her. "Don't you recognize an old friend, when you see one?"

"Of course," Zoey replied with some relief. "You have always been our oldest and dearest friend."

"No, no," Madame replied impatiently," an old friend who was far younger, when you first met."

"I'm not following you." Zoey said.

Madame took a piece of paper, wrote something on it and slid it over to Desiree. "Read it aloud."

"Revanj'?"

"Is this French?" Zoey asked.

"Haitian Creole," Ravonjay replied. "I spell my name phonetically, so I can protect my identity."

"Protect your identity? Why?" Desiree asked.

"I had been on the run from the police for major crimes I committed. So when I came to New Orleans, I needed a new identity, an alias, if you will. The fake name you know me by is pronounced Ray- von - jay, but the Creole name I chose as an alias is spelled, 'Revanj,' and, of course, pronounced differently. Madame studied the girls intently. "Can you guess what it means?"

"Revenge?" Zoey asked.

"Perfect!" Madame smiled. "Revenge."

"Revenge on whom?"

Madame leaned back in her chair with an arrogant look of strained patience. "Many, many years ago, I was betrayed and robbed by persons whose names," she sneered, "you may recognize—They left me for dead." She paused, savoring the moment. "All these years, I've spent my time, trying to find out about the foreigners who betrayed me and robbed me. I knew they were from another place, and different from anyone I had ever met. I came to understand who they were, and where they really came from." Ravonjay paused and smiled. "As I told you many years ago, we lead many lives. We meet many people in each of our lives, some with whom we have unfinished business. The karmic wheel turns, and in the wink of an eye, they meet again."

"What do you mean, you told us many years ago about past lives? When did you say that?" Zoey shook her head. "Why are you telling us any of this, anyway?"

Ravonjay ignored her question. "After I was almost killed, I was blessed with the gift of clairvoyance. For years, I have known that I would meet this pair of murderers again—So, I have waited, patiently."

Zoey rubbed her hands together nervously. A look of uncertain fear filled Desiree's face.

"I recall that when you first came to me, I used psychometry

… holding your hands and your jewelry and absorbing your essence. Do you remember?"

"Yes," Zoey replied.

"And what did I tell you of yourselves?"

"Intimate details of our entire lives …"

"You even described our childhood home, and the town we were from," Desiree added.

Rayvonjay nodded. "Yes," she said. "What I did not tell you is that I saw far more. I saw two houses that you lived in when you were young girls."

"That's not true," Zoey stated

"She's right. We were born and raised in the same house."

"Oh, really?" Madame said with manic glee. "I saw a second house. I saw a winding driveway that led up to a lavender Victorian House with window boxes and flowers. It overlooked an impressive seaport city …. Tabula Rasa it's called, I believe."

Both sisters felt nauseous and dizzy, reeling from Ravonjay's revelations.

"Oh my dear Zoey! Oh, my dear Desiree!" Ravonjay cried. "Or should I call you Mandy and Lizzy?" She broke into psychotic laughter. "I told you, I have learned the secrets of the many lives we lead."

With the mention of their names, Mandy and Lizzy's consciousness buried that of Zoey and Desiree. The sisters braced themselves for the worst.

"As for me, I think you have already guessed who I am." Ravonjay's 'raspy Creole accent disappeared. The terrifying voice made it impossible to deny.

"You were … Queen Ant LaRouge."

"No, my dear children, I *am* Queen Ant LaRouge…. I survived that little cave in you caused. Badly scarred and broken … but I survived." LaRouge laughed. "Have I aged well? I think not. Look at the scars and mangled bones on my face." She took a scarf and wiped off layer upon layer of make up. Then she removed her tignon and revealed a heavily scarred, bulb shaped skull. As she fastened her tignon back in place, Ravonjay railed, "You did this to me! You! But now I have the opportunity to undo what you have done and stop you from getting the Crystal Heart. If I kill you during this lifetime, your next lifetime will not happen … History will change and your next life will not be as Mandy and Lizzy. There will be nothing that can stop me from getting the Crystal Heart … and I suspect," she sneered, as her snake-like eyes bored into the sisters, "that Flora and Dora can perform the same service that you were supposed to … unleash the power of the Heart into my hands." There was no sincerity when she said, "I am so pleased that you finally found your way to me … Zoey and Desiree … Flora and Dora, the soon to be snuffed out Mandy and Lizzy," she said angrily, "or whatever you want to call yourselves!"

Queen Ant opened her robes and pulled out a thirty-eight pistol. Lizzy and Mandy were terrified, staring down the barrel of the gun. LaRouge licked her lips, like a hungry predator eying its trapped prey. "By now, my misguided murderers, you must know that I could have ordered D'Quad to kill you at any time, but it is a selfish pleasure that I have waited so long to savor and enjoy."

Knowing they had but one chance to survive, the sisters grabbed the edge of the table and flipped it over, knocking LaRouge from her chair.

"Come back here, you little cowards," she screamed.

The minds of Mandy and Lizzy disappeared in that moment. It was Zoey and Desiree who took flight. Bullets ripped through the table, shattering the glass in the door. It was impossible for them to escape that way. Desiree took a chair and smashed it through the window. Zoey followed her through the shattered frame and shards of glass. Down the street, D'Quad's men stood guarding their car. They were alerted by the gun shots and sound of crashing glass, as the sisters made good their escape.

"They've got our car, Desiree, and they're coming after us!"

"So how are we going to get out of here?" Desiree asked nervously.

Zoey spotted a motorcycle. She ran over to the old Harley and cried, "Oh, thank heavens! The key is in the ignition! Get in the sidecar, and let's get out of here."

Desiree heard the sound of footsteps pounding on the pavement behind her, coming closer and closer. She scrambled into the sidecar just as Zoey revved the engine and hit the gas. Desiree lost her balance and ended up sitting backward in the side car.

Victoria lurched to a stop on the side street next to Ravonjay's house. Gun shots told her she was too late to save her friends. Screeching tires squealed past. Armed men rode on running boards. In the distance, Victoria could see Zoey taking off on a motorcycle with Desiree in the side car. Gun fire chased them, as they sped off down the busy street.

"That old wreck they've just stolen is from World War One! They know they're never going to outrun those cars," Victoria thought. "So, with no means of escaping, they'll look for a place to hide."

Victoria knew this neighborhood well. She reviewed every possible place they could go—Someplace public—Somewhere they would be safe. Victoria put the car in gear, u-turned and roared up the street. "I know where they're going! I'll take the back road so D'Quad's goons won't spot me. I just hope I can get there in time and get them out of this mess."

CHAPTER TWENTY-SEVEN

Zoey leaned into the rushing wind. Desiree, facing backward, struggled to turn around. Her hair whirled and whipped the sides of her face. She couldn't see clearly for a few seconds, but then let out a blood curdling scream.

"What's the matter?" Zoey yelled

"There are three cars coming, and they're gaining on us!"

Bullets whizzed by. Zoey opened the throttle to the limit and feverishly wracked her brain. "I don't know where to go!" she shouted.

"I do! Turn down Pierre Alley and head for the movies! The street's too narrow for their cars to follow."

The bike banked hard to the right, and Zoey's eyes filled with terror. The motorcycle sideswiped a truck that sent the old wreck fishtailing and out of control. The side car broke away. Wobbling on only one tire, the side car hit the curb and flipped forward, launching Desiree into the air. "Oh no!" she screamed in terror, as she flew into a startled pedestrian.

"You infernal idiot," the angry man cried. "What is the rush?"

"I'm going to the movies!" Desiree groaned as she picked herself up off the ground.

The sisters abandoned the wrecked motorcycle and raced down the street.

"The movie theater will be the perfect place to hide out for a while."

Desiree grinned. "No one would imagine that when you're running for your life, you'd go to a movie."

The sisters reached the glittering marquee. The huge overhang was framed in light bulbs that flashed around the film's name, "It," starring Clara Bow.

With tickets bought, Zoey breathed a sigh of relief. "Let's go," she whispered.

Once inside, Desiree groaned, stopped and took off her shoes. "My feet are killing me!"

Zoey nodded and removed hers too. But Desiree was not done. "I hate these clunky heels!"

Zoey laughed as she rubbed one foot over the other, the soft plush carpet easing the pain. "Let's go inside."

Desiree grabbed Zoey's shoulder and whispered. "We don't have our Colts with us. But I have an idea. These heels might be useful after all … as hammers," she said with a devilish smile. "You know what I mean?"

"You bet, I know what you mean. The signal is 'Hammerhead Shark.'"

"I love it," a delighted Desiree replied.

The sisters left the lobby and slipped into the darkness.

"Where should we sit?"

Zoey's eyes found the exits. "In the center row, in the center seats. That way we'll have equidistant access to both emergency doors."

Desiree nodded. They managed to find four seats in the center row. They took the middle two and placed their coats on the seats that bordered them.

"This will look like the seats are taken, and their owners have gone to the powder room."

The film was already on. Desiree giggled and whispered, "Oh, the 'It' Girl, my favorite movie!"

"We should have bought snacks!"

Desiree stifled a laugh.

The sisters tried to focus on the movie but could not. Both were lost in a maze of conflicting thoughts. They did not notice two men bumping their way to the seats behind them. Their reverie was suddenly interrupted. Aware of D'Quad's goons,

Zoey inched closer to Desiree. Both men leaned over the back of the seats that bordered the sisters.

"Well, well, well," one of them whispered. "If it isn't the flighty little Flappers, Zoey and Desiree Daniels. We've been looking for you. The Big Boss requires the pleasure of your company."

"Shhh. I'm trying to watch the movie," Desiree replied.

"Are you telling me to shut up?" he asked in a gruff voice.

"I wouldn't have to tell you anything, if you'd stop talking. But, since you won't stop talking, shut up!"

"You little tramps," the other man growled." I advise you to come along quietly, or else!"

Zoey's eyes flashed in the celluloid shadows. In a bored whisper, she said, "You're not going to kill us here, because your Big Boss wants the pleasure of doing it herself."

"That won't stop us from beating you up!"

"Hammerhead shark!" they both screamed.

Loud cracks echoed across the theater, as Zoey and Desiree's "hammer heels" smashed into each man's face. While they clutched their bleeding and broken noses, the sisters leapt up, scrambled and squeezed their way past those seated, and spilled out into the aisle. Zoey glanced back and saw their assailants already up and stomping across a row of people. As the sisters reached the emergency exit, Desiree cried, "Fire!Fire!"

Patrons screamed and stampeded into the aisles, joining the crush of the crowd struggling to get through the exits. Ravonjay's men were left behind in the full blown panic. Zoey and Desiree burst out into the street, rattled and desperate. A terrified mob streaked past them.

"Which way now?" Desiree asked.

Zoey looked frantically up and down the street, trying to maintain her composure. "Well, let me think ..."

"Come on, Zoey!"

"I'm thinking—I'm thinking."

Desiree's head was spinning, scanning the streets and buildings, expecting danger on every side.

"I know!" Zoey pointed. "Why don't we get a lift from her?"

"Come on, you idiotas!" Victoria cried.

"Oh, thank heavens!"

The girls scrambled into Victoria's car and sped off.

"How did you know we'd be at the movies?" a still winded Zoey asked.

"I saw you taking off on your stolen motorcycle, and D'Quad's boys following you. Knowing the wacky way you think, where else would you go to hide?"

"We have something to tell you," Desiree said somberly. "The Big Boss of this whole shebang isn't D'Quad. It's ..."

"Ravonjay ... that's the reason I came after you." Victoria told Zoey and Desiree of Andre's visit and revelation. "We both knew you had to be warned. Andre went to tell Kongo. I went right to your house. When I saw the remnants of a voodoo charm, I knew you had gone to Ravonjay."

"Speaking of going somewhere," Zoey said." We can't go on the Warehouse raid in these dresses."

"We have clothes in our car."

"You can't go back there." Victoria said. "Ravonjay and her men will be waiting for you. You'll be the first two casualties of this turf war."

"I know it's a bit of a risk," Mandy said, "but I think we should go to our house."

Desiree agreed. "I don't think we have much to worry about. D'Quad's boys are too busy with their big haul. Ravonjay plans to take over the French Quarter tonight!"

Victoria leaned forward and hit the gas. She did a screeching two wheel turn onto Chartres Street and lurched to a halt in front of the Daniels' house. Zoey and Victoria hurried through the courtyard and in through the front door. A shoeless Desiree limped far behind them. When she finally got inside, Victoria was beside herself.

"Come on, come on!" Victoria groaned. "Fishbowl's ship will be leaving soon. Get dressed!"

Zoey grunted as she helped Desiree into the kitchen and then to the bathroom. "Desiree has a nasty cut on her foot, and we need to bandage it up. She's not going to be able to make it tonight."

Desiree groaned, "You're starting to irritate me, Zoey. Nothing will stop me from going to the Warehouse."

Zoey ignored her and said," Victoria, you head down to the docks. Once you get there, tell Fishbowl what happened."

"Are you sure?" Victoria asked anxiously.

"Yes, but get going, now! I need to look after Desiree in case any of Ravonjay's assassins show up."

As Victoria closed the door behind her, Zoey shook her head and laughed. "Your side trip to the kitchen did the trick. Along with our incredible gift for straight face lying."

Desiree giggled, as she wiped ketchup from her bloody looking bandage. "For now, we need to get into our exotic evening wear."

Zoey nodded. "We're going to have to come back here later to put on street clothes. We can't hook up with Eric, in our Midnight Shadows get up."

Moments later, the sisters guided their motorcycles out of the garage. Through the eye slits in their masks, the sisters took a last look at their home. Both wondered if they would live to see it again.

"Let's ride," Zoey said somberly.

For one last time, the Midnight Shadows zoomed out of their driveway and into the uncertain darkness.

CHAPTER TWENTY-EIGHT

The Midnight Shadows streaked across the city. The full moon nudged it's way through puffy clouds. A short distance beyond the Warehouse, the sisters secured their bikes and disappeared into the crystal speared shadows. They made their stealthy way back toward Warehouse Road. Suddenly, they made a startling discovery.

"Well, well," Zoey whispered. "What have we here?"

"This is a freshly cleared dirt road."

"Let's follow it and see where it leads."

The sisters navigated their way through the darkness. The narrow road was bordered by swamps and marshes.

"There are gators and snakes and blind bogs in there," Desiree thought. "I just pray we don't have to slosh through them if we have to escape."

Zoey saw lights in the distance. She stopped and looked through her binoculars. "I see the Warehouse and the *Eclipse*—and a lot of cars. Take a look."

Desiree did. "You're right—and lots of men hauling crates from the *Eclipse* and loading them into trucks."

"I sure hope the police and Coast Guard arrive here on time—And Fishbowl too."

Desiree nodded, knowing that without help, they would have to fight D'Quad alone.

****

"The current is swift and easy rollin." Fishbowl smiled, as he pulled away from the dock.

Andre and Victoria stood side by side at the rail, searching the sky for the signal from the police. Diego roamed the deck, telling jokes, assuaging fears; keeping the men loose but focused. Kongo huddled with Eric at the rail.

"What a day, mi amigo," Kongo said wearily. "We have linked seventeen missing or killed to the stolen jewelry at D'Quad's store. Before today, Madame Ravonjay was a saint to the poor in the French Quarter. No one would have believed that Madame Ravonjay was a ruthless killer. She duped the poor of the Quarter. She extorted protection money and inflicted violence or death on those who would not pay."

Eric nodded somberly. "Revenge is a dangerous motivator, Kongo."

A bloodthirsty look filled Kongo's face. "All of my friends on this ship share that thirst for revenge. I want it badly." Kongo stared into Eric's eyes. "My only fear is, if my friends trap Ravonjay's gang, even if they try to surrender, they will kill them anyway."

Eric stared out over the moonlit water and frowned. "I cannot let my feelings about the murders of Agents Buck and James cloud my judgement. Neither can you. You've got to keep your friends in line."

Kongo looked down at the dark water's depths, as if he was looking into an uncertain future. "You are right, amigo. We must take down Ravonjay's entire smuggling operation, if the Quarter is to rid itself of violence for good. That will have to be enough to quench our thirst for revenge."

The night was indifferent to the ship. One minute there was darkness and mist. The next, the full moon cleaved the clouds, destroying any cover the *Goldfish* had. Fishbowl deftly played the currents. His ease with the wheel, in light or in darkness, made it seem like the boat was piloting itself. The ship cut its lights as it drew closer to the Warehouse. A quarter mile away from their destination, two dinghies were lowered into the river. Kongo, Victoria and the Street Sweepers squeezed on board.

Before Eric disembarked, he asked Fishbowl, "You sure you have enough people to man the guns on this ship if the *Eclipse* tries to escape up river?"

Fishbowl winked and smiled. "I've defended this boat with just me and some big river rats."

Eric patted Fishbowl on the shoulder. "Well, that's good enough for me. Just make sure you're here when we come back."

"I'll be waitin 'cap'n. Just try not to sink my boats."

****

Although H. T. Franks had only been the New Orleans Police Chief for a short time, he had made it clear that he was a no nonsense leader. In his first speech to the officers, he stated his position: "If any of you are involved in corrupt activities of any kind, you are a criminal. Have no doubt that I will catch you, arrest you, and you'll be facing prison time." Since Ravonjay's gang had been laying low, she was not aware of the Chief's threats, nor did she realize that her gang had lost all of the support from the once corrupt, but now reformed, officers.

Chief Franks had selected his team members for the raid. He trained them well for all potential complications and knew this was a team he could count on. On the night of the twenty-ninth, the Captain received his message from the Coast Guard. The officers flashed searchlights that cut through the clouds, then ignited a fireworks display that boomed and lit up the night sky in a brilliant display. Delighted residents of the Quarter rushed outside to admire the impressive surprise.

With search warrant in hand, the team departed from the police station. The Jackson Square contingency was sent out to barricade the streets that led to the docks, while the rest of the team silently surrounded the Carriage House. The Captain banged on the door. The minute it opened, he and his men pushed through with their weapons drawn, announcing:

"Police! We have a search warrant—Do not move."

Billy the Goat raised his arms in stunned surrender. Big Boy drew his weapon and fired a bullet that grazed Billy's shoulder and brought him to his knees, completely missing the Chief and his men. The police quickly handcuffed both Billy and Big Boy and pressed forward. The rest of Ravonjay's men inside scattered like rats. Some ran for cover, while others tried to escape through the back door. They were greeted with a police surge that pushed them to the floor. The officers began handcuffing the men and opening crates of illegal liquor, yelling: "You are under arrest, do not move."

In a panic, a small number of the remaining men broke windows and jumped outside. A few escaped, running towards the Square, while the others were shot or rounded up and detained by the police outside. Aside from capturing the men on the run, the entire Carriage House operation was over in less than thirty minutes.

****

While the police were heading to the Carriage House, Eric and his allies inched closer and closer to the Warehouse. Hidden in dense foliage, wading through marshland, they waited for the signal. A searchlight scanned the heavens like a beacon of hope. Suddenly, fireworks lit up the sky.

"Well, well," Gizmo said to Bilious. "Will you look at that. Those fireworks will keep all the French Quarter residents and the police occupied, while we take over the Quarter." Gizmo didn't have much time to savor the moment. Eric's band burst out of the shadows.

Bilious opened fire with a machine gun. The Street Sweepers returned fire. Bilious was hit with a rain of bullets. He did not get up again. Gizmo's men were being gunned down like dominoes.

The Coast Guard ships came into view. A megaphone mingled with the sound of gunfire. "Attention! Prepare to be boarded. Surrender, or face the consequences."

Eric's friends surged toward Ravonjay's goons, as the Coast Guard boarded the *Eclipse*.

"We've got to get out of here," Gizmo cried, "and now!"

Gizmo and some of his associates jumped into cars. Other heavily armed men rode the running boards, heading toward the freshly cut road where the Midnight Shadows waited.

"Gizmo's men are falling back, heading right towards us," Desiree said.

Zoey nodded. "It's time to make some noise and send them right back into Eric's arms."

Fleeing figures streamed around the Warehouse heading toward them. As they did, matches flickered in the darkness. A hissing sound gave way to a flurry of firecrackers, exploding in erratic bursts. Fugitives mistook them for machine gun fire. The men ran wildly back toward Warehouse Road. Two cars, however, were undeterred by the noise. They plowed over the muddy ground and roared onto the dirt road.

"Time for a dignified retreat!" Desiree cried.

Both sisters bolted up the road. The cars were not far behind. Gun toting gangsters, on running boards, opened up with machine guns. Bullets fractured tree branches, and kicked up tufts of dirt that seemed to be chasing the Midnight Shadows. Shells whizzed by the fleeing sisters. Crouching low, they dodged from side to side, slipping into the muddy marsh, then scrambling back onto the road again. Once they reached the highway, they stopped and watched the cars bouncing and careening toward them.

Zoey reached into her pocket.

"Time for some pineapples." Desiree said solemnly.

"On my signal."

The cars raged closer and closer.

"Now!"

The sisters pulled out two pins, counted to five and hurled hand grenades at the fugitives 'cars. They both exploded into a whirlwind of shrapnel, flames and smoke.

The sisters stood and stared for a moment. Both breathed

sighs of relief, as they mounted their motorcycles. Their diversion had worked. The Midnight Shadows had forced the last of Ravojay's men to jump into trucks and try to escape up Warehouse Road.

"Aim for the tires!" Eric cried.

Machine gun bullets sparkled like uncut diamonds, sharp and deadly. Vehicles careened into muddy bogs, tires blown to smithereens. Fleeing fugitives ran right into the police who had blocked off the road. Ravonjay's men dropped their weapons, put up their hands and surrendered.

Kongo, mud splattered and grinning, put his arm around Eric. They both sighed with relief. "That diversion over there sent Ravonjay's boys right into our trap."

Eric nodded. "Without that ball of fire, a whole lot of goons would have escaped."

"Whoever it was who did this, we'd better check to see if our savior is dead or dying."

While the police made their arrests, handcuffed the fugitives and stuffed them into paddy wagons, Kongo, Diego and Eric inspected the dirt road. What they found were strips of red shredded paper, two hand grenade pins, and the charred remains of bodies in and around the burnt-out cars.

At first, all three men were astonished.

"Those machine gun bullets turned out to be firecrackers!"

"Those pins are from WW1 surplus hand grenades."

"Now," Diego asked with delight, "who would use firecrackers and grenades to stop an onslaught of killers?"

Eric pointed to tread marks in the mud. He shook his head and smiled. "Motorcycle tracks."

"The Midnight Shadows!" Diego cried.

Kongo patted Eric on the back and said, "Look's like they saved your ass, again, mi amigo—and our's."

"Let's get back to the dinghies and Fishbowl's ship."

CHAPTER TWENTY-NINE

The *Goldfish* steamed back upriver. The soaked and spent Street Sweepers sprawled across the deck, looking up at the menacing clouds gathering over the river.

"If I was a superstitious person, I would say this darkness we are riding toward is not a good omen," Eric said.

"No need for them gloomy thoughts," Fishbowl replied. "You're a landlubber. You're gonna be just fine when you trap Ravonjay's gang. No doubt about it. As for old Fishbowl, I ain't no landlubber. I'm a child of the river. Every time I go back on land, bad things always happen." Fishbowl pointed to his cheek. "See this scar? I got this one from a knife-carrying D'Quad boy. I got a bullet lodged in my back from another."

"And what did those two assassins get?"

"Lemme just tell ya that neither of them went home for dinner that night. In fact," Fishbowl laughed," they never ate any dinner again."

Eric pointed to the sky. "Look! Fireworks! Searchlights! Captain Franks has taken the Carriage House!"

"At last!" Fishbowl cried.

Kongo huddled with Diego and the Street Sweepers. "Don't you forget Eric's list of our friends and family that are connected to the stolen jewelry," he whispered. "Every one of them disappeared. Every one is dead: My sister, Rose—Andre's cousin, Consuelo—Diego's best friend, Raoul—All of you have lost loved ones. This is the night when we make Ravonjay's assassins pay for what they did."

Meanwhile, the Midnight Shadows guided their motorcycles through the narrow alleyway behind their home and secured them in their garage. Once inside the house, they took off their muddy clothes and changed into black jackets, pants and boots. As they got ready, their grim reflections in the mirrors only made the silence more unbearable. They had not spoken a word since they watched the cars explode into flames. Both stood up, checked their ammunition and shoved their thirty-eights into shoulder holsters. They tucked their Colts into a jacket pocket. The sisters hurried down to the docks. They were just in time to see the passengers of the *Goldfish* disembark. As they did, Fishbowl said to Eric, "Don't worry 'bout a thing, cap'n, me and my crew ain't gonna let nobody, no how, reach any ships."

Eric nodded, patted his friend on the back and said, "I'll see you after we clean up this situation. I'll buy you a drink."

"I'm gonna hold ya to that, buddy."

After hurried greetings and sighs of relief that no one had been hurt, Victoria told the sisters about the raid on the Warehouse. Though the Midnight Shadows already knew all about it, Zoey and Desiree feigned ignorance.

"Desiree, is your foot okay?"

Desiree nodded. "It's a little sore but fine."

A thick fog filled Jackson Square. Jagged clouds hung like butcher knives, slicing the air. The gloom was so thick that Eric could barely see Fishbowl's ship. Eric looked over the grim, determined men and women around him. He spotted Zoey, Desiree and Victoria. Eric tried to suppress his feelings, as he walked over to them. He already knew that Victoria was armed. Desiree seemed touchy, and tonight, there was something about her that wreaked of a wound up cobra. She was not the one to ask.

"Zoey, are you armed with something other than Desiree's powder puff derringer?"

Zoey gave him a half smile. She pulled out her thirty-eight and her Colt.

Eric nodded but said nothing. Neither did the cobra. Desiree showed Eric her thirty-eight and Colt pistols, with a far away look in her eyes. As they crossed the street, she wondered if any of them would come out of this fight alive.

****

As Zoey and Desiree entered the Square, the world, as they knew it, disappeared. The thick fog had turned street lamps into disembodied heads, peeking out of the milky gloom. Spires atop St. Louis Cathedral looked like mountain peaks poking through clouds. Smeary outlines of Christmas lights framed the shop windows that bordered the Square. Eric was determined to keep an eye on the Daniels sisters. But as soon as they entered the Square, he lost sight of Zoey and Desiree.

"I'm not sure where we're going," Desiree whispered.

"The safest place for Ravonjay's men would be under the balconies," Zoey replied. "Keep an eye on the shop lights. When Ravonjay's boys enter the Square and pass by those windows, we'll be able to see them."

Sightless and soundless, the sisters inched their way toward the Cathedral at the top of the Square. They pulled out their thirty-eight pistols from their shoulder holsters.

"I wish we would hear something," Desiree whispered. "This silence is killing me."

Desiree didn't have to wait long. In the distance, they heard a cacophony of screeching tires, angry shouts and gunfire. Desiree spotted shadows sprinting toward the docks. "There!" she whispered.

The sisters fired, and two men went down.

Gunfire filled the Square as desperate fugitives ran through the smokey haze. Zoey had disappeared from Desiree's sight. Glimpses of shadows undulated in the impenetrable mist. One caught Desiree's eyes, barely a few feet away. It was Eric. Before she could reach him, she saw the silver flash of a gun barrel and lunged. The gunman fired, as Desiree knocked Eric to the ground. Desiree was hit. Eric returned fire. His bullets smashed through the gunman's chest.

Eric leapt up. "You could have been killed!"

Desiree struggled to her feet and felt her bloody hip. "Is that any way to thank me for saving your life?"

"Desiree!" Eric cried. "You've been shot!"

"Duuur … I know I was shot," Desiree replied with a groan. "The bullet only grazed me."

"I'm going to get you out of here to someplace safe!"

"I just saved you from getting shot!" she growled. "I should be the one to take you to someplace safe."

"But you're bleeding!"

Desiree pulled a hankie from her jacket and tucked it into her jeans to stop the bleeding. Bullets whizzed past them. In a split second, Desiree disappeared from view—But a new face came out of the mist.

"Put your hands up and drop your gun." Eric ordered.

T.M. raised his arms, the gun still in his hand. "Well, well, well," T.M. leered. "If it isn't Eric Strand, the photo boy, the little fed and the card cheat."

"Drop the gun."

"Sure, sure I will. But let me tell you a little story about your two agent friends," T.M. smiled. "Before I drop my gun, I want you to know that I was the one who killed both of your agent friends. Me and Digger dragged their bodies into the swamp. It was a great pleasure to see them become gator bait."

Eric's blood boiled, as he thought of his dear friends, Agents Buck and James. Eric sank into the clutches of blind rage.

T.M.'s gun hand came down. "Here ya go, photo b…"

Eric fired twice. T.M. dropped down dead. Eric went over to his body and stared. "One bullet was for Agent Buck," he said savagely. "The other bullet was for Agent James." Eric walked away. Then he stopped, turned around and smiled at T.M.'s body. "By the way, I don't cheat at cards."

****

While Zoey looked desperately for her sister, Diego found Zoey. The din of shouts and gunfire filled the Square. "Santa Maria, at last I have found you, and you are alive!"

Zoey hugged Diego and said, "I am so glad we found each other!" Zoey looked over her dear friend. "Well, Diego, despite the fact that you are covered in mud, I see you are wearing one spiffy outfit for some pretty dirty work."

There was a moment of nervous laughter. "Ah, my precious muchacha, I have an image to maintain. If I am to die tonight, I will die Diego, the dashing, debonaire corpse, the star of my own joyous funeral parade." Diego's bravado filled Zoey with renewed confidence. That was shattered by a shotgun blast. Diego was hit, reeled, spun around and went down.

"Diego!"

"I am fine, my love," he said, as he got up from the wet pavement. "Alas, my trousers are ruined. As for my wound, judging from the hole in my pants, I have a little buckshot in by buttocks."

Zoey's concern melted into a sigh of relief. "Can you walk?"

"I do not need my ass to walk, mi amore."

The pair couched low as they crept through the mist and toward the shop where the shotgun blast had come from. They heard the man reload, and ducked for cover just in time. Another shotgun blast cut through the mist. Zoey and Diego fired back, running as they did. The shadow, framed by blinking Christmas lights, struggled to reload his weapon. Bullets whizzed past him, blowing out the window of an antique store. The gunman jumped through the jagged frame. Then there was silence.

Zoey and Diego followed, avoiding the shards of glass, and took cover behind a display case. The shop was filled with antiques: elegant furniture, Tiffany lamps, mountains of jewelry, glassware, and even an array of weapons that lined the walls. Zoey and Diego heard the click of the gun, cocked and loaded. They peeked toward the back of the store. They spotted a bullet riddled violin case on the floor.

Zoey and Diego looked at each other. "It's Digger."

Digger opened fire. Buckshot buzzed like a swarm of bees. The display case exploded. A shower of shattered shelves, crockery and china rained down on them. Diego was knocked senseless. Zoey knew there was no time to wait. She crawled across the aisle and found cover behind a roll-top desk. Digger opened fire again. The buckshot thudded into solid oak. Zoey rose and fired back, hitting a barrel on Digger's weapon. He spotted her.

"Well, well," he laughed, "it's Zoey Daniels, and I've just reloaded!"

Digger's blast toppled a huge Grandfather clock, hitting Zoey across the face. Stunned, she lost her grip on her gun. Digger rushed toward her, wielding his weapon like a club. Zoey pulled a Persian broad sword off the wall. Digger's gun came down on Zoey. She parried it with the long steel blade.

"So, little pest, do you want to turn this into a Three Musketeers' duel? I'll carve you up like a pig."

Digger swung his gun. With a two-handed grip, Zoey slashed back, chipping a piece off his gunstock. Digger was furious and lunged. Zoey side-stepped him and swung her weapon, slashing his jacket and his side. Digger shoved Zoey to the floor, grabbed her by the throat and started to strangle her. While she gasped for air, one hand blindly searched the floor. She felt dizzy and thought she was about to pass out. Then her fingers found what she was looking for. Zoey jammed her 38 into Digger's side and fired. Digger struggled to get up. A series of shots rang out, killing Digger.

Zoey slumped in cold-sweated relief. "What took you so long, Diego?" she rasped, trying to catch her breath.

Diego smiled and said," I would have perished under that deadly debris, my chiquita. But the mere sight of your golden hair, drove me to a crime of passion!"

****

Kongo and Victoria fought their way through the gloom, searching for the last of Ravonjay's men. Few had escaped from the Carriage House. Only Ravonjay's elite body guards made it to the Square. Kongo, Victoria and the Street Sweepers shot them down, one by one. Three took cover under an archway. A straw hat had fallen to the street. Kongo and Victoria recognized it immediately. It belonged to the man who had destroyed Victoria's speakeasy. This was the man who had gunned down so many of their relatives and friends. Their bloodlust and thirst for revenge overwhelmed them.

"Come on out, Louis D'Quad, and give yourself up."

"How ya doing Kongo?" D'Quad shouted from the shadows. "How about you Victoria? When I'm done with you," D'Quad laughed, "I'm going to find all of your speakeasy riff-raff and kill every one of them."

D'Quad and his men sprang from the shadows, guns blazing. Kongo fired, cutting down both of D'Quad's goons.

Victoria shot D'Quad in the shoulder. He reeled backwards. A look of astonishment filled his face as he fired at Victoria. Off balance, he missed. Victoria did not. D'Quad slumped to the ground and tried to raise his pistol. Victoria smiled down at him. "This is pay back for all the innocent people you have killed."

D'Quad leered at Victoria. A gunshot took the grin off his face. Kongo joined his friend, put his arm around her and said," I have waited so long for this moment, and yet ..."

"... and yet, how come we don't feel any better?"

"Because, my dear muchacha, we have satisfied only our lust for revenge."

Tears filled Veronica's eyes. "Yes," she rasped. "But for all this bloodshed, we cannot bring back those we love."

****

Though all the roads were blockaded, the police did not stop one familiar automobile. "That's the Daniels sisters 'car coming," Chief Franks said. "Just wave them on through."

Their gleaming, maroon, Deusenborg X cruised to a stop under a flickering street lamp. Wisps of fog and smoke rolled over the steaming street. A single figure stepped out of the car and walked toward the entrance to Pirate Alley. An aura of light silhouetted its shadow.

The Square had gone eerily silent. Desiree looked away from the sight of bodies lying all around her. She paused to reload her 38. She reached into her pocket. She had no ammunition left.

"Oh, this is just so freaking divine," she wailed." This is just perfect, and the worst of luck!" She looked around, nervously. The Christmas lights on St Louis Cathedral sparkled in the mist. Desiree said a silent prayer.

"Well," she sighed, "I'll just have to make do with my Colt pistol." It was fully loaded. Desiree frowned. "Now I've got a 25 caliber gun that's only accurate up to twenty feet. I hope to heaven that if I come across any of Ravonjay's men, they are intimately close."

As Desiree hobbled past the Cathedral and turned into Pirate Alley, a pair of bug-eyed headlights made it hard for her to see. Only a single silhouette was visible. Desiree raised her pistol.

"Ah, my dear little Desiree," Ravonjay laughed sadistically, "I had a premonition that I would see you here. Oh, by the way. Thank you for the use of your fine car. You could have been more polite. If you had left the key inside, it would have saved T.M. the trouble of hot wiring it."

Desiree shielded her eyes and said nothing.

"Wonderful headlights on your Deusenburg automobile," Ravonjay continued. "I can see you quite clearly. Can you see me?"

There was no response from Desiree.

"Well, this is unfortunate that you are unable to say that you see me. Let me come a little closer." Ravonjay walked slowly toward her, gun in hand. She laughed. "Oh, Desiree, how stupid of you. That little Colt? Really? That little pop gun is no more than a toy—A fashion accessory for foolish Flappers like you. No matter, I'll step a little closer, so you can get a better view."

"Listen." Desiree warned. "The gunfire and the shouting has ceased. You need to give yourself up or else …"

"… Or else what, my misguided child? You threatened to kill me once, you and your pirate friends."

Desiree's consciousness crumbled. Lizzy now stood before Queen Ant LaRouge.

"Don't you recall that you promised to kill me if I came after you?"

"Yes, I do."

"You were a liar," Queen Ant screamed. "I was standing right in front of you in the Ant Hill, captured, without a weapon. You could have killed me right then and there. But you didn't. You are a coward who does not have the courage to kill me or anyone else."

Lizzy blushed with fury. "Don't come any closer."

"I don't take orders from worker ants. I must come closer, my dear Lizzy. Then I can see your terrified, hopeless eyes when I kill you."

Queen Ant walked slowly toward her. "Come, come, my dear frightened fawn. Fire at me."

Lizzy tightened her grip on the trigger.

"Kill me, now, you coward! I am giving you one last chance!"

"Desiree!" Zoey cried, as she stepped into the alleyway and stopped short. She dropped her pistol in shock. In that split second, Zoey disappeared. It was Mandy who heard Ravonjay's chilling words.

"Unarmed! Oh, how wonderful. What joy! A family reunion —and I, Queen Ant LaRouge, will have the pleasure of shooting you both!." Queen Ant turned her pistol on Mandy.

Six shots rang out in succession. LaRouge, with a look of disbelief, grabbed her bloody chest and collapsed to the ground.

Mandy looked down at the bullet riddled body of Queen Ant LaRouge. Then she looked over at her sister.

All she saw in Lizzy's eyes was a lifeless stare.

Lizzy dropped her smoking pistol. She sank to her knees,

blood streaming from her hip.

CHAPTER THIRTY

There was no chance for sleep that night, or for most of the day on the thirtieth. The police station was filled with Ravonjay's captured henchmen who had been arrested and booked. Interviews had to be conducted and affidavits signed. Crime scenes had to be cordoned off, photographed and investigated. Medics at the Square treated the minor injuries, and ambulances took others to the hospital. Many more were taken to the morgue. Well before dawn, newspaper reporters from the *Nitpicker* and other local papers filled the lobby of the police station to get information for their headline stories.

Kongo and Victoria worked the streets of the Quarter, calming the nerves of the residents in their neighborhoods who had heard rumors of the night's events, and the deaths that had occurred. They were in shock as they learned that their dear Madame Ravonjay was not only responsible for the threatening juju charms that they had found on their doors, but that she was also the "Big Boss" of D'Quad's murderous gang. They cried about her loss, as they shook with anger over how they had been deceived.

All of the morning papers sold out as soon as they hit the newsstands. The people rushed back to their houses to "read all about it" at their morning breakfast tables. Zoey, Desiree, Victoria, Eric, and Fishbowl met at Kongo's place in the late afternoon. None of them had slept a wink. After all they had been through, their energy was low, but the love and respect among the group was palpable. Kongo and Diego had prepared a table of food for their exhausted friends. When everyone was seated, Kongo raised his wine glass for a toast: "Here's to my amigo, Eric, for his bravery and leadership that helped us free the Quarter! Here's to the police and our friends who risked their lives to protect each other and our city ... And here's to good riddance of D'Quad, his Boss and his gang ... Amen!"

Everyone raised their glasses. "Amen!"

After everyone had eaten and said their goodbyes, Eric drove Zoey and Desiree home.

"Do you mind if I help you inside?" Eric asked Desiree.

"Yes, please," she answered. "This is one time I will take all of the help I can get. My hip hurts. In fact, I ache in places I didn't know I had. Even with old Doc Brown patching me up, it still burns like hell!"

Desiree winced as Eric gently lifted her from the car and helped her inside. After he and Zoey had made Desiree comfortable, Zoey headed to the shower. Eric arranged Desiree's pillows and brought her a glass of water and aspirins.

"You need to rest, but if you want me to come back anytime tonight, just call."

"Thank you, Eric."

"I'm so glad to be able to help you. I have told you how I feel about you ... and I hope you're reconsidering coming to Baton Rouge with me. I'll even rent a house for you and Zoey, if you want."

"I'm just too upset and tired to talk about that right now."

"I understand. Are you going to the Square for the big New Year's Eve celebration?"

"Everyone goes to the New Year's Eve celebration, silly!"

"Great! We'll meet there. It will be a bit chaotic with all those celebrators, and it might be difficult to find one another."

"Yes." Desiree replied. "I am a bit slow moving now."

"Well, just to make certain," Eric smiled, "I'll meet you in front of the Cathedral at eleven thirty. That will give you plenty of time to hobble over there."

Desiree gave Eric a sad smile. She looked away as she said," I will give you my answer then, my dear Eric Strand."

Eric reached out, gently kissed her hand, rose to leave and said, "I look forward to our next meeting, Madam Desiree Daniels."

"Till the next time, my sweet."

As Eric closed the door behind him, Desiree sank back into her pillows and closed her eyes. "Oh, my God," she said. "What have I done?"

****

Unlike the gloom of the past few days, dawn smiled with a brilliant sun. Live Oaks, Pawpaws and flowers gleamed with morning dew. Even the streets and sidewalks glowed. The Cafe D'Monde was packed with smiling faces. They scarfed down beignets, dusted with powdered sugar that looked like pixie dust. Coffee steam spiraled up into the blue sky. At a secluded table, three lovely ladies basked in the warm sunshine.

"All things considered," Zoey began, "we've come out of this pretty much okay."

Victoria nodded. "Most importantly, alive."

Desiree was slumped back in her chair, gazing at the only cloud on the horizon. Her heart-shaped sunglasses glimmered, as she blew perfect smoke rings into the sky. "I think that we are a whole lot crazier than before this all started."

"Can't we talk about something else?"

"Zoey's right," Victoria said. "Let's let the wounds heal into scars, before we revisit what we have been through."

Desiree smiled, nodded, sat up and took a deep draught of her coffee. "Ah, sweet nectar of the Gods! The air seems sweet today, too. All I have to do is breathe, and I give and receive all the joy that surrounds us."

Victoria gave Desiree a glowing smile and sighed. "It's like we've liberated the French Quarter. There is no fear, no sadness …"

"… just a whole lot of early New Year's Eve celebrating."

"I am so glad that your hip is feeling better," Victoria said to Desiree.

"Me too!"

"Do you think you'll be ready for your New Year's Eve soiree?"

"We sure will," Desiree replied. "All we have to do is lay out our clothing, get dressed, do our hair and makeup ..."

"... and go watch the fireworks light up the heavens!" Zoey added.

****

Eric spent the day down at the police station, tying up loose ends with Police Chief Franks and writing his final report for the agency. Finished, he went up to his attic dark room and removed all his photos and juju charms from underneath the insulation. He went out on the terrace and barely glanced at the stunning orange-blue sunset. He sat down and scrutinized each photo, reliving every special moment with Kongo, Diego, Fishbowl, Victoria, Zoey ... and most of all, Desiree. There was just something about her.... She was not just an "It" girl—though that made her even more dazzling—but she was more, much more; like an innocent angel. Eric laughed. "Who am I kidding?" he said to no one. "Desiree is irresponsible, irreverent, reckless, flirtatious, outrageous—She fights, she drinks, she smokes, she swears ... and yet," he sighed wistfully. "She is one of the most brilliant and beautiful women I have ever met ... the most passionate ... the most mysterious. I've fallen in love with her."

Eric went back inside. He finished packing his bags, placing the photos atop his carefully folded clothes. He shaved, got dressed and stepped outside into the friendly darkness. There was a discernible lightness that surrounded him. His footsteps echoed, without fear or apprehension. While Eric walked, he could hear the sound of revelers, screaming and laughing in the distance, coming closer and closer. Eric was a man who prided himself on emotional control. But he was leaving tomorrow, on assignment. There was no way of escaping saying goodbyes. His first stop was the *Nitpicker.*

Chuck invited him into his office. "Well, Mr. Strand," he smiled. "You're leaving us to clean up another gang mess."

"Yes. I would stay a lot longer, if I could. I'm going to miss your ugly mug."

Chuck grinned. "If you ever come back to the Quarter, there's always a job here for you."

"I may just take you up on that offer."

"I hope you know, you've just robbed me of my best photographer."

"You shouldn't have told me that. When I come back and accept your job offer, you're going to have to pay me a helluva lot of money."

Chuck pulled out a bottle of scotch and filled two tumblers. "A toast to you, Eric Strand!"

"A toast to you, Chief!"

Fishbowl was his next stop. Down by the docks, Fishbowl's ship, *The Goldfish,* was outfitted with a rainbow of lights strung around the deck and wheelhouse.

"Permission to come aboard," Eric called up to his smiling friend.

"Permission granted!"

After Fishbowl heard the purpose of Eric's visit, he said," I had a feelin' you'd be sent upriver soon. You're one helluva good agent. Lousy with boats though!" Fishbowl paused and said. "I'm gonna miss ya cap'n."

Eric looked into the sad eyes of a person who had become a dear friend. "I'm going to miss you too." Then Eric gave Fishbowl a sly smile. "No excuses, Fishbowl, there's no reason why you can't come upriver, now and then, to see me."

"Sure, I'll be comin' upriver. Sure, I'll come to see you! Though, for the life of me, cap'n, I'll be darned if I know why."

"What do you mean, you don't know why?"

"Cause," Fishbowl laughed, "every time I'm around you, you almost get me killed."

"You're tough as nails," Eric said as he sat down next to

Fishbowl, leaned back and looked up at the stars. The two friends sat in silence, enjoying the gentle sway of the boat, and the silent river rolling past. After a few minutes of enjoying the peace, Eric put out his hand to Fishbowl. "Till next time, buddy"

"You bet," Fishbowl nodded, shaking Eric's hand with a two handed grip.

As Eric entered Jackson Square, the happy din overwhelmed him. Madness and mayhem mixed with the music of the Cathouse Caterwaulers. The band was surrounded by drunken dancers, squealing, screaming, and flapping their arms like the wings of a giant bird. Eric found his way through the endless crowd, looking for some familiar faces. He found Kongo Kaminga, watching the dancers.

"Ah, mi amigo," Kongo cried. "It is so good to see you. I am so glad that you have joined us to welcome a brand new year!" Kongo took hold of Eric.

"I swear Kongo, you knocked the wind out of me the very first time I met you!"

"Back then, my hug was one of friendship, but it came with a friendly warning. It said, if you mess with me, amigo, this friendly bear will give you more than a hug!"

Eric laughed. "I assure you, it was a point well taken."

Kongo looked over his friend. "There is sadness around you on this night of nights."

"The agency is sending me on a new assignment. I leave tomorrow morning."

Tears filled the big man's eyes. "It has been a pleasure and an honor to call you my friend. I will miss you more than any man I have ever known."

Kongo gave Eric a gentle hug. "Until the next time, mi amigo."

Eric cleared his throat and rasped, "Until the next time, mi amigo."

Diego, sweaty and wild eyed, joined the duo. "Eric, my friend, Esmerelda will have me, now that I am a hero!"

"Eric has a new assignment," Kongo said somberly. "He's

CHAPTER THIRTY | 249

leaving tomorrow."

For a moment, Diego's wild eyes and laughter disappeared … but only for a moment. "Eric, though my heart is aching, let us not have our parting be a solemn affair. Come," Diego said. "We dance to celebrate our friendship and give you a happy send off!"

Diego took Eric by the arm and ushered him over to the dancers. "Look," he pointed. "It is my paramour, Esmerelda. Do you see the other lady over there?"

Eric nodded.

"That is Damita. A beautiful, buxom flower, is she not?"

Eric looked her over. "Yes! You have an incredible eye for the ladies."

"Alas," Diego said dramatically. "Both ladies think that I am their escort for the evening. I have been tormented, trying to spend time with each, discretely keeping them apart. That is why I have a New Year's Eve gift for you. I give you Damita to dance the night away! Then, my paramour and I will disappear into the crowd."

"And what will I tell Damita about your sudden departure?"

"Tell her that all of my passion has given me the vapors, and I had to depart for home."

"It sounds like you're not doing me a favor," Eric laughed. "You're asking me for a favor!"

"Ah," Diego pointed. "Look over there. That is Salma! Everywhere I go, I look for her. Her silhouette is that of a Goddess." Then Diego said emphatically. "I have made up my mind! I will no longer stray! I give my heart to Salma forever!"

"What about your paramour, Esmerelda?"

"Esmerelda who?"

****

As Diego tangoed his way toward the dance floor, Eric edged through the tangled throng of dancers, drinkers and a smiling conductor who had had one too many. So had much of his orchestra. Off-key playing matched off-key singing, but neither the musicians nor the merry chorus seemed to mind. Eric heard the St. Louis Cathedral bell tower chime the hour, eleven o'clock. As the minutes ticked by, Eric's heart raced. He checked his watch. He continued to check it every minute, as if it was a reflex action of love. As the clock ticked, one minute he felt a surge of excitement and anticipation that made him shiver. The next minute, he sank into a deep despair. Eleven thirty. Eric searched the crowd, hoping, praying that he would see Desiree. Eleven forty five. Eleven fifty. At last, he spotted Victoria. She saw him too.

"Victoria," he cried, as he embraced his friend. "Happy New Year!"

"Happy New Year to you."

Victoria tried to smile. Eric's heart sank.

"Eric …" Tears filled Victoria's eyes and she looked away. "Eric, it's about Desiree. She's not coming."

Eric struggled to maintain his composure. He now knew what it was like to be truly heartbroken, to feel an emptiness inside that was so deep and so wide that only Desiree's love could fill.

Victoria's own empathy crushed her. The sight of Eric trying not to break down left her speechless. Her gift for gab failed her in the one time she needed it most. Hands shaking, she awkwardly held out an envelope.

"It's from Desiree."

Eric took the envelope, opened it and turned away.

My dearest Eric,

I have written and rewritten this note so many times. I finally came to realize that anything I write, will not be adequate to describe all you have come to mean to me. In two short months, I have seen so many things in you: honesty, compassion, kindness, selflessness, bravery, charisma, your sexiness (blush blush), and the power of your love. Whenever I am with you, that power is overwhelming. That is why I purposely mislead you, implying that I would be in the Square and deliver my response in person. I could not see you, face to face, without falling apart. Love scares me. Especially yours. For all my reputation as the River Of Desire, I am, in many ways, an immature Flapper Girl, following silly dreams and chasing butterflies, masking my emotions with flirtatious behavior that has never failed to keep men at bay. But not you. You saw right through me. You rendered me defenseless. I can't surrender all of myself to you, because I am still trying to find out who I am. But please, Eric. Don't give up on me. I cannot bear the thought of not having you in my life. I refuse to believe we will not meet again. I had a dream last night. I was walking on a beach, just before sunrise. I could barely see my footprints in the sand. As the new day peeked over the edge of the earth, I saw footprints next to mine, but could not see who they belonged to. Then, as the sea turned to silver, I saw you. It doesn't matter that this was only a dream. It was a dream that confirmed my belief that some day, I will see you again. Four footprints in the sand, side by side, seeing the world in a new dawn....

Zoey and I need some time away from the Quarter. With all that has happened over the last few months, our spirits, our souls and our minds need a change. But what cannot be changed is my love and precious friendship with you. So, when we meet again, I'll probably still be coy and flirtatious with you, and bat my eyelashes. But I won't be batting my eyes seductively, but rather to hold back tears of joy.

I demand that there be no tears tonight. At midnight, watch the sky and think of me. I'll be watching the sky too ... thinking of you.
Your's forever, my dearest Eric,
Desiree

Eric turned to face Victoria.

"Desiree wanted you to have this too." She handed Eric a small box tied with a red ribbon. Eric could smell Desiree's perfume on the heart shaped bow. When he opened the box, his somber sadness turned into shocked disbelief.

"What is it?" Victoria asked.

Eric pulled out two black masks.

"Oh, my God!" Victoria screamed. "Zoey and Desiree? The Midnight Shadows? Oh my God, Oh my God!"

Eric shook his head in amazement. He ran his fingers over the shiny silk of the masks. "Somehow," Eric smiled, "I'm not surprised."

Eric and Victoria heard the cheering crowd count down the seconds to the New Year. The bell tower tolled. Fireworks and confetti exploded over the French Quarter. They lit up the night sky. They could be seen for miles.

Zoey and Desiree stared back toward the French Quarter. Rockets streaked overhead, leaving a trail of sizzling smoke and fire. A rainbow of light illuminated the empty highway.

Zoey knew her sister was distraught. She tried to cheer Desiree up. "Don't worry," she said happily, "I brought our spare masks. Just in case we need them...."

Desiree did not hear her. As they revved up their engines, Desiree looked back toward the Square and said softly, "I am thinking of you, Eric."

The sisters gunned their motorcycles and roared away, under a blanket of stars, into the western sky.

CHAPTER THIRTY-ONE

In room 566 of the Manchester Castle, the screen of the television showed two black SS100 motorcycles zooming into view. The two riders' hair whipped in the wind, and both wore huge smiles. The camera followed them as they sped, side by side, down the highway, until they were small dots on the distant horizon. Suddenly the screen went blank, and the portrait of Charles Manchester reappeared, gazing down on the room where Mandy and Lizzy lay in their beds. Lizzy suddenly shook and sat straight up. Mandy gasped and rolled out of bed, reaching for the trash can.

Lizzy rushed to her sister. "Let me hold your hair!"

Still on her hands and knees, Mandy shook her head. "No, I'll be okay in a few minutes. You know that when I get sick, it makes you sick too. Then we'll be sharing this trash can."

Lizzy collapsed on the floor next to her sister. "What a hotel! Their advertisement should say, 'Complete with soft, luxurious beds— and dreams that will make you hurl.'"

Mandy sat back on her knees, still holding her hair away from her face. "Did you dream of Desiree and Zoey again?"

Lizzy looked at her sister. "And Eric, Victoria, Kongo, Diego, Fishbowl, Chuck Hines—

"The Street Sweepers, D'Quad, T.M., Digger, Bilious, Gizmo— and last, but definitely not least."

Mandy paused and looked at Lizzy. Together they said, "Madame Ravonjay."

"Queen Ant La Rouge," Lizzy said softly. "We dreamed the

same dream again. Was it something on the TV?"

"Lizzy, I think the only explanation for this is that, somehow, we had past life regressions. Maybe the TV hypnotized us. Maybe this room is a time warp, or haunted or something. Maybe this is another part of our vision quest. Whatever it was, I wouldn't be surprised to find out that all of that stuff really happened in 1928. I think we were Desiree and Zoey."

Both girls rolled over on their backs and lay in silence for some time, until Lizzy started to shiver. "Mandy, did you notice that it is absolutely freezing on this floor?"

"No, I just thought my butt was numb because I fell out of bed to be sick."

They both laughed, as Mandy scrambled to her feet, put out her hand and pulled her sister up.

"I'll try to turn up this darned heat and start a fire," Lizzy said.

Mandy tied up the trash bag, washed her hands and face and then headed for the coffee pot to start the coffee. "What time is it anyway? We must have been asleep for hours."

Lizzy checked her phone. "Oh my gosh! It's already ten! We must have been asleep for about twelve hours."

"Yeah, and around two months passed during those twelve hours.... We've got to write down, as much as we can remember."

Lizzy put on her robe, filled their coffee cups and put their laptops on the table. "Just let me get a little caffeine in my system, and I'll be ready to write."

As they had done before, they sat in silence while they wrote and sipped their coffee. Both sisters recounted every event, person and conversation that they could remember from their dreams. After a couple of hours of writing, Mandy closed her laptop.

"Lizzy, are you almost finished?" she asked.

"Yes, I've just got a little more to write. What time is it?"

"It's almost noon, so I'm going to go ahead and take a shower and start packing up our things, while you finish. We promised to meet Lilly at the restaurant at one."

"Good idea ... I'll hurry, but I don't want to forget anything."

Just before one, both girls were dressed, and their bags were packed. As they left room 566, they took one last look around. "Wow, it seems like we have been here for so much longer than two nights," Mandy said.

"Yes, it does, and we have surely met a lot of new people—Both in the present and past." Lizzy put all of her weight into pulling open the stubborn door and finally succeeded in getting it to open wide enough to shove her bag through. She waved at the picture of Mr. Manchester. "Thanks for a great story, Charlie, and for not killing us."

"Let's get out of here before something bad happens!" Mandy exclaimed. Together, they pushed the door shut with a bang and headed for the stairs.

Slivers of sun streamed through the tall windows on the beautiful spiral stairway. "Hey Mandy, let's leave our bags here for a minute. I really want to see this view from the turret."

The sisters ran to the top of the stairs. After their long, unsettling night, the bright sun and amazing view of the crystal bay raised their spirits. Returning to their bags, they thumped their way down the stairs where they paused.

"There's one more thing we just have to do before we leave. Come on!" Lizzy grinned mischievously and motioned for Mandy to follow. She jumped up on the railing, side-saddle, and slid down. Mandy followed, colliding with her sister at the bottom.

Lizzy helped Mandy off of the rail and exclaimed, "Ah, that was good for the soul!"

Mandy just giggled and shook her head. "Lizzy, you sure know how to make the most of every day. Come on. Let's get our bags and check out, so we can enjoy some time with Lilly before we leave."

When the girls entered the dining room, they saw Lilly smiling and waving from her usual table. They rushed over to her and gave her big hugs.

"Oh you two look so pretty again today."

"Thank you," Mandy smiled. "You look stunning in that blue dress, and what an incredible Mistook necklace and earrings."

"Thank you! My dear friend, Rosethorn, gave them to me."

"Rosethorn!" Lizzy exclaimed. "I'm so happy to know you're friends. We have known Rosethorn since we were children. We were just adopted into the Mistook Tribe last month."

"What an honor! You two continue to impress me every time we meet. I hope that you know that you have a new friend in me."

"Now that is *truly* an honor," Mandy smiled. "You have been so wonderful during our stay. We can't thank you enough."

After ordering their breakfast, Lilly asked, "So how was your night in room 566? Any unsettling dreams?"

"Well," Lizzy stammered, "we sure did. We had the same kind of 'time warp' dreams that you said you and your husband had."

"It happened both nights," Mandy added, "and we both had the same dreams. It was like a past life experience in 1928 New Orleans. We were Desiree and Zoey Daniels, writers for the *New Orleans Nitpicker.*

As they ate their breakfast, Lilly encouraged the girls to tell her more about their dreams. When they finished, Lilly looked shocked. "Your experiences are absolutely astounding. When Alex and I slept in room 566, we both had vivid dreams of life in another time that seemed real. The main difference from yours is that we were not together in that past. Your experience is so unique, because you had the same dreams. You can verify what you dreamt."

"That's true," Mandy nodded. "We really haven't had time to talk about what we experienced, until now."

"I have an idea," Lilly said excitedly. "If you have enough time, let's go up to my rooms. I might have a way to see if any of the people from your dreams were real or not."

Lizzy grabbed her purse. "Let's go."

When they reached Lilly's office, she explained. "My mother was an archivist, a photographer and the most organized person you can imagine. We have a huge storage room of her albums.

Please let me show you."

Mandy and Lizzy were astounded at the size of the storage area that housed all of the one hundred year records of the hotel and the Manchester family's belongings. There were shelves of dated photograph books. Lilly showed them that at the front of each book, her mother listed each photograph by page, and the people in each one. There was also an alphabetical list of every name. Lilly removed the 1928 book. "Here you are," she smiled. "You can look up any name you remember and then find the photograph. Meanwhile, I'm going to contact my friend at the New Orleans Historical Research Library and ask her to send me any newspaper articles she can find written by Zoey and Desiree Daniels, or about the gang wars that you said took place in November 1928 through January 1929. This is so exciting!"

Mandy opened her laptop and called out names. Lizzy hit the jackpot on the first one she looked for and found the photo. "Oh my gosh, look at this."

Mandy and Lilly sat down beside Lizzy on the sofa and studied the black and white photograph. "It's from the food giveaway before Thanksgiving," Mandy pointed. "There we are, Desiree and Zoey, and there are Victoria and Madame Ravonjay."

"There's my mother," Lilly pointed to a beautiful, tall blonde, standing near the center of the group. "The description says, 'Thanksgiving food donations 1928, photo by Eric Strand.' Is he the one who was the federal agent?"

Lizzy leaned back and put her head against the sofa cushions. With a wistful smile, she replied, "Yes … yes he was. This was the photo he took for the newspaper."

During their search of the photographs, Lizzy found two others: one of Louis D'Quad in front of his Import-Export business, and one of Kongo and Diego Kaminga, smiling as they gave gifts to children at a community event.

Lilly had made a list of the names that Mandy called out. "I'm also going to give these names to my friend to see if she can find anything about them in the New Orleans historical records. Please give me your email address, so I can send copies of the photos, and anything she finds in the records. Girls, I have to tell you, I think your dreams really happened. This hotel holds so many mysteries, and I want to learn more. Mr. Knox will discourage me, but I think I'm going to spend another night in room 566, sometime soon."

Mandy wrote their email address and phone numbers at the top of Lilly's list, and gave her a hug. "We really appreciate your help."

Lilly opened her arms to both girls. "I told you that we would make a great team, but I didn't know we would be investigating 1928 New Orleans together. I thought I would just be giving you information to help with your article."

Lizzy looked at Mandy. "Oh no, the article! We really have to get home and start writing. We've got a deadline to meet."

"We sure do," Mandy nodded, "and Lilly, we promise that it is going to be great."

"Oh, I know it will be. I hope that you can drop by for the events on New Year's Day. I think it will be quite an extravaganza."

The girls gathered their belongings and paused at the door. Mandy smiled. "Lilly, we can't thank you enough for everything you have done to help us."

"We're so proud to be part of your team. I think we have great adventures ahead." Lizzy flashed a peace sign. Lilly laughed and returned it.

The girls walked slowly to the hotel lobby, pausing to admire and remember every detail. When they reached the front desk, the ever-efficient Mr. Knox bid them a cordial goodbye and escorted them to the door. "It was such a pleasure to have you as guests. Was everything to your expectations?"

"It was beyond our expectations, in so many ways," Lizzy said with a big smile. "It has just been beyond belief!"

The girls carried their bags down the steps of the hotel. There they paused for a last look, before they headed for home to the busy schedule that lay ahead before their New Year's Eve performance.

****

Eric and Victoria watched their world evaporate. The sky over the French Quarter, the people, the sounds of unabashed laughter and explosion of fireworks faded into soundless sepia. Eric and Victoria had the sensation of climbing up a pitch dark tunnel. Soon they found themselves standing on fluffy clouds, sparkling under a brilliant sun. As their vision acclimated to the light, the friends looked at each other. A sense of disorientation and fear filled them both.

"Victoria, is that you?"

"Um ... no. Eric, is that you?"

"No."

"Oh, thank heavens, Hugo!"

"Yerma, it's you!"

"It's us!"

A sparrow soared and called to the two friends. I'll-Go-Mine stood patiently on the clouds, grinning and wagging his tail. After an enthusiastic greeting for Hugo and Yerma, they set out on the long trek down Manitou Mountain. As they descended under the cloud cover, the bliss of the spirit world was replaced by Mother Earth, wintry and wild. Hugo and Yerma found no Mistook elders on their journey home. The pockmarked caves on Black Rock were dark and empty. They did not go across the precipice ledge, or the caved-in trail, or the rickety bridge. The two friends were not so much walking as spiraling down the mountain like a lazy tornado. The further they descended, the fainter the sun. It was all but gone when they reached the forest floor.

Yerma sighed with relief. "We made it back alive, and it's not dark yet."

"The trail was easier too." Hugo replied. "I'll-Go-Mine has a gift for finding the best way up and down mountains, through the woods, or anywhere else for that matter."

"I wonder what day it is."

"I wonder what month it is!"

The fire pit crackled with a pleasing warmth that enveloped them. They gradually opened their eyes. Hugo and Yerma's minds were flooded with memories and images of a time long gone. The flames illuminated the massive buttresses that reached up to the skylight of the Council House. Hand-carved totems emerged from the shadows.

Rosethorn sat opposite them in a lotus position. He gave them an inquisitive smile. "So, did you find what you were looking for?"

"Yes," a disoriented Hugo replied.

Yerma wore a puzzled look. "We found them. We found Mandy and Lizzy. We did have a life with them before … in 1928 … in the French Quarter in New Orleans."

"We sure did. I was an agent for the federal government, Eric Strand. My job was to take down a gang of smugglers and killers."

"And my name was Victoria Guerrero. I ran a speakeasy. I was an ally of Hugo … I mean Eric."

"And what of Mandy and Lizzy?" The Shaman asked.

"Well," Hugo said, "that's a little more complicated."

"As Zoey and Desiree Daniels," Yerma began, "they were notorious Flapper Girls and crusading journalists. Their column exposed the criminal activities of the gang and helped to bring them down … but … that's not the whole story."

"It sure isn't," Hugo said. "By night, they were armed and masked vigilantes, fighting a guerrilla war with the gang. People called them the 'Midnight Shadows.'"

Rosethorn chuckled. "Today, they would name a comic book after them!"

Yerma laughed. "Bats-girl and Batty."

"Yes, sometimes I think the both of them have bats in their belfries. But we have laughed enough at their expense. Please go on with your story. It is a very good one."

"The leader of the gang was a psychic named Ravonjay. But it turned out she was not who she professed to be. She had been in a terrible accident that left her face scarred."

"She had aged, too," Yerma continued. "That is why we did not recognize her. She was the boss of the gang ... much older than when we first met her. She was Queen Ant LaRouge."

"She believed that if she could kill Zoey and Desiree, that their life pattern would change, and they would not be reborn as Mandy and Lizzy."

"Without them being reborn as the Elegant sisters, they could not go back in time to stop Queen Ant from getting the Crystal Heart."

"And what happened to her?" Rosethorn asked.

Yerma shuddered. "You know, Rosethorn, we all detest violence. But, when we battled the gang ..."

"... We had no choice but to kill gangsters. The lives of everyone in the French Quarter were in jeopardy."

"And Queen Ant?"

"She was killed ... by Lizzy."

Hugo and Yerma hung their heads and sank into an uncomfortable silence. The Shaman stroked his chin and thought for a moment. "I see that you are troubled by the violence you inflicted. But there are times when there is no other path to take. I will tell you a story that will wash away the guilt that fills your spirits. When the U.S. Cavalry took away all of the Lakota land and killed all of the buffalo, they were not satisfied. They wanted to rub out all of the Lakota Nation. Soon, the Indian warriors were cornered. The holy man, Sitting Bull said, 'We were so hemmed in, we had to fight.'" Rosethorn paused and watched his young friends, still struggling to forgive themselves. "You were fighting for defenseless people whose lives were in danger. You were fighting for your own lives. And ... in a sense ... you were fighting to save the Crystal Heart. Knowing your brave and loyal spirits, you would not abandon your friends and neighbors ... even if it meant killing gangsters, to save their lives."

"It is still so unpleasant, so debilitating ... so horrid."

"Sometimes that is the way of the world," Rosethorn replied.

"Sometimes, that is the way of threads in the tapestry."

The two friends looked puzzled.

"Do you not remember when we started the ceremony of the triangle? Do you not remember what I chanted?"

"Across time, we remember the threads in our tapestry."

Rosethorn nodded. "Each of us has a tapestry woven from multicolored threads, born of our experiences over time. There are many threads that each of us has woven, good and bad. You have found one of your own, a blood red one. It is the thread of experience each of you have had with Queen Ant LaRouge. That thread was ended with her death."

"I understand what you are saying," Yerma began. "What I can't understand is why I feel this meeting with Queen Ant, and the one in Port Orion, is not the whole story. It's like we need another side of the triangle, before we can go forward. It's like we're in the middle of the story."

Rosethorn grinned. "You are correct. So, to go forward, you must walk backward."

"I assume that you don't mean that literally," Hugo said with a smile.

"Yes, I do!"

Yerma groaned. "I'm too tired to try and figure out what you just said. But please, let me ask you, when and where will we be going when we're walking backward toward it?"

"How did you find out that you had to go on your journey today?"

"In our dreams," Hugo replied.

"Dreams are one place where the Great Spirit calls to us. But there are many others: your spirit animal, or a voice in the wind, autumn leaves rustling through the trees, a crumbling temple, a rushing river ... any of these things can speak to us. You will know when it is time to continue your vision quest. Do you understand?"

Hugo and Yerma nodded.

"Speaking of time, my friends. This journey is unlike your journey through the vortex, where you left and returned at the same moment. You have been here since seven this morning. It is now after four o'clock."

"That's a relief!" Yerma said. "We thought we had been gone for months."

"In some ways, you were!"

As the pair rose to leave, Yerma said, "Wow, this has been some day, Rosethorn. I can't wait to tell Mandy and Lizzy about it."

"This will blow their minds," Hugo exclaimed.

Rosethorn shook his head. "That is something you must not do."

"Why?"

"Mandy and Lizzy cannot be told about this. They must experience it themselves, first hand, as you did. Then and only then, can all of you walk backward, so you can go forward."

"You have our word to keep silent, Rosethorn," Yerma said.

"In the meantime," Hugo smiled, "I think I'll walk backward out to my car and head on home for dinner."

Hugo and Yerma stepped carefully across the icy parking lot. After a goodnight hug, they hopped into their cars and headed home. Later that night, Yerma called Hugo. "Hey, I just had to tell you something that just happened to me that was so weird! I couldn't believe my eyes. A Sparrow was perched on the Alder tree, outside my bedroom window. I swear it was the same one we saw going up Mount Manitou!"

"Oh, wow! That is really something. I've got a story for you too. When I got home today and went inside, I'll-Go-Mine was asleep in front of the fireplace. My mom greeted me at the door and told me that he was exhausted. Apparently, I'll-Go-Mine got out of the house and was gone for most of the day. Guess what time he left and when he got back?"

"Around seven this morning?" Yerma asked tentatively.

"Yep! And he got home at around three thirty."

"Oh, my God, Hugo. In trance or awake, our spirit animals are by our sides. Bless my Sparrow and I'll-Go-Mine!"

"Well, there are advantages to having a Sparrow for a spirit animal and not a dog. Your Sparrow is outside sitting on a tree limb. I'll-Go-Mine is sprawled across my lap, eating my potato chips. He got into my father's mug of beer, too. His ears are sagging, and he keeps groaning and rubbing them. I'll-Go-Mine is bombed out of his mind!"

CHAPTER THIRTY-TWO

Thursday's weather was a waiting game. White clouds had ominous gray-black edges. They hung heavy and low. It wasn't a question of whether it would snow or not. It was when and how much? For now, the streets had been cleared. Mountains of snow, pushed off roads by tractors, were heaven for little kids on sleds. After a dreamless sleep, Hugo awoke with I'll-Go-Mine at the foot of his bed, staring and smiling at him.

Hugo sat up, rubbed his eyes, yawned and stared back. "No hangover, eh, I'll-Go-Mine?"

At the mention of his name, I'll-Go-Mine bounded onto the bed and was all over Hugo, nudging and licking and jumping on him. Finally, he leapt to the floor, grabbed his leash in his teeth and headed for the bedroom door.

The telephone buzzed. "You're going to have to wait buddy. Hello?"

"Hi, Hugo, I hope I didn't wake you."

"No, I'll-Go-Mine did that. How about your sparrow?"

Yerma laughed, then asked, "What are you doing today?"

"I need to finish my term paper for English class, but I may give myself a break and take I'll-Go-Mine out on my iceboat instead. How are you feeling today?"

"I'm feeling here and back there."

"Yeah, I can relate. I feel like Eric Strand is a shadow of myself."

"Me too, like there's a ghost of someone else living in my room."

"Speaking of ghosts and our Manchester Mansion reporters, I'm not waiting any longer. I'm going to call Lizzy today and ask her out."

"You can't do that, Hugo! Think about it. What will happen if Lizzy is still going out with Lou Solo? He will be upset. Lizzy will be upset. You will be upset. It could ruin our New Year's Eve gig."

Hugo was silent for a moment. Yerma let him have his space. Finally, she asked, "Hugo, are you still there?"

"Yes, I'm here," he sighed. "I can't disagree with you."

"You'll know when, and *if* the time is right to talk to Lizzy."

"For right now, I'm feeling lazy. No term paper! Just some iceboating with I'll-Go-Mine. Speaking of my canine friend, he's standing by the door with his leash in his teeth. His signal for 'I've got to go, really bad.' You have a good time teaching your dance classes today."

"Oh, yeah. Twenty little girls with boundless energy. I think I'd better get going."

****

Lizzy was awakened by giggles and conversation coming from Mandy's bedroom. She glanced at the clock and moaned, "Eight thirty—After what we went through the past few nights, it's way too early to get up." Frustrated, she got up anyway, straightened her t-shirt that read, "What?" and pulled up her baggy sweatpants. She quietly tiptoed over to Mandy's door to listen:

"Okay, I can't wait to see you. Please drive carefully, there's a good chance that it will be snowing…. Okay, bye-bye, Zak."

Lizzy pushed the door open, and Mandy jumped. "Lizzy, I can't believe you're up so early."

"Oh, I can't imagine why," Lizzy grinned. "Maybe it was the giggling and 'Oh Zaks,' I heard coming through the wall. When you're flirting, you have a high, squeaky voice."

"Oh Lizzy, he's so great and funny. I can't believe he's really coming. He said he watched the videos you sent from our practice, and he's really impressed. He has also learned 'When Ya

Gonna Wake Up,' so he can play that with us too."

"Well, that is exciting, but I know that you're excited about a lot more than playing music with him."

Mandy's cheeks turned red, as she covered her face with her pillow. "Is it that obvious?"

"Are you kidding?—Come on, my love struck sister. Let's go down to the kitchen and get this day rollin'."

As they sat at the table and had their breakfast, Mandy checked her email. "Oh my gosh, Lizzy. Lilly has already forwarded a link for information from the New Orleans Historical Society. In her email, she says they had already scanned all of the available issues of *The Nitpicker* into their historical records, so her friend just selected all of Zoey and Desiree's columns, and all of the local news from November 1928 through January 1929 and sent it to her. Lilly says she has been reading it, and it is fascinating to see how it confirms what we told her—I'll write her a thank you note, right now."

"Lilly is absolutely amazing. It would have taken us months to figure out how to get that information. I can't wait to read it all, but we have so much to do already. Aunt Billie wants us to come in to help her at the store this morning, and we have to get the article finished and turned in at the *Tabula Rasa Times* office."

Mandy continued to scroll through the articles on her computer. "Wow, Lizzy, there are over thirty columns by Zoey and Desiree here—I remember us writing them!" She continued to scan the articles, then stopped. "Lizzy, come over here, you have got to see this article in the *Nitpicker* editorials from January 15,1929."

A Thank You to The Midnight Shadows.
From the citizens of the The French Quarter of New Orleans

During the past two years, the French Quarter was plagued with gang wars, murders, bombings and destruction of property. Residents feared for their lives when they found dreaded juju charms

on their doors. Businesses were forced to pay protection money to thugs and were punished when they refused. During those dark times, the Midnight Shadows rode the streets late at night and brought us light. They have been called vigilantes, Robin Hoods of the French Quarter, or The Two Musketeers, all the while remaining anonymous. Since the raid on December 29th that took down the gang headed by Madame Ravonjay and Louis D'Quad, the Midnight Shadows have gone dark, but we thank them for their bravery and selfless acts to protect our community.
Sincerely,
Kongo Kaminga, Diego Kaminga, Victoria Geurerro, and Oliver "Fishbowl" O'Brien

Mandy and Lizzy looked at each other in stunned silence. Finally, Lizzy said, "This is absolutely amazing. I don't even know how to feel about it—Proud—We were there, and we did those things."

"But," Mandy said, "it wasn't really us. It was Zoey and Desiree. We were them, but we weren't— It's going to take some time to try to understand all of this." Mandy shook her head, and closed her computer.

****

At the dance studio, Yerma rounded up her wild group of tiny dancers, turned on the soft piano music and began the barre routine. They immediately lined up with their left hands on the barre and stood in first position, as Yerma counted off the beats to begin the routine. She smiled while she watched their concentration and movements. She took a deep breath, exhaled and said, "This is just what I needed."

A lone iceboat glided across the frozen bay. Hugo shielded his eyes and squinted through his goggles. The sun had been a rare sight lately, and though angry clouds were gathering, there were patches of blue sky. The wind was bracing, turning his cheeks a ruddy red.

Piloting the craft absorbed his concentration. But more often than not, Hugo's mind drifted. He had not said a word or uttered a sound since he set out this morning. His goggle-wearing shipmate did not seem to mind. I'll-Go-Mine couldn't talk, but he was a good listener.

"Did you ever get the feeling that you are here right now, but you are somewhere else?" Hugo asked. He looked over at his passenger. I'll-Go-Mine was staring straight into the wind, a blissed out look on his face, his lips flapping in the breeze, enjoying the zen moment and the pleasure of Hugo's company.

Hugo and his father had built the boat years ago, using the traditional Netherland's design that his father knew so well. Hugo's sails caught the wind, and he glided and made figure eights across the smooth, silver-white surface. He smiled as he watched I'll-Go Mine place his front paws on the bow and lean left and right with the movement of the craft.

"This is exactly what we needed," Hugo yelled to his loyal friend.

I'll-Go-Mine rarely barked, but at this special moment, he turned his head and howled in agreement.

It was exactly what Hugo needed to hear.

****

When Mandy and Lizzy arrived at their mother's Antiques and Oddities store, Aunt Billie was on a video call with their mother, Eleanor. They all gathered around the counter and exchanged stories from the last few days. After reassuring their mother that they were absolutely fine, again and again, Mandy and Lizzy blew goodbye kisses to her and hung up.

"Boy, I'm so glad that you two are able to help me this morning. Thank you so much for coming," Aunt Billie said. "We've had so much new inventory arrive in the past two days, and the store has been super busy. I've just had to pile up the boxes in the storage room."

Mandy grinned. "Well, it just so happens that Lizzy and I are the most experienced box-cutting, inventory-logging, experts in the city."

Lizzy laughed. "We'll have that merchandise priced and on the shelves before you've had time to finish your cup of coffee ... if you drink slowly."

"Oh, thank you. I've never run the shop by myself, and I don't want to let Eleanor down. Plus, the shopping this week has been crazy. Everybody must have gotten a whole lot of Christmas money this year, because they sure want to spend it."

The girls started walking towards the storage room as Lizzy assured her aunt, "Okay, we'll get this done as quick as we can. Don't worry."

As soon as they had finished their work, Mandy and Lizzy headed out the door and to their favorite store.

"Let's look at dresses," Lizzy said. "Everything is on sale, and we need to get something to wear tomorrow night—Something sparkly and special for New Year's Eve."

"Lizzy, look at these black, lacy garters. Let's get a pair, and each of us can wear one under our dress—Just like in the very old times."

"That's a great idea! So where are we buying our Colt pistols?"

Mandy laughed, "Or maybe boomerangs?"

"No problem, we know that we can get them online."

Lizzy started gathering dresses to try on, and Mandy joined in the fun. When their fitting room was loaded with options, the fashion show began.

Mandy tried on her first dress and turned to Lizzy with a frown on her face. "This is awful, isn't it?"

"Yep! You look like you're six, and you're on your way to an Easter egg hunt."

Lizzy tried on her first dress and started to laugh. "Well, this one looks fine, if I'm thirty and on my way to a cocktail party."

Mandy laughed. "Here Lizzy, try on this one."

Lizzy held it up and grinned. "Yes, this one just might work. I really like it."

Lizzy put on the short, black dress, accented with an art deco inspired, gold sequin design and fringe at the bottom. A smile spread across her face. "Oh yeah, this is it, Mandy. It is the perfect modern-take on the dress Desiree wore to Kaminga's the night of D'Quad's hit."

"Oh, my gosh, it is! I love that dress on you. Now, I want to find a Zoey dress ... something short, silver and shimmery, in the same style as yours!"

"Let me get one for you," Lizzy said. "I know where I found this one, and anyway, I want to see how I look in the big mirror in the store."

Lizzy returned with the perfect dress for Mandy. It was made with a soft, light silver-gray fabric and accented with a beautiful art deco design in silver sequins. A silver-gray fringe hung from the short, zigzag hemline.

"Oh Lizzy, I love it!" Mandy exclaimed when she tried it on. "It's like these two dresses were made just for us. Let's put the others back on the racks. We have found our dresses for the party ... and even the garters!"

To celebrate their shopping success, Mandy and Lizzy made their way to their favorite coffee shop for a late afternoon snack. After that, they picked up a pizza before returning home to work on their article. Once finished, the sisters emailed it to the *Tabula Rasa Times*. After it was sent, Mandy had misgivings about the article's content.

"Do you think we said too much about the paranormal stuff that happened in room 566."

"I hope so! Of course, after it comes out, everybody in town might think we're crazy."

"You don't have to worry about that, Lizzy. People already think you're crazy!"

CHAPTER THIRTY-THREE

The next morning, Mandy gazed out of the kitchen bay windows with growing concern. The gray-black sky was an ominous warning of a whopper of a storm. Steady snow began to fall. The weatherman said it would continue into the night. Mandy was filled with excitement, mixed with a sense of dread.

"I'm so looking forward to tonight," Mandy said to no one, "partying with our friends and playing our big New Year's Eve gig." Then she sighed. "And I'm so excited about being with Zak … but with all this snow."

Lizzy tiptoed into the kitchen, hearing her sister's every word. "Oh, stop worrying," she said, with the wave of her hand. "Zak will get here, safe and sound, and we're going to rock the rafters of the Solstice Ballroom! I guarantee it!" She joined her sister on the window seat and patted her on the head. "Think happy thoughts."

"Well, there is something that should make both of us happy. We just got an email from the editorial staff down at the newspaper. They loved our article and photos. We're going to be on the front page of the *Tabula Rasa Times* on New Year's Day!"

"That's fantastic! That is so freakin' cool! Let's celebrate! We need some fun!"

"Well," Mandy began, "Mother will be home tomorrow, and before we start celebrating and having fun, we've got one thing we have to take care of."

"When you said 'Mother will be back' and 'we need to take care of one thing,' I got a sick feeling in the pit of my stomach.

What un-fun thing do you have in mind?"

"Well, we're lucky old Mr. John is a friend of Mother's. He cleared the driveway for us. But we have to shovel the sidewalk and the front steps."

Suddenly, Lizzy's whole demeanor changed. She looked distraught and tired. "I had planned on a relaxing day," she said softly. "It's windy, and there's a driving snow out there." Lizzy paused. "Even though I'm jazzed about tonight, the whole emotional impact of our trip back in time is beginning to hit me. Love, hate, death, killing ..." Lizzy's eyes glazed over.

Mandy nodded empathetically. "I'm feeling that too, but we've got to try to put that out of our minds. We should be focusing on this lifetime, and the wonderful night we can have — Not a lifetime that is behind us. Maybe, what we need is something to clear our heads."

"Okay," Lizzy said brightly, "Maybe that's exactly what we need! Let's shovel us some snow." She put on her coat, hat and gloves, pulled on her boots and then broke into a devilish grin. "I'll take the snow blower," she giggled, and ran out the door. Mandy followed, rushed across the porch, slipped on the steps and bounced her way to the bottom.

"Are you all right?" Lizzy asked with a laugh.

Mandy got up in a huff, brushed herself off and chased her sister toward the garage. Lizzy stopped short, picked up some snow, ground out a snowball and hurled it at Mandy.

"Yahoo!" Lizzy shrieked, as she ran into the garage and started up the snow blower.

"You're going to pay for that snowball!"

Lizzy cupped her hand to an ear, as she pushed the snow blower out of the garage. "I'm sorry," she laughed, "but I can't hear you!"

Mandy grabbed a snow shovel. After days without tending, about two feet of snow covered their walkway. "Lizzy hates housework," Mandy smiled, "but when she gets behind that snowblower, look out!"

True to form, Lizzy plowed into the sidewalk, sending an

arcing, arctic shower up into the air. Every time Lizzy passed Mandy, she purposely altered her direction, so she could bury her sister in a tsunami of snow. While Lizzy went in the other direction, Mandy filled her shovel. As Lizzy turned around, Mandy side stepped the wall of white and hit Lizzy in the face with the shovel full of snow. Lizzy paused, laughing hysterically, and wiped the snow out of her eyes. While she did, Mandy picked up another shovel full and dumped it on Lizzy's head.

"That does it!" Lizzy cried, as Mandy dropped her shovel and ran off into the deep snow on their front lawn. Lizzy chased her, flinging up an old faithful of snow and gaining on her stumbling sister. Mandy lost her balance and fell face first into the snow. She got up shrieking with laughter and tackled Lizzy. The sisters rolled around and around, each trying to pin the other, each rubbing snow in the other's face. Finally, the breathless, giggling sisters stopped. They helped each other up.

"Well," Mandy smiled. "Not only did we clear the sidewalk and the steps, we blazed a trail down the lawn. We're finished with our chores, so you should be happy with that."

Lizzy perked up. "So, now can we have some celebratory fun?"

"Yes, that's a great idea. I do have something fun in mind," Mandy laughed. Lizzy winced, as her sister smashed a snowball into the side of her head.

"I'm going to get you for that!" Lizzy revved up the snowblower and zigzagged her way after her fleeing sister.

As soon as they were inside, Lizzy, seeking revenge, gave Mandy a wild grin. "How about a good old fashioned hair pulling contest?"

Before Mandy could respond, Lizzy wrapped her arms around her sister and dragged her to the floor. The only thing that stopped the hair pulling, pinching, tickling, slapping, screaming, ouches and manic laughing, was the ring of a telephone.

"It's Yerma," Mandy said, as she rubbed her sore head. "Hi Yerma, it's so good to see your smiling face."

"What ya been up to?" Lizzy asked.

"Well, as I've told you, Hugo and I still have questions about our part in our vision quest. We went to see Rosethorn to see if we could get a little clarity. But, as you know, every time we go to see him with a question, he doesn't answer it, but creates a new question that is even more puzzling."

"We feel your pain," both sisters groaned.

"Anyway, I'm dying to hear all about your nights in the Manchester Castle! I can't wait to read your article. But can you give me a little hint of what's going to be in it?"

"Sorry," Mandy said with a smile. "Lizzy and I swore ourselves to secrecy, until the article comes out on New Year's Day."

"Ooooh, come on you two! Can't you give me a little tidbit about your two nights in the Manchester Mansion of Terror?"

"No," Lizzy replied hesitantly. "But I am terrified of what might happen tonight. Not with our playing … with Hugo."

"That's one of the reasons I called you. I talked to Hugo. He was going to ask you out tonight, but I talked him out of it. I told him the kind of drama it could cause. I also told a little white lie," Yerma giggled. "I kind of implied you're still going out with Lou. So you can rest easy. Tonight is going to be dynamite."

Lizzy breathed a sigh of relief. "I am so, so, so, happy to hear this."

"You have nothing to fear, so let's rock, my dear."

"We can't wait!" Mandy exclaimed. "See you later Yerma … Bye, Bye."

"See?" Mandy said, as she patted Lizzy's hand. "You don't have to worry about Hugo asking you out tonight."

"I'm not completely convinced, so, as soon as the gig is over, I'm going to get out of there fast."

"Oh, Lizzy, your such a worrywart. Hugo won't do that, not now. Tonight is going to be a night to remember."

"Yes," Lizzy replied sarcastically, "I'm sure Zak will see to that."

"Oh," Mandy blushed. "Sometimes you are such an idiot!"

"Well, at least it's not all the time," Lizzy laughed. "I'm going upstairs to get out of these wet clothes."

"Good idea."

After they both had changed into comfortable clothes, Mandy and Lizzy came back downstairs. Mandy wrapped a blanket around herself, sank into the sofa and turned on the TV to the Weather Channel. Lizzy flopped down into an easy chair and looked out the window, up into the face of an angry sky. Neither could ignore the snow anymore. Mandy feared that the snowplows were waging a losing battle. Lizzy did not. She had an undeniable gut feeling that they would rock with Zak that night. As the sun went down on the long day, Lizzy said, "It's almost time for dinner. We didn't have lunch, and I'm starving!"

"Me too!"

They went into the kitchen and right over to the fridge to look inside. Mandy laughed. "How about our traditional 'we don't give a crap' buffet?"

"Yes! Let's haul out some of this crap and see what horror we can create in the microwave!"

After the food turned into lukewarm, overcooked rubber, the sisters served themselves and sat down. "Perfect," Mandy giggled. "Leftover Chinese takeout, leftover burritos, leftover pizza and some stale Christmas cookies."

"It's an international buffet! China, Mexico, Italy and Santa's North Pole!"

The sisters laughed their way through their delightfully bizarre dinner. It was the perfect capper to a day that was just what they needed. They cleared the table, washed the dishes and put them away. Both looked at the clock. They stared at each other, shivering with excitement. "I can't believe it's time to get dressed."

Once they had showered, done their hair and makeup and put on their new dresses and high heels, the sisters emerged from their bedrooms. Each gave the other a minute inspection.

"Oh, wow, Mandy! You look gorgeous!"

"So do you! With these dresses, shoes and our twenties accessories, it's like we're Zoey and Desiree Daniels."

In that moment, the consciousness of Mandy and Lizzy sank under the shadows of Zoey and Desiree Daniels. In dizzying disbelief and with trembling hands, each pointed at the other.

"You are the Angel of Allure."

"You are the River of Desire."

With that said, the shadows of Zoey and Desiree disappeared. All that remained was the Daniels sisters' devilish behavior; perfect for two girls who were poised to raise hell.

"Let's ride!" Lizzy cried.

CHAPTER THIRTY-FOUR

Zak carried his guitar case out of the casino and hurried across the snow-covered parking lot to his car. It had been a great night for his band, The Phoenix. Two encores, and the crowd wanted more. Thankfully for Zak, the next band was waiting to begin their set, so he was able to make his getaway to head out for Tabula Rasa. Since Christmas Eve, when he first met Mandy and Lizzy, he had watched the Mols' videos over and over, and knew he was ready to rock with them tonight. He also couldn't wait to spend some time with Mandy. She was certainly beautiful, and after talking to her on the phone, she was definitely funny and smart, and so delightfully different from any girl he had ever met. He knew he had never felt like this before. From the moment he saw her, he was inexplicably drawn to her.

Before leaving, he sent a quick message to Mandy: *"I'm on my way. Can't wait to see you and rock with the Mols."* Zak started the car, turned on the music and eased out of the parking lot, singing along with his favorite song. It was snowing, but he was confident that with his car's all wheel drive, he wouldn't have any problems along the way. However, as he reached the more mountainous areas, the snow started coming down more heavily, and the twisting curves made him slow down. His grip on the steering wheel tightened, and he turned down the music to focus on the road.

****

When Mandy told Lizzy about Zak's message, they were both so relieved.

"He's really coming! This is too good to be true!" Mandy's cheeks flushed with excitement.

"I know!" Lizzy exclaimed. "This is going to be a great night."

They had just arrived at the Solstice Hotel's New Year's Eve Ball, dressed in their stunning nineteen-twenties style dresses and new shoes. When they entered the ballroom, heads turned to admire the beautiful sisters and their dresses.

Noticing the attention they were getting, Zoey whispered, "I love these dresses. I'm so glad we bought them yesterday. They are just perfect for tonight."

Lizzy nodded and said, "They're perfect in more ways than one. When I think about it, we've always been drawn to the history and styles of the nineteen-twenties. We learned to do the Charleston by the time we were five. Do you remember performing it on stage when we were in kindergarten?"

Mandy laughed. "Of course I do. We adored those little costumes with the headbands, and thought we were stars." She grabbed Lizzy's hand and pulled her into the crowd of jubilant revelers. "With the band onstage playing Dixieland jazz, let's see if we can get the crowd going."

Lizzy nodded and broke into a devilish smile as they started doing the Charleston with unbridled energy, pent up from their recent experiences. The crowd parted to watch them, and then, two friends from their dance ensemble joined them on the floor. In an amazing, unrehearsed choreography, they matched Mandy and Lizzy's dance steps with ease.

Throngs of laughing teenagers and tipsy adults joined them, struggling to mimic the four girls. Tragically, they could not. Instead, they looked like each of their legs and arms had a mind of its own. Flapping hands hit surprised faces; as the sound of smacks and screams filled the air. Things got worse. Soon, everyone was trying to do the Charleston, howling with unmitigated joy. When the band saw what was going on down on the dance floor, they were delighted and kept playing Dixieland Jazz to keep everyone in a Charleston frenzy. They accomplished that. Some uncoordinated adults were downright dangerous. With their legs flailing away, they became marshal arts monsters; bruising kneecaps, kicking calves, and stomping feet. Many of the dancers were hopping on one leg around the dance floor, struggling to, at least, keep on beat. They could not. Some dancers were casualties of gravity, slipping and falling on the slick dance floor. But this did not deter any of them. Bad as they were as dancers, they celebrated their clumsiness and ineptitude. They were having the time of their lives! Chaotic flailing mingled with manic laughter, shrieking, stumbling, falling and the occasional cry of pain. The band, seeing the mayhem unfolding before them, mercifully ended the song. Mandy and Lizzy, laughing hysterically, exited the dance floor unscathed.

"Let's sit out the next dance," a winded Mandy said.

"I was just about to say the same thing."

"I'm thirsty. Let's go over to the refreshment table."

As they recovered from the dancing madness, Mandy and Lizzy spotted Hugo and Yerma.

Mandy was shocked. "Do you see what I see?"

"Yes," Lizzy replied. "Oh, Mandy, this is melting my brain."

"Mine too! Yerma's got on a Flapper dress. Hugo's wearing a suit that is similar to the one Eric wore!"

"This is too weird."

Not far away, Hugo and Yerma were thinking the same thing.

"This is unbelievable," an astonished Yerma said.

"Both of them are wearing Flapper dresses. I think they're screwing with our heads."

"That can't be," Yerma laughed, "unless they snuck up Mount Manitou, and we didn't see them."

"And we both know that is ridiculous."

"For now, let's just accept that we all have excellent taste in clothes, and head for the dance floor!"

"You go ahead. I'll catch up."

Hugo strolled over to Lizzy. Mandy made herself scarce.

"Hi, Lizzy. Wow, you look terrific."

"Hiya! You look so cool in that suit!"

"Thanks," he said nervously. "Um, would you dance with me?"

Lizzy extended her hand. "Echanté, Mr. Stra... um... Mr. Strongly Attractive Man."

"Huh?"

Lizzy's mind was reeling. "What a dumb thing for me to say!" she thought. Lizzy felt her cheeks turning red. Instantly, she regained her composure. "Derrr, Hugo," Lizzy said with a sultry smile. "You're supposed to kiss my hand. What are you waiting for?"

A stupefied Hugo gave her a vacant stare. "Um, yeah, sure ... I'm sorry." He took her hand and kissed it. Lizzy grabbed his and dragged him to the dance floor. The band broke into "Jumpin' Jack Flash."

"Oh thank God, this is a fast dance," Lizzy said under her breath.

"Oh, damn," Hugo thought. "I wanted this to be a romantic slow dance!"

****

Zak made it to the top of the mountains and breathed a sigh of relief as he rounded a curve and headed down the slope. In the distance, he saw the taillights of a car round a curve and then disappear. Unfamiliar with the road, he thought nothing of it, turned up the music and started singing again. When he reached the curve, everything changed.

"What—Oh, no!" Zak said out loud.

He saw a break in the guardrail and taillights in the brush and forest below. He pulled over, put on his emergency flashers and jumped out of his car. He slid down the snow-covered slope and fought his way through the thick brush to the car, down in the gully. He saw that it had been stopped by hitting a tree, and the front end was extensively damaged. He ran to the driver's side window and looked inside—two people. With the airbags almost deflated, he could see that the driver was slumped forward and not moving. He knocked on the window and heard a woman's scream, "Help! Please help."

The door was blocked by brush and a small tree, but with adrenaline-fired strength, Zak was able to pry it open far enough to see inside. He immediately saw that the driver's leg was bleeding, but the woman appeared to be uninjured.

"I got you," Zak said to them both. "You're going to be okay."

"My husband is hurt! Please help him!"

Zak pulled harder to open the door. The interior lights were on, but he needed more light. "Do you have a flashlight or an emergency kit?"

The woman bent with a groan and reached under the seat to retrieve their emergency supplies and handed them to Zak.

"Thank you," Zak said in a calm voice, realizing that although he was scared, she was trembling and relying on him. "What are your names?"

"I'm Sandy …."

"I'm Jason," the husband groaned. "I think I'm okay."

"Great," Zak said, placing his hand on Jason's shoulder. "Let's take a look at that leg and get you two out of here."

Luckily, the flashlight worked, and Zak was able to use the emergency kit to wrap Jason's leg wound tightly. Although it was a large cut and would need stitches, he was pretty sure the bleeding wasn't too bad.

Zak took a deep breath and nodded to the couple. "Okay, I think we're ready to go. You're too far from the road for me to pull your car out. We'll have to get you up the hill and to a hospital. Then we can call for a tow truck."

"Thank you," Jason said. "We were on our way to the hospital. Sandy is pregnant and was having pains, but it's too early for her to be in labor. Please help her up the hill first. If she needs to get to the hospital, just call an ambulance and leave me here."

"No way!" Sandy exclaimed.

"Let's get you up the hill. We'll take it easy," Zak said calmly to Sandy.

Zak used the flashlight to make his way around the car. The brush was thick, and his arms and legs were already scratched and bleeding. He stomped down the brush to make a path and was able to help Sandy out of the car. She was a small lady, so Zak carried her, until the terrain was too steep. Together, they slowly made their way to his car, and he helped her into the back seat.

"We made it," she said with an exhausted smile.

"You're a real trooper," Zak said with a grin. "How much pain are you in?"

"It comes and goes," she groaned.

Zak grabbed his phone and said, "I'm going to call for an ambulance and get you to the hospital, right away."

"No, we can't leave Jason … please help Jason."

Zak saw that there was no cell signal in this remote location. Rather than adding additional stress to the situation by revealing that there was no way to make a call, he smiled and nodded. "Okay, here's a blanket. You wrap yourself up, and if you need me, just open the door and yell. I'll go get Jason, as fast as I can."

Realizing what a bad situation they were in, Zak skidded down the slope and found Jason already standing by the car, balancing on one leg.

Jason shook his head in dismay. "I don't think I can put much weight on it, but if you can give me some support on my left, we'll make it."

They got into a position that seemed to work and started up the hill, Zak pulling and lifting, while Jason hopped. Jason was a big strong guy, and so was Zak, so they made good time and scrambled up to the road with only a few short stops for rest. When they reached the car and saw that Sandy was still okay, they broke into exhausted laughter.

"Oh, man," Jason huffed. "You are one strong guy. I never could have made it up that hill on my own. We owe you big time."

"You don't owe me anything," Zak smiled, while he helped Jason into the back seat and checked his bandage. It was soaked in blood, but no blood was running down his leg. "How far is it to the hospital?" Zak asked.

"About ten miles, but the road is curvy."

"Okay, let's take it slow and easy and get you two there safely. By the way, Jason and Sandy, I'm Zak and it's nice to meet you. I wish it had been under better circumstances." At that, they all started to laugh.

Zak ran to the driver's seat, started the car and eased his way onto the snowy roadway. During the time he was under the trees, helping Jason and Sandy, Zak had hardly noticed the snow. Now on the roadway, he could see that it was still coming down heavily, and it would be a slow trip. He glanced at his watch, 10:45 PM. He would be cutting it close, but thought he could still make it to Tabula Rasa on time.

****

Back in Tabula Rasa, the Mols were about to go onstage. Lizzy, Hugo and Yerma, nervously checked their watches. Mandy could not help but notice them.

"Listen, you guys," she stated emphatically. "I know all of you are worrying about how disappointed I'll be if Zak doesn't make it here tonight. We can't worry about that now. This is our biggest gig ever, so let's focus on the Mols and forget about Zak."

All three nodded and broke into excited smiles.

"One for all," Mandy shouted.

"And all for one!" the others cried, fist bumps and goose pimples all around.

The next thing they heard was the voice of the MC, "Let's welcome Tabula Rasa's most popular rock and roll band, The Mols!"

Thunderous cheers ricocheted off the rafters of the ancient ballroom. As Mandy sat down behind her drums and picked up her sticks, she snuck a quick look at her watch. "Focus," she said desperately. "Good grief, Mandy, focus!"

****

Zak was encouraged as they made it down the mountain, and the visibility improved. Glancing in the rearview mirror, he could see that although Sandy never complained, she was wincing in pain. They finally reached their turn, and Jason directed him to the hospital. Zak skidded to a stop in front of the emergency room and ran inside to get a wheelchair for Sandy. Lifting her into the chair, while Jason struggled to get out of the backseat and hop around the car, they finally made their way inside. Zak ran to the desk for help, and the nurses quickly wheeled Sandy in to see a doctor. Jason checked them in, and afterward, Zak and Jason said their goodbyes and exchanged phone numbers.

"Get yourself stitched up and let me know what the doctors say. If you need my help, I'm just a phone call away."

Extending his hand for a handshake, Jason expressed his gratitude. "I don't know what we would have done without your help. You may have literally saved our lives—There's no way I can thank you enough."

Zak smiled and nodded, "Just glad I was there—right time, right place. Tell Sandy I said goodbye."

Zak ran to his car, checked the time and sent another message to Mandy: *"Unexpected delay, but I'll be there."* He started the engine, turned up the music and drove like a man possessed. When he finally made it to the parking lot of The Solstice Ballroom in Tabula Rasa, it was twenty-five minutes until midnight. He jumped out of the car and hurriedly opened the trunk. The clothes he was wearing were ripped and encrusted with blood, so he had to change. He pulled the first t-shirt and pair of jeans he could find out of his suitcase, closed the trunk, grabbed his guitar case, started running towards the hotel—and slipped and fell. As he sat in the frozen slush, holding his guitar above his head, he started laughing hysterically. "Man, I'm a freaking mess," he said, as he closed his eyes and tried to center himself. He rubbed some snow on his face, got up and made it into the hotel men's room, where he changed and threw his mangled clothes into the trash. After a quick look in the mirror, he was out the door and juking his way through the crowd toward the stage like an NFL running back.

Mandy was the first to see him appear. Her face broke into a smile that could light up a room. At that moment, Zak's heart melted, as he gave her the thumbs-up. He thought to himself, "It was a heck of a ride, but it was worth it. I'd do anything for this girl." Watching Mandy and lost in thought, the next thing Zak heard was Lizzy's voice.

"Hey folks, thank you so very, very much. I just wanted you to know this will be our last song of the night."

The crowd yelled back," No!"

Lizzy paused and looked over at Mandy. Mandy gave her a big smile.

"No, no," Lizzy laughed." We've got to go, so we can all make it outside for the countdown to New Year's—and don't forget, the fireworks. No way we can miss that." The crowd cheered, and Lizzy motioned for silence.

"This is a song written by a dear friend of ours, Zak Davis, called, 'There's No Such Thing As Never In Forever.' We are so, so proud to be able to perform it for you tonight and to welcome to the stage, Zak Davis!"

Out of the wings came Zak, carrying his guitar. The Mols exploded into the song. Singing rode on golden cymbals. Bass and bass drum thumped like an excited heart; keyboard flourishes flowed like a happy carnival's calliope. The crowd went out of control, screaming and shouting and wildly waving their arms around, jumping up and down like pistons in an engine. The reaction fueled the band. The Mols pumped up the energy. Mandy, usually steady as a metronome, found her hands were shaking and sweaty. What she saw was like a fairy tale ending. Just when she had almost given up, there he was, an electric guitar in his hands, smiling. When Zak strode up to the microphone and sang, Mandy thought she was going to faint. She knew that voice:

"My love will keep it's promise to the letter,
there's no such thing as never in forever."

The band was a runway freight train on two wheels, screaming down the tracks. Zak broke into a blistering guitar solo. Yerma added a searing harmony riff, matching him, note for note. When he returned to the vocal, Yerma's guitar punctuated the power of his voice with withering licks that pushed his passionate singing to new heights. Lizzy played and sang with eyes closed. Sweat rolled down her blissed-out face. Mandy's shaky composure had exploded into a fury of cymbals and drums. Hugo was dancing with his bass, every step punctuating the ear-splitting rock and roll that was swirling around him. The band segued into a ferocious take of "When Ya Gonna Wake up?" Each time the band sang the title, the crowd shouted back. "Now! Now!"

"When ya gonna wake up?"

"Now! Now!"

Then, in the final dazzling crescendo, Zak, Hugo, Yerma and Lizzy jumped up and came down on the last beat. The song ended to a deafening roar of the crowd.

"Thank you and Happy New Year!" Lizzy yelled into the microphone.

As the first chords of *Imagine,* by John Lennon, sounded on the speakers, both inside and on the outer terrace overlooking the bay front, it was nearing time for the countdown to the new year. The ballroom doors were flung open, and many moved to the large windows or out to the terrace. In the midst of the chaos, Mandy grabbed Zak's hand and pulled him through the laughing crews and their families partying backstage. She led him up a winding staircase. Then, Mandy opened the door and led him out onto the building's upper deck. The air was cold and clear. Neither said anything. They just held hands, listened to the music and looked up at the full moon and sparkling stars —content to be in the perfect place, at the perfect time, with the perfect person. They heard the crowd below chanting the final countdown. Just as one second remained, Mandy and Zak embraced. Fireworks exploded over Tabula Rasa, and colorful confetti streamed down from the city rooftops. At that precise moment, Mandy and Zak kissed. After quite some time, Mandy pulled away and whispered. "Where the heck have you been? It feels like lifetimes."

Zak took Mandy in his arms and kissed her again. Then, they just held onto each other in an embrace that was gentle but passionate. It seemed like they stood there for centuries. They didn't want to let go.

Meanwhile, out on the loading dock, two figures sat two feet apart. They too had escaped the backstage bedlam. Minutes before, Lizzy was frantically trying to push her way through the crowd to get to the backstage exit. She was startled when Hugo's hand closed around her wrist.

"Why?" Hugo pleaded. "Why have you been avoiding me all week? You won't answer any of my texts or emails." Hugo felt exhausted. He couldn't tell if it was from playing tonight, or an emotional collapse. "Why?"

"You know why, Hugo."

Hugo let go of her wrist. "This place is bedlam. Let's go outside and talk."

Lizzy nodded and they exited through the backstage door. They joined in the countdown to New Year's and watched the beautiful fireworks display that lit up the sky over the twinkling lights of the city.

As the last streamers of confetti on New Year's Eve fluttered down on Lizzy and Hugo, they stared off into space, dangling their feet off the loading dock.

"All I wanted to do, Lizzy, was to ask you to go to the New Year's Ball with me."

"And then?" Lizzy asked, still refusing to face Hugo

"And then what?"

Lizzy finally looked over at him. "What I am asking you is … after our first date…. Then what, Hugo?"

"Well …" Hugo hesitated. "We'll just see how it goes."

Lizzy shook her head sadly. "Hugo," she replied. "We have been friends since we played in the sandbox together."

"So?"

"So … you're like a brother to me … to Mandy…"

"That doesn't mean we can't be more than that."

"Yes, but we could end up being less than that."

"No we wouldn't," Hugo said soothingly." We could never lose our friendship."

"Hugo …" she replied, preparing to give the final blow that would surely hurt her best friend. "Hugo … I'll say it one last time…. It would be like dating my brother."

"In that dress, you sure don't make me feel like your brother."

"Oh, Hugo, for heaven's sake, let's get this over with!" Lizzy slid over, grabbed an astonished Hugo by the shoulders, pulled him toward her and kissed him. It was not a quick peck on the lips. It was Lizzy giving it all that she had, and Hugo giving it right back. After a few seconds, their lips slowly parted. They looked at each other with shy smiles. Then they looked up to the heavens and couldn't help but laugh. Their frozen breath rose up in great clouds. Its vapor trail looked like a question mark, as it disappeared into infinity.

ABOUT THE AUTHOR

Kenneth Nichols Fecteau
And Judy Nichols Fecteau

Kenneth and Judy Nichols Fecteau are career educators and authors. Kenneth holds a B.A. in history and a master's degree in social science from William Patterson University. Judy holds a B.S.Ed. degree in biology from The University of  Georgia and a master's degree from Georgia State University. They are married and live in Washington State.

BOOKS BY THIS AUTHOR

There's No Such Thing As Never In Forever

There's No Such Thing as Never in Forever is an exciting, must-read, young adult book by authors Kenneth and Judy Nichols Fecteau. In this imaginative, action-packed adventure, four teen rock musicians set out on a vision quest, where they must navigate their way through time to retrieve an extraordinary talisman, lost centuries ago by their adopted Native American Tribe. Captured by the maniacal leader of a pirate gang who also seeks the talisman, they rely on their own wits, and a little help from new-found friends, to execute their daring escape through a world of present and past with death nipping at their heels.

REVIEWS

"There's No Such Thing as Never in Forever is a paranormal urban fantasy story filled with action and adventure. The story is geared toward the young adult audience, so the dialogue, discussions, scenes and details are created to attract the young adult mind. It is filled with intriguing and exciting descriptive passages. The concept of the storyline is intense, and you quickly find yourself self-hooked on the ordeal, hoping things will pan out for all four of them. I recommend this book to action adventure young adult readers. "
S.J. MAIN, REVIEW TALES MAGAZINE

THERE'S NO SUCH THING AS NEVER IN FOREVER
BOOK REVIEWS

"This book keeps the excitement going all through the journey ...Don't want to put it down!"
POSTED BOOK REVIEW, AMAZON

"I love this book. The authors allow you to use your imagination during this adventure. Wittily written, the book takes you every step of the way through a fantastic adventure."
POSTED BOOK REVIEW, AMAZON

"It felt as though I was right along with these characters and a part of their adventure. It is an entertaining and enjoyable book and would make a great movie!"
POSTED BOOK REVIEW, AMAZON

"Rooted in spirituality, There's No Such Thing as Never in Forever is a delightful book of non-stop action, entertainment and substance. The authors hit all the right notes keeping you hooked from beginning to end.

Intended for young adults, clearly this book appeals to all ages. Read it and become inspired by the four friends; you too may discover wisdom and powers that just might change you and sustain you on your life journey.

As the book nears its end, a pleasant surprise awaits, setting up anticipation of a sequel. I can hardly wait."
POSTED BOOK REVIEW, AMAZON